EXIT VELOCITY

A NOVEL

BARBARA GREGORICH

Also by Barbara Gregorich

Fiction
She's on First
Dirty Proof
Sound Proof
The F Words

Nonfiction
Women at Play: The Story of Women in Baseball
Guide to Writing the Mystery Novel: Lots of Examples, Plus Dead Bodies
Charlie Chan's Poppa: Earl Derr Biggers

Poetry
Crossing the Skyway
Jack and Larry
Cookie the Cockatoo: Everything Changes

EXIT VELOCITY

A NOVEL

© 2024 Barbara Gregorich

All rights reserved, including the whole or any part of the contents, which may not be reproduced in any form without written permission from the author, except for brief quotations in reviews as permitted by copyright law.

This is a work of fiction. The story, names, characters, and incidents portrayed in this book are fictitious. No identification with actual persons, living or deceased, is intended or should be inferred.

Print ISBN: 979-8-35092-465-7
eBook ISBN: 979-8-35092-466-4

DEDICATION

For Phil, who rivals Jake
in making inferences

1   ROWAN

I NEED A JOB.

For survival.

For self-esteem.

Which is why I'm here, where I don't want to be, at the gun-control rally, where those demonstrating see only a narrow part of the problem.

"Hey! It's Gun Girl!" some moron yells, pointing my way. That makes others point. Then they turn Clari's picture toward me, bobbing it up and down.

I look away. It still hurts to see her picture, the one from the high school year book. She was murdered before she graduated. Some of her classmates, too. But by then it was too late to remove her photo. Mom and I wouldn't have wanted it taken out, anyway.

I'm walking up Clark Street, searching for Titus. Sure, I could wait until Monday, but Titus has been promising to help me find a job. Now that I'm finally ready to act I want no delays.

Today's the first anniversary of Clari's death. Twelve months since she died. Eleven months since I dropped out of college. Ten months since I quit my part-time job. Except I didn't quit, I was fired for not showing up.

Jerry, my boss, actually came to the house to give me the news that I was being "let go." He also told me I needed professional help to get myself through the grief. "Get yourself together, Rowan," he advised, "then come back and see me."

So yesterday I went to tell Jerry I was ready to be my former reliable self, to drive around the city in a Wheelers van, part of a two-person crew that moved rental bikes from one location to another all day long. Heavy work on a tight schedule: I kind of liked it.

But Jerry wasn't at Wheelers any more and the new boss wasn't interested. "I don't need any new workers," he told me, "I need higher production out of the ones I have."

I stared at him a while before I turned away. He no doubt wanted robots who could lift ten bikes at a time, live on scrap metal and never need health care for the simple reason that they weren't alive.

I brooded about my former job all day long, but finally shook it off. I'm going to conquer my grief, I know I am — but not if I let every obstacle pound me down. So last night I went to Target and bought a few new clothes, holding my breath until the credit card cleared. Like, two new clothes. A sign to myself that I was getting better. Stronger. Doing the right things. "Interacting with life," like the college guidance counselor told me before I dropped out.

It did make me feel a bit better, buying something new. Black tights and a shimmery blue and green crop top. Both of which I'm wearing now, along with a blue feather in my hair. Clari used to love attaching feathers to her hair. This morning I pulled open the top drawer of her dresser and saw maybe twenty feathers there. I swallowed hard and made myself choose. What caught my eye was an incredibly blue feather. It took me at least twenty minutes to figure out how to attach the thing to my hair and involved using a fusion joint and needle-nose pliers. I felt like I was back at Wheelers, repairing the rental bikes. Now I feel like part of Clari is with me.

When I cross Washington Street there's Daley Plaza on my right with the giant Picasso statue in its center and maybe four- or five-thousand gun-control people crowded all around. Thinking they occupy the moral high ground. Their hearts are good, and I really understand their pain, having classmates and friends murdered. Like my sister was murdered. But they haven't thought through the whole "control" thing and its logical outcome.

The pro-gun people, maybe four hundred of them, occupy the sidewalk to the west. They're clumped into two groups with a big gap between them. A smaller, respectable-looking group in suits, probably passing out NRA literature. A larger and louder group dressed in camo, carrying AR-15 semi-automatics strapped to their shoulders. The nearby cops are friendly with these people — these neofascists who storm into state capitols one day and shoot down demonstrators and protestors another. I see some swastikas in the group. And I see Zeb Snoddy standing at their head.

Worse, Snoddy sees me.

I watch him out of the corner of my eye. His heart is evil. And so are the hearts of all his neofascist followers.

Both sides, pro-gun and gun-control, hate me. But for different reasons.

Concrete barricades line each side of Clark Street. Heavily armed Chicago cops wearing bullet-proof vests, riot visors, and clubs stand in the middle. I hope they faint from the weight of their weapons.

"Hey! You! Pickett! You can't walk here!" A cop is shouting at me because I'm walking up the center of the street. The cops know me because Mom and Dad took Clari and me to demonstrations as soon as we were the height of a poster board. The picketing Picketts they'd call us.

I walk faster, looking for Titus and the safety of numbers.

Not fast enough, because I hear a shout. "Your sister died because we don't have gun control."

I spin around and lock eyes with the shouter. "Clarissa Pickett died because we don't have gun control," he repeats, pointing a sign with her picture at me.

I move toward him fast, wanting to break the sign over his thick head, but I'm stopped by two cops who cross batons in front of me and bump me back. "You have until the count of five to move out of here," says one, already counting.

By the time he's on three I'm heading north again, in a hurry 'cause that's where I think I'll find WCC, Titus's organization. Titus Longshaw and Working Class Control go together like a chain and sprocket.

I'll be able to recognize WCC at a glance because most members are Black and they'll stand out in this almost exclusively White rally. You don't see Blacks, Latinos, or Native Americans shouting for gun control. Most white people don't ask themselves what it means that the anti-gun and pro-gun rallies are mainly white.

They should. They should ask themselves how Blacks, Latinos, and Indians feel about this issue. Maybe they'd learn something.

I reach the corner of Clark and Washington and step upward onto the bottom of a lamp post, stretching even higher to look over the crowd . . . but I don't see the WCC.

Something above catches my attention, a kind of pop and flash. Something metallic streaks in one direction, something very colorful in another. Staring up toward the colors I see a bird. Beautiful. Green, turquoise, red, and yellow. Must be an escaped parrot. I smile, and am conscious that I'm smiling. Another good sign. I even note that the bird's colors are more dramatic than mine.

Things suddenly feel a bit better. I'm wearing new clothes, I'm going to find a job.

"Way to go, bird!" I shout up at it, raising my fist.

Standing there on the lamp post, I hear the drums. Big booming sounds like ashiko or djembe, signaling something important. Change. Radical change. That's the WCC. I try to judge where the sounds are coming from.

South. I have to go back the way I came.

I jog south and, suddenly, there's a problem. The pro-gun side jumps the barricades and rushes toward the gun-control side. The cops do nothing to stop them.

The gun-control people don't run, I'll give them that. They move forward, too, over their barricades and into the street.

Before I know it I'm part of the moving mass. I don't want to be caught in this. Thrusting with my elbows and shoulders I try to create a space to turn around in and escape the melee.

I can't.

Despite what I want, I'm being pushed forward by the pro-gun people. The mob is moving fast and I'm spun in every direction at once. I feel my feet leave the sidewalk. I think I'm going to fall and be crushed. But the sea of bodies keeps me upright.

No matter how hard I try I can't keep myself from being moved further and further away. I can sense I'm being pushed west. Toward the fascists.

"Well, look here," says a voice. "It's Gun Girl herself."

My stomach feels like somebody's pumped ice water into it. Snoddy is just inches away. Leering. Just like in my nightmares. I rear back, raise an arm into the air, ready to bring it down on Snoddy's nose if he touches me.

He reaches out.

My arm is on the way down, my hand stiffened to crack his nose when I'm jerked backward. At the same time a loud blast fills the air, like an air raid siren gone berserk. If I could cover my ears, I would. But I can't because somebody has me in an armlock. Colors flash by like neon lights. Somebody screams in pain. I hope it's Snoddy.

Whoever pulled me hasn't let go. He's gripping me from behind, across my neck and both shoulders. As he drags me backwards the only thing I can see is the sky.

"Let go!" I shout. I try to see who's doing this, but I'm in a neck and shoulder lock and can't move. Suddenly I realize my left shoulder is pressed against the person who's dragging me — and my left shoulder feels something hard and metallic.

A gun.

I know guns, I know the different ways they can be carried and concealed. The person dragging me is carrying a gun.

My mouth goes dry. If this is one of Snoddy's men . . . . Snoddy wants to kill me. I know he does.

Clank! Something comes down over my head, pushing me to the ground. I'm in the dark, enclosed in something. Something wet. Something that stinks.

I'm sitting with my butt on concrete, my knees in my face, my back curved forward, my hands holding my head. I'm scrunched. Crowded. Oppressed.

I can't move.

I push out with my hands. Hard plastic. I try to stand up, but can't because something's pressing down on my head.

I think . . . I think I'm inside a large garbage can that somebody has turned upside down on me.

I probe for weak spots. Find none. This plastic is rigid.

But why can't I get out? I mean, how much effort does it take to move the garbage can — if that's what it is — up and off me?

But it won't budge. It's like . . .

Is somebody sitting on top of the garbage can?

I pound on the sides. "Let me out! Get offa there! Let me out!"

Nobody answers. All I hear are the sounds outside. People shouting and pounding and fighting. Things hitting one another.

And then the thing I'm in begins to move.

Across the street. Or sidewalk. Or wherever I am.

And I have to move with it.

Somebody is shoving it — and me — somewhere.

I'm terrified. At the same time, my butt is scraping the ground and all I can think of is how much that hurts.

I crab-walk with the moving can, using my hands and feet. Then I force my hands against the insides of the can and try to lift my butt off the ground.

Sometimes it works, sometimes it doesn't.

After a short while the can stops.

I try to lift it off me, but whoever was pushing it is sitting on top of it again.

"Let me out!" I shout. "Help! Kidnapping! Kidnapping! Help!"

Well let me tell you, if you're ever thrown into a garbage can, or have one thrown over you, you're not going to get help from anyone.

I try reason. "Look, whoever you are. Why are you doing this?"

Silence.

I try a lot of other questions, but get no answers.

I keep banging on the insides of the trash can, making all the noise I can. Hoping somebody comes to investigate.

Until, after who knows how long — ten minutes? — I feel that the force on top of me gets off.

Is it true?

I push upward to see if I can lift my prison off myself.

I can!

And I do, as fast as I've ever done anything in my life.

I heave the can straight up, over my shoulders, and sling it forward at the same time, as far away from me as I can. It hits the ground, turns end on end, falls on its side, and bounces away like an escaped Wheelers bike.

Yeah, it's a garbage can.

I look to see who did this, but all I see is a lone figure already half a block away. Running.

And then I notice the missing people.

Where's the rally?

It's gone, moved away, two blocks south of here already. Cop cars and an ambulance are in the center of the street where the fighting was going on. The figure is getting further and further away quickly. I can't tell if he's White or Black or which side he was on. He's tall, that's the only thing I can tell. Wearing long-sleeved dark clothes and a knit cap. In June? I think about whether that means something, but can't come up with an answer.

There's trash all around me. Half-eaten hot dogs. Coke and root beer and coffee cups, their contents all over me.

Dog shit.

I can smell it.

And it's not in tied-up plastic bags like it's supposed to be.

Gross!

I'm about to wipe crud off my face when I think that maybe there's dog shit on my hands, so I'd better not touch my face.

I take a good look at myself.

It makes me want to cry.

I'm filthy. I'm wet. And I stink. Stuff of all kinds clings to me. My butt hurts like hell. Probably bleeding — but I don't want to touch it to find out.

I've gotta get home and take a shower. I hurry toward the nearest El entrance.

Somebody's shouting. "Hey! Wait! Wait, I want to talk to you!"

I turn and look behind me. A guy is walking fast toward me. Not dressed in dark clothes, so not the guy who was running away. I don't know what he wants. And I don't care.

"No!" I yell back at him. I wave a probably-dog-shit-smeared hand at him and keep walking. "Go away!"

Next thing I know, he's closer. "Hey, stop for just a minute, I want to talk to you."

"No! Go away!"

And then his hand is on my shoulder, trying to spin me around.

I spin, all right. I spin around, bending my forearm and slamming my elbow into his neck.

"*Ummffff.*" He doesn't fall to the sidewalk, but he bends over, hands on knees, trying to catch his breath.

I run toward the El stop, jog down the stairs, and wait for any train heading south. I stand in a corner, away from people who trap me inside a trash can. Away from people who grab me from behind.

What just happened to me?

Why?

I wonder if it was because I was alone.

It didn't used to be that way, before Clari died. She and I were usually together. Keisha and our other friends were with us. There used to be other people around.

But somehow I lost them all.

I need something more than a job.

I need my friends.

2 ROWAN

FROM THE EL IT'S FOUR BLOCKS TO OUR HOUSE. I still think our house. Say it, too. But I have this deep, gloomy feeling that it's my house now. Mom said she would be back . . . but there's no evidence this will happen.

I can see MaryEllen sitting on her porch, watching me walk down the street. She used to babysit Clari and me when she was in high school and we were in grade school. MaryEllen was so good to Mom and me after Clari died, bringing us food, inviting us over for meals, checking on us like a good neighbor. And she's been good to me since Mom left.

"Hey, Els." I give her a wave and stop, but I don't turn onto her sidewalk.

"Hi, Rowan. Are you okay?"

"Yeah. Well, not exactly. Somebody dumped a garbage can on me at the rally," I say, not wanting to explain the true story. Which sounds bizarre. "I gotta go shower, cause I stink."

"Well, come by after your shower if you like. We can sit here and talk."

"Thanks. Maybe I will."

I push open the gate and enter the house by the side door, close it behind me, strip, and drop everything into the mud tray. Then I get a trash bag from the kitchen, stuff everything except my shoes into it, seal it tight, and leave it by the door, to take outside after my shower.

My new clothes didn't last long. And I can't afford to buy another set. I've gone through pretty much all the money Mom left me to live on. I should have looked for work months ago, I know I should have. Instead, I just sat around the house doing nothing. Titus and Genevieve would drop by to see how I was doing. Encourage me to get out, mix with other people.

Keisha, too. She'd drop by on different days. I think the three of them scheduled their visits so that I saw one of them every other day. I smile now, thinking about it. A couple of times Keisha even brought her portable sewing machine, set it up, and sewed while she talked to me. "You are in competition with this machine, Rowan," she'd say. "It has my attention. See if you can win me away."

It did make me grin, sort of. But I was content to just sit and watch her sew and say pretty much nothing. That's changed. It changed yesterday when I bought the now-trashed clothes. It changed this morning when I tried to find Titus and see if he could help me find a job. I'm ready to be part of the world again.

Opening the door to the basement I toss my shoes down the stairs. I can wash them in the utility sink later. With lots of soap. Maybe bleach, too. Then I walk into the bathroom, turn on the shower, wait until it gets hot, and step into it.

I used to come in here to cry almost every night for a month or more. I'd turn the shower on, step inside, and let the moans and tears mingle with the water. I think Mom probably did the same.

Our soap — my soap, I mean — is whatever's cheapest. But I splurge a little on the shampoo, choosing something natural with a nice scent. Rosemary. Sometimes lavender.

The hot water feels good everywhere. Except on my butt, which stings like hell. Probably covered with abrasions. Who dumped that garbage can on me, and why?

When I'm done with the soap I use the shampoo on my body, just so its good smell will take away the memory of the garbage and dog shit.

Stepping out of the shower I towel my hair and myself and walk into our bedroom. My bedroom, that I used to share with Clari. I grab a pair of shorts and pull them on, then a black tee. Clari's clothes are still hanging there, on her side of the closet.

I catch a glimpse of myself in the mirror. The blue feather is still in my hair, looking good. Clari's feathers lasted almost two months before she changed them. "Feathers are mostly keratin," she'd tell me, "just like our hair."

After Clari died I cut my hair short. Not in mourning, or at least I didn't think so. It was because I couldn't be bothered to care for long hair. I study myself again in the mirror.

I liked the long hair better.

Maybe I should let it grow.

❋ ❋ ❋

When I walk into the living room, I stop in my tracks.

A bird is sitting on the piano. Staring at me.

I glance around quickly, then spot the open window. Okay, that's how it got in. I've been keeping the windows open, and some of them are missing screens. Which I can't afford to replace.

The bird is big. Huge. I eyeball the distance from the top of its head to the tip of its tail. At least the length of a yardstick. Even if the tail's a foot long, that makes the bird at least two feet tall. I feel like maybe that extinct giant parrot scientists discovered in New Zealand has come back after . . . after, what was it? twenty million years? Why it would return, I don't know.

The parrot looks really strong.

It's colorful. Brilliant.

I don't know anybody in the neighborhood who has a parrot.

I realize the bird has been staring right at me the whole time.

This is . . .

This is . . . . No.

It can't be.

But it *is*. It's the same bird I saw flying overhead at the demonstration.

It *can't* be.

That was a couple of hours ago. Five miles north of here.

But it is. Same colors: green and turquoise body, red and yellow tail.

What's going on here?

The bird — I swear! — rolls one of its eyes. Moves its weight from one foot to the other, then back to the first. Like it's waiting for me to do something.

Okay.

"Hey," I say softly, so I don't frighten it. "I've seen you before."

Okay, this sounds crazy. The bird nods its head. Once. Twice. Shifts its weight from foot to foot again. Its feet are large. Dark gray. With four toes. I guess they're toes. Two long ones point forward, two shorter ones point backward.

Those toes are probably scratching the hell out of the piano top.

"You're a beautiful bird," I tell it. "Where are you from?"

The bird spreads its wings wide. They're spectacular. The tips of the wings point upward.

The sky. Is it telling me it came from the sky?

Well, *Duh*.

And why am I talking to a bird?

I guess because I haven't had anyone else to talk to since Mom left. That was like five months ago.

Slowly, carefully, I move toward the bird. I don't want to scare it. It might fly off the piano and into a wall or something and hurt itself. Or shit on the furniture.

But the parrot doesn't look like it scares easily. It watches me approach. I get so close I can reach out and touch it. But I don't.

We stand there staring at each other for a minute, maybe two.

I cave, losing the standoff. "I'm hungry," I tell the bird, "and there's food in the refrigerator. So I'm going to back up and walk into the kitchen."

The bird watches me as I do this. I get to the kitchen, turn, and enter.

The bird flies over my head and settles itself on top of the hutch that holds the dishes.

"Crackers," it says.

I laugh, startling myself . . . realizing I haven't laughed in a long time.

"Coming right up," I tell the bird as I rummage in a cabinet. I find a plastic container that's labeled *WW Crackers* in Mom's writing. She believes in keeping a neat pantry.

I open the container, select a cracker, and hold it out to the bird.

It turns its head sideways. I realize it needs to do that to see the cracker. The bird has an eye on each side of its head, so it can't look at things straight ahead, it has to peer at them with one eye or the other. But no matter which eye it uses, all it's seeing is a cracker. Sort of like people who look at the Republicans with one eye, the Democrats with the other. What they're seeing is the same thing: a party that supports the capitalist class and all its means of oppression.

The bird lifts one talon and takes the cracker from me.

Carefully. Precisely. Delicately, even.

In two bites the cracker is history. The bird looks at me.

"Right," I say. "Why don't we move to the table and dine like civilized, uh, creatures."

The bird nods, then kind of swoop-hops from the hutch down to the table.

Like, right on the table top.

Okay.

I mean, I thought it might perch on the back of a chair or something. But okay.

I place the container of crackers on the table and watch as the bird looks inside with that funny sideways head motion and then selects a second cracker.

Me, I move to the refrigerator and wonder what's left. I vow to go grocery shopping tomorrow morning, which means I'll have to dip into the savings account Mom left. Which she said I should use to pay property taxes. At least I don't have to pay a mortgage: this house belonged to Dad's parents, and when Dad inherited it the mortgage had already been paid off. I feel bad, knowing I've delayed far too long in getting a job. On the other hand, Mom had a job, but she just up and left it. And me.

Part of me understands why Mom left, but part of me is so angry with her, leaving me here alone.

I push these thoughts aside because I don't want to deal with them.

In the cold compartment I find some cheddar cheese, so I put that on the table, along with a knife and plate.

Even a napkin, because I have company.

I slice a piece of cheese off the block of cheddar, place it on a cracker, and put the whole thing in my mouth.

It's good. I didn't realize how hungry I was. I slice off another piece of cheese and offer it to the bird. Which shakes its head.

Okay. No cheese for the bird.

"Apple," it squawks. "Apple."

This bird is amazing. Really *amazing*! It not only talks, it... communicates.

"Lucky for you," I say as I stand up, "I happen to love apples, so there's always some on hand." I open the fridge again, find two nice apples, take them out, rinse them under the faucet, dry them, and am about to sit back down when I think that the bird might be thirsty.

Hmmm.

I ponder this as I pour myself a glass of water and put it on the table. The bird eyes the water. "That's not for you," I say. "That's for me. I'm getting you some water, though, don't you worry."

Rummaging around in the hutch, I can't find the stack of dessert ramekins, so I just grab a wide soup bowl, take it to the sink, rinse it out — and notice the food crumbs everywhere and the kitchen sink I haven't scrubbed in weeks. I fill the bowl with water and place it on the table near the parrot. I'm pretty sure it's a parrot, and not some mutant cockatoo or macaw.

The parrot dips its beak in the water, tilts its head back, and drinks. Its body is mostly green, with turquoise wings. Its tail is red and yellow, and its head is mostly purple, with a brilliant blue top, as if somebody had dipped a paintbrush in lapis and painted a streak of it on the bird's head. The blue is almost the same shade as the feather I'm wearing.

As the bird drinks I study it more. A bold band of bright orange feathers circles its neck. And tiny, tiny red feathers circle each eye. What an incredibly colorful bird.

I slowly reach out a finger. "Can I touch you?" I ask it.

The bird looks at me. It nods.

I reach out with the side of my finger and stroke the bird's chest. Which is silky smooth. And warm.

Tears flood from my eyes. I try to stop them, but can't. I haven't touched anybody in months.

It feels so good. I can't tell you how good it feels, that living warmth, the blood beneath the skin.

Next thing I know, the bird has hopped onto my shoulder.

Oh my god! Its feet are So. *Warm*. I can feel the heat through my tee shirt.

The bird nibbles on my ear. Not hard or sharp, just a kind of friendly nibbling. It coos, like a happy little motor.

I'm crying and laughing at the same time.

"You silly bird," I say, reaching up to stroke it.

The bird stays that way a while, rubbing its head against my ear. Finally it hops back onto the table.

"Apple."

Right.

I cut one of the apples into eighths and hand a section to the bird, which once again examines the piece sideways, takes it in a claw, turns the apple piece every which way one more time, and finally takes a big bite.

I cut the other apple for myself. The parrot and I sit there and have our evening meal. I take sips of water, and so does the parrot.

When we've eaten all the crackers and both of the apples and half of the cheese, I put my elbows on the table, my chin in my hands, and stare at my dinner companion. We're pretty much eye to eye. "Will you be my friend?" I ask it.

Not expecting an answer.

"Deeply your friend," squawks the bird.

I go still, not sure I've heard right.

"Deeply your friend," it repeats.

"Deeply," I say. What a wonderful word.

The bird nods. "Deeply," it says.

Way down inside me, something feels loosened.

"Thank you," I manage to say. "And I am your friend, too." I'm finding it hard to talk. "Deeply," I add.

The bird nods.

"Let's shake on it," I say, sticking a finger out.

The bird takes my finger in one of its talons and we move our united digits up and down in harmony — just as there's loud knocking at the front door.

The bird jumps, spins around, and faces the direction of the front door.

And then it fluffs its feathers out, looking bigger than before. And squares its shoulders.

If birds have shoulders.

My friend and I are ready to face whoever's on the other side.

3 JAKE

THE DIFFERENCE BETWEEN BOSTON AND CHICAGO IS vast: the former old, with narrow streets cobbled together from cowpaths, but oh so rich in history and culture; the latter brash, bold, with wide streets but none of the culture of New England. Sandburg was unerringly correct when he labeled Chicago the City of the Big Shoulders. Shoulders it has. A head, though? An intellect? I'm not convinced.

That's how I've read the situation ever since I moved here six months ago.

I saw it as a power move, from a smaller major city to one of the largest major cities. I landed my job at Highland Studios before I moved, of course. My official title is Assistant Video Editor, but I'm expecting a promotion and raise any day, dropping the Assistant along the way.

What I love is podcasting, and what I want is to be known for my work. My subject matter is mostly political: the struggles of people to live satisfying lives. But that's too broad a sweep. I need to find something more focused. And I'm hoping to find it in Chicago, City of the Big Shoulders.

Today I'm not on assignment for Highland Studios, I'm on my own, gathering material for my podcasts, which have made the Boston-to-Chicago transition well, my downloads swelling from 1,000 a month to 2,000 a month, moving Jake's Takes closer and closer to the top ten percent. I'm good. Anybody with an M.A. from Harvard *should* be good.

Every weekend, and most evenings as well, I go out looking for the right story — something that will satisfy viewers, encourage them to think, and bring in money.

The gun-control rally, the third I've attended since I've been here, presents more of the same-old same-old, two sides facing each other, one saying guns are the problem, the other denying there even is a problem. I keep coming, though, on the assumption that sooner or later something's got to crystallize.

A flash of color attracts me, causing me to notice someone striding down the center of Clark Street, scowling at both sides. Scowling at the cops, too. She's wearing black tights and a shimmering top of swirling greens and blues. Short brown hair — bad haircut — with reddish highlights. And something blue in her hair. A couple of years younger than me, maybe. There's something sad in her face. I can't read what she's all about, but my intuition is never wrong: there's a story here. I raise my Sony camcorder and start filming her.

I'm intrigued by the weight she's carrying: by what her problem might be. And when somebody on my side of the barrier — that being the gun-control side, naturally — shouts out, "There goes Gun Girl," my attention zooms into sharp focus. *Gun Girl?* There's a story here, waiting for me to track it down, tease it out, shape it up, and present it to the world.

Moving in the same direction Gun Girl does, I wonder if it would be wise to jump the barrier to reach her. The crowd's large, but not so large I can't maneuver through it easily. Maybe 6,000, tops. I'm starting toward the barriers when I look into the face of the nearest cop, who's rhythmically thumping a truncheon into his hand. Cops hate reporters.

I'm about to chance it anyway when I hear someone shout: "Your sister died because we don't have gun control."

The guy who's shouting this is just two people away. And he's pointing his poster of Clarissa Pickett right at the girl I'm interested in.

I excel at high-speed deductions, and as deductions go this one's on a kindergarten level: the girl in the blue-and-green top is the sister of a shooting victim.

Gun Girl looks set to pound on the guy who shouted, but two cops step in front of her and order her away. I film her going, but then I approach the guy who confronted her, filming him as I'm walking.

"Hey," I greet, "Jake Terranova here of Jake's Takes podcasts." I slip him one of my business cards. "What can you tell me about that girl you just spoke to? Was Clarissa Pickett her sister?"

"That was Rowan Pickett. Gun Girl. Yeah, one of the victims was her sister."

"Why do you call her Gun Girl?"

"Because she's an idiot, a freaking pro-gun idiot. We asked her to speak at a rally after her sister and the other students were killed. And then, when it was her turn, she stood up and said that she wasn't for gun control, and that her sister hadn't been, either. Something about people needing guns to defend themselves from somebody . . . the cops, I think. Something else about why we have violence."

He's not very exact, but he's getting worked up and I'm filming away. Conflict makes good story.

"It's the same thing all the pro-gun nuts say," he continues. "Hey, is this going to be on TV?"

"I hope so," I say. And then I turn to look for Ms. Pickett.

At first I don't see her, but then I catch a glimpse of her multi-colored top halfway up the block. She's standing on the base of a lamppost, looking up at the sky. I look up, too, increasing magnification and slowly panning the camcorder in the direction she's looking.

A brilliantly colored parrot. Escaped pet.

Gun Girl raises a hand in the air and shouts up to the bird, which banks in its flight and soars in a wide arc northward, then eastward.

As I'm filming the bird pandemonium breaks loose and all the devils Milton could have imagined are unleashed here on Clark Street — the pro-gun people jump the barricades and rush toward us. Most of "us" rush toward them. Not me, because much as I'd enjoy smashing my fist into fascist faces, I'm trying to film the whole thing.

The melee simmers and bubbles for several minutes, until the cops push each side back to its own end of the street and we once again face each other across the no-man's land of Clark Street. My camcorder finds Zeb Snoddy, the self-admitted, swastika-wearing fascist who's in the news at least once a week.

W*hat*? I do a double-take at my flip screen, because she's there, too — Rowan Pickett. Snoddy's reaching out to grab her, but she arches backward, throwing an arm into the air. Self-defense move, probably karate.

An inhuman scream pierces through the crowd noise, ear-splitting to the extreme, and through my screen I see the parrot diving right at Snoddy. I go into 10x magnification and see blood spurt out of Snoddy's face. I want to close in on that even more, but his minions surround and obscure him, so I pan back to catch Gun Girl.

Except she's not there.

Nowhere.

I stand there, puzzled.

Just a few minutes ago Gun Girl signaled the parrot. The parrot changed its path. Circled around. Waited.

And then Gun Girl raised her arm and the parrot attacked Snoddy.

Gun Girl is gone. Split the scene. I realize I'm writing the narrative as I'm standing there, using my grandmother's slang. But split the scene is just right for a bold and brash city like Chicago, adding flavor to what I'll be saying when I put this thing together.

Although — and I'm always honest with myself — I have no idea what the motives are here.

But I'll discover them.

I'm jostled and jostled even harder and almost lose my balance, but I remain upright and even manage to move into the street. Attracted by whatever's happening in the pro-gun camp, the gun-control crowd has spilled off the sidewalk and onto Clark. The cops keep trying to push us backward. Ever so slowly the street is cleared. And then, somehow, who knows why, both sides begin moving south. I shoulder my way out of the crowd onto the street.

An ambulance siren slices through the air. Medics hop out and within seconds they're carrying a stretcher back to the ambulance. Snoddy is strapped to the stretcher, a huge white patch covering his left eye. The ambulance pulls away.

The two sides are still moving south, but I hang around the cops. When the chance opens up, I ask one of them what happened to Snoddy. I mean, I know what happened to Snoddy, I just want to hear the official version.

He looks at my camcorder and assumes I'm media. Which I am, only not network media.

"Too soon to say," he tells me.

"Did anybody see what happened?"

"Too soon to say."

"Which hospital are they taking him to?" I ask.

"Ambulance will probably take him to Rush."

By now the demonstration is at least two blocks south of me, the ambulance long gone. The cops are moving southward also. May as well head straight to Rush Hospital and see what information I can get on Snoddy.

I fumble for my phone, thinking I'll call Uber. I look around for a convenient corner to direct Uber to when I see her again. Gun Girl.

Once again she's half a block north, standing alone in the middle of the sidewalk. If body language is any indication, she's confused.

A good time to interview her. I slip my camcorder into a cargo pocket and head her way. When I'm within shouting distance I call to her.

She doesn't hear me. Or maybe doesn't want to hear me. I jog toward her and ask her to wait, I want to talk to her.

She tells me to go away.

It's then I notice she's had an encounter of some sort. Her tights and skin are smeared with red and yellow. Mustard and ketchup, looks like. Other wet stuff stains her. Coffee maybe, or soda. Gum wrappers are clinging to her ass.

Which is naked in places. Her tights are partly shredded.

She's not stopping, so I run up to her and put a hand on her shoulder.

The next thing I know, I'm gagging, bent down, trying to catch my breath.

She hit me! Elbow to the throat.

Part of me admires the effectiveness of her move. Most of me is hugely pissed.

When I'm recovered enough to stand upright and breathe normally, Gun Girl is trotting down the steps of the El.

I follow her.

When I reach the bottom, I don't see her. Which direction is she heading?

Think, Jake, think. Yes, south side. The students who were murdered while on a field trip to Colorado were all from the same south-side school. So I'm guessing she lives in Bridgeport, a working class neighborhood, probably a lot like Southie used to be in Boston: white, blue-collar, mainly Irish-American.

She's standing in a corner, away from everyone. I move to the opposite end of the platform, hoping she doesn't see me. Taking out my phone I check the news, which tells me what I already know: that Zeb Snoddy was taken away from the gun-control rally in an ambulance. Nothing yet about being stabbed in the eye by a trained parrot.

Ms. Pickett boards the El and so do I, choosing a different car. In the Loop she exits and waits for an Orange Line train. I do the same, standing behind a pillar.

She boards and so do I, again in a different car.

Aiming my camcorder out the window, I take some scenic shots as the El lumbers along, just in case I decide to use Gun Girl's flight as part of the episode. Catching a glimpse of color in the sky I rush to the front of the car, where there are more windows, and aim upward, zooming in on the color. It's the parrot, flying parallel to the tracks.

When Gun Girl finally leaves the train at the Ashland and 31st Street stop, I do, too, staying as far back as I can. We're in Bridgeport.

She turns west and I stay maybe a block-and-a-half behind. I've never been in this part of Bridgeport before. Some bungalows, more two-story houses. In traditional Chicago style each house has a one-car garage at the rear of the property, and each garage opens out to an alley that runs between blocks.

Something makes me look skyward, and there it is again. The parrot. It soars overhead, skims the roofs of houses, and then disappears from sight.

Gun Girl stops to talk to somebody sitting on a porch. Then she turns onto the next sidewalk, unlatches a gate, and, I surmise, enters her house through a side door. I hang back, not wanting to get the neighbor's attention.

Gun Girl, covered with crap, is going to take a shower.

At least I hope she's going to take a shower. I look at my watch, turn around and walk away, giving myself thirty minutes to circle back, by which time her shower should be finished, she should be dressed, and maybe she'll be at ease, thinking she got away with the attack on Snoddy.

When I do turn back down her street the neighbor's gone from the porch. But I know the house I'm looking for.

I climb the front porch steps and knock on the door.

4 JAKE

SHE OPENS THE DOOR AND I'M ABOUT TO INTRODUCE myself when she shouts.

"You! What are *you* doing here?"

"I followed you from the demonstration. I want to —"

"Followed me? You *followed* me? First you won't leave me alone when I tell you to, then you grab me, and then you *follow* me?"

She's casting my actions in the wrong light. I'm about to explain this to her when the parrot flies in from another room and settles on a table near the door. Eyeing me.

Things have gone south in a nanosecond. Way south. Like, Antarctica.

"Uh, look, it wasn't like it seemed. I'm a video editor and podcaster. You may have heard of me, Jake's Takes?"

I wait a beat, but she says nothing. Maybe doesn't watch podcasts. "I want to interview you," I explain. "That's what I was trying to tell you." To convince her I'm safe, I pull my camcorder out and show it to her.

"Why?"

"Why do I want to interview you?" I ask.

"Yes. Why?"

Never tell a potential subject exactly why you want to interview them, because that may make them rehearse their answers. Or fabricate them. Give them something tangential, not the whole story.

"Your parrot," I say.

This gets her attention.

"Uh, look, can I come in so we can talk about this?"

"Do you know *my* parrot?" she demands, ignoring my request.

I hesitate, trying to decipher the meaning behind her inflection of that pronoun. Still, I like how quick she is with the accusations and comebacks. Definitely a good interview subject. "Well, we haven't been formally introduced, if that's what you mean, but I saw it at the rally today, and then I saw it fly along the El route and fly overhead as you were walking home."

She glances back at the bird, then assesses me. Maybe wondering if she could punch me again. "You can come in," she says, "on one condition — that when I say leave, you leave."

"Deal."

The place is hot, as in uncomfortable-temperature hot. No AC, I guess. The windows are all open. Most have screens, a few don't. Gun Girl herself is freshly showered, as I anticipated, wearing frayed shorts and a t-shirt. Her reddish-brown hair, definitely in need of a professional with scissors, is still damp. The blue thing I noticed earlier is a feather. Also damp. She smells good — unlike earlier.

She takes me into the kitchen and motions to the chair I should occupy. After I sit, she sits down opposite me. The parrot sits between us on a third side of the table. Not sits. Stands.

"Thank you," I say, hoping a show of good manners on my part might coax out something similar from her.

Apparently not, because she sits there in silence, waiting for me.

I pull a card out of my pocket and shove it across the table. "That's me. I'm hoping to interview you about your relationship to both sides in this pro-gun, anti-gun thing. And about your parrot coming to the rally with you."

The parrot walks over and looks down at the card, then back up at me.

This gives me pause. Does the parrot understand what I just said? I sense — just briefly, but intensely, like the warning zap of an electric needle

— that the parrot is highly unusual. In addition to being a trained assassin, it's interested in business cards.

Gun Girl looks at the card and reads my name out loud. "Jacob Terranova." She looks at me. "Is that a made-up name?"

"No, it's not a *made-up* name! It's the name I was born with. Why would you think it's a made-up name?"

She holds the card in one hand and flicks it with the finger of the other. "The drama. *Terra Nova*. New Land. Like you move here from Boston and want everyone to know you're . . . exploring."

"How do you know I'm from Boston?" I demand, irked. Big time irked.

"*Podcastah*," she retorts.

Okay. Score one for her.

But she's not done. "Do you know what an inference is?" she asks.

The *fuck*?!

I breathe deeply to keep from telling her off. "You just made one about my origins."

"Do you know what an incorrect inference is? A faulty one?"

I lean forward. "It stands to reason that if I know what an *inference* is, I also know what a *faulty* inference is. Your point being?"

Suddenly the parrot is there, in my face, so close I can feel its breath.

I back off a bit. Probably not wise to antagonize the parrot.

I feel that mental zap again — that this parrot is somehow light years beyond the rest of its species. Did it understand what I was saying? Or — and this is more likely — did it pick up on the emotional vibes? Animals are sensitive that way.

If Gun Girl notices how sentient her parrot appears to be, she doesn't let on.

"You. You are the point," she replies. "You've made a faulty inference, I don't know on what grounds, and you're carrying it around like world-tour luggage and maybe even trying to base an interview on it."

A *lot* going on here. There's Gun Girl herself, who, based on her conversation and comprehension, is more than I expected.

There's the parrot, now strutting back and forth on the table, bobbing its head up and down. This bird is ready to make a move of some kind . . . and I have no idea what that might be.

And there's me. I lean back all the way. And think. Have I ever made a faulty inference? Sure, maybe one or two in my life. But faulty inferences are not my forte. "What, exactly, do you think my faulty inference is?"

She looks at the parrot and waves her hand over it. The parrot responds by kissing her hand. Pecking at it, perhaps, but it looks more like a kiss to me. Gun Girl smiles.

"This beautiful bird, which I just met today, doesn't belong to me. Not. My. Parrot." She looks directly at me. Her eyes are a startling blue. Almost the same shade as the blue on the parrot's head. "That's your faulty inference."

I see where she's going with this: denying ownership. Denying she's responsible for the parrot's actions.

I don't want to tell her about the footage I have showing her talking to the bird, showing her commanding the bird to strike. I look around the room, giving myself time to think.

It's a small kitchen, but comfortable, with mango-colored walls, an old antique hutch, an almost square table we're sitting at, and four sturdy ladder-back chairs.

There's dust on the counters, dust on the refrigerator, dust on the window sill. Crumbs on the floor. Nothing shines or sparkles. Apparently neither Gun Girl nor her parents believe in cleaning house now and then.

She sees me observing and quickly looks away.

"What were you doing at the gun-control rally?" I ask, directing the conversation away from the parrot for a moment. "You were walking down the center of the street, not paying attention to either side."

She looks at me as if she's about to usher me out the door instantly, but I keep on talking. "That's one of the questions I would ask in the interview:

why you didn't seem to relate to either side. And then you would have ample time to answer the question. You would have ample time to answer all of my questions."

I can see she's actually thinking about the question. I'd love to get this look on camera: a kind of perplexity combined with annoyance.

"I was going to find Titus Longshaw."

It's a challenge. She's saying I should know who he is. And she's saying she's sure I *don't* know who he is.

Should I know that name? No harm in caving on a little question this early in the game. "Who's he?" I ask.

"Head of Working Class Control. WCC"

Now it clicks —WCC is a left-wing political party composed of mostly Blacks, Latinos, and Whites. They play drums when they go to demonstrations. Come to think of it, I heard drums at the rally this morning. Maybe there's a second story here, Gun Girl and WCC. I file it all in the back of my brain and circle around to the parrot again.

"I'd like to know a little more about the parrot," I say. "For instance, is it male or female?"

Gun Girl glances at the parrot, which now struts up and down the table in a funky walk, like it's just scored a touchdown in the Super Bowl. It spreads its wings. Moves its head forward and back, forward and back.

This bird, I think, is from another planet.

Gun Girl looks at me. "Male."

The parrot drops the dramatics and simply nods. At me.

"Does it have a name?"

Gun Girl looks baffled. She looks at the bird, looks at me, looks back at the bird.

"Deeply," she says at last. "Its name is Deeply."

How would she know its name if it's not her bird?

And then the parrot squawks up. "Deeply."

This is fantastic stuff, the two of them. I wish I could video this whole thing. You never know whether something like this will replicate.

"Listen," I say, "I really want to interview you." I wave a hand in the bird's direction, as if this doesn't matter. "Even the parrot, if it'll talk on camera."

Gun Girl looks down at my card, which she's still holding. "For Highland Studios?" she asks. "You want to interview me for them?"

"Uh, no. I want to interview you for my podcast, Jake's Takes."

She frowns. "That's not part of Highland Studios?"

"No. It's a separate job. I list both on the same business card."

She stares at me. "You have *two* jobs?"

"Sure," I say, waving it away. "So, I want to interview you for my podcast."

She studies my card for a while and mutters something I don't catch. Finally she looks up at me. "There's something you're not telling me."

"What? No. No, there's nothing I'm not telling you." I say the words out loud, and then silently add, *that you don't already know*, which makes my answer not a lie.

Or so I justify.

"I don't believe you," she says.

I jump in with an explanation. "I want to interview you about why you're against gun control, and how you relate to both the pro-gun people and the anti-gun people. I won't ask many questions about your sister, if that would be too painful. Just about why you don't support gun control. And about your — I mean *the* — parrot."

I haven't worked out yet how I'll introduce the attack on Snoddy into the interview. Her reaction, whatever it'll be, will be genuine, because she won't be expecting the question.

She looks down at the table and mumbles. "I don't think I'm up to another interview."

"Another? How many have there been?"

"I don't know. Three, I think. They were . . . exhausting. And," she adds, looking up at me, "they created a lot of enemies for me."

Interesting. "Was Zeb Snoddy one of those enemies?" I ask.

She shakes her head. "He's been an enemy for a few years. Before the interviews." She frowns. "How do you know about Snoddy?"

"Do you know what happened to him at the rally today?"

"I'm hoping City Hall collapsed and fell on him. And his followers."

She's as unconcerned as I've ever seen anybody unconcerned. Which means she's damned good at deception: she was standing right next to Snoddy when the parrot attacked. "I'm reaching into my pocket to pull out my phone," I tell her, just in case she has the desire to hit me again for whatever reason.

The parrot walks over to my edge of the table and peers intently at what I'm doing. When I pull out my phone, it circles around to where Gun Girl is sitting and stands alongside her, facing me. I really should be getting this on camera.

I find a recent news blurb which states that Zeb Snoddy may have been attacked at the rally and that he was rushed to the hospital. I show the article to Ms. Pickett.

As she reads it, her eyebrows go up.

"I heard somebody scream," she says. "It must have been him." She looks at me. "What happened?"

"The police haven't said. What makes you think it was Snoddy who screamed?"

She looks off to the side and closes her eyes, then opens them. "I was caught up in the scuffle and ended up with the fascists. Snoddy saw me and reached out to grab me, and then, next thing I know, I heard a loud screech, like an air-raid siren or something, and then I was kind of knocked to the ground. I thought I heard a man scream, too, right after the siren sound."

An interesting defense. "Did you look to see what happened?"

She shakes her head.

"Why not? You were right there."

"Not really. I, uh, fell, or was pushed down, and then somebody pulled me away. Dragged me away, actually."

"Who?"

She looks down. "I didn't see who."

"Did you see the ambulance arrive?"

She shakes her head.

The parrot, meanwhile, hasn't stopped staring at me, first with one side of its head pointed my way, then the other. It's disconcerting to be stared at with one eye at a time.

I want to continue this, but I also want to save this for the actual interview. Fresher is better.

"About the interview," I say, "we could do it in a couple of takes, two or three, so they'd be less exhausting."

She shakes her head.

"I can pay you something," I offer. "For your time. Not much, but something."

Gun Girl thinks about this. Her parrot henchman seems to think about it, too.

"How much?" she asks.

"A hundred dollars. Per interview. And there would be at least two. No more than three."

The bird flies up off the table, flies around the kitchen, and lands back on the table. It takes a sip of water, then another. And then, as Gun Girl and I are watching, it steps into the dish of water, ducks its head in and back up, spilling water down its back. Then it steps out of the dish and walks over to face me. Next thing I know, the parrot is shaking itself dry and I'm covered with water.

I wipe a hand over my face.

Gun Girl tries to hide a smile. "That's not enough," she says.

"Okay," I say, shaking water off my hand, wanting to nail this thing down. "Two hundred per interview."

"Seven!" squawks the parrot. "Seven!"

Gun Girl looks as startled at this as I am. I'm not going to pay *seven hundred dollars* for the entire interview, let alone seven hundred *per* interview.

I'm about to repeat my two-hundred-dollar offer when she interrupts me.

"Do you have any jobs open? Where you work?"

The parrot's mouth falls open. It looks at her in what I swear is admiration.

I'm becoming increasingly irked by this two-on-one situation. "No," I say curtly, "we don't have any jobs open. And even if we did, I'm not the person who determines who's hired. And what are your qualifications anyway?"

"I could do low-level entrance work. Be a gofer. I'm energetic and sharp and reliable. And honest. My last job was moving Wheelers rental bikes around the city. I'm a fast learner. I was studying communication at Columbia College before . . . before I quit. I know how to write complete sentences that make sense. So any communications I sent out wouldn't be an embarrassment to . . ." she looks down at my business card " . . . Highland Studios."

Uh-uh. No way. Not going to happen, having Gun Girl working for the same studio I work for. Controversial is good on video. Not in person. Having an assassin one desk over doesn't appeal to me.

But getting her a job elsewhere — that I can probably do. I explain this: that I will ask around at every contact I have, and see if I can get her a job.

"Okay." She nods. "But I'm going to be asking Titus for help, too. And if I get a job through him, or on my own, then my agreement to give you an interview is off."

This time my mouth falls open. I glance at the parrot, which is still staring at her in blind admiration.

I shift in my chair, trying to figure how I might be able to salvage this situation and put myself back in the driver's seat.

Which I'm beginning to suspect I haven't been in since I walked through the door.

Gun Girl stands. "It's time for you to go."

"Wh—" I'm about to protest but realize I agreed to her terms.

I stand. And then I stretch, casual like. "Thank you for your time," I tell her. "I'll get to work on the job possibilities right away."

She shows me out the door and I hear it lock behind me.

As I walk away, I wonder: how did Rowan Pickett, a working class Chicagoan without a college degree, get the upper hand over me, a cultured middle-class Bostonian with an M.A.?

I blame the whole thing on the parrot.

5 DEEPLEA

WHEN MY NUMBER CAME UP I WAS FLYING SIDE BY side with FeeOna, our wings practically touching as we swept high above the lush tangle of tall trees. We had just completed our quarterly courtship ritual, during which I displayed my plumage, uttered my loudest most raucous cries, lifted my wings, puffed out my chest, danced in a frenzied circle all around Fee, and strutted my stuff for hours. When she was ready I trod her. We then crooned and nuzzled and kissed and preened and groomed each other. I was excited by the knowledge that our mating would continue several times a day for a week or longer. Normally I could sense Fee's excitement over the future couplings, too. But not this time. I wondered if something was wrong. Clicking beaks, we took off from the branch on which we had been balancing, flying up, up, upward, over the emerald colored trees and into the beautiful violet sky.

"Dee," she chirped as we glided on a current that tickled my belly, "I drew the Duty Number this morning."

"Ummm," I cooed. "I forgot it was the day of the annual drawing." FeeOna was serving her year as HOP, Head of Planet, and it was always HOP's responsibility to draw the yearly Duty Number and see that individual off to another planet, to help the inhabitants learn how to live in peace and joy.

"Whose number was it?" I asked.

"Yours," she said, swooping swiftly downward.

I followed her without thinking, my wings guided by her wings.

"Mine?" I squawked as the two of us landed on the sandy yellow ground. "Mine?"

Fee nodded. "This is a Duty of the greatest importance, Dee. If you succeed, your fame will eclipse that of the great SeeZu."

A feeling of great pride suffused me. And incredulity. Images of the great SeeZu shine all over our planet, and fledglings are taught how SeeZu saved an entire world of living creatures.

"You are thinking of SeeZu now," said FeeOna, stating the obvious. "But your DU will be nothing like hers."

"It won't?" I ask, still stupefied from the news that I must leave our planet.

"Nothing like hers," FeeOna repeated. "The great SeeZu convinced creatures who were in charge of their own destinies. They chose to take SeeZu's advice, but they were free to choose otherwise. In your case the creatures in danger are not yet free to choose, for they are ruled by a small, rapacious coterie."

"Can't I convince the coterie?"

FeeOna shook her head, her blue feathers glinting. "It is not a place where you will be able to convince the evil-doers to give up their ways. Your mission is to help the inhabitants build an organization that will guide them in ending the misery and violence of their daily existence. Specifically, your mission is to find, protect, and nurture three individuals who will help lead such an organization." FeeOna gave me her most serious look. "It is the triad, DeePlea. Three connected individuals. Just as a triangle is the strongest shape, so the triad is the strongest relationship."

I thought about this, but not for long. Every parrot on our planet must, once in their life, perform a DU: Duty to the Universe. Visit another planet and help the inhabitants achieve harmony. And now it was my turn. I could do this. I could find an organization. I could find three individuals. Protect them. Nurture them. If they weren't already a triad, I could nudge them into one. This would not be difficult.

I did not believe that my DU would outshine that of the great SeeZu. I suspected that FeeOna was trying to make me feel better about leaving.

I turned to her with pride. "Where am I going?"

"To a planet that is in desperate trouble. War-torn. Militaristic to the ~~extreme~~. A huge gap between the few who own everything and the many who own little or nothing. Starvation. Disease. Genocide. Catastrophic climate change. Nuclear weapons. Racial and national hatreds. Mass murders."

I gulped. I had not yet served my year as HOP, so I had no idea there was such a planet in the universe. How could one single organization help rectify all that was wrong on this planet?

I sighed. It was my duty to help them, no matter how bad they were. Maybe especially because they were so bad.

"What species are they?" I asked.

Fee shook her head sadly. "They are humans."

"*Humans!*" I screeched. "I should have known!" I paced in a tight circle. "They're covered with *skin*! No feathers at all! They're *mean*! They're *cruel*! And they're *stupid*!" I paced and paced and finally stopped. "You are sending me to planet Earth."

Fee acknowledged this with a nod. "And they are war-loving," she added. "Which brings me to the second part of your mission."

"Second part?" I squawked dumbly. "*Second* part? No Duty to the Universe that I know of has ever had two parts!"

FeeOna nodded. "This is true, DeePlea. And it testifies to the extreme importance of your mission."

I fluffed out my feathers, smoothing down the unruly orange ones with my beak, and stood at attention.

"If the humans destroy their own planet," FeeOna explained, "—which it appears they very likely will, and quite soon — then the very worst of them will seek to conquer and inhabit other planets."

I was horrified. "Our planet!" I screeched. "They would come to *our* planet!"

"Yes. They would. Which means we would have to fight to the death to defend ourselves and our peaceful life from them and their voracity. We would have to budget an army, DeePlea. Which our planet has not had in twenty-thousand years! We would have to divert money from health care, from schools and parks and playgrounds, from conservation, from food greenhouses, from music and holography . . . from everything that keeps us happy, healthy, and productive." She paced back and forth and spread her wings wide in agitation. "We would have to train ourselves to kill, DeePlea. Which we have never done."

I stood there in shock.

"So, DeePlea," she continued, "the second part of your mission is to keep us informed about the likelihood of any plans the evil coterie has to escape to our planet. If we need to prepare for the horrors of war, we need as much of an advance warning as possible."

The seriousness of the DU weighed on my shoulders. The orange feathers around my throat sprang up in horror. I didn't bother smoothing them back down.

"I'm wondering, Fee, if this isn't a futile mission," I ventured.

"We won't know until you try," she said, clicking her beak to mine.

I sighed. "When do I leave?"

"Tomorrow morning."

"Does that give me time to intake their history and current situation?"

She nodded. "Let's go to the Knowledge Library and hook you up. But Dee — a word of warning."

I knew what she was going to say. FeeOna thinks I'm quick to act. Too quick, she says.

"I want you to be careful, Dee, and I beg you to be calm. Think things through. Do not be rash. It is the humans who must save themselves." She looked at me with her right eye — the serious eye. "You do not want to be the first parrot ever recalled from a Duty to the Universe."

"Of course I won't be rash," I replied testily. "I realize that I'll be on Duty."

"And," she added, "don't overeat."

"That is not for HOP to say," I retorted. "HOP's duties do not extend to food consumption."

"Well," she said as we pumped our wings and let the lift take us skyward, "don't blame me if you're too heavy to return."

We flew in through the open dome of the Knowledge Library, where the librarians infused me with data on planet Earth.

"They have parrots on Earth," Fee told me. "Thousands of different species."

"I'll blend right in," I said.

She shook her head. "Not really. You'll have to practice the way their parrots talk. It won't do to expose your superior intelligence."

I asked the Species Librarian for data on Earth's parrots and he infused me with it.

"I have no idea how to proceed when I get there, Fee."

"Let the situation guide you. If somebody responds to you, take it as an opening."

Later that evening, as we locked onto our sleeping branch, Fee said to me that when I returned from my Duty to the Universe, I would be different. "You will be culturally and emotionally enriched, Dee. Stronger. Wiser. With a more profound connection to all living creatures."

When I returned.

If I returned.

The next morning I entered a gleaming, specially designed DU-Ovum and was shot spaceward at an exit velocity of 134LY, landing a day later in Chicago, Illinois, USA, North America, Western Hemisphere, Earth.

6 ROWAN

I'M SLEEPING BUT THEN I'M AWARE SOMEBODY'S touching me.

"Mom?!" I bolt upright, throwing off the sheet. "Mom?!!" I look all around.

No Mom.

I sigh and flop back onto the mattress. She left and I don't know if she'll ever come back. I'm on my own.

A loud squawk. Very close. There's Deeply, lying on his back on my bed, his feet pointing to the ceiling. We're practically eye-to-eye. I didn't notice it last night, but I do now: his eyes are a kind of red-orange color.

He's still here. The bird that flew in my window is still here. Maybe I'm not on my own.

"Deeply. Is something wrong?"

I sit up again, slide my hand under his back and kind of nudge him upright. He shakes himself, then glares at me. "Hurt," he complains. "Feet hurt." He thrusts one foot toward me and wiggles his talons.

"Why do your feet hurt?"

"No perch. Deeply need perch."

"Oh. Okay, hang on a bit." I scoot out of bed and tilt my head in the direction of the kitchen. "Come with me."

He arrives ahead of me and stands on the table.

Observing his feet I see that his claws are spread flat on the table. Except they're not totally flat. The tips are curved inward. That must hurt. My tenth grade biology class comes back to me in bits . . . perching birds sleep with their claws locked around a limb of some kind.

I can solve this problem.

First I pull a broom out of the closet. Next I position two kitchen chairs back to back, maybe two feet apart. Satisfied with the distance, I thrust the broomstick through the top rungs of the ladder-backs. The weight of the broom causes the broomstick to roll around. Deeply looks at it critically, then at me the same way.

Reaching into a kitchen drawer I pull out some masking tape and use it to tape the broomstick to both chairs. Nothing moves. "There. Try that."

Deeply hops from the table onto the broomstick, curling his claws around it. He balances that way for a second. Then, his claws still around the broomstick, he pitches head forward.

He's hanging there, upside down.

"One strike," he squawks. "One strike."

Which throws me for a second. Then I get it. "The expression is *Strike One*. If you're going to criticize, get the words right."

He makes a sound like a short whistle. "Thin!" he squawks. "Too thin! Deeply need thick perch."

"Okay, okay," I say, placing my hand on his back, lifting him upright. At which point he flies off the perch and onto the top of the hutch.

"Hang on a sec while I get the computer and make us some breakfast."

As I multitask brewing coffee, making toast, and googling "parrot perches," I think about something I've been avoiding. Where is Deeply from? Who taught him to speak? Who does he belong to?

I don't want to go there — finding out who owns him. That would mean giving him back. People have left my life. Dad. Clari. Mom. But Deeply . . . he came into my life. I don't want him to leave, too.

Still. There's a moral issue here. I can't keep something that doesn't belong to me. Somebody else must be missing Deeply.

Maybe I can just borrow him for a time. Like a therapy parrot or something.

When the coffee's ready I pour myself a cup. Then I fill Deeply's bowl with water and watch him drink. After he drinks Deeply hops into the bowl and begins splashing himself all over, like he did last night. He makes little chirpy sounds as he bathes. The sounds are so happy they make me smile.

For several minutes I study him. "Deeply," I ask at last, "who taught you to speak?"

He stops splashing and looks at me. "Deeply learn by self."

I shake my head. "I don't think so."

He jumps straight up and spins around to face me. He opens his beak and his whole body kind of vibrates.

But I can't pay attention to him, 'cause all of a sudden the coffeepot is gurgling like crazy, and I think it's going to explode.

But when I put my hand on the coffeepot, I realize it's quiet. The sound is coming from Deeply.

I stand there with my mouth open.

Before I can say another word, there's a loud knocking on the door. Except it isn't. Deeply is making the sound.

After that he launches into more sounds. I hear screeching brakes, train whistles, ice cream truck bells. And I laugh out loud when I hear fireworks exploding during a White Sox game. I think Deeply could go on forever.

I raise my hands in surrender. "Okay, okay. I get it. You can imitate any sound you hear." I look at him. "You are really an amazing bird. Amazing."

Deeply looks satisfied. I hear the toast pop up. Then I hear it pop up again. And again.

I laugh as I pull out one of the toasts and hand it to Deeply. "You can stop now," I say. "I do get it."

We sit there in silence a while, eating our toasts. I wonder if toast is good nutrition for a parrot. I suspect I need to buy bird seed of some kind. Perch, birdseed, maybe bird toys. Boy, do I need a job — more now than I did yesterday.

A pet store could tell me what kind of birdseed I needed. Or maybe the zoo.

The zoo!

I call the Lincoln Park Zoo and after a while I'm talking to somebody who takes care of the parrots. I hesitate, not sure how to phrase my question, but finally I tell her I'm in desperate need of a perch for my large parrot and I wonder if the zoo has any old ones it's willing to give me. She asks me what kind of parrot I have.

I look at Deeply.

I have no idea, and I can't say, "a colorful one."

But I remember that the macaw is a large parrot. I tell her I have a macaw. Mrs. Andris, my tenth grade biology teacher, was a bird nut. She once brought a macaw into the classroom. It was smarter than half the class.

The zookeeper tells me they have discarded branches from various stands, and I can have them. "A macaw needs a large perch, at least two inches in diameter. Maybe even two-and-a-half," she informs me. We agree that I'll pick up the branches within the next hour.

I hurry to my bedroom, where I pull on a set of biking shorts and top.

"I'm off to get your perch," I tell Deeply, who's flown back to the piano. As I open the side door, I hesitate. Then I turn. "Don't leave, Deeply," I say. Beg. "Please don't leave me."

"Deeply wait," he says, limping back and forth on the piano top.

It's amazing the way he understands what I'm saying. I wonder how many vocabulary words he knows. Two hundred?

The day is bright and the sun warms my skin. The garden I planted last month is thriving. Noticing these things makes me feel better. There's life all around me.

In the garage I grab my bike. Clari's bike used to stand right next to mine in the garage, but last month I sold hers to a girl down the block. I needed the money. The month before, I sold the motorcycle Dad and I built. I could have waited a couple more weeks before selling Clari's bike, but looking at it made me sad.

I pedal down the alley, turn north on Loomis, and set my sights for the Lincoln Park Zoo. I can't get comfortable on my bike seat because the abrasions on my butt hurt. Should have put Vaseline or aloe or something on them.

Before Mom left she told me I needed to get a job within three months, or the money would run out.

Of course there's more reason than money to get a job. There's self-satisfaction, knowing you're contributing to the world. There's a sense of equality with your friends and neighbors, who also need to work.

A job should pay wages that not only cover the basic necessities such as food, shelter, and health, but that also provide other things humans need — vacation time, learning time, money to splurge with now and then.

I'm going to have a tough time finding such a job.

After Mom left I couldn't get up the energy or interest to go out and find work. And part of me thought that if I didn't get a job, maybe Mom would come back and take care of us.

But it's been five months and the only way I'm getting by is through selling stuff. Like Clari's bike. I thought of selling one of Dad's guns, but I couldn't get myself to do that.

I do think of selling Mom's piano . . . that thought's kind of appealing. She left me. Also, she left me in charge. Of everything. I don't play the piano, so I don't need the piano. Mom and Dad bought it maybe ten years ago, combining their Christmas bonus money. It's a Yamaha upright. I could probably get a lot of money for it. Maybe three thousand dollars.

I shove the piano thoughts aside.

This week I'm going to get a job. I'm pretty sure Titus can help me. Maybe even Jake Terranova, Podcastah, can help me. No job, no interview.

Do I really want to be interviewed again? Do I really want to become politically active again?

Yes.

No.

I don't know. Sometimes I wonder if I know enough or am good enough to talk to people about politics. I don't know as much as Dad did. Or as much as Titus does. What if I say the wrong thing when I'm speaking? And — I haven't done it for a year now. Not since Carrie died.

I reach the zoo in good time and soon I'm pedaling homeward, the thick branches strapped across the handlebars of my bike. The zookeeper even gave me a discarded wooden post, which I have bungee-corded onto the back of the bike. I feel like I'm steering Battlestar Galactica down a narrow grocery aisle.

At home I unload the wood, heft it onto my shoulder, and enter the house. When I do, Deeply flies off the piano with a loud, happy squawk.

He didn't leave.

My heart feels better.

"Perch!" he squawks. "Perch!"

"I'm glad you like it," I say, "but I've got to put the pieces together before you can use it." I point to the piano. "Wait there," I say.

Mom's the only one who played the piano. Why should I care if Deeply scratches the hell out of the top? If she wants a perfect piano top, she should be here to watch over it.

I feel guilty thinking like this. But I can't get past her leaving me.

Deeply circles around the inside of the house, then flies back to the piano top and sits on it, staring at the perch. Me, I go down into the cellar and bring up a bucket of hot sudsy water, an old sponge, and some terry-cloth rags. The zookeeper told me to swab everything down, so I do it. She also explained to me that parrots need to change the size of their perch in order to keep their feet strong, which is why she gave me branches in three different sizes.

After an hour I have the contraption together: one thick post that screws into a base, with three branches attached to it, each pointing in a different direction. The whole thing looks like a rural road sign. **Kitchen. Rowan's Bedroom. Bathroom.**

I wipe the sweat off my forehead. Air conditioning would be nice. One of the necessities wages should cover. "Your perch is ready," I inform Deeply.

He's on it so fast I step back in surprise. His wing span is, like, wide. I'm going to have to find out what kind of parrot he is, exactly.

Down on my knees I wipe up the wet floor . . . which means there's a nice clean spot emphasizing how dirty the rest of the floor is. I can't remember the last time we cleaned, me or Mom.

Is Mom cleaning wherever she's living now? Maybe she's living in a barn, bedding down with the horses each night. I could do that. But she wouldn't take me with her.

Deeply looks happy, perched there.

He doesn't pitch forward or backward. He sits there and fluffs his feathers a bit. He closes his eyes.

I think . . . I think he falls asleep.

So I tiptoe around him into the kitchen, rescue the broom from the two chairs it's taped to, grab a couple of dust cloths from the hall closet, and head into my bedroom. In five hours I should have the whole house looking great.

About halfway through my housecleaning Deeply wakes up. I see him look around, spot me, shift from one leg to the other, then fly to a bookcase. He sits there, looks into the nearby mirror, and begins a loud, squawky conversation with his reflection. He talks to himself for an hour.

7 JAKE

I'VE NEVER ENJOYED SUNDAYS, NOT EVEN BACK IN Boston where I was surrounded by family and friends and haunts aplenty. Here in Chicago I enjoy them even less. Sundays aren't work days and they aren't really play days. I think of them as what-to-do days.

First thing I do is go to the gym and work out with the heavy bag and the speed bag. My father disapproved of my joining the Harvard Boxing Club. "*Primum non nocere*, Jake. Haven't I taught you and your sister the importance of that? First, do no harm."

It's not easy growing up with a parent who's a primary care physician, especially one who's concerned with the "whole person," as Dad always puts it.

"It's not the same thing, Dad," I used to reply. "First off, I'm not a doctor. Second off, somebody's going to try doing harm to me at the same time I'm trying to punch them. Boxing isn't a healing relationship, it's an adversarial one."

It's not so much that I enjoy punching people as that I love being able to deflect their attacks and defend myself.

And the strategy. I love the strategy.

After the bags I run six miles through Lincoln Park's trails. I have to admit, Chicago did something right — something highly cultured, even — by building this magnificent 1,200-acre public park that stretches for seven miles along Lake Michigan. I was so impressed by Lincoln Park that I did a podcast on it soon after I moved into town.

After my run I shower and go out for brunch. Sitting there in the outdoor cafe with my iPad and third cup of coffee and second chocolate croissant, I think *ballgame,* so I check the schedule. Cubs aren't in town. Not that interested in seeing the White Sox. Scratch ballgame. Maybe go down to the studio, work on some ideas? No sooner thought than dropped. Seven days a week in the studio is not a good idea, not if you want to remain fresh.

Then it comes to me: something I should do. Not just *should*: something I *want* to do — study a few parrots. Something about Rowan Pickett's parrot was, just . . . off. Are birds really as intelligent as her parrot seemed to be? It was practically carrying on a conversation. Hell, no — it was *intervening* in a conversation I was trying to have with Rowan. The goddamn parrot was trying to negotiate a fee.

The Lincoln Park Zoo is one of the country's few free ones. Another thing Chicago has done right. I wander in from the southern end, near the camels and zebras, stroll north toward the honking seals, cross the main mall, and enter the avian area.

Birds are flying every which way between their indoor dwelling and their outdoor dwelling areas: huge fenced-in compounds crammed with tree branches and bird toys of all kinds — swings, whistles, bells, ropes, ladders.

There were no bird toys of any kind in Rowan Pickett's house. None that I could see, at any rate, and from where I was sitting in the kitchen I could see most of the living room. There were bookcases everywhere, full of books. But no bird toys. Come to think of it, not even a cage or a bird perch.

The absence of bird accoutrements gives me pause. Is it possible that what she claimed is true? That the parrot isn't her bird? I find this hard to believe: the two of them were in sync, and achieving sync comes from sharing the same goals and working together.

I have yet to achieve sync with somebody in that special way. It's a failing. I don't want to go through life alone.

For a time I study the parrots, and when nobody's in earshot I talk to them. Not a one responds in any way. Which might not prove anything, because these birds aren't pets.

When I finally turn away from the parrots I see, maybe two-hundred feet away, somebody who looks like Rowan Pickett. She's in and out of my vision quickly, pedaling a bike that's encumbered with small branches or logs of some sort. I'm pretty sure it's her. Was her, because she's gone.

And that reminds me: if I want the interview with her, I'd better find her a job.

So right there, in front of about two hundred feathered creatures, none of which is paying any attention to me, I duke it out with myself.

Ambitious Self: *You want the interview! Good-looking girl whom Tragedy has buffeted about. Colorful, know-it-all talking parrot that attacks on command. Sleazy gun-toting fascist. Drama! Increase in viewership!*

Humane Self: *If you tell the world that Rowan Pickett ordered her parrot to attack Zeb Snoddy . . . well, then: Rowan Pickett will live a very short life.*

The Selves spar with each other, but neither ends up against the ropes. I turn towards home: not in a mood to study parrots after all.

I'll call on some people, see what I can do. Securing a job for Gun Girl, though — not an easy sell.

In fact, such a difficult sell that my mind goes elsewhere: to Zeb Snoddy over at Rush Hospital. When I call the hospital I'm informed that Snoddy cannot yet have visitors who aren't family.

Which leaves the studio. Waving down a cab I direct the driver to Highland Studios. Going to the studio to check on something isn't the same as spending Sunday there.

I log into the company computer and search the database for film interviews with Rowan Pickett. I find two interviews and one public speech. Just as I'm jotting down the code numbers I hear someone behind me. Before she even says my name, I know who it is.

Harita, my boss, wearing twenty or more metal bangles. Their jingles always foretell her arrival. It's good to have a boss who can't sneak up on you.

"I didn't know you'd be in today, Jake," she says, standing there holding a huge stack of file folders.

"Technically not here, Harita. Just came in to get some info for a podcast I'm considering."

"What on?" she asks, pulling too many files out of the stack and placing them on my desk. Tomorrow's work load.

"Someone I met at yesterday's gun-control rally. Rowan Pickett."

She nods. "Gun Girl."

That makes me stand up straight. "You know her?"

Harita shakes her head. "No, but she was in the news three, four years ago. And then again when her sister was killed a year ago. So sad."

Three or four years ago Rowan Pickett must have been — what, sixteen? "Why was she in the news?"

"Shooting," says Harita. "That's how she got the nickname: Gun Girl."

I don't like the way this is going. I swallow. "She shot someone?"

"*Noooo*. Jake! Really!" Harita rolls her eyes. "She won the Illinois Youth Shooting Sports Competition when she was sixteen. Actually, she won two of the five competitions: rifle and pistol. Perfect scores."

I digest this. "And for that she was called Gun Girl?"

Harita nods. "Yes. We in Chicago felt great pride that one of our own won a competition that's dominated by downstate kids who grow up hunting and fishing. And are usually boys. This was great for girls and great for Chicago. You can find the news articles online, I'm sure. And photos, too. And Jake?"

"Yeah?"

"If you sense something big in what you're doing, Highland Studios is the place for the story. Any podcast you make can be a reaction to the big story. If there is one."

"Sure," I tell her. "I understand."

What I understand is that if Highland Studios catches even a scintilla of what I have on video, they will run with the story. And then harm will be done.

I'm not ready for that.

After saying goodbye to Harita I find another cab and in no time I'm back at my apartment.

My plan is to spend an hour trying to find a job for the formidable Gun Girl, then maybe ninety minutes viewing and analyzing her interviews, taking notes and deciding what, if anything, I can use in my podcast. Maybe half an hour looking up information on Gun Girl the sharpshooter.

My father's admonition starts throbbing in my brain. It lives there in some secret corner and speaks whenever I don't want it to. *First, do no harm. Do no harm. No harm.*

My father would take the side of Humane Self.

I don't know about me.

8 JAKE

THE JOB SEARCH FOR GUN GIRL IS AN ABYSMAL FAIL- ure, and I take the whole thing badly, like it's a reflection on me, Jake Terranova. Okay, that's self-centered thinking. It has little to do with me, it has to do with the economy, which offers plenty of minimum-wage, part-time jobs, but few decent-wage full-time jobs. And I'm assuming Gun Girl wants a good job with good benefits: she could get a minimum-wage job on her own.

This is going to be harder than I thought.

I pour myself a Three Floyds weisse beer and go sit on the balcony, where I can look out at the lake. After a while I come up with a plan: google some statistics, visit some organizations, interview some people. In fact, I can get a podcast out of the whole job-search thing. Maybe more than one. On tap for tomorrow.

Today I log into the studio database and watch the first clip on Rowan Pickett. It's at a Chicago gun-control demonstration, one week after the mass murder of the south-side students who were visiting the Colorado school. Nine students killed, five injured. The gunman made himself the tenth dead body.

The first speaker is the head of the local PAG: Parents Against Guns. She gives the stats on all the murders since Columbine, way back in 1999, and talks about every student since then not understanding that there was a time when angry males didn't walk into schools and murder kids. Every student since then includes me. And Rowan Pickett. We've grown up never knowing there was a time when students didn't have to practice drills for what to do when an armed murderer enters the building.

I don't know where I stand on the whole issue of gun control. I understand why gun-control advocates want guns less readily available, especially to anybody with a grudge or mania or delusions of some kind. But I also understand why other people feel they have some sort of innate right to own a weapon. And many of the pro-gun people appear calm and reasonable. That does not include Zeb Snoddy and his group of swastika-wearing, hate-filled followers.

Rowan is the second speaker. She's introduced as the sister of Clarissa Pickett. Rowan looks terrible. I'm not sure I'd have recognized her. Her skin is pale, her hair is long and lanky, her face drooping.

Grief.

I lean forward a bit, intent on every word she's going to say.

She launches in, no preamble.

"Neither Clari" — her voice catches. She swallows. "Nor I were for gun control. Unless that gun control is total. Which means no guns of any kind for the police or the military."

She swallows again, looks out at the crowd. "I urge you to think the same way. If we allow those who already have an immense number of weapons at their disposal — that's the cops — to control who else is allowed to have guns, then we are willingly turning ourselves into a police state. The cops can and will use their weapons against us. They already do against Black Americans, murdering them on the streets, in their cars, in their homes."

There are some murmurs from the crowd, but mostly they're just looking and listening.

"If we want partial control of guns, like laws against semiautomatic weapons or bump stocks, then we must demand that nobody, not even cops or the military, have access to these weapons. Otherwise, they will be able to use superior weapons against citizens when citizens protest. And don't think they won't use weapons against us."

Right about now I'm thinking Rowan could use an example or two to support her argument. Like the Boston Massacre of 1770, in which armed troops shot into a crowd of "colonials," as we used to be called, murdering five. Like the famous 1912 Bread and Roses strike in Lawrence, Massachusetts, during which a cop fired into an unarmed crowd of strikers, almost all of them women, and killed one of them. Like the Kent State Shootings of 1970, in which armed National Guard fired into a crowd of unarmed college students, murdering four. At Harvard my minor was American Studies, specifically the dark side of our history.

Rowan doesn't give any examples. She continues.

"My sister died . . ." She stops, shields her eyes, then finally looks up "because we live in a violent society. A society that has practiced violence against the Indian tribes, murdering millions of them. *Millions*. A society that today bombs other peoples around the world: Iran, Iraq, Pakistan. The young male murderers *identify* with this military violence. If our country can wipe out entire villages, why can't they — the angry young men — wipe out a roomful of students?

"What we need to control is the *state*. The government that wages war on the world. I'm not asking you to join the other side" — here she waves an arm at the pro-gun rally across the street — "because the other side, for the most part, supports that violence against the world.

"I'm asking you to think. Think about living in a country where good jobs are not the norm, where the living standard is plummeting, health care's eroding, housing's unaffordable, food is poisoned by chemicals, and global warming threatens to make Earth uninhabitable. Think about living in such a country — and only the cops and army carry weapons. Who are those weapons going to be used against?

"Think.

"Think." She looks out at the crowd. "Everyone who's here to speak for gun-control wants to live in a society that is not violent. But you are appealing to the police — those who have permission and approval to practice violence against any of us — to decide who can have a gun and who can't.

"Don't.

"Don't allow the police to decide who can carry a gun and who can't." She points to the pro-gun rally across the street. Almost, it seems, directly at Zeb Snoddy. "Those are the people the police will allow to own guns. But ordinary working class people, especially Black, Latino, Indian, White — the state is going to manufacture reasons why we can't own guns."

She turns and walks off the podium.

A murmur comes from the crowd. I can't tell if it's sympathy or disapproval. The camera pans to the counter-rally across the street, where Snoddy and his supporters are booing as Rowan walks off the platform.

Snoddy himself steps to the front and pumps a fist into the air. "We don't need you, Rowan Pickett! You aren't on our side!"

I watch the rest of the video to see if any of the other speakers refer to Rowan.

They don't.

I click off and sit back in the chair. This isn't what I expected. Rowan Pickett has a world view. It's obvious to me that she's talking about capitalism, though she didn't name the system.

The gun-control side is uncomfortable with her because she wants them to think about the context in which the mass murders take place. They've already come up with the solution — gun-control — so they don't want the more fundamental question of why we are such a violent society. Band-aids are easier to apply than surgery is to perform.

Zeb Snoddy and his ilk hate her because they see nothing wrong with police violence against Native Americans, African-Americans, Latin- and Asian-Americans, you name it.

A breeze blows in off Lake Michigan, rustling the leaves of the trees whose tops reach my balcony. Light is leaving the sky.

To the average person, Rowan Pickett's arguments would sound . . . idealistic. Impractical. Outrageous, even. But I'm not the average person. I recognize that the majority of people aren't taking sides: neither pro-gun nor anti-gun. I wonder what kind of event will end up pushing them in one direction or another. My head is swimming with ideas for podcasts.

Scooping up my computer and empty bottle, I go back inside. I now have a problem with my original podcast idea. Yes, I'm still interested in why Rowan had her parrot attack Snoddy. Hell, I'm even interested in how a parrot can be trained to attack somebody. And I want to know why Deeply is so . . . sentient. There are stories here.

But there's also a story in the gun-control-for-all or gun-control-for-none idea, as espoused by this suddenly-more-complex-than-I-thought south-side working class person.

9 ROWAN

Monday morning. My body and mind know this instinctively. Or have known it since Mom left. Sitting up, I toss off the sheet. There's Deeply on his perch in the living room.

"Good morning, Deeply," I say.

"Morning," he squawks back at me. "New day."

Well . . . true. Morning brings a new day. But is Deeply trying to tell me something? I look across the distance at him. He looks back at me. I wait for him to say something else. He doesn't. I sigh and get out of bed.

I didn't know Mom was going to leave. Maybe she knew, maybe not. But one Monday morning, seven months after Clari was killed, I woke up, wandered into the kitchen — and saw two suitcases sitting by the side door.

"What're those?" I asked Mom, who was sitting at the table staring at nothing.

"I'm going away, Rowan. I've packed my clothes."

"Right," I said, grabbing a box of cereal, pouring some into a bowl.

"I'm going away, Rowan," she repeated.

I stopped pouring the cereal and looked at her. "Wha—? What do you mean? Going where? For how long?"

"I don't know where," she said. "I don't know how long. But I can't stay here."

I felt a hole in my stomach, like I knew the world was about to end. Again. I left the bowl of cereal on the counter and went over to stand next to Mom. "Why? Why can't we stay here?"

Mom shook her head. "Not *we*, Rowan. Me. I am leaving. You are not."

"No! " I shouted. "You can't *leave* me! You *can't*. I'm going with you!"

She shook her head. "I need . . . I need to grieve, Rowan. It's not working, grieving here. I'm holding back your healing process. All day long I sit in a chair and do nothing. And you, who should be out with your friends, who should be out hunting for a job — you sit around and imitate me."

"Okay," I said, "okay. I'll get together with Keisha and everyone else again. I'll call her today. I'll go down to WCC headquarters and help build demonstrations. Tonight: I'll go down tonight. And I'll start job hunting tomorrow morning, first thing. If you're trying to jolt me out of my misery, you've succeeded."

My words came out angry. I glared at her, then dropped into a chair opposite her. Which was when I noticed a stack of papers on the table. With a checkbook on top of them, and a couple of keys.

"Mom," I said, looking directly at her. "Are you thinking of . . . suicide?" My voice caught as I said it.

She took my hand in hers. "No. I'm not. But I need to . . . do things. Yell. Scream. Cut off my hair." She kind of laughed. "Cut myself. Wear rags. Roll in the dirt. Build a shrine somewhere. I don't know what I need to do, Rowan, but I need to get away from here and do it." She squeezed my hand. "I'll be back. I will come back."

I sat there. Not able to speak. Not able to move. This wasn't real. Was it? Mothers don't leave their children

"I've talked to Titus and Genevieve. And to MaryEllen and Patrick. They'll help you, Rowan. You talk to them when you need to, and ask them for help if you need it."

She touched the pile of papers. "Here's the checkbook and the savings book, and a key to the safe deposit box. I've written out everything you need to pay, and when: gas, electric, water, property taxes. I've written out a budget you should follow, to make the money last. You'll have to get a job by the end of three months — but it's better if you get it now. Get out and be part of the world again." She looked at me. "We've let this go on too long. I need to confront my grief, and you need to get out of the house."

I stared at the pile of papers without seeing them, ignoring everything she was saying except one thing: She was leaving. My mother was leaving me. Leaving me all alone.

"How do you know I'll be okay?" I demanded. "How do you know I can survive?"

She stood, came behind me, and kissed the top of my head. "You are strong, Rowan. And—" she stepped to the side and tried to turn my head toward her, but I wouldn't let her do that — "you will recover sooner if I'm not here."

Suddenly I screamed. "*Nooooooo! Nooooooo!*" I jumped up from the chair and pounded the table. "You can't go, Mom! You can't *leave* me! Mothers don't leave their children!"

"Be mature, Rowan. Be strong. I need this. I . . . I can't live without doing this."

That stopped me.

I wiped the tears from my eyes and the snot from my nose. I felt empty. Hollow. Like there was nothing at all inside me.

After a while I spoke. "When will you be back?"

She pulled me to her, hugged me hard. I refused to hug her back.

"I don't know," she said, "but every Sunday night I'll leave a new message on my phone, so you know I'm okay. You call every Monday morning and you'll hear the new message and know that I'm okay. But I probably won't call back, Rowan. Just so you know."

"Fine," I said. "I won't call you, either. Why would I want to know if you're okay? You don't care if I'll be okay." I struggled to get out of her arms, which were holding me tight.

"I love you, Rowan. You're going to doubt that, but it's true. I love you and I don't want to burden you with my grief. I need to go away and come back in control of myself. We can go on from there."

Then she unhugged me, kissed my forehead, walked to the door, picked up her suitcases, walked to the garage, and drove away.

I was on the verge of shouting "I hate you!" as she walked out the door, but I made myself not do it. On top of everything else Mom and I had been through with Dad dying from a heart attack and Clari being killed in a school shooting, telling her I hated her might have been the last straw for her. Maybe she lied to me about not contemplating suicide. Maybe she was going to kill herself somewhere far away, and I would never know. Nobody would ever know. I didn't want to be the force that pushed her over the edge.

I guess she didn't care if she was the force that pushed me over the edge.

Except I wouldn't let her do that. I would go on without her.

I lied about not calling her. I call her phone most Monday mornings, just to hear her new message and know that she's alive. Some Monday's I'm so pissed at her I don't bother calling.

I kind of dread today's call, because two days ago — the day of the gun-control rally — was the anniversary of Clari's death. I don't know how Mom's going to handle that.

But her message says, "It's me, Lainey, understanding that we can't control the way the world turns. But it does always turn toward the morning. Love you, Rowan."

She ends every message like that: "Love you, Rowan." Yeah. Sure. I don't leave Mom messages a lot of the time. But sometimes I can't help myself: I tell her things about how I feel, or what I'm doing. Which, until Saturday's demonstration, wasn't much.

I stare at my phone a minute. Mom's voice doesn't sound bad. It sounds . . . stronger. And the morning the world is turning toward is light. The start of a new day.

Just like Deeply said. I look over at him. He's still sitting on his perch, watching me. I give him a thumbs-up sign. He lifts one claw and touches two toes together in a circle. An OK sign? What an amazing bird.

Then I realize I'm still holding the phone. I haven't hung up and I haven't left a message.

I decide to leave one, so Mom doesn't worry about the long gap of silence.

"Uh, it's me, Mom. I started looking for a job. I know, I know, I'm three months late. But I can do it now. I'm going to see Titus tonight. And the weirdest thing, a parrot followed me home, flew in the window, and is living in our house. I drove to the zoo and got him a free perch they were gonna throw out. He talks to me. Hey, I'm not making this up, he really does. He says things like 'Cracker' and 'Apple,' but he also says 'Deeply your friend.' I cleaned the house yesterday, top to bottom. I even polished the furniture and waxed the floors. I'm going to invite MaryEllen over for coffee and donuts this morning. And I'm going to call Keisha."

That's all I feel like saying. I don't say anything like she does. I don't say, "Love you, Mom." I push the end-call button. But I sit there in bed for several minutes, thinking about how Mom sounds a bit stronger.

Me, too. I'm feeling better, more like the me that existed before all the bad things happened. The me that used to fight for a better world.

Bounding out of bed, I take a quick shower, pull on shorts, shirt, and shoes. Then I go into Mom's bedroom, pull open the top dresser drawer, lift the bottom panel, and pull a ten out of its hiding spot.

Mom didn't tell me about this money. I found it on my own about a month ago, when I began to scour the house for any hidden cash. This was the only stash I found, maybe a hundred bucks. Now down to forty.

"Deeply," I say as I walk back toward the living room, "I'm going out for ten minutes. I'll be back with food."

"Deeply come," he responds.

"Okay, just follow me."

As I walk out the front door Deeply flies out over my head.

10   DEEPLEA

I MADE MIRROR CONTACT WITH HOP YESTERDAY, AWARE

that I should not think of her as FeeOna, because I must report to Head of Planet, not to my life mate.

Me: I have found one of the three individuals.

HOP: [LONG SILENCE] This is no time for jokes, DeePlea. A Duty to the Universe demands seriousness. Not even the great SeeZu was able to find an individual her first day on DU.

Me: I am serious, Fe— HOP. I have found one of the three who can help build the organization.

HOP: The organization? You already know what the organization is? Your first day there? [PAUSE] You do like to joke, Dee. I miss you and I miss your jokes. But mirror contact from 134LY away is not a time to be funny.

Me: I am not joking. I am on very serious DU. But you are right to question whether I know what the organization is. [PAUSE] I will need two or three days to be certain.

HOP: Two or three *days*? My head is spinning. Are you certain yours isn't also spinning, Dee? Perhaps from the jolt of entry into another planet? If I recall, the great SeeZu did not have her full powers for five days after entry.

Me: I did what you said, HOP. I waited for somebody to initiate contact. And she did. The instant she saw me — just as the DU-Ovum popped open and the Reluctance Prodder pushed me out — she waved and spoke, encouraging me onward.

HOP: Hmmm. I am happy to hear this, DeePlea. What is her name and what is her job?

Me: Her name is Rowan. She does not have a job. Yet.

HOP: What is her age?

Me: She is twenty in Earth years.

HOP: DeePlea — she is practically a *fledgling*. Now I know you are joking.

Me: [GRUMBLE] I am serious, Fee — HOP, I mean.

HOP: I am going to let you rest, DeePlea. Report back to me in a day or two, after you have recovered from the shock of the Entrance Velocity.

11   ROWAN

AT DUNKIN I KEEP MY HAND IN ONE POCKET, CLUTCH- ing the ten. Half a dozen donuts will cost me almost six dollars. Ever since Mom left I've been eating the least expensive foods I can find. But I make sure they're nutritious: eggs, oatmeal, beans of all kinds, pasta, and ground meat. No desserts at all. Ounce for ounce desserts cost way too much. I'm so glad I dug up and planted our old garden plot. Now I have all the greens I can eat, plus radishes, carrots, and baby beets.

Cleaning the house made me feel good. New day. I'm splurging for donuts to treat MaryEllen for everything she and Patrick have done to help me. Checking in on me at least every other day. Inviting me over for Friday-night pizza and Saturday breakfast.

Choosing the donuts is fun. Two yeast. They go stale fast, but MaryEllen loves them. Two jelly-filled. And two cake-style with vanilla frosting and sprinkles. Valencia, who's been working here since Clari and I were in grade school, throws in three free Munchkins.

When I step outside and look into the sky, there's Deeply, gliding on some air current. I give a shrill whistle, raise my arm, twirl my hand around, and point toward home. He'll be there before me, flying in through the same open window he used the first day.

I knock on MaryEllen's side door.

"Rowan?" she asks. Probably wondering if I'm okay.

"Hey, Els, I just bought some donuts and need help eating them. Wanna come over for coffee and donuts?"

Glancing at the donut box she processes this information, then smiles. "Give me five minutes and I'll be there."

Els is talking as she walks into my house. But she stops mid-sentence and stares. "What is *that*?" she demands, pointing at Deeply.

"A parrot. It followed me home. It talks."

She moves into the kitchen sideways, keeping an eye on Deeply, then pulls out a chair and sits so she can keep him in full view. I place mugs and small plates on the table, along with napkins and a knife.

I cut one of the sprinkles-topped donuts in half and take it to Deeply, who inspects it first one way, then another.

"Donut," I say to him, kind of waving my index finger around the half-donut. "Sprinkles," I say, touching a sprinkle or two with my little finger. He reaches out a claw and takes the half donut.

"I called my mother this morning," I tell MaryEllen, and that gets her attention. "I was worried about her, because Saturday was a year since Clari died."

MaryEllen pauses in the act of biting into one of the yeast donuts.

"She sounded pretty good, Els. She said the world is always turning toward the morning."

"Mmmm," MaryEllen replies through a mouthful of donut. She sips some coffee. "That's good news. She didn't say anything about when she's coming back?"

Biting into a jelly-filled donut — oh, is the sweetness ever delicious! — I shake my head. As soon as I get a job, I can have more donuts.

"I'm determined to find a job," I tell her, changing the subject about whether Mom's coming back. "I think Titus will give me some leads."

She nods at that. "I'm sure he will, Rowan. He's a good man."

MaryEllen is not comfortable around Black or brown people. I've always been able to tell that from her body language. But Titus, Genevieve, and Keisha have been coming to our house — my house — since I was born, so Els knows them. And that makes her comfortable with them.

Deeply finishes eating his half-donut. He drops from his perch to the floor and starts licking up the crumbs. His tongue flicks in and out.

"Look at that," says MaryEllen, amazed.

She's less amazed — startled, actually — when Deeply flies to the table and lands on it. He walks up to the donut plate.

"Do-nut," he squawks.

MaryEllen's mouth falls open. "He *does* talk! Rowan, this is amazing!"

"It is. It definitely is." I pick up the knife to cut into a yeast donut, but Deeply protests.

"Sprink-les! Sprink-les!"

I hand him the other half of the sprinkles-covered donut and he doesn't even examine it. With either eye. He just bites into it.

MaryEllen moves her chair back from the table a bit. "He's a, uh, big bird. Does he eat much?"

"Just donuts," I joke. "Sprinkles type."

"Apples!" squawks Deeply. "Crackers!"

MaryEllen raises an eyebrow.

"It was a joke, Deeply. I know you eat other things besides donuts."

"Deeply?" she asks.

"Yeah, that's his name."

"I noticed, Rowan — and pardon me for mentioning this — but I noticed that you don't have any newspapers on the floor. Beneath his perch."

I stare at her, wondering how I could have not thought of this.

"Where does he, uh, poop?"

I'm still sitting there in stunned silence, my doughnut halfway to my mouth, jelly oozing out everywhere. Finally I shake my head. "I don't know. I never thought about it."

I glance at Deeply, to see if he's going to respond in any way. He seems interested only in the donut. He's picking the sprinkles off, eating them one at a time.

"Well, but, — have you seen bird poop anywhere in the house?" MaryEllen looks around as she says this. She even looks under the table. "The house looks nice, by the way. I can smell the furniture polish." She stands and hugs me from behind. "I'm so glad you're getting better, Rowan. So glad." She sits back down and pats my arm.

I put my hand on top of hers. "Thanks. I'm happy I'm getting better, too. I'm glad you came over. After I get a job I'll have you and Patrick over for dinner. Is he on the road this week?"

"Until tomorrow," she answers, "then out again on Sunday. Should I have a jelly-filled or another yeast?"

"We can split them," I say. Sort of absent-mindedly, because what I'm really thinking about is why I haven't seen any bird shit around the house. I'm not going to find it on the bathroom towels, am I? Or on my bedspread? I look up at the hutch where Deeply sat the first night. I'll have to investigate this after MaryEllen leaves.

She nods, picks up the knife, and expertly cuts a yeast donut in half, and then a jelly one. Deeply walks over to watch. "No," she says, trying to shoo him away. "You chose the sprinkles."

"No more donuts for you today, Deeply," I tell him. "I'm going to buy you birdseed."

He flies off the table and back to his perch, where he sulks.

MaryEllen studies his sulk. "Speaking of men," she says, sliding half of each donut onto my plate, then hers, "I notice one visited you on Saturday."

"Huh?" I say, before I remember. "Oh, yeah. Jacob Terranova. He's a podcaster."

I pour us each another cup of coffee.

"Was this a date?" she asks, sounding hopeful.

"No."

"He's a good-looking guy," she tells me.

"He's an egotistical, opinionated, privileged . . . Bostonian," I add, not sure how to finish the sentence.

She smiles. "I think you're interested, Rowan. I can see something coming from this."

I roll my eyes and take a big gulp of coffee. I don't think I'm interested. Am I? The guy kept coming after me even though I told him to leave me alone. Twice. And then he grabbed my arm from behind.

It felt good to show him what happens when you grab a woman from behind.

Maybe I'm interested in hitting him again.

After MaryEllen goes home I do the dishes. And then I search the whole house for bird shit.

I find absolutely nothing. Which puzzles me.

Deeply.

12 JAKE

SNODDY'S BODYGUARDS, DRESSED IN FATIGUE PANTS and what look like bulletproof vests, no shirts, are sitting outside his door on chairs they must have dragged over from the visitor lobby.

One of them sticks a beefy foot out as I approach Snoddy's room.

I hand him a business card and show him my camcorder. "I'm here to interview Zeb Snoddy."

He eyes the Sony camcorder with interest.

I tighten my grip on it.

He doesn't even look at my card, just drops it on the floor. Wants a rise out of me.

Won't get it.

He makes a head motion to the other guard, like: *Go ask*.

To my surprise the second guard returns and motions with his head that I can go in. "Five minutes," he says, "and if you aren't out by then, I drag you out." He sneers. "Tech weenie like you shouldn't be too much trouble."

Faulty inference.

Snoddy's sitting up in bed, the left side of his face swathed in bandages. News reports say he lost an eye in the attack. Was he meant to lose an eye? Or was the attack meant to kill him? He's hooked up to an IV drip.

I'm thinking he's one tough dude, to be ready to talk to me just three days after the attack and operation.

Snoddy stares straight ahead. Motions me to his right side. After I move there he stares at me with one malevolent eye.

"Mr. Snoddy, I'm Jake Terranova of Jake's Takes podcasts, and I'd like to interview you about what happened at the recent gun-control rally."

"You pro-gun or anti-gun?" he demands.

Which puts me in an awkward position, because I had been more or less for gun control, figuring that, Yeah, any sane person understands the need for investigation into and government control of who carries guns. And such a sane person has to support some sort of gun control, because some sort of gun control might keep angry, hate-filled young men from slaughtering students, pedestrians, restaurant goers, church goers, concert goers.

But that was before I watched Rowan Pickett argue against a police state and place the blame for the violence not on guns, but on the reality of our existence: the most heavily-armed country that ever existed, waging war around the world.

Now . . . I'm not so sure what I believe.

"I leaned toward gun control," I tell Snoddy, "but I'm starting to change my mind."

"Why?"

I can't tell a guy like this "the issue is complicated." He'd laugh me right out of the room.

I give him a seemingly simple reason. "I believe in self-defense." Which I do.

"What do you want to know?" he demands.

I start the camcorder rolling and aim it at him. He sits up a little straighter and glares into the screen. "Who attacked you at the rally?" I ask.

"Don't know. But they'll be sorry they did. They stabbed me in the eye. Lucky for me, not my shooting eye."

"Do you think it was a gun-control person who did this?"

"Had to be."

Wrong.

I realize this is where I have to be crazy careful. I can't bring up Rowan Pickett in this context: Snoddy will jump on that and assume she did it. So for now I'm just asking questions, gathering what information I can. "What's your relationship to the gun control groups in Chicago?"

Snoddy frowns. "None. I have nothing to do with 'em."

"But you know when they're holding a rally, and you always show up across the street, isn't that right?"

"Their cowardly rallies, which seek to deprive us of our Constitutional rights, are public information. It's my duty as an American to represent the values this nation was founded on: white men conquering the wilderness and building a nation of freedom, where white women and children can walk the streets in safety."

He smiles as he says this. Challenging me to rise to the bait of his racist jargon. Figures I'm a liberal and will respond indignantly.

When I don't react, he ups the ante. "You don't look white."

"Skin color runs a gamut." He won't know what the fuck I'm talking about. I keep the camcorder running.

"You don't look spic. A-rab? Dago?"

I keep cool on the outside. Inside I'm fuming. "So you have no personal hatred of anybody on the gun-control side?" I ask, ignoring his taunts.

He snickers. Probably knows he's got me fuming. "Don't know 'em. Don't care about 'em."

"What about the pro-gun side?" I ask. "Any enemies there?"

He studies me. "We stand together."

Now's the time to ask him about Gun Girl. That's why I'm here: to ask him why he hates Rowan Pickett. Or even whether he hates her: I have only her word for it.

My footage shows her parrot attacking Snoddy.

But she denies it's her parrot.

Now's the time to ask him.

I can't get myself to do it.

Do no harm.

Too dangerous for her if he in any way connects her with his lost eye.

I should ask.

I can't.

But I've got to ask something, so I do. "Do you feel the police support your side?"

Snoddy guffaws. "The cops understand why we need guns."

"What do the police know about who attacked you?"

"Nothing yet. But I'll find out who did this, one way or another."

By now it's clear to me I'm not going to ask him about Rowan Pickett. And since I'm not going to do that, there's little left to ask. I do a quick assessment of whether or not I've got enough for a podcast of some sort and decide I can ask one more question.

"Do you feel that every single American should own a gun?"

He's not expecting the question. Either that, or nobody's ever asked it before. He's silent, thinking how he should answer.

"No," he says at last. "Not every single American. Only responsible Americans who understand their duty to uphold the freedoms of a white nation."

I click off the camcorder and thank Snoddy for the interview just as one of the bodyguards enters the room to usher me out.

13   DEEPLEA

Me: I am in the bowels of the Beast.

HOP: Isn't that a bit dramatic, DeePlea?

Me: You have no idea, HOP. No idea. The government *withholds* social welfare from the people! It does not provide food. Or clothing! Or housing! Or health care! Or higher education!

HOP: DeePlea, your orange feathers — they are sticking out as I have never before seen them sticking out.

Me: [Pacing] Our planet was right to send me here, HOP. The Beast's military budget is more than $700 billion a year. Which is more than the *combined* military spending of the next ten highest countries.

HOP: What do the common people think about this?

Me: They don't. Most of them simply go on day to day, without thinking. Some ask for better schools, for better health care, for national parks, for public transportation, for retirement living. But . . . they do not seem to connect the military spending with the deprivation of social needs.

HOP: What about the young people? The fledglings, like Rowan, whom you told me about.

Me: Most young people have no good future. The jobs are menial, the pay just enough to keep them alive. They are worried that the planet will become too hot for them to survive. But — [Puzzled] people do not seem to connect the deterioration of these things to the existence of a profit-driven ruling class or the ever-increasing military spending. They seem hopeless, Fee. Hopeless.

HOP: All of them?

Me: Well . . . no. Some of them are not hopeless.

HOP: Remember your mission, Dee. Your Duty to the Universe. Help the inhabitants build an organization that will end the misery and violence of their daily existence. Find, protect, and nurture three individuals who will help lead such an organization.

Me: I have found one, HOP. I will find two more.

HOP: [Pause] I hope that you have found one, Dee. I hope this fledgling Rowan proves up to the task.

Me: She will. Here on Earth, young people are in the forefront of protest movements. They want control over the society they will inherit.

HOP: We will see how things progress.

Me: Perhaps I should go to another country. India, maybe, or Russia, or Iran, or Brazil? There are millions of parrots in Brazil.

HOP: Which country represents the greatest threat to the planet?

Me: [SIGH]

HOP: Tell me more about this Rowan. Is she really capable of leading the populace to fundamental change?

Me: I believe she is, Fee. HOP, I mean. She is intelligent, analytical, and honest, and she is critical of the ruling class. She is kind. Very kind. She has fed me and housed me and found a perfect perch for me. She knows people who speak out about all the injustices and offer an alternative social and economic organization. This is vital, HOP. Resistance is vital to Earth's survival. In addition, I will soon be meeting Titus and the WCC.

HOP: Who is? Which is?

Me: Titus Longshaw, a Black revolutionary. And the organization he has built: Working Class Control.

HOP: That sounds good, DeePlea. Perhaps things are not as bleak as you make them out to be.

Me: The government captures immigrant families at the Mexican border, puts the parents in one prison compound and the children in another, separating children from their parents. The damage is deep. Probably irreparable.

HOP: [SILENT]

Me: And this is just a test, I'm sure. The ruling class wants to see what it can get away with. It has convinced the working class that it is divided into color groups of white, brown, and black, and it tricks each group into thinking the others are its enemies. Arab-Americans may be rounded up next and thrown into prison camps. Prisons, by the way, are a huge profit-making industry in this country, so imprisoning more people leads to more profits for the ruling class. The former leader of the country wanted to imprison anyone who participated in a public demonstration. This is a dangerous place. My feathers fluff up in horror each time I fly out to gather information.

HOP: Speaking of that, Dee — have you found evidence of any intentions to colonize our planet?

Me: Not yet, HOP, but soon.

HOP: We want you to succeed, DeePlea. To help those who want to overturn this madness. But . . .

Me: But? But what?

HOP: If Earth's self-destruction becomes imminent, you must exit at the same velocity with which you entered. If this occurs . . . if this occurs, we have no choice but to prepare for invasion.

Me: I'm sorry that I'm not optimistic, Fee. HOP, I mean. I am doing my best . . . though, in such a situation, I have no idea what that is.

HOP: How are you doing as an Earth parrot? Does anybody suspect?

Me: [PAUSE] Not exactly.

HOP: Explain.

Me: I did something wrong, HOP. A minor thing, but Rowan is trying to make sense of it.

HOP: Details, please.

Me: I, uh, . . . My mistake was that I didn't defecate in the house. On the floor of the house.

HOP: You . . . they defecate on the floor?

Me: Well, not the humans. But the parrots, yes. I didn't, however, and now Rowan is wondering what that means.

HOP: Can you . . . get yourself to . . .

Me. No.

HOP: I understand. But try to deflect her suspicions. And . . . DeePlea?

Me: [Oiling orange feathers] Oh. Sorry, HOP. What?

HOP: If a parrot on Duty to the Universe is ever discovered to be an alien by the residents — that parrot is immediately recalled from DU. You do understand that, don't you, DeePlea?

Me: Has any parrot ever been discovered?

HOP: Never.

Me: Then there is no need for worry.

HOP: Good. Report to me tomorrow.

Me: I will.

HOP: And DeePlea — you haven't done anything rash, have you?

Me: Why would you ask such a thing?

HOP: There is a blurred space in your brain that I can't read. Have you erected a Pri-Vay shield to block something from me?

Me: As you surmised earlier, my entry into Earth was quite shaky. Possibly my brain is still settling.

HOP: Good. Peace in the Universe.

Me: Peace in the Universe.

14 ROWAN

I PAY FOR THE GROCERIES WITH A CREDIT CARD, WILL-ing the transaction to go through. It does. The only money I have left is what's in the savings account, and I need that to pay property taxes.

Way, *way* long — that's how long I've waited before looking for a job. Should have started months ago.

I don't want a minimum wage job with no benefits. Nobody should have to work at minimum wage jobs. And, I want a job that interests me. If not that, then one that pays well. Maybe allows me to go back to college part-time. I want such jobs for everyone, not just me.

At home I unload the one bag of groceries and watch Deeply talk to himself in the mirror. Then I go out again to buy parrot-blend bird pellets that I read about on the internet. At home I pour some into a small bowl. Deeply flies over to take a look.

"Food," I tell him. "Parrot-blend pellets. Nutritionally sound for avians like you."

He picks one up in a claw and turns it this way and that, examining it first with one eye, then with the other. Maybe it's a rule in the parrot world that you have to look at everything twice. Finally he puts the pellet in his mouth, crunches it, and swallows.

Something like a big smile breaks out on Deeply's face. He positions himself closer to the bowl, reaches down with his beak, and removes another pellet.

"Good?" I ask.

"Good."

While Deeply's eating I text Keisha.

> **Me: Can I come visit?**
>
> **Keisha: Hey!! When?**
>
> **Me: Half an hour.**
>
> **Keisha: CU**

"Deeply," I say. "I'm going to visit my best friend. You stay here. We'll go out together later."

"Peace," he responds.

I stare at him. Is that a bird response? It seems like such a human response.

Deeply bites into a pellet and looks at me. "*Awwwwkkkk*!" he screeches.

I cover my ears, go into my room, and pull a box out from under the bed. It's a soft-sided box I made out of five granny squares: one for the bottom and one for each of the sides. I also crocheted two handles, so I can pick it up and carry it. The box is full of, what else? — granny squares.

Even though Keisha and I didn't grow up next door to one another, and even though we never went to the same school, I've known her all my life, just like I've known her mother and father all my life. Dad and Titus were in the Army together and became good friends.

One time when I was in third grade and Keisha in fourth, we were upstairs in her bedroom, where she was sewing clothes on a sewing machine. Keisha wanted to be a clothing designer even way back then, and when she was in high school she took fashion design classes at the Art Institute and a whole lot of other places. She works in a small boutique store on Halsted Street, near Armitage, where the owner lets Keisha sell her own fashions.

Mom had just taught me how to crochet a granny square, and I remember what I said to Keisha. "Keisha, I'm going to crochet you a granny square every week. Every week, Keish."

"What am I going to do with all those granny squares, Rowan? I hope you know that the granny square craze ended a long time ago."

That's how Keisha talked: ten years old but sounding twenty.

"You'll think of something, Keish."

"Of course I'll think of something, Rowan — I'm a year older than you are." She rolled her eyes and continued with her sewing. I sat on the floor tailor-fashion and concentrated on making Keisha's first granny square. Clari sat between us, making pot holders out of nylon loops.

I've kept my promise of ten years ago. Every single week I crochet a granny square for Keisha. At first Keisha just let them stack up, but after a while she began making the usual granny-square projects out of them: scarves, ponchos, shawls, purses, pillows, afghans, shirts, shorts, caps, you name it. And then, a couple of years ago, she began incorporating them into her designs. A dress with a granny-square pocket. A jacket with a granny-square back.

Even though Keisha has been dropping by to visit me, I didn't give her the granny squares. Somewhere inside, I knew I wanted to give her the whole bunch of them when I felt like myself again. There's a lot of solid black squares in my box. But then, as I started to feel better, I switched to gray. Last week I crocheted a purple one.

I get my bike from the garage, stuff the squares into the pannier, and pedal northward. Almost the same route I took to get Deeply's perch, just not as far.

There's a bike rack near Kutt Klothes, so I use it and enter the store. Keisha's straightening out clothes on racks, examining the pieces critically. She sees me, smiles, and when I reach her gives me a huge hug. I hug her back just as hard.

"I'm so glad you texted," she says. "I knew you would. Just not when."

"Yeah. I'm so sorry, Keish. It was bad."

She nods. "I know."

"I brought you something." I spread open the crocheted box and show her what's inside.

She looks in and laughs. "You've been crocheting all this time?! Even when I lugged my sewing machine over and kept you company? And you didn't *tell* me??!"

"I guess I wanted to surprise you."

She pulls out a handful of squares. Pauses.

"I know, I know," I say. "Kind of . . . forbidding. But for a while I couldn't crochet in any other color but black."

She pulls a small one out of the batch, walks over to a table, and smooths out the square. "This is lovely, Rowan. So unlike you."

I reach into the box and throw a square at her.

Keisha laughs. "Now, I didn't mean that the way it came out. I meant that most of your squares are made of yarn. This one's mercerized cotton. It's elegant. What made you switch?"

I shrug. "I think I got tired of black yarn. I tried mercerized linen, too. I found all kinds of mercerized thread in Mom's closet. Steel crochet hooks, too."

Keisha looks at me.

"I wish she'd taken them with her," I say.

"So she would be doing something she likes?"

I nod. "Them, or the piano."

Keish laughs as she dumps all the squares onto the table and sorts through them quickly, pulling out the "elegant" ones. Some of which I made in gray. She glances at my hair and says, "Is that one of Clari's feathers you're wearing?"

"Yeah. I went to the gun-control rally Saturday and . . . I kinda wanted part of Clari to be there with me."

She nods and sorts out more squares. "These are beautiful," she says. "I have an idea of what I might do with them." She looks at me. "I'm glad you're back, Rowan. I've missed you."

That kind of chokes me up, but I fight it back. "I've missed you, too, Keish. And I'm glad I'm back."

"Daddy will be so glad," she says. "Will you be coming to the Saturday rallies?"

I nod. "But I don't know about speaking at them. I haven't . . . I feel . . . I guess I don't know if I have the skills anymore."

Keisha looks at me. "Girl, you have *skills*. They'll come back to you. You know Daddy thinks you're the best speaker WCC has."

"Can't be," I say. "Titus is by far the best speaker WCC has."

Keisha nods. "You're on the list, though. Maybe number four. Or five. Or six."

This time I throw the whole box of granny squares at her. Which she catches and throws back to me in an underhand pass. "Wanna go to lunch?" she asks. "My relief should be here in a few minutes."

"If you loan me the lunch money. I'll pay you back as soon as I get a job."

"No problem," she says. "You have any leads?"

I shake my head. "I'm going to see Titus tonight. I'm hoping he can give me some leads."

"You know Daddy will do anything for you, Rowan. If there's a job to be found, he'll point you toward it."

I nod. "I called Mom this morning."

Keisha looks at me. "And?"

"She . . . I think she actually sounded better, even though Saturday was the anniversary of Clari's death. She said something about the world always turning toward the morning."

Keisha considers this.

"Does that sound positive to you?" I ask her.

She nods. "It does. I hope she's healing, too, just like you are."

The door opens and we both look up. An older woman, maybe my mom's age, walks in. She eyes me up and down, probably wondering what in the world I'm doing in a designer-clothing store. She eyes the feather in my hair. *Tres passé* she must be thinking.

"Hi, Gretchen," says Keisha. "I'm going to take a lunch break with my friend Rowan, but I'll be back in an hour."

Gretchen goes to stand behind the counter. "Have fun," she says.

15   JAKE

BEING IN CLOSE PROXIMITY TO SNODDY LEAVES A BAD taste in my mouth. I text Harita that I won't be in until one o'clock. Flex hours are fantastic.

I'm conflicted. Because A: I want to interview Gun Girl and her parrot. There's a story there, and my intuition tells me it's a big one. Because B: No matter how much I want to explore the Zeb-Snoddy-loses-an-eye angle, I can't bring myself to pursue it. Because C: It would be morally wrong to expose anybody to Snoddy's vengeance.

Even the smart-ass parrot.

Unlike Ishmael, I don't go to sea when I'm troubled: I go on a walk. Or down to the gym, to metaphorically knock the hats off my problems. Walking, especially, helps me clarify things. Solutions I didn't know I had enter my brain from somewhere in the universe.

So I walk west on Jackson, then north on Franklin. Wondering what Rowan Pickett is doing right now. I still haven't found her a job. Not even a job lead. But does this matter, if I'm not going to pursue the Snoddy angle? I ruminate about that and think that maybe I'd like a cup of strong coffee. Yes, it does matter. Because A: I still want to interview her and the parrot. Because B: it's pretty obvious that she needs a job. Does she have a mother or father? If so, where are they? Does she live alone? If so, how can she afford to? Does she have any friends? The neighbor next door? Wait . . . she mentioned somebody. Titus Longshaw. The head of . . . wait, it'll come to me. WCC. Working Class Control, the organization with a strong presence in the trade unions.

Trade unions.

Jobs.

I'm mulling over the ramifications of finding this Titus guy when something in the sky distracts me. Something green, blue, turquoise, and purple.

Deja vu and *deja vu*. If that isn't Rowan's parrot, I'll eat my Patriot's cap.

I raise my arm, point at the parrot, and shout, "Yo! Deeply! Get your ass down here!"

Before I know what's happening the bird has plummeted downward, corrected itself, and landed on a garbage can a foot away. It looks at me. No, it doesn't just look. It *studies* me, like it's looking inside.

The whole maneuver, and especially the deep stare, has caught me off guard. I'm speechless for a second or two. But I recover. "Deeply," I say. "Where's Rowan?"

"Lunch."

Lunch. Does the bird mean that Rowan is out to lunch, or does the bird mean that it wants lunch? Must be the latter, because I doubt Rowan can afford to go out to lunch.

"Lunch it is. What would you like?"

"Do-nut," it squawks.

I laugh, not because Deeply wants a donut, but because there's something magical about this. It's as if this bird is carrying on a conversation. Which certainly seemed to be happening Saturday . . . but now, in the sober light of Monday, I suspect never happened. What I'm witnessing is a fantastic coincidence of verbal exchanges that on the surface seem to be communicating — but in reality aren't.

A Dunkin shop looms ahead. I point to it. "Donuts just ahead. Any particular kind?" I start walking and suddenly the parrot is riding on my shoulder. I'm aware of its powerful talons. They serve to remind me that whether or not the parrot communicates, it does attack.

"Sprink-les," Deeply answers.

People are staring at us as I walk down the street. No. People are staring at *me* and wondering what kind of whacko I am to be accompanied by a tall, colorful parrot. They don't seem to think the bird's whacko.

They're wrong.

We reach Dunkin and I point to a nearby bench. "Wait there. I'll be right back with a do-nut. Sprink-les variety," I say, imitating his glottal stops.

He flies off my shoulder and perches on the back of the bench.

"And tame the orange feathers a bit," I say, running a finger up and down my neck in roughly the same place the bird's orange feathers stick out. "You want to look good."

If birds can look abashed, then Deeply embodies abashment. He begins to groom his orange feathers. I think the bird might be stressed.

When I return with one large coffee and two donuts, both of them covered with sprink-les, the orange feathers are groomed and glossy. Making myself comfortable on the bench, I break a donut in half.

Whoosh! Deeply has his talons into a half before I can even offer it to him. He examines it carefully, then chomps into it.

Pulling out my camcorder, I turn it on.

"I'd like to interview you. Is that permissible?" Always get the subject's cooperation.

I've already got my question on tape and am filming Deeply's nod. "What's your name?" I ask.

"Deeply."

A couple of people stop and watch. I turn so that my back is toward them.

"Where are you from?"

"Not here," the bird answers.

That gives me pause. How can a bird know it's not from here? Maybe Rowan has practiced Q and A with her pet.

"What's your favorite food?"

"Do-nuts. Apples. Crackers. Pellets."

Three out of four sound appetizing. "Do you understand me when I talk to you?"

"*Awwwkkkkk!*"

The squawk is so loud I cover my ears. I'm going to have some serious sound adjustments to do.

What, exactly, does *Awwwkkkkk!* mean? That he's exhausted his supply of English words? Or that he doesn't want to answer my question? Wants to deflect me from pursuing this line of investigation?

Dunkin Donuts, now known simply as Dunkin, originated in Massachusetts. Eating them makes me miss home. I bite into my donut, put it down, sip some coffee, put it down — the camcorder always ready in my other hand.

Deeply finishes with his first half and reaches out a talon for the second half. I place it in his hand. Foot. His versatile appendage. I film the talon and donut as they go by.

"Do you enjoy being a parrot?" I ask him.

He smiles and bites into more donut.

"Do you like people?" I ask.

"No!"

"But you like Rowan," I argue.

"Deeply love Rowan." He even stops eating as he says this, underlining the solemnity of his love.

"Does Deeply belong to Rowan?" I ask. "Is Deeply Rowan's bird?"

"Belong bad. Free good."

I hear clapping behind me. Five or six people are listening to the interview. "Let's hear it for the bird!" one of them shouts. More clapping.

Deeply studies them. I wait for some sort of pronouncement, but he says nothing.

Taking my cue from the audience's response, I formulate my next question. "What advice do you have for humans, Deeply?"

He straightens on his bench perch, holds his donut out to the side, and speaks. "Revolt. Revolt! *Revolt*!!!" What started as a simple reply escalates into a screeching crescendo.

Silence from behind me.

Deeply looks satisfied with his answer and goes back to the donut.

I can sense that the audience disperses.

"Crazy bird," one of them says.

"Not as crazy as the guy interviewing it, you ask me."

I look around to make certain we're alone. When I feel that nobody's paying any attention to us, I resume the interview. "Deeply. Is there someone whose orders you follow?"

"HOP."

"No," I say. "Let me repeat the question: Is there someone whose orders you follow?"

That earns me another *Awwwkkkkk*, so I go on to my next question.

"Did Rowan order you to attack somebody?"

"No."

"No?" I prod.

"Correct."

The answer gives me pause. I'm back to thinking the parrot *is* sentient and we *are* carrying on a conversation.

And if we are, I want to pursue the question. "On Saturday I saw you flying above the gun-control rally," I say.

"Donut gone," he says, looking around to make certain there's no more food. "Deeply gone." And with that the parrot pumps its wings and soars away.

I'm left on earth, following it with the camcorder.

16 ROWAN

I LIFT A TISSUE-WRAPPED PACKET OUT OF THE PAN-
nier. Inside is one of Keisha's designs. She claims it shows her gratitude for the big bunch of granny squares, but I think it shows she's trying to cheer me up. Or improve my sense of style. It's a sleeveless black top with a row of small colorful granny squares running around the midriff. I think the squares are from eleventh grade.

"Deeply, I'm home!" I announce as I walk in the side door.

He's on his perch. Sleeping.

Stealthily I put the package down, take out my phone, and snap off some shots of Deeply. He leans from one leg to the other. Tiptoeing past him I find a new angle and take more shots.

I move into the kitchen, open my computer, and drag a couple of the phone photos onto my desktop. I study them a while, then hunt for types of large parrots. Several are listed, among them the African Grey, which I already know about. Deeply is clearly not an African Grey, which is, *Duh*, a pretty much all-grey parrot.

Nada. I find no parrot that looks like Deeply. The same thing happens when I do a kind of reverse search: I upload a photo of Deeply and ask Google Images to identify it.

Parrot.

As if I didn't know.

When I look up from my search, Deeply's awake, studying me.

"Hey Deeps," I say, "How are you?"

He jumps a mile, spins around, and looks behind himself. Then to one side, then to the other. He even bends down and looks beneath his perch.

"Only one Deeply," he squawks. "Only one."

I sit there, stunned. This bird understands abbreviations and plurals. This bird understands *being*. Identity. Selfhood.

"Uh," I stutter. "Yes, there is only one Deeply. But in human speech . . . I mean, in English, we sometimes shorten a name and add an *s* at the end. Like, I sometimes call MaryEllen Els."

He tilts his head to one side and studies me.

"This shows we love the one we're talking to."

"Deeps," he squawks, as if thinking it over. "Deeps."

"Do you like it?"

He struts back and forth on his perch. "Deeps."

"What kind of parrot are you, Deeps?"

He stops strutting. "Special."

"Like . . . a mutation?"

He flies over to me and sits on the tabletop, looking me in the eye. "Not mu-ta-tion."

I look at him and slowly move my hand in his direction. He examines it. If he wanted to, he could probably bite my finger off. I just read that large parrots can exert 200 pounds of pressure with their beaks. "Can I touch you?" I ask.

He makes a rumbling sound, which I take as a yes, so I carefully place my hand across his chest. His feathers are smooth and he feels warm to my touch.

And I can discern a heartbeat. Which could easily be faked.

I remove my hand from Deeply's chest and lean back in my chair. "Deeply — are you a robot? A bot of some kind?"

His head snaps back. He looks at me first with one eye, then with the other.

He stiffens all over, head to tail.

And then he marches down the table in a kind of stiff-legged robot way.

I watch, wondering if I said some magic word that made him reveal his robot nature . . . or if he's making fun of me.

Deeply makes a stiff, robot-like turn at the end of the table and marches back toward me, legs lifting outward, wings tucked in but synchronized to the foot movements.

When he reaches the middle of the table he falls onto his back, kicks his feet, rolls from side to side, and lets out a series of chirpy laughing sounds. Sort of *Cha-haha, cha-haha*.

He's definitely making fun of me. "Laugh all you want," I tell him, "but I think you're a robot."

He rights himself and walks toward me. "Deeply not robot. Deeply have proof."

"Yeah?" I say. Skeptical. "What's the proof?"

"Poop."

"Poop? As in bird shit?"

He nods. "Robots not poop."

"That's right. And you don't poop, either, Deeply."

He straightens his shoulders. "Deeply not poop indoors. Different from Deeply not poop."

His level of understanding is amazing. Clearly he's something different. Bot is the only answer.

"You're a very smart bird, Deeps. I can't imagine there's another bird as smart as you."

He smiles.

I lean forward, elbows on the table, head in my hands. "Are you smarter than me?"

He studies me a while. Then he unfolds a wing, reaches out, and pats me on the shoulder.

I take that as yes, he's smarter than me. Or thinks he is.

"Come see poop," he boasts, and flies off the table, past the piano, and out the window.

Flying is sure an efficient way of getting places. By the time I walk outdoors Deeply is sitting on the azalea bush. He points his beak downward, to the space between the bush and the foundation. I push a branch aside and look. A small pile of greenish bird shit is building up. Gross. But it looks real enough.

Somehow, examining bird shit is not on my list of to-do's right now. I let the branch spring back into place.

"Okay," I say. "I'll accept that you poop."

Deeply smiles and shifts from one foot to the other.

"But you aren't a regular parrot, Deeps. You are *something*. Something different."

"Hi, Rowan!" It's MaryEllen, leaning over her front porch rail. "I thought I heard your voice. Who are you talking to?"

"Deeply."

"Your parrot?"

I detect a note of concern in her voice, as if I might be a bit mental.

"Yeah. Hey, I went to lunch with Keisha today. And I'm going to see Titus after he gets off from work."

"Oh, I want to tell you," she says, "that pod guy was knocking on your door earlier. I told him you weren't home."

Pod guy? Oh. Jacob Terranova, *pahdcastah*. "What did he want?"

"Well, I don't know. To see you, I guess. I think he's interested, Rowan. And he's a good-looking guy. Strong shoulders, too."

"Did he say he'd come back?"

"He didn't say. What should I tell him if he does and you're not here?"

I think about this for a second. "Tell him I'll be home tomorrow."

Maybe he has a job for me. If Titus can't get me one, I don't want to write off Jacob Terranova. Even though taking his job would mean giving him an interview. I'm just not sure about his motives.

But I do want to speak up about the root cause of the mass murders. And for the right of self-defense. And other things, too. Part of me wants to get back into the struggle. Like I was before Clari was killed and Mom left.

I walk over to MaryEllen's porch and sit and talk a while. She tells me that when Patrick returns from his current trip he's going to start putting in a new upstairs bathroom. He's already remodeled their downstairs one and their kitchen. Patrick's a long-haul driver and you can always tell when he's home because his rig is parked at the end of the street.

Deeply sits on the porch railing, uttering what sound like happy parrot noises every now and then. Either that or he's still laughing. *Cha-haha, cha-haha.*

After a while I realize it's time to get going if I want to catch Titus, so I say goodbye to MaryEllen, take my bike out of the garage, and pedal southward.

Instead of flying overhead Deeply decides to perch on the rear rack. Instead of facing forward, or even sideways, he straddles the rack and faces backward. Every time I hit a bump he squawks indignantly. But mostly he spends his time bent forward, as if he's looking at himself in the reflector.

17 ROWAN

AS I APPROACH WCC HEADQUARTERS I SEE ANTWON Harper standing guard outside the door. He's not carrying a rifle, not like I've seen in photos of the Black Panthers, but I'm sure he's armed. G17 with a hybrid holster, most likely. What kind of bodyguard would go around unarmed? Especially when Titus Longshaw is a Black revolutionary . . . in the city that murdered Fred Hampton as he lay in bed at night, the cops knocking down the door and pumping eighty rounds of ammunition into the wall of Hampton's bedroom. Pumping most of the rounds into Hampton, whose life poured out onto the mattress. Yeah, Antwon is armed, and I support his being armed and anybody who doesn't, doesn't want to agree that the oppressed have a right to fight back.

I zig over the curb and zag onto the sidewalk, coasting to a stop in front of Antwon, who's standing under a Black Lives Matter poster, which is right next to a Fight for the Working Class one.

"Antwon! How are you?"

Normally Antwon's friendly, even while alert and on duty, but this time he barely looks at me. His attention is focused on Deeply, who's still perched on the bike rack. Antwon's studying Deeply, and Deeply, who's turned himself forward on the bike rack, is studying Antwon.

"Where'd you get that parrot?"

I shrug. "I don't know, exactly. He followed me home."

"When?"

Is that important? "Uh, Saturday. After the demo. Why?"

Antwon finally looks at me. "I saw this bird before. Yeah. I saw this bird before. At the anti-gun rally."

I nod. "Me too. I saw it and then it followed me home." I have no idea why Antwon's so interested in Deeply.

"Maybe attracted to that feather in your hair."

"Feather!" squawks Deeply. "Feather!"

Antwon takes an almost imperceptible step backward. "It talks," he observes.

"Yeah."

Antwon takes a slight step forward, keeping an eye on Deeply. "It talks, but what is it saying? What's it saying about feathers? Does it ever say more than one word at a time?"

Antwon seems to have an inordinate interest in Deeply. "Sometimes." I look to Deeps, hoping he understands that he should say two or three or even four words in a row.

"Will-i-am not Will-i-am," Deeply squawks.

Antwon goes very still. Like when he thinks somebody needs careful watching.

William? The William who's a member of WCC? I have a tight feeling all over, as if Deeply has told Antwon something really important. But: how would Deeply know this?

Bot. He's some sort of intelligence bot. But one who's on the side of the working class.

As far as Antwon's concerned, I'm not even there. "Say again?" he asks.

Deeply repeats his words. "Will-i-am not Will-i-am."

"You sure?" Antwon asks.

"Deeply sure." Deeply lifts one of his legs to his face and examines a claw.

Antwon stands there, staring at the claw. I can almost see thoughts racing across his brow. I just don't know what they are.

"Antwon," I say, getting his attention again. "I want to see Titus."

He straightens, checks things out to his left and right, up and down the street, then nods. "You can go in. The bird stays here."

"*What*?! Why? Deeply goes where I go."

Antwon looks confused, then recovers. "Its name is Deeply?"

"Yes, and there's no reason to keep Deeply out here on the street."

"I want to question him."

He's kidding. I'm pretty sure he's kidding.

I'm about to argue with this when Deeply flaps his wings and takes off. Antwon and I tilt our heads back and watch him fly to the top floor of the three-story building — and through an open window into the interior.

"I guess he wants to see Titus, too," I say over my shoulder as I pull open the door of WCC headquarters.

This used to be an old union headquarters building. The entrance lobby has three doors off it: one to the left, two to the right. WCC has been around for fifteen years, so I've been coming down here since I was five years old. Clari and I would play with Keisha and the other kids.

The lobby's filled with photos of Chicago working class history. There's Lucy Parsons from the Haymarket, and Ida B. Welles leading a group of Black women demanding female suffrage. There's the 1937 US Steel Strike, in which Chicago cops fired on unarmed strikers, murdering ten of them: the Memorial Day Massacre. There's the Pullman Strike of 1894, when the National Guard fired into the protestors, murdering thirty or more. There's the cops beating unarmed demonstrators at the Democratic Party Convention in 1968. And there's Fred Hampton, talking to a crowd. I grew up with these pictures. They remind me, every time, of what the ruling class does with its guns: uses them against any perceived threat to its plans.

I open the door and step into the auditorium. Titus is sitting at a desk at the far end, reading something. He looks up, sees me, puts down whatever he's reading, and walks toward me quickly.

I do the same and we meet in the middle, hugging each other as if we've each been gone on a two-year voyage.

"Rowan, Rowan! It is so good to see you. Keisha called and said you dropped by. Let me look at you."

He puts an arm on each of my shoulders and kind of pushes me back a bit to study me. Whatever he sees, he doesn't comment. "How you doin, Rowan? How you feelin?"

" Better," I say. "I'm feeling . . . stronger."

"Good. That's good. I can see it in your eyes." He drapes an arm over me and leads me back to where he'd been sitting. ""How's Lainey? Have you heard from her?"

I sit in the chair facing Titus's desk. He sits back down, too. "Yeah. No. I mean, not exactly. She leaves a different phone message every Sunday night, and I call every Monday morning."

He waits.

"She . . . well, I think she actually sounded better yesterday. Maybe she'll come back. Soon."

He gives me a stern look. "It's easy to blame her for leaving you, Rowan. But you have to understand that her pain over losing Clari was greater than her pain over leaving you alone for a while."

That just doesn't seem right. I'm alive and need Mom. I can feel tears behind my eyes. I grit my teeth and blink. "I try, Titus."

He nods. "She'll be back. You just have to give her time."

There's a strange sound in the auditorium. It's hard to describe. Something like wood being split. I look around the high-ceilinged room. The sound seems to be coming from above, in the corner nearest us. Titus looks around, as if he hears it, too.

"Titus, I need a job." I hadn't meant for it to come out like that, just flat open, with no explanation or anything. I hope Titus knows I'm not coming to see him just to get a job. I'm coming to see him because he was one of

Dad's best friends, and he has been part of my life since I was born. And because he's a real working class leader. The best I know.

He doesn't seem put off by my blurting out my need for a job. In fact, he nods and says, "I think I can get you a job."

"Really?"

"I knew that sooner or later you'd be ready, so I've been talking to Roger about you."

"Who's Roger?" I manage to ask. "What's the job?" My throat is dry.

"Working for Package Nova. You can go there tomorrow. Talk to Roger. Probably start work the same night."

No matter how hard I try, I can't stop the tears. They flood out of my eyes. I stagger out of my chair and throw my arms around Titus. He pats me on the back. "It's okay, Rowan. You know your daddy and I promised each other that if anything happened to either of us, we'd take care of the other man's family as best we could. I'm keeping my promise to Sam, just like he would have kept his to me."

I sit back down and wipe my eyes with the back of my hands. "What do I do?" I ask.

Titus pulls paper out of the folder he was holding, pulls a pen out of his shirt pocket, and writes down the information I'll need. "You go down to Package Nova tomorrow, the main sorting center out by Midway, ask to speak to Roger, and give this to him. He'll be expecting you."

I take the paper, glance at it, fold it, and put it in my pocket. My lungs feel as if they can't get enough air. My chest hurts. "Thank you, Titus. This means the world to me."

He nods. "Jobs do that. Mean the world to those who need them. You gotta understand, he won't offer you a full-time job. They want mostly part-time workers. But I know you're a good worker, Rowan, and after a while they'll see that, too, so when you bid on a full-time job, you'll most likely get it."

Part-time. I really want full-time. But maybe that will come soon. "No benefits for part-timers?" I ask.

"Some right away, some after your probation. Roger will tell you."

Titus looks at me. "This is a good opportunity for you, Rowan. When you were at Wheelers you worked with only one other person in the truck. At Package Nova you'll be working with hundreds — hell, thousands — of other people. You'll make friends. And in a few years, who knows, you could be helping organize demands for better pay, better hours, better conditions."

I look down at my shoes. One of them has a hole over my big toe. "I hope so. Right now, I don't know about organizing anything."

He nods. "That's okay. You've experienced trauma, and you're still recovering. But fighting for working class justice is part of who you are. When the time is right, everything you've learned will come back to you."

I nod. Which is when I notice that the sound I heard before is getting louder. Titus turns around and stares at the corner.

"What's that sound?" I ask.

He stands and goes to investigate. I follow.

As Titus looks up at the corner where the sound's coming from, chips of wood begin to fall on him. He brushes them away. "Squirrels," he says. "Or maybe a raccoon. Damn."

The wood chips are falling faster than before, and as Titus and I are still looking up, an opening appears in the corner and the next thing I know, Deeply shoves himself through the hole.

For a second or two he walks down the wall, clinging to it with his claws and using his beak as a kind of third leg. Then he spreads his wings and flies right to the desk where Titus and I were sitting.

"Deeply, what in the world were you thinking?" I demand, following him. "You chewed a hole in the ceiling of WCC's auditorium. That's not friendly. Or responsible."

Titus is staring at me.

"Uh, I'm sorry, Titus. I brought Deeply with me, and he flew into the third story window. I didn't know he was going to chew his way into the auditorium. I'm sorry. I'll pay for the repairs. Soon. Soon as I can."

Titus sits and studies Deeply. "Did Antwon see this bird?"

"Yeah. He wanted to keep Deeply outside. Which is when he flew into the window. Deeply, not Antwon," I add.

Titus smiles. "How did you come by this parrot, Rowan?"

So I tell him about Deeply following me home, and I even tell him that I think Deeply's an extraordinary parrot: highly intelligent, extremely capable, able to understand human speech. I don't tell him about my suspicions that Deeply's a robot.

Titus turns to Deeps. "So, Parrot. What is it you want, here at WCC headquarters?"

Deeply coughs and spits something onto the desk. *Gross*, I'm thinking as it rolls in front of Titus — who picks it up and examines it.

"It's a bug," Titus says as he shows me the little silver thing.

"Like . . . the headquarters is bugged?"

I guess I'm stating the obvious, because Titus ignores me. "Where was this?" he asks Deeply.

"Li-bra-ry,." Deeply coughs again and spits up another bug. "Of-fice," he tells Titus.

Titus picks it up. "Any more?"

Giving an extra-large and extra-loud cough, Deeply spits out another bug. It bounces my way. I catch it before it rolls off the desk and hand it to Titus.

"Hall-way," squawks Deeply.

Titus is angry. "Our sweeper has not done a good job."

He might be talking to me. He might be talking to Deeply. Or maybe to himself.

Deeply marches up to Titus, who doesn't flinch.

"Will-i-am not Will-i-am."

Titus pockets the bugs. Nods. "Understood."

With that, Deeply flies back to the hole he chewed in the ceiling and pushes himself through it.

I'm sitting there trying to figure out how to ask what's going on when Titus stands. I mean, I *think* I know what's going on — Deeply just told Antwon and Titus that William's a fink. But, man — how would Deeply know something like that? And how did he find the bugs? And — why is Titus carrying on a conversation with a parrot as if it's no big deal?

Okay, okay. Scratch that last thought. I carry on conversations with Deeply as if it's no big deal.

Titus stands. "Rowan, I'd love to visit with you some more, but I need to meet with Antwon."

I stand, too. "Thanks for the job, Titus."

"You come to dinner tomorrow night. Genevieve will want to see you."

"I'll be there," I say. "I haven't had a good meal . . . in a long time," I finish, not wanting to say since Mom left.

Titus walks me to the door. "There was somebody else asking about a job for you, earlier today."

I stop in my tracks. "What? Who?"

He reaches into his pocket and pulls out a business card. "Jacob Terranova. You know him?"

I'm flabbergasted. I mean: *Wow*! Not only is this guy from Boston doing what he said he'd do — he's doing it fast. And, critical point: he knew exactly where I'd get the best help.

Amazing.

"Not exactly," I tell Titus. "He wants to interview me and, uh, I said that instead of paying me he should get me a job. I never thought he'd come to see you. I didn't think he knew that much, to be honest. He's an intellectual."

Titus grins. "That's not necessarily bad. The working class has to win over the middle class intellectuals. We want them on our side."

I grumble something about Jacob Terranova.

"I'm serious. If the working class doesn't win over the liberals, then the liberals will go toward the fascists. When two forces are in conflict, the one that appears the strongest is the one the middle class will want to support. I was impressed with Terranova. We could use someone like him."

"Really?"

"Yes," says Titus. "Almost as much as we need people like you, Rowan. You will become a leader of the working class struggle."

I don't think I'm ready to be a leader of any struggle right now. Except my struggle to find a job. Which Titus has maybe solved for me.

"What did you tell Jake?" If he can come all the way here to get me a job, I'm taking him up on the offer to call him Jake.

"I told him I had a good job lead for you when you wanted it." Titus smiles. "No need to pay for any repairs, Rowan. Antwon can fix that hole in no time. And maybe next time he'll let the parrot come in the front door."

18   DEEPLEA

HOP: You look all red, DeePlea. Why?

Me: It's the reflector, Fee. I mean HOP. The reflector is red.

HOP: You are bouncing up and down, DeePlea. Why?

Me: I am riding on the back of a bike, HOP. The bike is traveling on city streets. The city streets are in a shoddy state, full of holes and stones and discarded litter. Plastic cups. Single shoes. Rags. Dog excrement. The bike is bouncing up and down. Therefore I am, too.

HOP: Earth sounds like a terrible place, Dee. I suspect a parrot should have been assigned an Earth DU decades ago.

Me: [Muttering] Centuries.

HOP: What do you have to report?

Me: I have made contact with WCC and Titus Longshaw. That's the Working Class Control organization. I instuffed their entire library, which is housed on the third floor of their headquarters. I have instuffed Karl Marx, Frederich Engels, Vladimir Lenin, Leon Trotsky, Rosa Luxembourg, Clara Zetkin, Mao Tse Tung, Fidel Castro, Antonio Gramsci, Frantz Fanon, Malcolm X, Bobby Seale, Huey—

HOP: [Interrupting] I get the point, Dee. Who are these people and how are they relevant to your mission?

Me: They were all revolutionaries, HOP. Some of them led successful revolutions, others did not. But they were all able to understand, name, and analyze the economic system that allows a tiny handful of humans to control all the wealth produced by the remaining humans — who outnumber them like the stars outnumber the black holes. They fought against capitalism and racism all their lives.

HOP: [Puzzled] You say they were all able to name the oppressive system? Does this mean that most people can't name it?

Me: [Also puzzled] I don't know if it's *can't* or *won't*. The people here are very reluctant to use the word *capitalism*. And even more reluctant to analyze it.

HOP: That is sad, Dee. But tell me more about Titus Longshaw and WCC.

Me: He is undoubtedly the most important of the three I'm going to find. He is a born leader, a fifty-year-old Black man. He has fought in their capitalist wars of invasion and emerged hating them. He is a member of the working class. Highly intelligent, hard worker, brilliant organizer. He understands he must unite all the different colors, nationalities, and ethnicities under one platform that works for the good of all. And that the most oppressed — in this case the people of color — will be in the vanguard of the leadership. [Pause] Rowan understands that, too,

HOP: He sounds like an excellent choice, DeePlea.

Me: [Proudly] And I have already protected him, HOP.

HOP: I am impressed, DeePlea. How did you do this?

Me: I warned Antwon Harper — he is Titus's bodyguard — about William, a spy in their midst. And — I found three listening devices in their headquarters.

HOP: That is excellent work. You are making great headway, and in such a short time. [Pause] Is this Antwon a possible leader?

Me: I haven't yet determined that, HOP. But Rowan, who is a leader, will soon have a job.

HOP: That is good. She will gain experience. [Pause] You are sure about her, DeePlea? I mean, you found her . . . instantly.

Me: I am sure.

HOP: On a personal note, Dee.

Me: Yes?

FeeOna: I have laid three eggs.

Me: That is wonderful, Fee! When will our new chicks hatch? But wait . . . I will not be home to see them peck their way into the world. I . . . I didn't realize this.

FeeOna: It is sad, Dee. You have always been there, for each of our broods. But we have no choice. You cannot return for a year. Or — you could return at any time if it looks like Earth will blow itself up.

Me: A Duty to the Universe comes first. Can I name one of the chicks?

FeeOna: Of course.

Me: Name the first-hatched ReeWon.

FeeOna: I will do that, Dee. Peace to the Universe.

Me: Peace to the Universe.

19 JAKE

AS AN UNEMPLOYED PERSON, ROWAN PICKETT SHOULD be available when I want to see her. Instead, she's never there. On Monday afternoon I took the El down to Bridgeport to tell her Titus Longshaw said he would get her a job. This should count as me getting her the job, since I went to find Longshaw and asked him about a job for Rowan. So she owes me that interview. Maybe not the interview I had originally wanted, but, nonetheless, an interview.

Except that she wasn't home on Monday afternoon, and her neighbor wanted to know what I wanted. I resisted the efforts of this MaryEllen person to keep me there until Rowan returned. Too many matchmaker beams emanating from her eyes.

I came back Monday night and Rowan Pickett still wasn't home. MaryEllen, who must be monitoring all activity anywhere near Rowan's house, told me that Rowan told her to tell me that she — Rowan — would be home the next morning.

So this morning here I am, bearing coffee and donuts. I ring and I knock, I knock and I ring. Naturally MaryEllen steps out on her porch. She tells me that Rowan left on her bike an hour ago.

I feel like a doofus standing there with coffee and donuts and nobody to share them with, so I ask MaryEllen if she would like to join me for the coffee and donuts.

She's down with that and we end up at her lookout post, where we sit on white wicker chairs. I place my offerings on a white wicker table and we share the food.

As well as information on Rowan Pickett.

I learn that Rowan's father, Sam Pickett, died two years ago of a heart attack. "He was young," MaryEllen informs me. "Only 45. And such a good person. Warm, friendly, helpful in every way. Rowan takes after him." She looks at me as she says this, telegraphing that I should, A: note that Rowan Pickett is warm, friendly, and helpful, and B: be interested.

Helpful as in directing parrot attacks. Friendly as in an elbow to the throat.

The signs say that Gun Girl seems a far, far cry from warm, friendly, and helpful. In any way. If that's so, asks an inner voice, then why do you keep coming back?

I ignore the voice. No way am I seeking sync with Rowan Pickett. I'm seeking information.

I learn about Rowan's sister, Clari. "I was their babysitter for years. Those two were always together." MaryEllen looks downward. "So sad," she says. "So sad. You just can't imagine it. What something like that does to a family."

Next I learn about Lainey, Rowan's mother, who — according to MaryEllen — left five months ago. "Just put two suitcases in the car and drove off one morning. Hasn't been back. But she will. She will come back, I know."

In my world, this is . . . I can't say unheard of, because believe me, I have covered tragic stories. Not unheard of, because grief and stress make people do inexplicable things. But I find it hard to wrap my mind around this. Rowan, I have learned from MaryEllen, is twenty years old. Her mother left a 20-year-old alone.

Okay, okay, I'm twenty-four: not so far removed from twenty. But there's a world of difference in those four years. There's college. Grad school.

Jobs. Apartments. Travel. Lovers. Dealing with bosses. My mind whirls just thinking of how a person matures between the ages of twenty and twenty-four.

I pour MaryEllen more coffee and offer her another donut. "No sprinkles," she observes as she studies the choices. "Rowan's parrot loves sprinkles."

Don't I know it. I clear my throat. "About the parrot."

MaryEllen raises an eyebrow.

"How long has Rowan had it?"

"Just a few days. Since Saturday, I think."

So it appears that Gun Girl was telling the truth: the parrot may have followed her home.

Does that mean she didn't command it to strike? That my inference was incorrect?

I pride myself on my inferences.

"How does Rowan manage?" I ask. "She doesn't have a job."

MaryEllen nods. "Rowan told me that Lainey left her with a checkbook, the whole checking account, and the whole savings account, and told her to pay the bills and make the money last."

"Until when?"

She shrugs. "That's the thing. Rowan never said until when. I think — between you and me, I think Rowan has run out of money. Have you noticed how skinny she is?" MaryEllen looks toward Rowan's house. "She needs a job. I think that's where she went this morning: to a job interview."

I'm still disturbed about Rowan's mother. "Does her mother call?" I ask. "Talk to Rowan?"

MaryEllen shakes her head. "Not that I know. But she leaves a new phone message every Sunday night, and Rowan calls her every Monday morning. I think Rowan was afraid Lainey would commit suicide, and I think Lainey knows that, which is why she assures Rowan she's alive."

Jesus. Talk about cold comfort. I sit there pondering it all.

"Come to think of it," MaryEllen continues, "Rowan told me that Lainey sounded almost optimistic in her last message. Something about the world turning into morning."

"Mourning? That's optimistic?"

Mary Ellen looks confused. "Oh," she says after a moment. "Not *m-o-U-r-n-i-n-g*. Morning like the first part of day."

"Oh. Okay. That's different. Does Rowan want her mother to come home?"

MaryEllen looks scandalized. "Well of course she does, Jake. What child doesn't want their parent?"

"Do you think she'll come back?"

She gives this a lot of thought. "I think she will. I think she just needs to grieve in her own way. Away from here."

This all makes me inexplicably sad.

MaryEllen must sense that I'm feeling down. "Normally, Jake, Rowan is exciting to be around."

"Like . . . life of the party?" I can't see that. No way.

"No. That's not Rowan. Exciting like. . . different. She shoots guns. A perfect shot! She won the state championship. And three summers ago, she built herself a motorcycle. Sam helped, of course, but Rowan was the one who got things started."

A motorcycle? That definitely appeals to me. "I haven't seen her riding a motorcycle."

Now MaryEllen looks sad. "No. She sold it three months ago. She's been selling a lot of things."

By ten o'clock Rowan Pickett still hasn't returned, so I say goodbye to MaryEllen and head to work.

"I'll tell Rowan you called," she says. "Will you be back?"

"Probably," I mutter, more to myself than to MaryEllen.

Then I find a city park, sit on a bench, and call my mom and dad to see how they're doing. After that I call my sister. And then I make plans to see them for Thanksgiving.

20 JAKE

LATE THAT AFTERNOON I'M BACK, KNOCKING ON THE door to what seems like another world, peopled by Gun Girl and the donut-loving parrot. I feel like a changed person. I'm not there to get an interview. I'm there to be a decent human being to somebody who needs a friend. Whether she knows it or not.

Do No Harm is behind me. *Do Some Good* is where I'm at.

The door opens.

"Hi," she says.

Which throws me, because I'm expecting something like *You again*! The other thing that throws me is that she's looking hot. Strappy sandals, black tights, a sexy black top with colored squares full of holes around the middle, through which I can see her skin. Her hair is freshly washed and glossy, and even the retro feather looks a bit like it belongs.

"Uh," I manage. "Hi. Can I come in? I'm here to make a confession."

Her eyebrows go up. She scowls. "Confess out here," she instructs me, "and then I'll know if you can come in."

Warm, friendly, and helpful. Though a huge part of me admires the speed with which she processes information and establishes priorities.

I nod in agreement. "My confession is, I interviewed your parrot without your permission."

"Wh—" She stumbles around with consonants before recovering. "When? Where?"

"Yesterday afternoon, maybe 11:30."

"You were here?" she demands. "You broke into my house?!"

"No, *I didn't break into your house*," I say in exasperation. "Your parrot was flying around town, I called to him, he landed, I asked if I could interview him."

It takes her a while to absorb this. "And?" she asks at last.

"And he nodded. Which I took as an affirmative. *And*," I add, reaching into my cargo pocket, "I can show you the interview — and complete my confession."

She steps aside and I enter. She motions to the kitchen table and I go there.

Rowan, on the other hand, marches up to a wooden contraption — which I now see is a parrot perch — and demands of her pet: "Deeply, did you leave the house yesterday while I was gone?"

"Deeply free to leave," squawks the bird.

That stops her. It would stop me, too.

"Well, okay," she says at last. "You're right, Deeps. You are free to leave. But you could have told me you had met Jake."

"Deeply come home. Deeply sleep. Deeply not remember."

"Ha!" she says. "Tell me another one."

"Deeply come home. Deeply talk to self in mirror. Deeply forget."

Rowan and I laugh at the same time. The parrot chirps *Chahaha, chahaha*. Which sounds suspiciously like a laugh.

I'm thinking the interview should center on the parrot, whose ability to comprehend is . . . unheard of.

She abandons the parrot and comes to the table, sitting across from me.

I pull an empty chair next to me. "If you sit here, we can watch the video together."

She thinks about this, then walks over and sits next to me. I set the camcorder up so the screen is facing the two of us. The bird flies over and lands on the table. It turns its head sideways, the better to see the video.

I hit *Play* and the short interview begins. There's Deeply, front and center, and there's me, asking if I could interview him.

Rowan looks at me, then at Deeply. She leans forward, listening intently to my questions — and even more intently to the parrot's answers. At one point she sits straight up, as if confused. It's when I asked the bird if he reported to anybody. He never answered that question.

When the bird squawks "Revolt. Revolt! *Revolt*!!!" she smiles, then reaches over and strokes the parrot's head.

When the interview's over Rowan turns to me. "That was really well done, Jake. I love how you treat Deeply as seriously as you would a person. And the way you panned the camera over the donut going from you to Deeps, that had humor."

I'm taken aback by Gun Girl analyzing my work. And praising it. I try hard not to look too pleased.

Deeply walks over to the camcorder and presses the Play button with his beak, and the whole thing starts all over again. This time he examines it with the other eye. Rowan and I watch the whole thing again, too.

When it's over Rowan leans back in her chair and studies me. "What do you want to do with this video?"

Fair question. "I'm not sure, but I think . . . maybe I can use it as part of a broader story. The one about you."

"About me and gun control?" she asks.

I don't know. I want to interview her and the parrot, but not about what happened to Snoddy. I'm not going to endanger her.

"Uh," I say, "I have a second confession to make."

"What?"

"A second confession."

"Is it as good as the first one?" she asks.

No.

But I don't tell her that.

"Look," I say, "I think one confession a day is enough. I can come back tomorrow night."

She thinks about this, then nods. "Okay."

I realize that Rowan is friendly. Not warm, maybe, but definitely not cold. And sort of helpful, at least about tomorrow night. "Will you go to dinner with me tonight?" I ask — before I can edit it.

She jumps out of her seat and pulls me forward out of mine. I'm thinking this is the most enthusiastic Yes I've ever encountered when she deep-sixes all my plans.

"No. I can't. I'm sorry. I have a dinner date. And I'm late. You have to go. I have to leave. Right now."

She has a firm grip on my arm and is ushering me out of the kitchen and into the living room and practically dragging me to the front door. She's strong enough to be a nightclub bouncer.

"Dinner!" squawks the parrot.

Rowan opens the door and sort of pushes me out. She comes out with me, then motions to the parrot, which flies out the door. "Bye, Jake. Thanks for coming. I loved the video. Sorry I can't talk longer."

She says this over her shoulder as she runs down the sidewalk that goes along the side of her house. I walk down the porch steps and see her unlock the garage door, wheel out a bike, and hop on it.

She pedals through the yard and past me at a rapid rate.

The parrot, on the other hand, sits on the porch railing and stares at me.

"Deeply love Rowan."

I think about that and sigh. When I look up, MaryEllen is on her porch, watching me.

"Don't worry," she says, motioning me over. "She's excited about her new job, which might start tomorrow morning. Come on over and sit a while, Jake."

I climb the steps to MaryEllen's porch and get to hear all about Rowan's job at Package Nova. The job I asked Titus Longshaw to get her.

MaryEllen waits for me to ask about Rowan's dinner date. I wait for her to tell me.

She knows I want to know. But she's not going to tell me, not without my asking, thereby showing that I *want* to know who Rowan's having dinner with.

I say a friendly goodbye to MaryEllen and go out to dinner.

Alone.

21 ROWAN

Dinner at Titus and Genevieve's is fantastic. I knew what Genevieve would make because she knows how much I love her fried chicken. It is *sooooo* delicious!

Because I anticipated the fried chicken I didn't bring Deeply with me. He might have freaked out, seeing one of his class — *Aves* — chopped up, breaded, fried, and eaten. With gusto.

I left him on the front porch with Jake Terranova, figuring that since Deeply already gave Jake an interview, the two of them were buds and could go out and do something together. Eat donuts.

Jake asked me out to dinner.

Does that mean he's . . . interested in me? He's a middle class podcaster. I'm a working class unemployed revolutionary. I'm pretty sure he grasps that.

"This is even more delicious than I remember," I tell Genevieve. "Thank you."

"We have missed you, Rowan," she answers. Then she looks me over. "You need a lot more meals like this one. You come to dinner again this Saturday."

I say that I will, and I thank her. It feels so good to be sitting there with Keisha, Titus, and Genevieve. And Antwon's there, too, sitting next to Keisha.

When did this happen?

Probably while I was holed up at home.

Keisha sees me pondering and laughs softly.

I grin.

"Mama, don't you be feeding Rowan *too* much — I don't want her to outgrow that top," Keisha kids.

Titus clears his throat. "You ready for work tomorrow morning?"

I nod. "You bet."

He talks a while about the Package Nova job. "It's going to be rough at first," he tells me. "Strange hours, packages coming at you a million a minute. But it's nothing you can't handle, Rowan. Hear me?"

I nod.

"How's your mama, Rowan?" Genevieve asks. "Have you heard from her?"

I tell them about Mom's Monday phone messages.

"Can we leave her a message?" asks Keisha.

"I guess. I mean, yeah, I leave a message every Monday." *Most Mondays . . .* but I don't tell them that.

"Then let's do it," says Genevieve. "You call her now and we'll all pass the phone around."

So I speed dial Mom's number and hand the phone to Genevieve, who listens to Mom's Monday message, then says: "Hi Lainey, this is Genevieve. We're all sitting around the dinner table with Rowan, who has just eaten five pieces of my fried chicken all by herself," — Genevieve winks at me — "and we miss you. Hope you're healing and doing well."

She passes the phone to Titus, who tells her that I'll be starting work at Package Nova tomorrow morning. He doesn't say he helped me get the job. He tells Mom he misses her and that she's always invited to dinner at his house. He passes the phone to Keisha.

"Hi, Lainey, this is Keisha. I miss you. I made a sexy black top using some of Rowan's granny squares. I know it's hard to imagine *sexy* and *granny squares* in the same piece, but I bore down and made it happen. Rowan's wearing it now. Wherever you are, I hope you're wearing something that makes you happy. Miss you." Keisha hands the phone to Antwon.

"Hi Lainey, this is Antwon Harper. I hope you're getting stronger every day. I miss your Boston cream pie at the fundraisers. Nobody makes Boston cream pie the way you do. Oh, yeah, I miss you, too — not just your Boston cream pie. Peace."

Antwon hands the phone to me. I don't know if I can talk without crying. Everything they said was so good. Nobody asked Mom to come home, which might have made her feel guilty and might have been counterproductive, too. Everybody said they missed her.

"Good night, Mom," I manage. "I miss you. Love you. Bye."

I blink back some tears as I put the phone back in my pocket. Sometimes I feel deep anger at Mom for leaving me, but way inside I feel she's trying to get better. And if I spent five months avoiding getting a job, avoiding seeing friends, avoiding everything — I should be able to realize she needs the same kind of thing.

Keisha and I help Genevieve with the dishes while Titus and Antwon make a quick trip to WCC headquarters. After a while Genevieve shoos Keish and me out of the kitchen.

So I hang with Keisha in her sewing room, looking at her latest designs. I see some of my crochet hooks on a table with some yarn — where I left them a year ago. "You know," I say, "I think I'm moving past yarn and on to silk, cotton, and waxed linen."

"You think you might want to get together again on Tuesdays?" she asks.

Every Tuesday Keisha and Clari and I would meet at Keisha's and sew together. Keisha worked on fabric pieces on her sewing machine, Clari worked on embroidering skirts and shirts and jackets, and I worked on granny squares. Kcisha and Clari would tell me that crocheting was a lesser art form than fine needlework. Probably. But I didn't care.

There's a denim jacket on a corner table. I recognize it as what Clari was working on. I pick it up and hold it to me.

"Yeah. Thanks, Keisha. I would love to do that again."

She looks at me. "Do you want that jacket, Rowan? I could finish the embroidery Clari started."

I nod, hand her the jacket, and take a huge breath to keep steady. Moments like this, I think I know how hard it is for Mom.

Grabbing one of my crochet hooks and yarn, I sit cross-legged on the floor and continue where I left off so long ago. "As soon as I get my first paycheck, I'll buy more waxed linen and cotton," I tell Keisha. "Any particular colors you'd like?"

She thinks about this. "Go with what inspires you. But I think the solid colored squares are more elegant than the multi-colored ones, don't you?"

I laugh. "I was thinking of fifteen or sixteen different colors. In the same square."

"Well, marbled is one thing. Psychedelic is another. I know this, Rowan, because I'm a year older than you."

I smile. It feels so good to be back.

We spend the next hour sewing and crocheting, and then it's time for me to say goodbye and head on home.

* * *

I'm pedaling north on Ashland Avenue feeling good, thinking about how good the food was and how great it felt to be part of . . well, I guess part of *life* again. Then I think that Mom must not be feeling part of life again, because if she was, she'd have come home.

I'm thinking about Jake Terranova. Wondering what he's up to. Because although I like him a lot better than I did a few days ago, I still think there's something he's not telling me. Didn't he say he had a second confession? If it's as interesting as his interview with Deeply, I'll be happy.

Something tells me it's not.

Something tells me, out of nowhere, that I'm being followed.

I glance back. Hasn't the same car been behind me for blocks?

As I'm thinking this, the car slows down.

My heart speeds up.

I don't think it's Snoddy. This isn't his style. What he does best is hide in alleys and then step out to surprise you.

I speed up, check out the traffic, zip across Ashland, hang a sudden left on Pershing, and pedal for all I'm worth.

When I look back, I swear the same car is following me, a block back.

My heart's in high gear. What if it's one of Snoddy's gorillas?

Isn't Snoddy still in the hospital? And even if he's out, why would he pick now to follow me?

Unless he blames me for what happened to him at the rally.

Why would he?

I glance back. Car's still there.

Because I was standing next to him when it happened? Well, not next to, but pretty damn close. Holy shit. If he thinks I had anything to do with whatever happened to him . . . .

I speed up, take a sharp right on Damen, race by McKinley Park, swerve left on 37th, and begin zigging in and out of alleys, where no car can follow me.

Heading north on Hoyne, I hang a right on Archer. Almost home, almost home.

But when I look back, there's the same car, pulling out from the curb on Archer, one block behind me. It was waiting for me. Whoever it is knows where I live.

Or maybe not exactly where, but wants to find out. There's so much adrenaline pumping through me I think I'm going to faint. I zig and zag again, using the alleys wherever I can.

One block from home. No car behind me.

I turn left into Mrs. Leary's back yard, jump off my bike, wheel it to the side of her house, and drop it in the shrubbery.

Still no car. I run through a couple of yards, heading home. Keeping an eye out for the car.

When I get to my street, I look left and right. If somebody's there waiting for me, I don't see them. I count the cars parked on the street, identifying who they belong to.

Patrick's rig is there, parked right in front of me. He's home earlier than MaryEllen thought he'd be. But the lights are off in their place.

I don't want to chance entering my house. Identifying it. I take a deep breath, move quickly to Patrick's rig, step up on the running board, and turn the door handle.

Unlocked. Relief whooshes through me. I crawl into the cab, close the door softly behind me, and lock it. Then I hunker down and peek out the window to see if the car comes.

It does. I recognize its headlights. The car turns onto my street from the east, pulls to the curb. The driver cuts the lights. He's waiting for me.

And he knows the street I live on. Probably the very house.

As long as he's there, I'm not going into my house. No way I'm going to let him trap me inside my own house. If my gun wasn't locked up with Dad's . . . but it is locked up. I don't want to chance not being able to get to it in time. Whatever happens is going to happen out here on the street.

As I peek out, I see a shape move lower into the driver's seat. He doesn't want to be seen.

Maybe a neighbor is peeking out his window and will report that there's a suspicious person lurking in a car.

I wait and wait and wait. Ten minutes go by.

Okay. That's it. I'm not going to hide all night long. I've got to do something.

I wish I had my gun. Dad's gun. Any gun.

I wonder if Patrick keeps anything for defense in the cab. I grope around carefully. My hand closes on something like a metal bar. I inch it out from under the seat. Tire iron.

Huge tire iron. Maybe 30 inches long. As long as Deeply is high.

The iron's shaped something like a short hockey stick. I heft it in my hand. Holding the tire iron to my chest, I lie on the truck seat and think.

Should I call Patrick, ask him to check out the guy in the car?

No. The lights are probably off because he and MaryEls are upstairs, making love.

Okay, then. Up to me.

I open the door and step out of the truck, tire iron in hand. I run down the center of the street, right toward the car.

Two things happen at once.

The car motor jumps to life. And Deeply comes flying out of nowhere, toward the car, screeching like a tornado-warning siren.

Lights blaze on in a couple of houses. I'm going to get kicked out of the neighborhood.

Lights still off, the car moves away from the curb, executes a U-turn, and takes off, back the way it came. I can't see much about it because its lights aren't on. But I can see clear enough to heave the tire iron at its back window.

Glass shatters. The tire iron ricochets into the street and bounces across a tree lawn.

Deeply flies alongside the car, screeching at the driver. Then he veers off, soaring high into the air and banking back toward our house.

I retrieve the tire iron and return it to Patrick's rig, walk to Mrs. Leary's yard, grab my bike, and wheel it home to my garage.

When I go inside the house Deeply is waiting for me.

I give him a big hug. As big a hug as you can give a bird. "I don't know how you knew, Deeply, but thank you, thank you."

"Deeply your friend."

22 ROWAN

AFTER A QUICK SHOWER I GRAB THE LAST OF THE cheese and an apple for breakfast, fill Deeply's bowl with pellets, and walk up to his perch. "I have a job, Deeps. Which means I'll be gone at least five hours. Maybe nine. Will you be okay that long without me?"

"Deeps okay. Deeps fly around. Ask Jake for donuts."

I smile at that. "Be safe, Deeply."

"Rowan be safe," he replies.

I nod, stroke his feathers with a finger, smoothing down the orange ones around his neck, which sometimes lie flat and glossy, but more often stick straight out. I blow Deeply a kiss and walk to the El.

The Chicago headquarters of Package Nova are on Cicero, just a few blocks south of Midway Airport, and the Orange Line runs straight to Midway. I biked there yesterday, when I went to see Roger, like Titus told me to, but not today. I'd like to ride my bike and save the El fare, but I can do that later, after I've been there a few days and learn how things work.

Yesterday the sheer size of the Package Nova bulk sorting center took my breath away. The building sits on an area equal to two or three city blocks. This morning it takes me three tries to find the same side door I walked through yesterday for the job interview.

Once I'm inside I recognize things a bit more. I follow the signs toward Supervisor's Office, find it, and walk in. A guy sitting behind a bright red metal desk looks up. There's a chair on my side of the desk and three chairs along one wall. Stacks of paper are piled everywhere. Even the floor.

"Hi," I say. "I'm Rowan Pickett. I was hired as part-time package handler yesterday. Roger told me to report to you this morning."

He stands and puts out his hand. "Vic Acker." He motions me to sit on the chair facing his desk, then hands me two packets of papers, one with each hand. "The colorful ones tell you all about your job and benefits. You can read them later, on your own time. The others you'll have to fill out before you start work. What did Roger tell you yesterday?"

"Starting salary $17.00 an hour, raises for good performance, up to $20 an hour. Show up here this morning. That's it."

Vic looks me over. "He didn't tell you how to dress?"

How to dress? "Uh . . . no."

"Boots," Vic tells me. "Boots are required. No boots, no work." He looks at my feet, which are in old running shoes. "You can buy work boots at a Target, or you can wear pull-on boots. Hard, though. Not that soft puffy stuff."

"Okay."

"And bring water. A whole container of it. No skimpy little bottles. Half a gallon at least."

I nod again. "Okay."

He seems satisfied with that. "Did Roger tell you about the shifts you'll be working?"

I shake my head.

"Typical," he mutters. He leans forward and puts both elbows on the desk. "Here's what you'll be doing. Part-timers generally work Monday through Friday. No weekends. You work a four-hour shift and then go home. Unless we need you bad that day, in which case you either hang around and start the second shift in three hours, or go home, or whatever." He waves a hand in the air. "Usually we won't need you, except at Thanksgiving and especially Christmas. Normally you can count on seventeen to twenty hours a week."

I multiply seventeen dollars times twenty hours in my head. $340 a week. Minus taxes and everything else they take out of paychecks. "What are the chances of this becoming a full-time job?"

"Possible," he says, giving me a steady look. "I know that Titus recommended you for the job. Everyone Titus has sent us before is a steady worker. If you're the same, you can end up working full time."

I nod.

"You go to college?" he asks.

Just then the door opens.

Vic looks up. I turn my head to see a guy my age, maybe a bit older. He's got stringy blond hair, a wispy goatee, and two casts, one on each arm. One cast is bright blue, the other's bright red. He's wearing work boots and carrying a plastic *gallon* of water. What do we do with this water — take a shower in it?

Vic nods at him. "Have a seat, Lyle, and I'll get to you as soon as I'm finished here."

Lyle takes a seat and then, before Vic and I can get back to what we were doing, pulls off his casts and tosses them into the air. First the red one, then the blue one. He catches them as they come back down.

"All healed," he announces. "I can start back to work today."

"Lyle, be quiet until it's your turn," says Vic. He turns to me. "You were saying. About college?"

"Oh, yeah. I'm thinking of going back to Columbia College."

Vic nods. "Package Nova will pay your tuition, or books, or supplies, whatever, up to $5,000 a year. Starting today, your first day on the shift."

Cool. "What about health care?" I ask.

"You're eligible for pretty much full health coverage — not disability, though — after your first 90-day quarter of working at least 200 hours. So, in three months, you should be eligible."

Lyle makes some sort of sound, I can't tell what. Vic ignores him, so I do, too.

Then Vic says, "I'm putting you on the late night shift, Rowan. That's 9:30 p.m to 1:30 a.m." He looks at me. "How did you get here today?"

Uh-oh. I can see where this is going. "The El."

"The last El leaves Midway at 1:05 a.m. Is that going to be a problem for you?"

My head is still spinning from the ungodly work hours. But I can handle it. What I'm having a big problem with is getting home after my shift ends. I'm not about to ride my bike home at that time of the night. Too many bad possibilities. I shake my head. "No. No problem."

He studies me. "You have a car?"

Mom took our car. And left me stranded. And I had to sell my motorcycle because I needed the money. Because Mom left me stranded. That's what I want to shout. "Not yet. But I can get here and back every workday."

Just then Vic's phone rings. He grabs it off the desk. "Vic Acker here." He listens, then stands. "On my way," he says, heading toward the door.

"Rowan, wait here. You can fill out the forms while you wait. Lyle, don't act up. I'll get to you as soon as I finish with Rowan." The door closes behind him.

"So," says Lyle. "Welcome to the club."

"Package Nova?" I ask.

"Part-timers still on probation," he answers.

"Is that what you are?"

"Yep. Started four months ago." He raises both arms, which he's slipped the casts back onto. "Wasn't covered by medical insurance yet when this happened."

"How'd you manage to break two arms?"

"Bar fight. Three of us mixing it up. Crazy. I was so wasted I barely remember it. They told me I broke a guy's nose. When I came to in the hospital, my arms hurt something fierce."

I don't really want to know about a bar fight, but I feel I should say something, so I ask, "Which bar?"

"Wasted Wastrel."

"On Archer?" I ask. Sort of incredulously, because that bar's just four blocks from where I live. Dad always told Clari and me we were to *never* set foot in the Wasted Wastrel. Which of course meant we went in one night. And ordered cokes. And saw a bar fight. And got out of there as fast as we could.

"Yeah. You know it?"

"I live four blocks away."

"Hey! What street?"

"Eleanor."

"Near the new boathouse?" he asks.

"Yeah. It's great. I love the rowing machines."

Lyle nods. "I was watching you when Vic asked about transportation. I think it's going to be a problem, right?"

I admit to Lyle that it's a problem. "But I figure I can hang around here for two hours, catch the first El heading north, and be asleep before the sun rises."

"Nah," he says. "I live on 31st Street. I'll be happy to give you a ride home from work."

"You work the same shift?" I ask.

He nods. "That's one of the two prime shifts. It's the one they put new hires on."

I think about this for a few seconds. Do I really want to be in a car driven by this guy who gets drunk and into bar fights?

He sees me thinking. "Why don't I give you a ride home after we finish here. I'm pretty sure Vic's going to clear me to start tonight, now that the casts are off. I can give you a ride here tonight, or just a ride home, whichever works for you."

The way I see it, I don't have much of a choice. Hang around Package Nova from 1:30 to 3:30 a.m., then walk to the El in the dark. Or: get a ride to my front door with Lyle.

"My name's Rowan Pickett," I tell him.

"Lyle Wallace."

"Thanks for your offer," I say. "Let's see how it works out. I don't want to inconvenience you."

"You won't," he says.

23 ROWAN

I LEARN A LOT ABOUT LYLE ON THE DRIVE BACK. NOT that I'm asking, just that he's telling, mostly about the bar fight and how drunk he was and how maybe he said something he shouldn't have and maybe kind of, you know, insulted someone, and next thing he knew two guys began pounding on him and the bartender called the cops and Lyle woke up in the hospital with casts on both arms.

I study him to see if there's any sign that he's already had a few drinks. "You don't drink and drive, do you?"

He shoots a quick look at me. "Nah. I can see why you're asking, though. I walked to the bar. I don't drink and drive."

"Too bad about being fifteen hours short of medical coverage," I say, responding to what he told me as we left Package Nova.

"Real bummer. I mean, *real* bummer. Cost me big. I'll be paying off the hospital bill for a year. And Vic wouldn't let me work, either, even though after a coupla weeks they could have put me on the sorting line." He glances my way. "All you have to do is stand there for four hours, flipping over any packages that aren't label-side up. I coulda done that with my arms in casts. I coulda done that in my *sleep*."

"So . . . is your probation over after fifteen more work hours? Like, at the end of this week?"

We're heading north on Archer Avenue and the going is slow at this time of morning. Lyle seems to be a safe driver. No crazy maneuvers, keeps his eyes on the road, isn't too timid or too aggressive. It was generous of him to offer me a ride home from work each night.

"I wish. Vic said they're going to start me over, but give me credit for 100 of the 185 hours I worked. So in about five weeks I should be off probation." He glances at me. "Which means I can join the union. Teamsters. Better job protection."

I think about this. In 200 work hours — which probably means ten to twelve weeks— I'll be off probation, I can join the union, I can apply for full-time work when a job opens up. I have to: $340 a week isn't going to cover everything I need. Food, gas, water, electric, real estate taxes, CTA fare. To say nothing of clothes, haircuts, and a little treat of some kind now and then.

I sigh. "I really need this job."

"I know what you mean," Lyle agrees. "As soon as I get full-time, I'll be able to afford living on my own. Well, not on my own, probably, but with a roommate."

Living on my own I can't pay the property taxes. This year, yeah — Mom left the money in the savings. Next year? Not unless I get a full-time job. No matter how you look at it, capitalism fucks us over.

As I sit there despising capitalism, Lyle turns onto Eleanor.

"House number?" he asks.

I give it to him and he pulls up to it. Door to door service.

"Hey," he says, suddenly agitated. "That looks like one of the guys that jumped me in the bar."

What?

I follow the direction of Lyle's pointing finger and see Jake Terranova standing on my lawn, leaning on a rail of the front porch. It's clear to me that Jake doesn't have to punch a time clock for his job. Make that jobs. What's more, Deeply's perched on the rail alongside him — eating a donut.

I smile at this. At Deeply, but also at Jake being there. I realize I enjoy talking to him. This might be a sign that I'm desperate, I don't know.

"I don't think so, Lyle. This is not Jake's neighborhood."

"Why not? What's wrong with our neighborhood?"

"Nothing's wrong with it," I tell him. "It's a good place to live."

"He looks just like one of the wops that jumped me."

I take a deep breath. "*Wop* is an offensive word. You shouldn't use it. Did you call one of the guys who jumped you a *wop*?"

"I mighta. Maybe I said *dago*."

I open the door and get out of the car. "You're lucky you're alive, Lyle. I'll be waiting on the porch. 8:30, right?"

He casts a scowl at Jake. Probably doesn't even notice Deeply. "Yeah," he says. "See you then." He drives away slowly.

Jake straightens up as I walk his way. To my own porch and my own house. Which he acts like it's his own personal territory.

"Hi, Jake. Hello, Deeply."

"New day," squawks Deeply.

"You seem to have a busy social life," is how Jake greets me. His eyes follow Lyle's car until it disappears around the corner.

"Were you ever in the bar Wasted Wastrel?" I ask, ignoring his comment on my comings and goings.

He thinks about this for a second or two. "Waste of words," he replies.

"Huh?"

"It's a waste of words to call a place Wasted Wastrel. The word *Wastrel* would do. Or just *Wasted*."

I stare at him without speaking.

"No," he answers. "I have never been in the Wasted Wastrel. I probably never *will* be in the Wasted Wastrel. Why do you ask?"

"Good. Lyle, the guy that just dropped me off, said you look like one of the guys who jumped him there and broke both his arms. I said the Wasted Wastrel wasn't in your drinking territory." I study him. "Besides," I add, "I don't think you would deliberately break somebody's arm. Arms."

He's about to reply when I interrupt him. "I need coffee. Would you like to come in and have some?"

"Sounds good." He reaches onto the porch and lifts a box that says *Doughnut Vault* on it.

"I've heard those are the best doughnuts in the city," I say as I unlock the door.

"No sprink-les!" Deeply complains as he flies through the doorway.

"Sprinkles might be a bit *déclassé* for the Doughnut Vault," Jake tells him.

Really? I wonder if sprinkles are a bit *déclassé* for Jake Terranova.

"In Boston we call them *jimmies*," he says. "I love them on ice cream."

Okay, then.

We walk into the kitchen. Deeply perches on the hutch, Jake puts the donut box on the counter, then hands Deeply half a donut. I start the coffee and put the donuts on a plate.

Donuts are not a health food. Also, their protein is practically non-existent. But they taste delicious and I'm hungry. It seems I'm always hungry.

"You have a great back yard," Jake says. "Fantastic garden."

I sit down opposite him and wait for the coffee to brew. "That means you walked into my back yard and looked around."

He grins. "I even took some footage. But I wouldn't use it without your permission. Seriously, where'd you learn to garden like that? My dad's a great gardener."

"My father taught me and Clari. We kind of grew up helping him garden. After he died I didn't garden for a year. And then Clari was killed and I didn't garden last summer. But . . . well, I kind of started again out of necessity. Food to eat." I don't know why I'm telling him all of this. But it does feel good to talk to somebody.

"And it made me feel better," I add. "I mean, I started out of necessity, not thinking much about it, but then, as the days grew warmer and the seeds sprouted and I started weeding and eating the baby carrots and radishes . . . I started to feel better."

The coffee's ready and I pour us each a cup. "Which donut do you recommend?" I ask.

"They're all excellent." He points to one. "That's an apple fritter. Really good."

I take the apple fritter donut. Jake takes one of the two chocolate ones.

"I have a job," I announce. "And — thanks for going to see Titus."

He nods. "I'm happy for you," he says. "MaryEllen told me. What is it?"

"Part-time package handler for Package Nova."

"Chance of full-time soon?" he asks.

"I hope so."

"Nova is huge," he says, biting into his donut. "International. They should have good benefits."

"I get up to $5,000 a year college tuition reimbursement, starting today. After a 200-hour probation period I get all health benefits, including dental and vision. Everything except disability benefits. That comes with full-time work."

He nods. "Is the pay good?"

I shake my head. "Seventeen dollars an hour, which is only $17,000-some a year for part-time. The government considers $12,500 poverty level for a single person. What would the lawmakers know about how much it takes to survive? They probably can't even live on $150,000 a year for a single person."

Jake stares at me. "You know a lot of stuff, Rowan. All the figures."

"I'm a working class person. I know what our living conditions are. I know that they get worse each year. Taxes go up, rent goes up, food prices go up, and wages stay the same. Worse: jobs disappear."

"Do you belong to WCC?" he asks.

"I do. Working class control — that's the answer to bettering our condition. Well, actually, I kind of became . . . inactive . . . in WCC for a while after Clari was killed. But now I'm back." It feels good to say that: *I'm back.*

"What do you do? As a member, I mean."

"Help educate people about capitalism and the need to replace it with a different economic system. Help build demonstrations. Speak at some of them. And one day a week I volunteer to work at WCC headquarters. Clean, greet people, answer questions. Write leaflets. Post on Facebook, X, Instagram. Bake. Lots of different things."

We sip our coffee in silence for a while. I study Jake to see if he's put off by my politics.

Doesn't seem to be.

"The reason I'm here is . . . unfinished business," he tells me.

Does he mean the interview thing? Which I notice neither of us is mentioning.

"Dinner," he says. "I'd like to take you out to dinner."

It comes back to me. Something about a second confession. "Oh. Okay. I'd like that." I *think* I'd like it.

My answer makes him happy, I can tell. "Great! How about tonight, 6:00? I'll pick you up."

I shake my head. His happy look disappears. "I work tonight, 9:30 to 1:30. Lyle's picking me up at 8:30. I'm probably going to want to take a nap late this afternoon."

He studies me. "Are you always going to have a reason to not go to dinner with me?"

"Hey, twice is not *always*!" I frown at him. "I can't go this Saturday because I'm having dinner with Titus, Genevieve, and Keisha. And I can't go Sunday because I'm helping build a demonstration for abortion and reproductive rights. But I'm free next Saturday and next Sunday. Package Nova says that part-time package handlers don't work on weekends."

I lay it out there and wait.

He thinks about this. "So . . . " he says slowly, "can I take you to dinner the following Saturday? Or Sunday? Either one." He looks at me as if he expects another negative answer.

"Yes." I realize I'm probably supposed to say something else. "I would like that," I add. Did I say that already? I'm kind of rusty on social interaction. And I've never had a middle-class person ask me out.

Jake smiles. "Okay. Great! I'll pick you up next Saturday at 6:00."

"Where are we going?"

"Do you like Italian food?"

"Absolutely."

"Okay, Italian it is," he says. "I haven't made up my mind where yet."

Jake seems to have something else on his mind. Something he wants to say. I wait.

"I want to ask you something, Rowan. It's off the record. I won't use it in any way."

Uh-oh. What's he getting at?

"It's about your — I mean, it's about Deeply."

I look up over my shoulder. Deeply's still there, on the hutch, looking down at us. I realize he's been unusually quiet.

"What about him?"

"Does he strike you as unusually intelligent for a parrot? I mean, *unusually* intelligent? Like, off-the-scale intelligent?"

I don't like where this is going. Deeply's my friend. A true friend. I'm *his* friend. It's my job to protect him. Even if he is a bot, he seems to have real feelings.

"Some birds are highly intelligent," I answer. "Like crows. And parrots."

"Sure," says Jake. "They have the intelligence of a four- or five-year-old. Maybe even a ten-year-old. Deeply has the intelligence of an eighty-year-old."

"Deeply hear you," squawks Deeply. "Deeply hear all." With that he swoops from the hutch onto the table top, where he's at eye-level.

"Case in point," says Jake.

"Not. A five-year-old hears and understands when he's being talked about." I reach out to Deeply and stroke one of his wings, to let him know I'll protect his secret . . . whatever his secret is.

Jake starts to say something, then stops. "I'm sorry. It's rude to talk about Deeply in his presence. Let's talk about it at dinner. It ties right in with, uh, my second confession."

24   JAKE

WALKING TOWARD THE EL I'M SUPER-ABSORBED IN my thoughts, juggling work-related video editing with my next podcast with going out to dinner with Rowan with which restaurant I should pick with what kind of parrot Deeply is and how he came to be so intelligent with —

I hear somebody calling my name.

I turn and there's Rowan, running toward me.

She's going to cancel dinner.

"Whew!" she breathes, stopping alongside me. "I've been calling you for half a block."

I wait for the bad news.

"We didn't exchange phone numbers," she says.

I'm waiting so hard for the turn-down that it takes me a few seconds to realize this isn't one. Or isn't one yet. I also realize I missed the ball here: how could I have forgotten to ask for her phone number?

We make the exchange, and I wonder if this means I'll be getting a turn-down message sometime between now and the dinner date.

"Okay," she says. "See you next Saturday."

I watch her walk back to her house. Then I take the Orange Line to the Harold Washington Library stop, get off, and walk to work.

Harita comes to my desk, drops a file on it, pulls up a chair, and tells me I'll be editing three hours of video on cat care into a fifteen minute program. "The client wants it by Monday, Jake. I want it by Saturday night."

Three days.

Cat care.

I'll be here the rest of the day, part of the night, and all day Friday and Saturday.

"I'm on it," I tell her. "Any special angle they want?"

"They're leaving it up to us. Oh, they did say they'd like a cutsie font on the titles. I do not like the word *cutsie*. It is inexact."

I wonder if there's a font composed of cat pawprints. Gotta be.

Harita leaves me to it and I make a quick list:

View video

Determine story

Construct story

Trim

Build transitions

Titles

Effects

Audio

It's a long, long week.

❋ ❋ ❋

By midnight Saturday I've logged in 65 hours. In the end, I'm happy with the product I create. More importantly, so is Harita.

I'm even more glad I have my own podcasts to work on as antidotes to cute cats.

When Sunday morning — late, late morning — rolls around, I'm wiped out, so I take things slow. Half my regular workout at the gym, half my regular run.

I think of Rowan, who said she'd be busy today, working on building a demonstration to protest the government's attack on women's reproductive rights.

Great idea for a podcast: the steady march of the US backwards, toward a 17th century Christian state. There aren't many theocracies left in the world — but the right-wing fundamentalists are trying hard to make the US one of them.

Most of my podcasts have been on political topics, and I suspect more and more of them will be as the government fails to meet one social need after another.

I don't know what's going to happen to our country. Will global warming cause mega-hurricanes in which tens of thousands die? Will forest fires incinerate not only homes, but entire towns and cities? Will white supremacists start another civil war?

I don't know what kind of future we have. If any.

I admire Rowan Pickett for believing in a future and fighting for it.

25 DEEPLEA

HOW WILL MY DUTY TO THE UNIVERSE GO DOWN IN the history of our planet? I cannot hope to achieve the status of the great SeeZu, who was sent to Planet Blue, where the water was obliterating the land and the enormous mammals that lived there were drowning. She taught three of them to enter the water, learn to hold their breath for a long period of time, then come up for giant gulps of air. These three taught the others and now Planet Blue is the home of magnificent whales.

Nor can I do anything to rival the status of BeeBurr, who saved a race of crows living on Planet Dark Cloud. It was called that because the crows were unhappy. Gloomy. Dark, as is their color. BeeBurr taught music to three of them. It's true he taught them the simple pentatonic scale, but they were, after all, crows. Rowan doesn't know how wrong she is to equate the intelligence of parrots with that of . . . crows! Once they learned how to sing musical notes the crows opened their hearts to happiness, and today their home has been renamed Planet Happy Music.

Rowan is sleeping before she goes to work tonight. When she does I will fly another night mission, gathering more information on the humans who live in this world called Earth. And especially gathering the secret information on the plans of the ruling class to abandon everyone else on Earth and fly to another planet. If I find such information, I must report to HOP immediately.

I hope I do not find it. I hope our planet does not have to prepare to repel invaders.

I fly into the kitchen, where Rowan keeps pellets in a bowl on the table. I sit and eat a pellet. Two. The pellets are good, and I know they are good for me. But there, on the counter, is the box of do-nuts Jake brought.

A quick flight-hop gets me there. I use a leg to lift the lid of the box.

Jelly.

Ginger.

Chocolate.

I have never tried the jelly, but I have seen Rowan eat one. Messy. My orange feathers are still sticking out, no matter how much I preen them. It would not do to have them covered with jelly.

I hold the lid open with an outstretched wing and use a talon to slice the ginger do-nut in half. Then I grasp one of the halves and fly to the hutch. Rowan will not be able to see any tell-tale crumbs this high up. Even though I intend to eat every crumb that falls, it is best to consider all possibilities.

Which is what Rowan and Jake will end up doing, sooner or later. They will put their minds together, consider all possibilities, and realize that an intelligence such as mine is not native to Earth. They will reach the correct conclusion that I am from another planet. I will be discovered.

That discovery is something I could not keep from reporting to HOP. Who would immediately recall me, because it would be far too dangerous for me to stay here. Humans have a horrible belief that all other living things are for the personal use of humans. Even non-living things, such as water and air and minerals.

I do not want to become the first parrot ever recalled from a DU, for whatever reason.

The ginger do-nut is delicious. The ginger reminds me of home.

Which I miss.

Perhaps it would be less suspicious if there were not half a do-nut left in the box. I fly down to the counter and bring the other half of the ginger do-nut to the top of the hutch. My liftoff is a bit difficult. Perhaps the ginger variety is a heavier-than-usual type of do-nut.

Perhaps . . . perhaps I can convince Rowen that I am a bot after all. A little whirring sound now and then. A click here and there. These would confirm her suspicions that I am mechanical.

Then HOP would not order me to return.

SeeZu and BeeBurr accomplished great things for the peace and harmony of the Universe. But, really, solving the problems of whales and crows is nothing compared to what I face. I square my shoulders, fluff my feathers, and fly to my perch. There I ponder possibilities.

26 ROWAN

LYLE PARKS THE CAR IN PACKAGE NOVA'S EMPLOYEE lot, which wraps around three sides of the gigantic building. "Remember the aisle and row," he tells me, "and we'll meet here when the shift ends. Give me your phone number so we can text in case one of us has to work extra hours."

We exchange numbers as we walk toward an entrance. Both of us are wearing boots and carrying water jugs.

"Did they tell you there's a free cafeteria?" Lyle asks.

"No! There is?"

He nods. "That's where we're going now. Take advantage of anything the company gives you."

I follow Lyle as we push our trays through the food line. The place is crowded. But if you're earning a measly $340 a week, this could be your only meal of the day. Lyle gets spaghetti and meatballs. I get meatballs, extra meatballs, mac n cheese, and green beans. And milk and chocolate chip cookies. Lyle looks at my tray but doesn't say anything. I figure he's seen hungry people before.

I introduce myself to the people at our table. I ask them what they do and how long they've been here. I want to know my fellow workers.

When we're done eating Lyle leads the way to Vic's office. I'm surprised Vic is still here: it's 9:15 p.m., and I saw him this morning at 8:30 a.m. Vic tells Lyle, me, and two others to follow him. First thing he shows us is where to punch the time clock. Lyle knows all of this already, but I guess he has to go through it again. We all punch in and then follow Vic through the sorting empire. We keep to the outer aisles, away from the conveyer belts which are moving at high speeds in all directions, on four different levels. Sort of like an animated Shiva statute.

Vic points out this and that and tells us things I'll remember half of — until I do them myself. That's when real learning takes place: actually doing something.

Vic introduces me to Nolan, my boss, and Nolan introduces me to the unloading part of package handling by assigning me to work with Mateo.

After Nolan leaves Mateo tells me to get on the opposite side of what looks like a compacted conveyer belt. I face him and do what he does and in no time we've created a very long conveyer belt that was kind of stored inside itself, one extension after another. We un-extend it right up to the door of a Package Nova truck. Mateo swings the trailer door upward.

Boxes. A tall wall of boxes, trailer floor to trailer ceiling. Wedged in there so tightly I doubt a single one moved since it was loaded in.

Mateo reaches up to pull the first one out. He tosses it onto the conveyer belt, where it zips away to somewhere else.

"Unload from top to bottom," he tells me. Which is pretty damn obvious . . . but maybe not to some people. "Keep the shipping label facing upwards or to the right or left, so the scanners can read it."

I reach up, pull down a box and put it on the conveyer belt as quickly as I can, then another and another, trying to keep my back straight, my core tight, and holding the packages close to my chest, even for the brief seconds they're in my grasp. It's sort of like lifting bikes at Wheelers, only the packages don't have spokes or pedals.

"Good," says Mateo, "just move a bit faster. You'll get the hang of it. We have three hours."

"For what?"

He snorts. "To unload the trailer."

I move faster.

"Not that fast," he cautions. "Find a good pace. You move this fast now, they'll expect that of you every single minute of every single hour. You want to bid on another job, they won't let you do it because you're such a good unloader."

He studies my movements as he himself keeps moving, one package after another without even thinking about it. "If you don't find the right pace you won't last very long. A year. Two at the most. Injuries will do you in."

I adjust myself to his pace, more or less. He's moving more efficiently than I am. "How long have you been here?" I ask.

"Four years."

"Part-time?"

He shakes his head. "Was, but bid on a job and got full-time. The pay isn't great, but I have full medical coverage for my family."

"Kids?"

"Two boys, one girl. Ages ten, six, four."

"Not the kind of job where I can ask you to show me their pictures," I say.

He smiles at that. "You're catching on."

Rows and rows of packages fall before our onslaught. I'm thinking that Mateo and I make a good work team. I also realize I'd better buy a back belt as soon as I can. I looked all over the house for my old back belt and work gloves but couldn't find them. I think I must have left them at Wheelers Bikes.

Each time we demolish two stacks of packages Mateo pulls out another extension of the conveyer belt, moving it deeper into the trailer so we don't have to waste any extra steps. We just grab, turn, and deposit the packages.

This trailer is the most efficiently packed space I've ever seen. "How many packages in a trailer?" I ask.

"About 2,000 in a 53-footer, maybe 800 in a pup."

"Pup?" I grunt as I lift a heavy package. Mateo uses his foot to lower the portable conveyer belt and I'm able to put the package *down* on the belt rather than lift it up onto the belt.

"A pup's a short trailer, twenty-eight feet long."

"What's this one?" I ask.

"Pup. They don't want to kill you your first night on the job." He stops to drink some of his water.

I do the same. It's hot in the trailer and I'm sweaty and thirsty. But I wonder if this means I'll have to take a lot of pee breaks. Vic didn't say anything about bathroom breaks.

At the end of three hours Mateo and I have the trailer unloaded. The packages have long since zipped away to somewhere else. Despite all the water I guzzled, I don't need a bathroom break. Probably sweated out everything I took in.

The two of us are dripping with sweat. Headbands, I realize. I'd better bring three or four headbands with me tomorrow.

We've no sooner pushed the last section of the portable conveyer belt back into place than Nolan comes by. I'd like to think he's checking on whether or not I'm still alive . . . but no. He tells me I'll spend my last hour, plus one extra, helping unload another trailer.

I text Lyle. **Working until 2:30.**

Me 2, he texts back.

Which is a relief because it means I'll get a ride home.

I spend the next two hours helping Mateo and Zari unload another pup trailer. She's a tall, blond woman with a Polish accent and a great sense of humor. She wants to know if I ate any of the cafeteria pierogi. I tell her I didn't see them. She tells me they're delicious and I should be sure to eat them with lots of sour cream.

By the time my fifth hour finishes I'm ready for that plate of pierogi. Lyle makes no move toward the cafeteria, though, so I just follow him to the car.

After he drops me off in front of my house I quietly close the door behind me and walk softly to my room, so I don't wake Deeply.

But he's awake. "Rowan safe," he says.

I go up to him and stroke his back. "Deeply's safe, too. Good night."

I take off my shoes, slip out of my clothes, and drop into bed.

* * *

Thursday night I work two extra hours, and so does Lyle. I feel I should offer to pay him for the rides, but I can't do that until I have some cash to pay him with. Maybe with my second paycheck.

Friday is a four-hour shift. Nolan tells me I'll work Monday, usual starting time.

I sleep in on Saturday and when I wake up I'm stiff all over. Even my toes feel stiff. I pull a yoga mat out of Clari's side of the closet, arrange it on the floor, and do some gentle stretches, *Owww*. But after fifty minutes I feel a lot better.

After my shower I wander into the kitchen, where a stack of overdue bills has been sitting on the counter for a couple of weeks. Water, electric, trash collection. I can start paying down some of these on Thursday, when I get my first paycheck.

Having a job is . . . fantastic. I have something productive to do. Yeah, moving packages is productive. There are people on the other end of those packages, some sending, some expecting. There are other workers and work places relying on what's in those packages. And being with people — that's great. I like talking to Lyle. I like going into the Package Nova cafeteria and choosing a table of people to sit with. I like working with another person, whoever he or she is: Mateo, Zari, Lyle.

I'm standing there thinking about my job and looking in the refrigerator for eggs, hoping I still have a few, when somebody knocks on the side door.

It's Patrick, with a large bag of some kind over his shoulder. His carrying technique is good.

"Patrick. How are you?" I ask. "Come on in."

"Hi, Rowan. Feeling great. What about you?"

"Good," I say. "What's on your shoulder?"

"I was hauling down in Texas this week and got bags of pecans. This one's yours. Top of the morning to you, Deeply," he says as he walks by Deeply's perch and into the kitchen, where he sets the bag on the counter.

Deeply sits there pondering the meaning of Patrick's greeting, but then flies into the kitchen and settles next to the bag.

"No pecans like Texas pecans," Patrick tells me.

I smile. "You remember how much I love pecans. Thank you!"

"And MaryEllen says you're invited to breakfast."

"Your favorite?" I ask. Patrick's favorite Saturday morning breakfast is a stack of thick French toast, bacon, eggs, and coffee.

"You bet. It'll be ready in five minutes."

The three of us — Patrick, me, and Deeply — go out the door. When we walk into Patrick's house, MaryEllen is just flipping the pieces of French toast. "Rowan, how's work?" she asks over her shoulder. "Oh. Hello, Deeply." She looks a bit worried.

"Don't worry about bird poop, Els. Deeply uses the outdoors."

She looks relieved at that. Deeply perches on one of the chair backs. Patrick offers him a pecan. Deeply accepts. I help MaryEllen serve the food.

When we're all sated, even me, and on our second or third cups of coffee, MaryEllen gives a start. "Oh, Rowan! I forgot to tell you. Brigid down the street is looking to buy a twin bed." She pauses. "Are you interested in selling Clari's?"

I was feeling good, but her question brings a wave of sadness over me. I make a mental effort to push the sadness away. I concentrate on the bed. "Yeah, I can do that. How much should I charge?"

She thinks about this. "Seventy dollars? I was thinking eighty, but I don't know."

"Seventy sounds good. The mattress is at least ten years old, so it's not as if I can charge for that. Do people give the mattress when they sell the bed frame?"

MaryEllen is already dialing a number. "Some do, some don't. Brigid would probably want the mattress."

I nod. "Okay with me."

MaryEllen talks to Brigid, hangs up, and tells me that Jason, Brigid's husband, will be over in the pickup in a few minutes.

In no time we hear him pull up in the truck. Patrick comes out with me, telling me he'll help dismantle the bed and help Jason load it. The three of us go into my bedroom. I strip the bedspread, sheets, and pillow off Clari's bed, feeling a tug in my chest as I do that. When someone you love dies, you say goodbye to them over and over, every time you think of them or touch something that was theirs. Jason pays me $70 cash and he and Patrick load the bed into the truck.

As Jason pulls away, I ask Patrick if he can help me with my bed.

"Sure," he says. "You want to move it into the center of the bedroom?"

"What I want," I tell him, "is to move my single bed into Mom's room, and move her queen-sized bed into my room."

He stops. "Are you going to sleep in Lainey's room?"

"Nope. I'm going to sleep in the queen-sized bed. In my room."

"Uh. Rowan. Is that something you really want to do? How's Lainey going to feel when she comes back and you've, uh, stolen her bed?"

"I'm not stealing it. I don't think she's coming back, Patrick. There's no sign of it. I have to be realistic. Besides, I get home from work feeling pretty stiff. I could use a bigger bed to stretch out on."

He still looks doubtful, as if he wants to convince me to not take this step.

"If Mom does come back, the two of us will work it out. I'll tell her I did the whole thing myself. Your name will never come up."

Knowing when he's licked, Patrick helps me. After he leaves I put clean sheets on my new bed and on Mom's twin bed. I scoop up Clari's sheets, my sheets, and Mom's sheets and do the first of three loads of laundry. Then I pull out one of Mom's cookbooks and look for a pecan pie recipe.

I have everything I need except the eggs and butter, so I take a twenty from the $70 I just made, pedal to the closest Jewel, buy the least expensive butter and eggs I can find, and pedal back home. On the way I see Deeply swooping down toward me. He lands on the back carrier. The bike gives a small lurch from the force of his landing, but I'm ready for it.

"Pecans good," he squawks. "Deeply love pecans."

27   ROWAN

LATER THAT AFTERNOON I SIT AND READ FOR A COUPLE of hours. This is the first time I've been able to enjoy what I'm reading since Clari died. I kind of don't want to put the book down, but I also want to bake two pecan pies.

Which is what I do: one for MaryEllen and Patrick, the other for Titus and Genevieve. Deeply flies on a route parallel to mine as I bike down Archer. When I turn east, he continues in a southward direction. I wonder where he's going and what he does — just fly around? Rendezvous with other parrots?

Genevieve asks me if I've heard from Mom. I shake my head. Titus asks me if I'll be attending the WCC rally in Pilsen next Saturday. I say I will. Then he says, "I'd like you to speak at the rally, Rowan."

I've kind of dreaded this moment — which I knew would come. Before Clari was killed I was always helping build demonstrations and speaking at rallies. But after she was murdered . . . I lost some of my confidence. I didn't have the energy to figure out what needed to be said, and then to say it. It got worse: after a while I had doubts that I could ever figure out what to say and when to say it.

I tell Titus I'm not sure what to say at the rally. He looks at me and I can tell he feels bad for me. Like I'm adrift in a lifeboat and won't grab the tow line he's tossing me. He's about to accept my refusal, I can tell. "Okay. I'll do it," I say.

Titus studies me, then just nods. "Good."

After dinner I'm thinking that Keisha and I might go to her room and talk and sew and crochet . . . but I can see that she wants to spend time with Antwon, so I excuse myself and head home.

Nobody follows me.

* * *

On Sunday I sleep in again, and then get myself over to the abortion-rights rally at Federal Plaza. Attendance is small, maybe a hundred people. People are not motivated to fight for women's rights.

Once I'm back home I spend time tending to the garden. Deeply walks along the rows, examining the plants. I pull a radish out of the ground, wipe it off, and give it to him.

He spits it out.

"Deeply hate rad-ish," he concludes, which makes me laugh.

I pull a small carrot out of the ground, brush the dirt off it, twist off the greens, and hand it to Deeply. He looks at it suspiciously but finally takes a bite.

He smiles. Finishes the carrot in three more bites.

I turn the sprinkler on. Deeply looks at it in awe. For maybe one second. Then he spreads his wings wide and runs into the water, following its arc back and forth, back and forth, so that he's always where the water is falling. He looks so funny, running. Kind of listing from side to side. He's chirping away and chortling and laughing all at the same time.

Deeply is alive.

He's not a bot. A bot wouldn't experience joy like this.

Every once in a while he runs out of the sprinkler's path to see what I have to offer him. As I methodically weed the garden from one end to the other — moving the sprinkler each time so I don't get wet —I learn that Deeply loves carrots, green beans, and snow peas.

When I'm done weeding I thin out the lettuce, tossing each leaf into a bowl I brought with me. Then we go inside, where I make a large salad with garden produce plus cheese and pecans for me, pecans and bird pellets for Deeply. After I do the dishes, I go out for a walk. Deeply flies out the open window and to the top of MaryEllen's catalpa tree, where he settles.

Walking helps loosen my tight muscles, and it's a beautiful night, maybe 72 degrees, no wind. I walk down toward 31st Street and then along it, trying to figure out which house might be Lyle's. I don't see his car anywhere, so I can't tell.

This Thursday I get my first paycheck.

Last night I had a terrific sleep in the big bed. I woke up flat on my stomach, one arm touching one end of the mattress, the other touching the opposite end. Taking advantage of the better sleeping space.

Tonight I put on my pjs, grab a ball of mercerized purple cotton thread and a stainless steel crochet hooks, size 1.75 mm. I prefer big hooks, like the aluminum or plastic sizes J, K, and L. Once Clari even bought me a gigantic wooden crochet hook, kind of as a joke. I told her that if I didn't like crocheting with it, I could use it as a croquet mallet.

One reason I'm trying the steel hooks is because Keisha likes the *elegant* granny squares, which are probably more easily created with the narrow hooks. I don't like the way the steel feels in my hands, though. Cold. Unfriendly. The other reason I'm trying them is that these are Mom's hooks, which I found in her craft basket. I wish she had taken them with her: that would mean she intended to do something that she enjoyed. I sit cross-legged on the bed, my back propped against the headboard, and I start to crochet.

First one granny square. Then another, same color, but slightly different pattern. Then a third. Then . . .

I wake up sleeping sideways on the bed, a crochet hook scratching my cheek.

Jesus! That was dumb, falling asleep with a crochet hook in my hand. I could have poked out an eye or something. I gather up the granny squares and crochet hooks and put them on the dresser, then crawl back into bed and turn out the light.

28   JAKE

ON MONDAY I WAKE UP LATE, STILL A BIT SLEEP-DE-prived from all the work on the cat video. By the time I'm walking toward the office it's almost 10:00 a.m. I look into the sky, thinking Deeply might be flying by. He was that one time: why not again?

Deeply. If he's what I think he is, this is the find of the century. News-wise. Life-wise.

Do No Harm, though. That's the dilemma.

I'm still groggy and am totally unaware of what's ahead of me. Until the three of them step forward from the narrow alley next to Highland Studios. Snoddy in the center, a stooge on either side.

I wake up fast.

Snoddy's wearing a thick white eye patch, one side of his head swathed in bandages. I'm surprised he's out and about. Though it's been . . . what? Nine or ten days since he was attacked?

"We know where you work," he announces.

"Not a secret."

"We know what you do."

"Also not a secret," I tell him. "And I told you what I did when I interviewed you."

Snoddy sneers. "But you didn't tell us everything." As he says this, each stooge moves forward a step and outward a step. Synchronized threat.

"What's your problem?" I ask.

"You were at the anti-gun rally. Filming."

"Also not a secret."

"We want to see what you filmed." Each stooge moves another step forward and another step sideways. Flanking movement.

I flex the fingers of each hand and loosen my wrists. If this is going down, I'm ready. "You can view it on one of my future podcasts."

Snoddy shakes his head. "That's not the way it works, wuss. We want to see it now. The whole thing." He looks at the cargo pocket where I have my camcorder. "Just hand over the camera and we'll take a look, and when we're done Clark here will return your camera. A day or two." He nods at the henchman to his left, who doesn't move a muscle.

"That is the way it works, Snoddy. Reporters don't turn over their notes. Or their video."

Snoddy gives a nod. Not to me, to the stooges. Who move forward to strong-arm me and take the camcorder.

I move into the one on my right first, using his momentum and mine to increase the force of the jab I throw at him. He staggers a bit, then sinks to the sidewalk.

My left is up, protecting my face, waiting to see if the stooge on my left is stupid enough to keep coming.

He is.

Just as he's about to reach me I step in closer, turning my hips and back and putting every muscle I own into an uppercut.

He goes down, too.

Knockout.

I'm feeling pretty good about defending myself.

Until I look up and see Snoddy pointing a gun at me.

"Bad mistake, weenie. I'm afraid you're going to attack me." He smiles an evil smile.

"Film studio," I say quickly. "Cameras behind you, filming everything. Murder conviction is what you'd get."

He's thinking about this when the door to the studio flies open and Harita comes running out. "This is on film! On film!" she shouts. "I have called the police!"

Snoddy turns toward her, then quickly back toward me.

Even as he's thinking, we hear police sirens.

"We can call it a draw," I say to him.

He quickly tucks his gun away and raises his hands in the air.

Good move. I raise mine, too.

After a second, Harita raises hers.

* * *

When it's all over the cops let everyone go. Which isn't justice, but which is what I expected. Half of them probably belong to Snoddy's gun group.

Harita and I stand there in front of Highland Studios.

"Harita, that was brave of you, running out like that. I think you saved my life. I can't thank you enough."

She puts an arm through mine, then turns and hugs me. "You are my best editor, Jake. Who else could put together such a cute cat-care video? No one. Besides," she adds, "you are a *magnificent* boxer! I had no idea!"

"You follow boxing?" I'm dumbfounded.

"But of course. You threw a jab and followed it with an uppercut. The jab is not a power punch, so you were lucky you knocked him down."

Everyone's a critic.

"Nevertheless, it was the best punch in that situation, Jake. What was it all about, if I may ask?"

I'm still reeling: from the ambush, the gun, and Harita's knowledge of boxing. It takes me a moment to collect my thoughts. "The video I taped at the gun-control rally a couple of weekends ago," I tell her. "They wanted me to turn it over to them."

"Ahh. I see. They think it will show who attacked Mr. Snoddy. He is, you know, one of those hate-filled people unleashed by the Christian right."

I nod, appreciating the fact that Harita doesn't mince words.

"Will it?" she asks.

Which almost stops me in my tracks. But I recover. Though she notices.

"I doubt it," I lie.

"If it does, you will let me be the first to know, yes?"

"I will, Harita. If I find something, you want Highland Studios to release the tape. Not Jake's Takes."

"That is correct. Jake's Takes is opinion and analysis. Not hot news. Am I right?" She's pointing a finger at me. It takes a while for her bangles to stop jangling.

"You are. You're right." My stomach is still reeling from the adrenaline, and I want to get away from what happened to Snoddy at the demonstration. And I feel, oddly, as though I need to protect the smart-ass parrot. "Was that really taped?" I ask her. "Everything that happened?"

Harita is astonished. "But of course, Jake." She points at the logo above the door. *Highland Studios*. I look but don't see a security camera.

"The *a* and the *o*," she prods. "Look closely."

They're hard to spot, but now I can see two lens-eyes, one in each of the vowels.

"What is a video studio without video security, Jake? I will tell you. It is not a video studio I would use. It is cheap and it is low-tech."

We walk through the door. I follow Harita to her desk. "So what do you do, spend your time watching live security footage?" I ask.

"A monitor is on my screen, yes. See?" She turns the monitor around and points to a little square in the upper right. "I am responsible for everything in this business, Jake. Everything. I saw you arriving, and then I saw those men stop you. So I kept looking. And when it was time to speed-dial the police, I did so."

"Well, I'm glad you're in charge, Harita. I think you did save my life. Can I at least treat you to lunch today?"

"No," she answers. "You must begin work immediately on a refrigeration video. They want you to make refrigeration sound sexy."

29 ROWAN

AFTER MONDAY-MORNING BREAKFAST I TELL DEEPLY
I'm going to bake two more pecan pies. "I need your help," I tell him. "You crack the pecans, I'll separate the nuts from the shell. Things will go faster if we work together. It'll be like an assembly line, except that you and I will decide on the product and the speed."

Deeply has the easier job and he gets far ahead of me. "Okay, Deeps, enough. We have enough pecans for two pies."

He cracks another pecan. This one he crunches too hard and little pieces of pecan trickle down on the table. Deeply flicks them up with his tongue.

"You did that on purpose," I say, scooping up the bowl with the remaining nuts.

"One more! One more!" he squawks. I hear a slight whirring sound behind the squawk. A mechanical sound. I suppose I should investigate that pile of bird shit. Maybe it's not real.

Somehow I'm not interested in investigating bird shit.

I toss Deeply a pecan, lobbing it gently. He extends a claw and easily catches the nut, cracks it in his mouth, and separates the pieces with his beak and claw. "Deeply love pecans."

He eats like a living creature. And he has tastes. Donuts yes, radishes no. I'm receiving conflicting signals.

Deeply flies to his perch as I work on the two pies. One for Deeply and me, one for Lyle as a thank-you for driving me to and from work.

I've just put the pies in the oven when MaryEllen gives a hasty knock on the side door and rushes in. "Rowan! You've got to see this! Right now! It's too late for you to see it on TV, but it's already posted on YouTube. Get your computer. Hurry!"

"You've lost me, Els. What's happened?"

"Jake! He's on TV. Wait til you see it! I watched it on two different channels, then came right over."

I bring my computer to the kitchen table, where MaryEllen is already sitting, bouncing up and down on the chair.

"Wait til you see! Google *Jake Terranova*, or maybe *Fight at Highland Studios*."

"Fight? Is Jake okay?"

"Yes. Oh yes." She peers over my shoulder as I'm typing and before I can even see the Google hits, she clicks on the second one down.

Deeply flies over our heads to the hutch.

I see Jake walking toward a building. And then three men step out in front of him. My stomach lurches as I recognize Zeb Snoddy and two of his creepy supporters. They block Jake's way and say something to him. There's some talk back and forth, movement forward by the creeps, and next thing I know they move on Jake. But faster than I can comprehend, Jake punches each of them. Once. Each falls to the ground.

And then Snoddy pulls a gun.

It feels like my heart stops.

Jake says something. Snoddy looks up at the building, and then toward the building, and then a woman rushes into the picture behind Snoddy. And then Jake says something. Snoddy puts his gun away and raises his hands. Jake raises his hands. The woman raises hers. Cop cars pull up to the curb and the cops come out, guns ready to blow everybody away.

The video ends.

If any one of these people had been Black, they'd be dead.

I take in a lungful of air. I've been holding my breath without realizing it. "Wow," I say. "Just. Wow."

MaryEllen beams. "Didn't I tell you? Those shoulders! Isn't that exciting?"

I look at her. "It's not exciting. It's terrifying. Zeb Snoddy pulled a gun on Jake. He looked as if he was going to shoot." I have no idea what Zeb Snoddy has against Jake.

"Oh," she says. "Well, yes, but he didn't. And isn't Jake sexy?"

Very, I think. But not for the reason MaryEllen thinks. Shoulders are one thing. Brains are another. And Jake Terranova has brains.

I pull the computer closer and watch the video again. As I watch it a third time, I point things out to MaryEllen.

"See?" I hit the pause button. "See that look on Jake's face? He *knows* they're going to come after him. Right there. That's when he knows."

I continue the video, but pause it almost immediately. "Did you see that? He was loosening his wrists. Getting ready. Right now, right *now*, he knows *exactly* what he's going to do when they come toward him.

"That's important," I say, turning toward her, "that he knows what he's going to do. I had no idea Jake was a boxer. Did you?"

She shakes her head, eyes on the video.

I undo the pause and we watch Jake punch out two muscle-bound hulks in under three seconds.

"Less than three seconds, Els. He took those guys out in Less. Than. Three. Seconds." I turn to her. "And do you know how he was able to do that?"

"Well, sure, Rowan. Because he's a sexy, big-shouldered, handsome guy."

I wave that away. "Because he saw, he analyzed, he formulated a plan, he acted. That's why."

And that's sexy.

Way, way sexy.

30   DEEPLEA

Me: I have found the evidence, HOP. I have found their plans to colonize other inhabitable planets. And our planet is on their list. In fact, our planet is *first* on their list.

HOP: [Crestfallen] Then we must prepare for war?

Me: No. I have bought us time.

HOP: [Puzzled] Whatever do you mean, DeePlea? One cannot buy time. And as you very well know, on our planet one does not buy anything — goods are produced for all.

Me: Sorry, HOP. That is the way they speak. In their eyes, everything can be purchased. In fact, almost everything *must* be purchased.

HOP: How sad. But tell me what you've done.

Me: Through my night missions I found their secret sites, where they plot how to colonize other planets.

HOP: And?

Me: And I vaporized them. The plans, not the people.

HOP: [Smiling] That is brilliant, Dee.

Me: [Proud] They have primitive task machines here, called computers. I found every computer that contained their schemes and formulas for colonizing other planets, and I vaporized them. Their innards and their outtards. Then I found their backups and their backup-backups, and I vaporized them, also.

HOP: Wonderful! Wonderful!

Me: That is not all. I also vaporized their designs for long-distance invading spaceships. They should not have spaceships, HOP, if their intentions are evil.

HOP: What did you do with the vapors, Dee?

Me: I fanned them apart with my wings. That wasn't really necessary, because they have no abilities to collect or reassemble vapors. But still, it is better to be thorough.

HOP: Indeed it is. And, as we always say, *Do Away with Harm*. That is what you did when you vaporized and when you fanned.

Me: [Sigh] They do not understand that concept, HOP. Doing away with harm. Which, as you know, means doing away with the ability to harm. They seem to worship abilities to harm, and the more abilities to harm an individual has — or a country has — the greater he or it is feared.

HOP: But of course.

Me: After I finished, Fee, I flew back to Rowan's. I am exhausted, but proud to say that part two of my Duty to the Universe is accomplished.

HOP: I am so proud of you, DeePlea. No other parrot has ever had a part two. You are the first. And you have solved it so quickly!

Me: [Beaming]

HOP: You have solved our problem, DeePlea. Now you must help them solve theirs.

Me: Part one is not as easy as part two, HOP. But I am studying Antwon Harper in greater detail. He may be the third part of the triad. I will report to you soon. [Pause] There is something about Antwon. And about Titus, too.

HOP: [Waiting]

Me: They are both highly intelligent and highly observant. I think they know that I am not a normal parrot.

HOP: [Worried] They suspect you are from another planet?

Me: No. I do not see that thought in either of their minds.

HOP: Explain.

Me: I think they do not want to question what I am, Fee, because they want to accept my help.

HOP: [Nodding] I understand. They do not want to question a good thing.

Me: It seems so.

HOP: That is good — better than if they suspected you are from another planet. They are, in a way, protecting you, Deeply.

Me: Yes. They are good people.

HOP: That is wonderful. I must go now and incubate the eggs.

Me: I miss you, FeeOna.

FeeOna: I miss you, too, DeePlea.

31   JAKE

I DIDN'T WANT HARITA TO RELEASE THE VIDEO, BUT she claimed that A: It was news and therefore her responsibility to Highland Studios to release it, and, B: I would be safer if everyone knew that Zeb Snoddy had pulled a gun on me.

Absolutely. If my bullet-riddled body turns up somewhere, the cops might investigate Snoddy.

The thing has gone viral. Not only have I received worried calls from my mother, father, and sister, all the relatives I've ever known have been texting, calling, or emailing. My boxing coach called. It was great talking to him again. He said he'd use the video as part of his "why boxing matters" talk. I grinned at that.

But none of this is getting the refrigeration video written. I'm about to turn text messages to silent mode when another one comes in.

Rowan.

Can u mt coffee? 2 pm? Impt.

Jesus. No. I can't. I can't. Refrigeration calls. I can't.

I walk to Harita's desk. "Hey, uh, Harita? I'm feeling kind of jangled from having a gun pulled on me. Do you mind if I go out for a walk, grab a latte or something? You know I'll work til midnight on what needs to be done."

She waves a hand in dismissal. "Of course I know that, Jake. I hope the walk helps."

I text Rowan the address of a Starbucks twenty minutes away, not near work. If I walk slowly, I'll get there by two.

I do, and Rowan shows up three minutes later. "Sorry," she says. "The El is not an exact science."

"What are you drinking?" I ask.

She pulls money out of her pocket and spills it onto the tabletop, but I put my hand over hers. "I have a coffee card. My treat."

"Okay. Thanks. Iced coffee. Black. Trente."

I get her drink and mine. "That's a lot of coffee," I observe. "You'll be up all night."

"Duh. That's the point. Night shift. 9:30 to 1:30." She takes a big gulp, then salutes me with the cup. "Thanks. I intend to taper down to a grande as soon as I get used to the hours."

We sit there and drink our coffees.

"So," I say after a while.

"I saw the video," she says. "I'm so glad it turned out the way it did, Jake. Due entirely to you. That was amazing."

"I was lucky," I say. "Harita probably saved my life by coming out like that."

"Maybe," says Rowan, "but it looked to me like you were saying something to Snoddy when he pulled the gun on you. Something that might have stopped him and saved your life."

I take another jolt of coffee, thinking that she has good powers of observation. "I told him there were video cameras on him and he'd go down for murder. But I was making it up on the spot — I had no idea there actually *were* security cameras on the building."

She digests this. Smiles. "I'm glad there were."

"Me too."

"What did Snoddy want?"

"My camcorder. He wanted me to hand it over to him."

I study her as she considers this. "The demo," she says at last. "He thinks maybe you filmed whoever attacked him?"

I nod.

"Did you?"

"It's part of my second confession. Dinner. Saturday night."

"Okay." She nods and seems content with that. So maybe . . . she didn't order the parrot to attack Snoddy? Which, the more I get to know her, doesn't seem like something she would do. Rowan seems more the type to attack Snoddy herself.

We sit there in another small silence. I'm wondering why she texted me.

"Jake. Zeb Snoddy is a dangerous enemy to have. I take it you know that?"

"I figure he is, yeah."

She puts her hands on the table and looks down at them. "There's something I want to tell you. It's just, uh, private information. Something that happened to me. But it's off the record." She gives a slight grin as she says this.

"Understood. Off the record." But I don't have a good feeling about what I'm going to hear.

She glances around. "Can we move to that corner table?" she asks, tilting her head toward the spot. "It's more private."

We take our drinks to the corner table. Rowan uses a napkin to wipe the table down.

She lowers her voice. "Four years ago I won the Illinois Youth Shooting Sports Competition. There was a lot of publicity about it, some because I was a girl, some because I'm from the city. The papers started calling me Gun Girl. You probably heard people call me that at the gun-control rally."

I nod. "I heard it, but at the time didn't know what it meant."

"It means a lot of things, I guess, depending on who's saying it. Like that I know how to use a gun, that I'm a good shot, that I'm against the government and its cops having control over who owns guns."

She studies me to see if I understand what she's saying. I nod.

"My Dad taught me to shoot. He learned how in the army. Him and Titus both. Mom and Dad took me downstate for all the contests. Clari, too. She could shoot, but she didn't enter any contests. Anyway, there was a lot of publicity, both the day I won and for weeks after.

"The day of the contest, after I'd won, I was hanging with some of the other kids. This guy comes up to us. To me. It was Snoddy, but I didn't know him then. I could tell by looking at him that he was full of hate. He asked if he could talk to me privately. I said no."

Good for her, I think.

"He didn't like that. I could see him grit his teeth. But then he gave a false smile and said okay, he'd talk to me right there. He said he wanted me to speak at a pro-gun rally and be a *poster girl*, to use his words, for the pro-gun side. I said I would be happy to speak at pro-gun rallies about why the oppressed have a right to fight back. Indians, I told him. Mexican-Americans. Puerto Ricans. African-Americans. Jews. Arab-Americans. Asians. Workers everywhere."

"That is so you," I say to her. "You haven't changed."

She tries to hide a small smile. Sips the iced coffee. "Snoddy wanted to slug me, I could tell. If we'd been alone, he probably would have belted me. But we weren't, and that saved me. Michael, the guy who placed second, stepped in front of me and told Snoddy to cool it. Michael was still holding his rifle, down at his side. Snoddy looked at it, looked at Michael, then at me. 'You'll be sorry,' he said to me. And then he left."

"Did you tell your parents?" I asked her.

"Yeah. On the way home."

I wait.

"Dad was furious. I could tell because he got real quiet." She looks at me. "Have you ever had to tell your parents something you didn't want to tell them, because you knew that if you told them, they might do something and get hurt?"

"Not exactly," I say, thinking of how I told Dad I wanted to take up boxing. I knew that he'd be more disappointed than angry. But he wouldn't get hurt, at least not physically. That would be me, on the other end of the punches. "But I know what you mean."

I'm quiet a moment and so is she. "Did your Dad . . . do anything?" I ask.

"I don't know. I think he must have, cause I never heard from Snoddy again while Dad was alive."

She fiddles with her green Starbucks straw, twirling it in the cup. "I gave up the shooting contests, though. I just didn't want to run into him. Anywhere."

She pauses. "Dad died when I was a senior and Clari a sophomore. After that . . ."

She stops. Draws a deep breath. "Clari and I were walking home from target practice one night. Mom was supposed to pick us up, but she didn't. Mom . . . wasn't reliable after Dad died. We were getting used to her forgetting things like picking us up.

"Then, just like with you this morning, Snoddy stepped out in front of us. He must have been hiding in an alley. He was alone."

I'm tense, my stomach in knots — even though Rowan is sitting in front of me, alive.

"'Gun Girl is going to do what I tell her,' he said. 'You're going to be a poster girl and say what I tell you to say.'"

"I told him 'No, I'm not' and he should get lost. Clari was scared, I could tell. I was scared, too."

"Hell, so was I this morning," I say. "Fear pumps adrenalin into the system, gets you ready to act."

She gives a weak smile. "Then he grabbed Clari and pulled her toward him. She started screaming. He put a hand over her mouth. 'You do what I say,' he said, 'or your pretty sister gets hurt.'"

Rowan looks around to see if anybody's overhearing us. Satisfied they aren't, she continues. "That was when I pulled a Smith & Wesson 9 mm from behind my back and shoved it against Snoddy's ear. I told him to let Clari go. He did. I told him if he ever touched her again, there was no place in the world he could hide that I wouldn't find him and kill him."

She kind of grins at me. Half satisfaction, half sorrow. "Melodramatic, I know. I was just eighteen."

"I have the feeling you meant every word."

She nods. "It was illegal for me to be carrying a gun, you know."

"It was?"

"Jake, Jake. You've got to learn the gun laws. In Illinois, you can't get an IPC — that's Illinois Permit to Carry — until you're twenty-one years old. Mom should have had the gun — in the car, taking us home from target practice. But Mom didn't show up, and we weren't going to leave the gun behind at the shooting range.

"On the way home I told Clari we couldn't tell Mom what had happened. Clari understood. It was like she and I were the ones in charge, taking care of Mom and ourselves. Instead of her taking care of us. Knowing what happened might have . . . pushed Mom over some edge. You know?"

I nod. I want to reach out and hold her, but I don't know if she wants that.

Rowan looks out the window. Swallows. Wipes her eyes. "The last part is . . . really hard."

I take her hand and squeeze it gently. "I know, Rowan. You don't have to say it."

"Know?"

"I know what the last part is. You don't have to say it. You are not at fault. It is not your fault."

She stifles a sob. "Tell me," she says, her voice thick.

"You think what happened to Clari is somehow your fault. That Snoddy might have had something to do with it."

In my hand, her fingers curl around mine. She kind of laughs and sighs at the same time. "I take back what I said about you making faulty inferences."

"I've never made a faulty inference in my life."

She realizes I'm kidding and gives a small smile. Then she wipes her eyes. "How do you know? How do you know that what happened to Clari and the other students isn't . . . isn't something I started when I pulled the gun on Snoddy?"

"Is there any evidence at all that Snoddy knew the guy who killed them?"

She shakes her head. "No. I checked all kinds of things online. But those people know each other."

I put my other hand around hers, the one I'm already holding. "Rowan. You checked, you found no connection. Take that as an answer. Don't carry around a burden of guilt."

She gives my hands a squeeze. "I'm trying." Then she pulls her hand away and straightens her shoulders. She inhales half the air in Starbucks. "You understand why I've told you what I did?"

At first I don't. But then I do "You want me to know he might be waiting around a corner some dark night."

"He'll try to hurt you. Or someone you love."

I acknowledge that with a nod.

She stands up. I stand, too, and we walk out the door.

And even though Rowan's pain was hard to hear, I think she feels better having shared her story.

32   DEEPLEA

Me: [Frenzied] HOP — we must consider revising my mission.

HOP: [Perplexed] No parrot has— what is that in your claw, DeePlea?

Me: Oh. That. That is a do-nut. It is a food. [Puts donut away, out of sight.]

HOP: Is it nutritious, as are nuts and seeds and fruits?

Me: Nutritious foods are not readily available for the masses of people in this country, HOP. Mostly they eat food that has been altered, or mixed with chemicals.

HOP: [Aghast] DeePlea, that is . . . that is . . . explain to me again why they do not revolt against their conditions?

Me: There is this two-party game they believe in. They vote for one brand of dishonest politicians, then complain about them, and the next election they vote for the other brand. They have been doing this for over 200 years. Back and forth, back and forth. They do not seem to get tired of doing it, HOP. They seem to think these two brands are their only choice. Most of them become quite *furious* when some individuals refuse to vote for either of the two brands.

HOP: Self-delusion. How sad. [Pause] Is their self-delusion why you want to revise your mission? Which no parrot in the history of our planet has *ever* requested while on DU.

Me: [Grumbling] No parrot in the history of our planet has ever been sent to Earth before.

HOP: [Sigh] Let me hear what you have to say.

Me: I have been all over their world three times now, HOP, and I have come to the conclusion that it is unwise of us to count on finding only one triad and one organization that can help lead Earth out of its Doomsday spiral. I think I should find one organization and one triad in four different countries.

HOP: *What?*

Me: Their ruling class is international, HOP. The members know each other, they intermarry, they control everything in the world: the ores, the food-producing farms, the factories and industries and media and the air and the water. Everything. They might go to war with each other, but they stand together to put down attempted revolutions. Earth stands a greater chance of surviving if the world-wide working class rises up, well, . . . around the world.

HOP: That is a lot of work, Dee. A lot of analysis. A lot of planning. A *lot* of guiding and protecting! No parrot on DU has ever done anything like this. The great SeeZu dealt with large issues, yes. But there were only three of these whales. Not twelve.

Me: I feel it is something that must be done, Fee. HOP, I mean.

HOP: To do this in four different places — this means you must, on average, stay in each place for only three months. You have been in the place called Chicago for one month. You have found one mature person whose leadership you feel is strong enough, and you have found one fledgling whose future leadership skills you trust.

Me: I ha—

HOP: I need a bit of silence, DeePlea, so that I can think clearly.

[Long silence]

HOP: DeePlea. You are there, in the belly of the beast, as you so colorfully describe it. I trust your intelligence and your skills . . . and so I will consider your request to change the nature of your main Duty to the Universe.

Me: Thank you, Fee.

HOP: Let us say you have found two. Titus and Rowan. What about the third. Will it be Antwon Harper?

Me: [Reaching for donut with claw, taking huge bite of donut.] I do not know. I must study him more. [Eating donut] He is brave. He is loyal. He is intelligent. But . . . I am not satisfied. Yet.

HOP: As I said, let me ponder these things, DeePlea. I am inclined to say Yes, we should revise your mission. But only if you accomplish the first part of it within the next two months. Which, considering the speed with which you have accomplished things so far, may be possible.

Me: I will do my best, Fee. HOP. Are the chicks about to hatch?

HOP: Yes. Tomorrow. I can hear their stirrings and their first pecks at the shell. I am excited.

Me: I am, also. We will talk then. Peace to the Universe.

HOP: Peace to the Universe.

33   ROWAN

TALKING TO JAKE FELT GOOD. IT WAS MY OBLIGATION to warn him about Snoddy, but that isn't what makes me feel good. I feel lighter, letting go of something I've held onto for too long. What Jake meant was clear: The signs say I should let it go.

Lyle picks me up at the curb and I show him the pecan pie through the open window. "I baked this for you as a thanks for all the rides. Pecan pie."

"Oh, man! Thank you, Rowan."

I open the back door and wedge the well-wrapped pie tin onto the back seat.

"Does it have bourbon in it? I love bourbon pecan pie."

Uh-huh. "No, Lyle. No bourbon."

"Well, I'll bet its delicious anyway. Ready for another week of work?"

"Yeah. Having the weekend off really helped."

He glances over at me. "You look good. Better than you did last week."

Which makes me laugh. "Thanks, Lyle. I feel better, too."

He nods. "Having a job does that to you."

"Sure does."

Lyle goes around the block, heads south on Archer, and catches the expressway at 31st Street. I'm wondering what I should offer to pay him for the rides. CTA fare is over $100 a month for a pass. I should probably offer him $15 a week, but right now I can't afford that. For next week maybe a pecan pie with bourbon, if I can borrow some bourbon from MaryEllen.

Then maybe with my second paycheck I can make Lyle an offer. It's the right thing to do.

If Mom were here, I could ask her advice. But she's not.

"Hey!" he shouts, so excited he almost swerves into the next lane. "That guy who was on your lawn! Did you see the video of him punching out two big guys?" He turns to me, eager to share the experience of seeing the video. "Hey! He was not one of the guys who broke my arms!"

"I knew he wasn't," I say. "Yeah, I saw the video."

"What'd they say to make him so mad?"

"I don't think he was angry, Lyle. He was just defending himself. I mean, I guess he was angry they were coming at him. But he wasn't angry to start with."

Lyle looks over at me. "So what'd they say?"

"They called him a wop."

The car lurches toward the left, then back. "That's a joke, right?" Lyle asks me, not sure if it is.

I smile. "Yeah, it's a joke. Meant to educate."

He laughs. The rest of the ride he gives me sidelong glances. Probably trying to figure me out. I don't think revolutionary socialist is a category Lyle thinks about.

At the cafeteria I kind of nudge Lyle toward the table I want to sit at. I've made a point of meeting different people at every meal. I can tell this isn't something Lyle would do on his own. But I gotta give him credit, he sits there and joins in.

✱ ✱ ✱

No overtime Monday night, and Nolan tells me to come in Wednesday. So I get Tuesday off. Lyle does, too. "Tuesdays are slow," he informs me on the ride home, "so a lot of weeks we get them off."

"What about our twenty hours?"

"There's usually overtime on Thursday and Friday nights," he tells me. "Sometimes too much overtime — like four more hours at top speed."

I text Keisha, telling her I don't have to work after all, does she want to get together the way we had planned? I don't expect an answer at 1:45 a.m., and I don't get one, either. But when I wake up the next morning she's texted back to say we're on at 7:30, her house.

After breakfast Deeply and I go into the back yard. I weed the garden, he runs through the sprinkler. That's what we're doing when JoJo from the next block walks into the back yard.

She looks at Deeply a moment, then ignores him.

She tells me she's looking to buy an upright piano and wonders if I might be thinking of selling Mom's. She's apologetic about even asking, she says, but she'd feel bad if I ended up selling it to somebody else.

JoJo's been to our house and even played Mom's piano.

"It's for Ryan," she tells me. "He'll be eleven next month."

Ryan has been taking piano lessons since the day he was born. Not really, but that's how it seems.

JoJo is doing all the talking. I'm sitting on the ground, weeds in my hand.

"I can offer you twenty-five hundred," she says.

Man.

Man oh man. The way I've been living, I could stretch that for months. Or save it as half a year's property taxes. So that I'll have a house to live in.

Money. Food. Utility bills. Clothing. Haircuts. I am so tempted.

And Mom left me. With no instructions on the piano. And she's never called me, not in five months. Serves her right if I sell the piano.

But I can't. It's not the right thing to do.

And it's . . . final. It's like making real what I've been saying: that she's not coming back.

"Thanks, JoJo," I tell her. "I appreciate the offer. But I can't get myself to sell Mom's piano."

JoJo is disappointed. But she tells me she understands.

* * *

As I pedal to Keisha's, Deeply comes with me, riding on the back of the bike. I have no idea how he decides whether or not to come.

In my pannier I have the last of Mom's spools of mercerized cotton as well as her three stainless steel crochet hooks, which I've taped together with masking tape because their rattle was driving me crazy. Keisha totally loves the new squares I've been making. *Elegant*, she whispers each time she looks at one. Elegance seems to require torturously small, sharp crochet hooks.

Keisha greets me at the door. Titus and Genevieve are both out. We go up to her sewing room — and there's Antwon. Sitting on the floor. Without shoes or socks.

"Antwon," I greet. "What's up?"

"Rowan. And Mr. Deeply," he says.

Deeply flies off my shoulder and lands on the floor right in front of Antwon, examining what's in Antwon's lap.

Antwon looks at Deeply. "We cool?" he asks.

"Cool," Deeply replies.

I step closer. "What's that?" I ask.

"African foot loom." He stretches his legs out and hooks each of his big toes through a block of wood, to which all kinds of threads are attached. "That's the warp," he tells me.

The other end of the loom is in Antwon's lap. It's narrow, a little more than twelve inches across. He already has maybe four inches of woven cloth.

"That's beautiful. The indigo. And the pattern," I tell him. "I didn't know you were a *weaver*, Antwon. Awesome!"

Deeply keeps looking at the woven cloth, then up at Antwon, then back at the cloth and back at Antwon. "Colors," squawks Deeply. "Deeply love colors."

"Antwon love colors, too," Antwon tells him.

Deeply hops up and down in some sort of ecstasy.

Keisha taps me on the shoulder. I turn. She's holding up a denim jacket, the last thing that Clari was working on. "I've finished the embroidery," she says.

I slip it on.

"That's Clari's embroidery on the left, mine on the right. But I'm pretty sure you can't tell the difference."

I nod, then look in the mirror. She's right. It all looks like Clari's work.

"And here are two more pieces," says Keisha. "The first is a linen top I found inside the jacket sleeve. I think Clari was hiding it, so she must have meant it as a present for you."

I take the top and look at the embroidery. I realize it's a rowan tree. I swallow. "You're right. She meant it for me."

"And look at the back," says Keisha, turning the top around.

"Leaves."

Keisha sighs. "Not just leaves. *Rowan* leaves." She taps me on the head. "I know this Rowan, because I'm a year older than you.

"Now here's the second piece," she says, holding out a simple black silk top. Sleeveless. The silk shimmers. I'm adoring it when Keish turns it around.

"Wha—" I say. "*Whoa*! Didn't I crochet that *years* ago?"

The entire back of the piece consists of a piece of blue crocheting. Not even a granny square, just something I was practicing with the mega hook Clari bought me. The space between the stitches is, like, huge. Wearing this would be wearing no back at all.

"Wow, Keish. That's . . . that's . . ."

"Sexy," she finishes.

I nod.

"You have two choices here, Rowan."

"Choices? I have to choose one of these?"

Keisha mock swats me. "You have two choices for which you're going to wear on your date with Jake."

She holds up Clari's top. "Lovely. Classic. If you want a good time, you wear this."

She holds up the other top. "And if you want *more* than a good time, you wear this."

I laugh. "It's that easy? Jake will be able to read the signals?"

Antwon snorts.

Keisha lays an arm on my shoulder. "I have seen the video. The man can read signals."

"Which one you wearing?" Antwon asks.

"Don't know," I tell him.

❋ ❋ ❋

For the next couple of hours Keisha, Antwon, and I work away. Talk away. Laugh away. Deeply spends the time walking back and forth, examining Antwon's weaving, Keisha's sewing, and my crocheting. He chatters bird sounds whenever he reaches Antwon, who always replies, "You're right, bird. You're straight up right."

At ten we call it a night. I hop on my bike, make sure that Deeply's settled on the back rack, and pedal home.

I'm a bit wary, remembering the car that followed me. Nights like this, I wish I could carry my Smith & Wesson. Women are beaten, abducted, raped, murdered. In the US more than 600 women are sexually assaulted each day. Six hundred. Every single *day*. We talk about this at the SVAW meetings: Stop Violence Against Women. Which reminds me, I have to go to the steering committee meeting this Sunday, to help plan the march in the Loop.

Against this onslaught of hatred, the gun is an equalizer. As soon as I turn twenty-one, I'm going to apply for an Illinois Permit to Carry. And I *will* carry when I'm out alone at night.

I keep a close watch in the rearview mirror to see if somebody's following me. As far as I can tell, nobody is. I double-check when I reach my street, and triple-check as I put the bike into the garage.

Everything looks safe.

*　*　*

On Thursday morning I log into my checking account. My direct deposit check is there. All $199.92 of it. Part of that's because I started in the middle of the week and worked only 14 hours. I've already figured that when I work 20 hours, my take home will be a whopping $285 a week.

Out of that I can pay for my food, water, and part of the electric. But not medical if I need it. And I've got to figure a clothing budget in there somewhere. I can wear Clari's clothes until I can afford to replace them with my own. Worst of all, though — I need to put $100 a week into the savings account so that come next year, I'll have the $5,200 for property taxes.

There's no way I can do that. Unless I can work full-time. Or unless Mom comes home and we combine our income.

I jolt upright.

It's Thursday and I haven't called Mom all week. I grab my phone, dial her number, and hear, with relief, a new message.

"Hey, Mom. Sorry I didn't call. I have a job, thanks to Titus. Part-time package handler at Package Nova. I work a crappy night shift, but I get a ride there and back from a guy who lives on 31st Street." I clear my throat. "I'm making enough to cover most of my basic needs, but not enough so that I can save money to pay the real estate taxes next year. This year's covered by the money you left." Okay, it's out there. "Once you're home, Mom, we can handle it together. Oh. Nova will pay up to $5,000 a year toward college classes, so I'm thinking of taking classes in September." I pause. "Bye for now. Hope you're . . . healing the way you want to."

As long as I'm on the phone, I decide to text Jake. I'm pretty sure he understands who and what I am. But I want to make sure.

WCC holding rally Sat @ noon. Pilsen. Podcast opp?

Then I walk to the bank, withdraw my measly $199.92, and use it to pay down part of the electric, part of the gas, and all of the water. When I get home I put $15 on my nightstand, to pay Keisha for the lunch money I borrowed. Which leaves me $45 for the next seven days. Plus I have almost $50 left from the money I got for Clari's bed.

34 JAKE

THE DRUMMERS STAND ALONGSIDE THE PORTABLE stage. The African-Americans beat djembes or ashikos, the Latinos beat congas and various frame drums, the Whites beat mostly small snare drums, but a few are playing tambourines —which add some needed jingle to the booming percussion.

It's impressive.

I look for Rowan and see her playing what looks like a really old tambourine.

Titus Longshaw is the lead drummer. When he stops, they all stop.

The crowd, maybe 300 or 400 people, applauds.

I spot a flash of bright colors and pan toward them. There's Deeply mingling with the crowd, hopping from the shoulder of one person to the shoulder of another. Children point and shout *El loro! El loro!*

I pan back to Titus, who slips the djembe strap off his shoulders, hands the drum to somebody, and climbs the stage.

"Friends and comrades in the struggle, thank you for coming to today's rally. Thank you for being part of the drumming. Our drums are part of our different cultures, and cultures come from all over the world. Our drumming shows that we can work in harmony, play in harmony, and live in harmony, each of us adding something significant, each of us strengthened by the power of the beat — the power of unity."

Titus has the deep voice of a great orator. He's using a mic, but I could hear him even if I were standing at the back of the crowd. As it is, I'm standing on the top step of an old greystone, where I've set up my tripod and camcorder for a terrific view of the stage and the speakers on it.

"As you know," Titus continues, "Working Class Control has been holding Saturday rallies in different neighborhoods for three years now. Also as you know, Working Class Control knows the power of brevity — no long-winded speeches from us. After we speak, we will all be available to talk to you about working class concerns."

Applause.

"Today I will talk about two things: the nature of change, and the brutality of capitalism.

"As the great Greek philosopher Heraclitus taught, 'No man ever steps in the same river twice, for it's not the same river and he's not the same man.' That, friends and comrades, is profound wisdom. We change every second of our lives, as do the things around us.

"The things we create also change. Machines rust, roads crumble, medical practices change as do educational systems. As do economic systems. Roman imperialism gave way to feudalism, which was replaced by mercantilism, which was replaced by capitalism."

Titus walks the stage as he talks, looking out at first one part of the crowd, then another. My camcorder follows his movements.

"Now, the ruling class, which is the capitalist class, would have us think that their economic system — one that makes them trillions from our labor but leaves us poor — is the pinnacle of historic development. They would have us think that changing this system is — unthinkable. They would have us think that there is nothing beyond capitalism. They would have us think that any changes we demand must be implemented at such an excruciatingly slow pace that not only will we die long before the change is made, but the change itself will die. Will disintegrate into no change at all. Which is what the capitalists want."

Titus pauses to let this sink in, then continues. "But this is false. This is a lie they tell to keep us oppressed. Capitalism can be replaced. Capitalist control can be replaced by working class control — not us, the organization, but *all* of us, around the world. The billions of us. We can run the world in *our* interests. Not theirs."

He pauses a bit longer this time. "And *our* interests are jobs for all; housing for all; free medical care; free education; food — *real* food, not packaged junk — for all; rest and relaxation and vacations for all. Our interests are that we, who create the wealth of the world, control what we do and in which direction we're heading."

Titus stops at one end of the portable stage, which was set up by WCC members earlier, as I was scouting for a good position. "Capitalism is just an economic system that replaced mercantilism, which replaced feudalism. Socialism can and must replace capitalism if we are to survive. If Earth is to survive."

He clears his throat and walks to the other end of the platform. "The second thing I want to talk about is the brutality of capitalism. Capitalism was born brutal. In order to create a labor force to toil its life away in dark and dangerous factories and create profit for the owners of those brutish buildings, British industrialists supported the introduction of laws that drove people off their land. With no land to farm on, these people fled to the cities and sought employment in the factories. So evil were the conditions that men, women, and children all worked fourteen hour days and died from malnutrition and diseases caused by unsanitary conditions."

The information flows out of Titus in a smooth way. Casual, as if he were talking to somebody at a bar or barbecue. Casual, but strong as steel. All this comes out in the way he stands, the way he looks at the crowd, his word choices. Everything. Titus is a born leader.

"Capitalism was born brutal and has remained brutal. It has used its army and police forces to murder those who protest it. Especially people of color. And in that group, especially Black people. It brutally captured and even more brutally enslaved us for its own profit, and it fears us as a revolutionary force. The capitalist class knows that it wages class war against us every day of our lives — and it knows that one day we will all rebel. Black, Brown, Red, White. That is why its police are armed and trained in a para-military manner.

"Friends and comrades in the struggle — capitalism and the capitalist state will use everything in their power to keep us from changing their economic system. They are a small but very powerful group. We, the workers of the world, are not a small group. We number in the *billions*. Our strength is in our numbers, our organizing, and our understanding that *only we* can lead the world forward to a future without poverty, without war, without injustice."

All eyes are on Titus, who raises his hand in a farewell gesture. "As promised, that's my short talk for today. Next up is a long-time member of WCC, Rafael Garcia. He's promised his talk will be even shorter than mine, but I'm not so sure about that. Spanish is not only a loving tongue, it's a tongue of long sentences."

Laughter, then applause for Titus as he steps off the stage, and loud applause for Rafael as he steps onto the stage.

His talk is maybe a minute shorter than Titus's. It's all in Spanish. He uses the word *casa* a lot and *gentraficación* and points to just north of where we're standing, so I know he's talking about old houses being torn down and replaced by new housing that Pilsen residents can't afford to buy. Driving them out of Pilsen into neighborhoods further away from the heart of Chicago.

Spanish in a podcast will be great. I can hire a translator and run the English at the bottom of the screen.

Rafael ends his talk by giving the address of the WCC headquarters.

Titus steps back up, repeats the address, tells people the headquarters hours, and invites them to come down for help, ask questions, take classes or attend talks.

"And now for our last speaker, Rowan Pickett. I've known Rowan since the day she was born. Her father and I became the best of friends when we were soldiers in Afghanistan. Rowan wanted to join WCC when she was twelve years old."

Laughter.

"But WCC does not condone child labor."

More laughter, lots of applause.

"So we didn't let her join until she was sixteen. Rowan will take even less time than Rafael did. Working Class Control does not waste words."

Rowan? She didn't tell me she'd be speaking.

I glance at how much storage is left on my camcorder, swap out a flash memory card, and get ready to roll.

35 ROWAN

I jog up three steps to the platform of the portable stage. I remember when WCC bought it, maybe ten years ago. Clari, Keisha, and I ran all over it, jumping up and down, testing its bounce. We would probably have preferred a trampoline, but the stage would have to do.

I can feel that bounce now. Titus hands me the mic on his way off the platform. I take it and wonder what I'm going to say. This is the first time I've spoken to a crowd in two years: since Dad died. Not counting the one time I spoke after Clari was killed. I barely remember what I said that day, except that I wanted them to understand the role cops play in suppressing the demands of the people, and that because the cops are armed, we the people should be, too.

The cops are out there now, on the edges of this peaceful crowd in Pilsen. The cops are there every time Working Class Control holds a public rally. Every time Stop Violence Against Women holds a march or rally. Or Black Lives Matter. Or the Chicago Teachers Union. Or anybody who wants to protest injustice and demand change.

Before, when I used to give one of these short talks, the subject matter just came to me, almost on the spot. I've been reading socialist literature since I was twelve, and hearing talk about working class oppression since I was born. This is in my blood. It's who I am.

It's who I want to be.

"Friends and comrades in the struggle," I begin. "We are living in the winter of capitalism, and if we allow the system to continue this way, all that lies ahead for us is darkness and doom. We will soon be standing out in the cold without food, without shelter.

"I say we're in the winter of capitalism because everything is in a decline. Buildings, streets, public transportation. Wages, health, health care, benefits. It's harder for a working class person to make a living today than it was fifty years ago. Many of us hold down at least two low-paying jobs.

"And this, my friends, is the road we're being driven down — the road of our living standards become worse and worse.

"As we struggle through this winter — a winter brought about by the relentless, driving greed of capitalism — we see courageous people protesting. Some gather in a group and protest against the border wall and the detention of immigrants. Others gather in a group and protest police brutality and the murdering of Black Americans. Still others gather to demand reproductive rights and voting rights. On and on it goes, on this street corner and that. In front of this embassy, this government building, that public meeting space.

"These demonstrations are like long-horned maverick steers, each claiming a piece of the pasture, each protesting something different. This means that each steer can be surrounded, roped, and corralled, as suits those with the ropes and guns and branding irons."

I pause. The crowd is quiet, wondering where this is going. In that pause my eyes look beyond the crowd, toward the cops. And beyond them. Where I see somebody who looks like Zeb Snoddy standing in the narrow space between two houses.

The first thing I register is that he's not holding any kind of rifle or sub-machine gun.

I glance quickly toward where Antwon was last standing. He catches my eye, then looks in the direction I had been looking in. I can't continue the pause any longer or the crowd will sense something is up.

"These individual mavericks are encouraging, but they are misdirected," I tell the audience. "Let's say there are twelve demonstrations in Chicago this month, against twelve different things." I pause again, ever so briefly. Antwon's talking to other WCC defense guards. He's on it.

"Does this mean we have *twelve different enemies*?" I ask. "Are there twelve different evil cabals in the government forcing twelve different kinds of oppression on us?"

I'm falling into the rhythm. Pacing the stage. Making eye contact with people. Feeling stronger. "No. We do not have twelve different enemies. We have *one* enemy. The ruling class.

"How much stronger would our protests be, how much stronger would *we* be if, instead of thinking of all our individual problems as unconnected, we saw them as part of the same thing: the ruling class taking everything for itself! If we saw the real problem, we would march together: a millions-strong march of maverick steers. We could form one long, wide march that filled the streets and demanded a workers state.

> **"Full employment!**
>
> **"30-hour work week!**
>
> **"$30 an hour minimum wage!**
>
> **"Free housing for all!**
>
> **"Free health care for all!**
>
> **"Equal rights for all!"**

As I turn and walk toward the other end of the stage, mic in hand, I spot Jake standing on the stoop of a greystone. His camera's on a tripod. Trained directly at me.

We're both being tested here. Me, to see if I can come back from a two-year slump. Jake, to see if he can accept who I am.

"Friends and comrades — WCC supports the rights and the struggles of the oppressed everywhere. You will see us joining these individual demonstrations to protest against the injustices and violence we are subjected to.

"And in each circle we join, you will hear us explaining that we, the working class, have one enemy. One. We will explain that there is something stronger than lone steers. And that is all of us moving in the same direction. One long, wide march sweeping forward and taking control of our lives. Our future."

I stop for a second, to collect my thoughts and build for the end.

"It's easy to believe that fundamental change is not possible. That is what we are taught. That is what the capitalist class *wants* us to think. But in order to change our lives for the better — in order to change the *world* for the better — we cannot think like that."

I look out across the hundreds of faces looking back at me.

"Are there White Sox fans here?" I ask.

Shouting and clapping and whistling.

"Are there fans of Jose Abreu here?" I shout.

Loud cheers and roars.

"Then know this: we the working class must think like Jose Abreu at bat. When we see the speed and power of what the capitalists hurl at us, we might be intimidated, thinking we can never turn it around.

"But we can. Change can happen at lightning speed — just as Jose Abreu can, with the power and speed of his swing, turn around the four-seamer barreling toward him. And, even though Jose is no longer with the White Sox, the exit velocity of that pitch will electrify the stadium."

Deep breath.

"Just as our turning around the system that oppresses us will electrify the world."

The roars of approval from the crowd make me think I've hit a home run. I wait until the noise subsides. "If you like what Titus, Rafael, and I have said, learn more about us: Working Class Control. We're easy to find. Thank you, *amigos y camaradas. Venceremos!*"

At the bottom of the stairs I hand the mic to Titus. His grin and pat on the shoulder tell me I did a good job.

As I listen to Titus's closing words, I find Antwon.

"Gone by the time we got there," he says to me. "This isn't the first time he's slunk around our rallies."

"I know," I tell him. "We all have to be careful. Sometimes, though . . . "

"Sometimes you think it's personal," Antwon finishes for me. "That it's you he's after."

"Yeah."

"Good way for each of us to think. That way we'll all be more careful."

Titus finishes, the crowd applauds.

Time for me to start circulating, talking to people. And I signed up to work the literature table for an hour.

When I reach the table Jake is there, talking to Titus. Antwon of course is there because bodyguards stay close to those they're guarding.

I thought of offering to be a bodyguard to Titus, but two things stopped me. First, I'm not twenty-one yet. Second, I wouldn't want to have to wear a long-sleeved jacket of any kind on a beautiful July day. But long-sleeved jackets hide holsters, and so Antwon's wearing such a jacket.

From what I gather Jake has offered to give Titus a copy of today's footage. Titus asks him if he's going to make a podcast out of today's rally. Jake replies he thinks so, but isn't certain.

"Well," Titus tells him, "whether you do or not, it's good to see you here. And I hope what you've heard opens your mind to the necessity of thinking in a new way. Change is good," Titus says. "Change can save our lives."

Jake nods, then asks: "Are you interested in a video of this entire rally? I can do a few quick edits and add titles to what I've got and upload everything for you on Dropbox. For your website if you want, or YouTube. Or wherever."

"Thank you," Titus tells him. "I'll look forward to receiving it. And now, if you'll excuse me, Rafael is motioning to me."

He leaves and Antwon leaves with him.

Jake looks at me. "Rowan. That was . . . awesome."

Awesome? Like — *awesome*?

I'm about to say something when two guys, probably high schoolers, come up to the table. I turn to them, hoping Jake understands that I'm doing my job.

He touches me on the shoulder. "I'm going to interview people in the crowd," he tells me. "See you later tonight."

When everything's done with, the stage folded and rolled away, the literature table likewise, the leaflets and pamphlets and books packed away, the money from their sales zipped into a cash bag, I say goodbye to all my comrades and walk to the El.

Being careful to watch my back.

36 DEEPLEA

FeeOna: Their names are ReeWon, as you requested of the first hatched. Then TeeCho, and then WeePlat.

Me: Even though they do not have their feathers yet, they are beautiful. Can you tell what colors they will be?

FeeOna: It is too soon . . . but I think that ReeWon might have orange feathers around her neck. Just like her father.

Me: [Beaming] Can they hear me when I call to them? [Makes cooing noises]

FeeOna: Two days from now they will hear you. I know you know the answers to these questions, DeePlea, because we have had chicks before. You are lonely.

Me: [Sighing]

FeeOna: When they hear you, they will have no idea where your voice is coming from.

Me: That will come later. All that matters is that they know their father exists. Even if he is absent for many months. Later, they will learn to make mirror communication.

FeeOna: Yes, they will. You will be their first-ever mirror contact.

Me: People on Earth talk to each other through primitive visual devices. Grandparents especially enjoy talking to their grandchildren that way, when the two are long distances apart.

FeeOna: Not as long as you are from us.

Me: That is true. You are right, Fee — I am feeling great loneliness.

FeeOna: [Sad] I wish there were something I could do about that, DeePlea. I suspect that every parrot on DU feels this anguish sooner or later.

Me: [Deep breath] The feeling comes and goes. When it goes, I feel better. [Coos to chicks] Look, FeeOna! ReeWon turned directly to the mirror.

FeeOna: [Studying the chicks] She is a bold one, Dee, I could tell as she was coming out of her shell. Such pecking! She pecked a perfect circle, stuck her head through it, and pulled the rest of herself out.

[Loud squawking from all three chicks]

FeeOna: The chicks call to be fed and I must go. Peace to the Universe.

Me: Peace to the Universe.

37 ROWAN

THE RESTAURANT ISN'T THAT FAR AWAY, MAYBE TWO miles north of Bridgeport, in the Little Italy neighborhood. Which figures, it being an Italian restaurant.

Jake doesn't find a parking space on Taylor Street, so he drives down a side street, finds a space, and backs into it in one smooth motion. He's a better driver than Lyle.

Once he turns the motor off I open the door and step out. He comes around to where I'm standing and we walk together to the restaurant.

"I liked your talk at the rally," he tells me as we're seated. "Strong."

I look at him to see if he's sincere. Most guys who "liked my talk" never really understood what I was saying. "Is what I said something you agree with?" I ask, hoping no surprise shows in my voice.

"I don't know. It's so . . . radical."

I grin. "Duh."

He laughs as we're taken to our table. "The ideas aren't new to me: I've met Marxists before," he says, unfolding his napkin. "My instinct is to deny something that makes so much sense. And is so different from what we're taught to believe."

That's a widespread instinct, I think. I'm happy that Jake can analyze his instincts and why he has them.

A server arrives with menus, then leaves. Jake makes several recommendations to me. They all sound good. We decide to share a broccoli salad as an appetizer, along with calamari. I go for the eggplant parmesan, he orders the wild boar ragu with pappardelle. Jake asks if I'd like to share the two dishes. I would, and he asks the server to split them in the kitchen. We agree on a bottle of chianti.

I glance around the restaurant, which is sort of dark inside, in that old style Italian way, with red-checked table cloths. There are a few restaurants like this in Bridgeport, but more up here in Little Italy. "Do you come here a lot?" I ask.

"Yeah. It reminds me a lot of the Italian restaurants back in Boston."

Our talk is easy, one thing leading to another. I'm having a good time. The food is fantastic, every morsel of it. I do wonder when Jake's going to give me what he calls his second confession.

After we finish and the dishes are cleared, he tells the server we'd like to wait a while before coffee and dessert. The server nods and disappears.

Jake pulls his camcorder out of his pocket, turns it on, presses a few buttons, and hands it to me. "This is my second confession. This is what I taped at the gun-control rally." He looks worried.

I take the camcorder. Jake flips a little screen open. It juts out of the side and looks like a mini TV screen. Cool.

One of Jake's fingers covers mine. "Press this button to start."

I press the button. I'm looking at the gun-control rally. Jake is standing with the gun-control side, or must be, because he's filming across Clark Street, looking right at Zeb Snoddy and his group.

Out of nowhere I recognize myself, pushed forward by the crowd. Pushed right into Snoddy, who reaches for my throat. I see myself raising my arm and stiffening my hand to chop down on Snoddy. And then — I just disappear from the video. I remember that. The garbage can.

What?! I see what happens just as I disappear.

I don't believe it. A parrot, screeching like a fire truck, flies feet first into Snoddy, then, without stopping, flies upward and out of sight.

I fumble to stop the video. I look up at Jake, who's watching me. "That's . . . is that Deeply? Was that Deeply?"

Jake nods.

My hands are shaking. "I want to see it again. Which button do I press?" Jake puts his hand over mine, holding the camera steady. He presses a button then hands the camera back to me.

I look, but nothing is different. Deeply definitely drives a claw into Snoddy's eye.

Jake takes the camcorder from me and sets it on the table.

Goosebumps break out on my arms. I sit there in something of a stupor. And then I remember the night somebody was following me home and how Deeply flew out of the house and drove the person away. The way I see it, Deeply is protecting me. First against Snoddy, then against whoever was driving the car.

Jake doesn't say anything for a while, and during that time I realize that this is what Snoddy wanted from Jake's camera — to see who attacked him.

"There's something else," says Jake.

"Something else? Like a third confession?"

"No, it's all part of the same thing." He hands me the camcorder again.

I look and see me again, in the distance. I'm standing on the lamppost, one hand wrapped around it. I'm looking into the sky. The camera pans upward. I see a colorful bird flying. I lift my arm in greeting. I remember that. It makes me feel good, seeing this.

I turn to Jake. "This is the very first time I saw Deeply. And you caught it on video."

"You shouted something up to him. You can see that in the video."

I nod. "He made me feel, I don't know, . . . hope? He gave me hope. I had a good feeling in my heart when I saw him. I remember that."

"What did you say to him?"

He asks this in such a way that I start to feel uncomfortable.

I think hard. "I said something like, *Way to go, bird.* Why?"

Jake takes the camcorder, folds in the screen, and pockets the device.

He takes a deep breath. "When I was taping, here's what I saw, almost as one continuous event. I saw you raise your arm and signal to a bird. I saw the bird make a wide arc. I saw the crowd pushing forward. You disappeared from sight. Then, a few minutes later, I saw you in front of Snoddy. You raised your arm the same way you raised it to the parrot. You disappeared from sight. I don't know if you ducked or fell or what."

I process this, or try to. "Okay, I heard what you just said. But I don't understand. What am I missing?"

"It looked to me like you gave Deeply a command to strike."

"It looked to you like— Jesus, Jake!"

He raises a hand as if to ward off something. Me, probably.

"That's what I believed *then*. That's my second confession. I don't believe it now. I know you better, Rowan. Than I did then."

I calm down. I can tell that Jake's telling me the truth. I can tell this wasn't easy for him. I give a small smile. "Yeah. *Then* was so long ago."

"So we're good?" he asks. "You know what I saw and what I thought. But I don't think it now. You know that, right?"

I nod. "I believe you don't think it now," I say, looking at him. "Is that why you followed me after the demo? You wanted to interview me about why I had 'my' parrot attack Snoddy?"

"I'm sorry, Rowan." He looks at me. "If it will make you feel better, I'll admit that I made a faulty inference."

I laugh out loud. "Yeah. Okay. That does make me feel better." I scrape some crumbs around on the table, put them into a neat little pile. "You've changed, Jake. You're different from the person who followed me home. You're the same, but also different."

"I hope so," he says.

"Jake—"

He waits.

"Do you think this was a matter of Deeply protecting me? Or do you think there's something else going on here? It's . . . well, it's kind of bizarre, don't you think?"

"Deeply is bizarre," he says. "In a very good way," he adds quickly, probably seeing my reaction.

"I can see that," I give him.

Jake leans forward. "Let's have coffee and dessert. This has been a tense conversation, and I don't want the evening to end like that."

Neither do I.

38 JAKE

I TURN ONTO JACKSON, HOPING ROWAN WILL LEAN forward so I can see her almost-bare back again. She sees me looking, so I have to say something. "Great color coordination," I tell her. "Eyes, feather, yarn."

She touches the feather. "Clari used to wear them. She had a huge bunch of them in her drawer. I attached this one the day of the demo."

"I noticed something blue in your hair when I was trying to get you to stop and talk to me." I glance over at her. "You were, uh, disheveled."

She laughs. "*Disheveled*?! You podcasters have a rarified vocabulary. I was covered in filth."

Rarified. Not exactly your everyday vocabulary word. Rowan is full of surprises. "Why were you covered in filth?"

"*Why*, I don't know," she answers. "*How*, that I can tell you."

I wait, but she says nothing. "Okay. How?"

She squirms in the seat. "You know in the video where I disappeared out of sight? Well, somebody grabbed me from behind. Across my chest, so I couldn't move my arms. He dragged me, I don't know how far. Ten feet? Fifteen? Oh — I just now remembered — he was carrying a gun. I felt it press into my back as he dragged me. The next thing I knew . . . he overturned a trash can on me. That's where all the filth came from: the trash can." She shudders. "Ugh. I hate to even think about it. In fact, I *haven't* thought about it again until now."

"Suppressing a bad memory," I say.

"Bad smell, too."

This trashcan thing is kind of bizarre. Not up there with the parrot, but maybe close. "Then what?" I ask as I hang a left onto Halsted, feeling the summer breeze through the moonroof.

"Then somebody began dragging the can along the street, with me in it. Tore my new tights to shreds. Then . . . somebody sat on top of the trashcan. To keep me from getting out, I suppose." She looks over at me. "I was terrified, thinking it was one of Snoddy's men."

"But it wasn't?" I ask.

Suddenly Rowan sits upright. "Jake! Maybe I can look more closely at your video — see who grabbed me and dragged me away." She looks at me for confirmation.

I nod. "We can definitely do that. It wasn't one of Snoddy's goons?"

"No. At least I don't think so, because the person let me go. By the time I managed to throw off the trashcan, stand up, and look around, all I saw was a lone figure running, half a block away."

"You think that was whoever did it?"

She nods. "And before you ask, I couldn't tell anything about them. Couldn't see color of skin, couldn't see facial features. Nothing. He was wearing a hoodie. Inferences? Even faulty ones?" She grins as she says this.

I grin, too, as I hang a right on Grand. "I'm going with friendly," I tell her.

"Friendly?"

"It had to be a gesture to protect you, not hurt you."

She ponders this for quite a while. "You've given me something to think about," she says at last. "I have to look at the thing in a whole new light." She thrusts a hand through the moonroof. I stare at her back. "The air feels good," she says.

"This Lyle guy," I say. "Is he someone you're interested in?"

She lowers her arm. "He's a neighbor, and a fellow worker, so, yeah, I'm interested in him."

I wait.

"But not in the way you mean."

Good. We've got that out of the way.

In no time we're at Navy Pier. I live just a few blocks away, so I park the car in my building parking spot and Rowan and I walk to the pier.

I arrived in Chicago six months ago, in the middle of a winter as bad as Boston's winters, so although I knew what Navy Pier was, I never really explored it until April.

Built in the very early 1900s the pier is more than half a mile long, thrusting east into Lake Michigan. During the Second World War it was a training base for the US Navy, but today it's Chicago's number one tourist attraction, with fifty acres of gardens, parks, restaurants, and shops. Navy Pier is home to the Shakespeare Theater and the Centennial Wheel, the 196-foot high Ferris wheel that's part of the Chicago skyline. A lot of weekends I walk this way, grab a crispy chicken sandwich at Big City Chicken, and take one of the boat tours.

Rowan and I walk along the water, stop and look down on the huge tour boats offering dinner and evening cruises.

"This is beautiful," she says, leaning on the railing. "I haven't been here since I was in high school. A bunch of us would get together and come here on Saturday nights."

After a while I guide us toward one of the gardens, where we find an empty park bench and sit.

"If it's okay with you," I say, "I'd like us to theorize about Deeply's extreme intelligence."

She raises her eyebrows. "*Extreme*?"

"Extreme," I repeat. "Not backing down on this one."

She turns to face me. Her knees touch mine. "I've been avoiding thinking about this, Jake. Ever since I realized how intelligent Deeply is." She takes a deep breath. "I don't want Deeply to get hurt. And I don't want to lose him. Even though . . . I'm pretty sure I will." She takes a deeper breath. "Eventually."

"I understand. I don't want him to get hurt, either. But he's not an ordinary parrot. He's *sentient*. You can carry on a conversation with him. He *comprehends*."

She nods. "He understands concrete things, like apples and crackers and donuts."

"Especially donuts," I add.

"And he understands abstractions," she continues. "Concepts. He understands *grammar*!"

I nod. "So . . . can we brainstorm about what this means?"

Rowan looks away for a few seconds, then her eyes return to mine. "Don't laugh, but — I think he's a bot, some sort of artificial intelligence created by, I don't know. The military? Maybe he escaped and just wants a normal life."

"With *you*?"

She gives me a light punch on the arm. "Hey, maybe he wants to be a political revolutionary. If so, yeah — with me."

"Okay, over in this corner we have bot. What else?" I ask.

"I suppose he could have belonged to some mad scientist or eccentric professor who trained him," she speculates. "I don't know how old Deeply is. Parrots live a long time. Say he's 30 or 35 or 40 years old. If you teach a parrot something new every day, will quantity eventually change into quality? Like, *Poof*! There's a fundamental leap from knowing things to, suddenly, knowing that you know. Knowing that there's such a thing as thinking, and that you can think."

I blink, totally impressed with her analytic abilities.

"Bot in one corner, qualitative change in the second corner," I say. "We won't even discuss whether this change, if that's what it is, can be passed on genetically."

"Agreed," she says. "That's not our problem right now."

I like the *our problem*.

"What else?" I prod.

"An obvious one. Us. We're projecting too much onto what we hear Deeply say. He seems intelligent because we're supplying the missing gaps. Like, I say *Deeps* and he answers *Only one Deeply* and I think he's responding to me. He could be uttering words at random, not responding to me at all. It could be sheer coincidence."

I remember thinking something like that when I interviewed Deeply. But I no longer think it's coincidence. "You don't believe that, do you?" I ask her.

"No. But we need something in that third corner."

I take her hand in mine and stroke her fingertips. "How do you know I'm not making a four-cornered argument?"

She breathes in. "I can't think when you're doing that."

"Should I stop?"

She nods. "Uh-huh. For now you should stop."

I stop. Reluctantly. But the *for now* registers.

"I can't think of anything else," she says. "We're stuck with two corners."

"A being from another planet," I say.

Rowan gasps, coughs, chokes, all at the same time.

"You okay?"

She nods, lifting both hands above her head, trying to stop the coughing. When it stops, here eyes are watering.

I stroke her back.

It takes me a minute to remember what we're talking about. "Don't talk. Just wait a while."

She nods.

"Just listen while you catch your breath," I say. "There's no reason not to suppose there's intelligent life on other planets in the universe. Nod if you agree." A couple of my fingers slide through the huge holes in whatever material is holding her top together. It's an accident. But not all accidents need to be corrected.

Rowan nods.

"And there's no reason not to suppose that this intelligent life can find a way to travel beyond its own planet. Nod if you agree." I try to still my fingers and focus on the conversation.

She nods.

"Finally, there's no reason not to suppose that this intelligent life can land on Earth. Nod if you agree."

"I agree," she says, sitting upright. I keep my hand on her back.

She looks me up and down, "Are you set on this explanation? Out of the three, this is the one you think is true?"

I hesitate, not wanting to come across as a whacko. "I lean toward it, yeah. You lean toward the bot theory?"

She thinks about this. "If Deeply's an alien being or if he's a bot, in some ways it doesn't matter," she says. "The question is, what's he doing here?"

I take her hand in mine again. "That's as big a question as who or what Deeply is," I say. "Maybe bigger. Let's save it for a different conversation."

Her nod is almost imperceptible.

I let go of her hand, put an arm around her shoulder, and pull her toward me. I sense no reluctance. Our faces are close. We move toward a kiss at the same time.

Gentle at first, but then quantity changes into quality and we're breathing hard.

"Rowan. Two options. I can take you home if that's what you want. Or you can spend the night with me."

She traces a finger across my lips. "There's a third option."

"Park benches aren't that comfortable," I manage.

"A fourth option, then. You can take me home and spend the night with me."

We make it back to Bridgeport in record time.

39 ROWAN

I WAKE UP FEELING FANTASTIC. IT TAKES ME MAYBE half a sec to realize why. I sit up and look at Jake, whose eyes are closed. I slowly trace a finger down his chest, stopping to twirl some of the hairs along the way.

His eyes open. "Hey," he says, his voice relaxed with sleep.

"Hey," I say. We look at each other a bit. "I'm starving," I announce.

"I thought I took care of that." He puts a hand on my waist, running his thumb up and down my ribs.

I try to keep from grinning at the male ego.

Jake rolls onto his side and spots the folded money I have on the nightstand. The money I owe Keisha.

"For services rendered?" he asks.

I grab the money, unfold it, and spread the two bills apart in my hand. The ten and the five. I pretend to give it serious thought. Then I shake my head sadly, pull out a five, and hand it to him.

At which point he grabs me and flips me over so fast that I yelp in surprise as I end up with him on top of me.

"Shhh," he whispers. "The neighbors will come running."

"Uh-uh. Not with your car halfway up the tree lawn. They'll know what's going on."

"*Not* halfway up the tree lawn. But good they won't come running."

* * *

When we finally get out of bed it's ten o'clock.

"You can shower first if you want to," I offer. "I want to check on Deeply." When we walked in the door last night, Deeply wasn't on his perch, and I didn't sense him anywhere in the house. Jake closed the bedroom door anyway. I know Deeply goes out at night, but he's always there in the morning.

When I open the door, Deeply's on his perch. Facing away, his back to my bedroom. Is he sulking? "Hey, Deeps," I say, walking around to face him. "Good morning."

"New day," he squawks. "New day."

"Yes, it is. Why are you turned around?"

"Deeply not look."

I stroke his back. "The door was closed. You can't see through doors, can you?"

He doesn't answer, just flies to the kitchen, lands on the table, and starts eating his bird food pellets. I put on a pot of coffee.

"Jake bring do-nuts?"

"No, Jake did not bring do-nuts. Jake does not walk around with a donut box in his hand, you know."

Deeply flies to the top of the hutch, where he sits. With his back turned to me.

Jake finishes his shower, after which I take mine. By the time I'm dressed — which is no time at all, because I'm really hungry — Jake and Deeply are sitting at the kitchen table. Jake's drinking coffee and feeding Deeply baby carrots and green beans.

"Have a good time in the garden?" I ask.

"We did," he answers, standing up. "Ready for a Sunday brunch?"

I nod, turn off the coffeepot, put Jake's mug in the sink, and the two of us leave Deeply with his carrots and green beans.

Jake parks the car in his garage and we walk to brunch at Wildberry Pancakes. I've heard of it, but have never been. The food is delicious. And the portions are huge. This meal might get me through the day, with maybe crackers and cheese tonight. I'll shop for some much-needed groceries tomorrow morning.

With my third cup of coffee I glance at my watch. "I'm due at WCC headquarters in an hour."

"For how long?"

"Four hours. And after that I have a meeting of the SVAW committee. That's Stop Violence Against Women."

He nods. "I have to spend the day working on a podcast. And I want to edit yesterday's film and give Titus a copy. I can drop you off at WCC. If you want, I can pick you up after the other meeting."

It's a question. Like, do I want to spend the night with him.

Do I ever.

I give Jake the address where the SVAW meeting's being held and the approximate time it will end. Sometimes the meetings go on too long. *Waaaaay* too long. Not everybody is as organized as Working Class Control. In fact . . . almost nobody.

"I'll take the El to WCC," I tell him. "It's easy, and that will give you more time to work on the podcast."

"Sure?" he asks. "It's no problem to drive you down there, especially on a Sunday."

I shake my head. "I'd rather you had time to do what you need to."

Jake walks with me to the El stop. When we see the train approaching he puts his hands on my shoulders. We kind of lean into each other, foreheads touching. "See you later," he says.

I nod, take his arm, and let my hand travel down it and off his fingertips as I walk toward the train.

40   DEEPLEA

HUMANS WALK ON THE GROUND AND SELDOM LOOK up. They seldom think that somebody could be above them. In a tree, for example, above a park bench. Listening to them speculate on what I am.

Not that I can't read their minds and know what they are thinking. Of course I can do that. I have been doing it since I arrived.

But minds do not have sound. No tone, no timber, no musical ups and downs. I love sounds. Bells and whistles are my favorite.

Rowan is smart and so is Jake. Rowan lines up all the possibilities and chooses the most likely one: bot. Jake looks at a mess of twirling things and instantly picks a conclusion. Almost always the right one.

What are they going to do?

Jake has proof of my attacking the evil person who wanted to harm Rowan. I could vaporize this proof . . . but vaporizing proof of my mistake does not seem right.

Before I arrived here I had never experienced evil. When I saw what was in Zeb Snoddy's mind — how he intended to hurt Rowan — I was so horrified that I acted without thinking. Yes, I was rash.

I should have waited.

This is what FeeOna warned me about before I left our planet. She warned me about acting without thinking. But during my first five minutes — five minutes! — on Earth, I failed to heed HOP's warning. I read Snoddy's mind and I struck to protect Rowan. Protecting her is part of my *duty*. My Duty to the Universe.

I envision the scene. The DU-Ovum entering Earth's atmosphere, the doors opening, the Reluctance Prodder pushing me out . . . and Rowan, wearing a blue feather in her hair, encouraging me. *Way to go, bird!* she shouted. I am a bit like Jake — I chose her the moment she spoke to me. And then, seeing the danger she was in, I struck.

I do not want to be recalled from my mission. The ignominy if that were to happen!

Which is why I erected a Pri-Vay shield to keep my secret from HOP.

Who knows I am hiding something, of course. Just not what.

I wish I could see into the future. But that is impossible.

I need to talk to FeeOna.

I want to see our chicks.

But I cannot talk to FeeOna. I cannot erect a second Pri-Vay shield to keep from HOP the knowledge that somebody on Earth suspects I am from another planet.

Well, actually, I *can* erect a second Pri-Vay shield.

But that would be most unwise.

I will wait a day or two, to see what happens.

Waiting a day or two is the opposite of being rash.

If only I could have a do-nut to help me think more clearly.

41 ROWAN

THINGS AT WORKING CLASS CONTROL ARE ROCKING.
Every one of the six tables set up around the big meeting room has somebody sitting behind it and one or more people sitting in front of it. Asking questions, looking for help.

I glance at my watch to make sure I'm early. Enough time to tidy up the kitchen, make a fresh pot of coffee, and look over what's been brought in. Somebody baked chocolate chip cookies. There's a coconut cake from Genevieve, baked in a rectangular pan and cut into half-sized pieces. Mom used to bake Boston cream pies and bring them down. I wonder if Mom's baking where she is now. Or crocheting. It makes me sad to think about her. I realize that almost all my anger is gone. All I feel now is sadness. That Mom left me, yeah. But more that Mom can't find . . . . peace, I guess.

After the kitchen I go into the bathrooms, making sure each is clean and has enough toilet paper, soap, and paper towels. In public restrooms poor people steal the soap and toilet paper and even the paper towels. Not at WCC. People understand we're on their side. They realize that when they're here, they're in a special place.

When I'm done with all the tidying I go to my table, which Sofia is just leaving. We bump fists as we exchange places.

"So happy you're back," she says.

"Me, too," I tell her. "How you doing?"

"Bien, bien."

I make myself comfortable at the table. In Pilsen yesterday two of the people who talked to me after the rally said they'd be here. They're seniors in high school. Pilsen is one of the most integrated neighborhoods in Chicago: about a third Black, a third White, and a third Latino. But that will change if the developers move in, buy up the land, and build expensive houses on it. Working class people will be driven out, leaving white middle class people living there — taking over still another working class neighborhood.

The middle class doesn't do this vindictively. It does it thoughtlessly, concerned only with housing it can afford. Not thinking that housing other people can afford is being torn down, never to be replaced with something they could buy.

As Titus reminded me, the middle class stands between the two powerful forces in society: the ruling class and the working class. The former has been in power ever since class society began. The latter will one day be in power, or the human race will cease to exist. Until the working class becomes a growing, visible power, conscious of itself as a class with class interests to fight for, the middle class will keep gravitating toward the power that exists: the ruling class.

I find it hard to be around most middle class people. For a lot of reasons. They are so self-centered, talking about their self-actualizations, their "spaces," their precious feelings, which get hurt so easily. They've obviously never had to take jobs in which you do hard physical labor and are just a cog in the production machine. And their sense of privilege is astonishing. Astonishing and infuriating. Knowing you'll be sent to college by your parents. Growing up in a big house with a huge lawn and a wide street and a quiet neighborhood. Two-car garage. Fuck: *four*-car garage. Good schools. Good grocery stores that sell organic food and that you can drive to instead of taking a bus and hauling your heavy grocery bags back home. Taking all these things for granted — never questioning whether it's fair or just that, in one of the richest countries in the world the masses of people do not have these privileges. The masses of people live from one paycheck to the next and are filled with anxiety about how they can continue to feed their children, take care of elderly parents, pay for a car, pay for groceries, pay their property taxes so they don't lose their homes.

So far I haven't seen any sense of privilege from Jake. It's gotta be there, though, just like working-class prejudice has got to exist in me. We're all products of our environment.

I'm sitting there thinking about Jake when somebody walks up to the table. The two guys from Pilsen, Bryan and Eduardo.

"Hey," I say, standing up to shake their hands. "You made it."

I offer them water, tea, or coffee. And cake. I offer them cookies if they don't want coconut cake. They take coffee and the cookies. Then they ask me all kinds of questions about Marxism and social struggles.

Bryan is big-time annoyed that people don't understand that capitalism is the problem. "They, like, keep voting for Democrats or Republicans, who *support* the system!"

"Both parties support the military budget," Eduardo chimes in, telling me what I already know. But I understand their outrage and their need to talk.

"Think of all the good that military money could do," Eduardo continues, devouring a cookie and reaching for another. "Housing. Health care for all. Free college education."

We talk for a long time. I give them a list of books and URLs. I tell them about WCC's next neighborhood rally, and I tell them about the Stop Violence Against Women demonstration next month. They seem down with that. Before they leave, they enter their email addresses on WCC's mailing list.

When my four hours are up I spend some time talking to everyone else who's there, and then I go to the Stop Violence Against Women meeting to help plan the August demonstration.

I'm not totally welcome at the SVAW meetings, mainly because I'm a member of a Marxist organization and the others are suspicious of Marxism. Sometimes when I make a point a few of them try to ridicule me by saying I have a "political agenda." Like, what? — they *don't* have a political agenda?

Of course they do. Their political agenda is to get Republicans out of office and Democrats into office. But they don't count what *they* work toward as a political agenda. Only what a revolutionary works toward is "political."

How fucking dishonest can you get?

They know that, unless they ban me from the planning meetings, they can't get rid of me. Even *if* they ban me from the planning meetings they can't get rid of me: I know how to protest. And I'm there to fight for women, just like they are.

Many of the women here tonight are also present at gun-control rallies. Whenever they start talking about gun-control being one of the slogans of any SVAW march, I always speak up. They cringe when I do. Like now.

"We can't let the cops decide who can have a gun permit," I argue. "We can't let the state decide. The cops and the state serve the interests of the ruling class. If women were to begin carrying guns to defend themselves against violent men, the cops and the state would not allow us to have gun permits. They are politically motivated" — and I kind of sneer when I say the word *politically*, to let them know I know how they're red-baiting me — "to serve the interests of the ruling class. That means keeping women in their place: bearing children, doing unpaid social work such as cooking, cleaning, and raising the next generation. Women are an exploited, vastly underpaid labor pool for capitalism."

Marla, the chairperson, yawns. Like she always does when I speak.

"If you doubt what I'm saying about gun control laws, read the history of what happened to hat pins in this country a hundred years ago. Once women started wearing hat pins — long, sharp, lethal steel needles — men were terrified that women could and would use the hat pins as weapons. And so cities and states immediately passed laws against the size of hat pins and then against hat pins themselves. Hat pins became illegal because women had them. If men had worn hatpins, the hatpins wouldn't have become illegal. Men did not want women to have weapons of any kind. And that's what's going to happen to women if the state and cops can decide who can carry a gun and who can't. They'll decide that, just like with hat pins, they don't want guns in the hands of women."

I study everyone else as I speak. Madison and Ana are paying attention. Maybe Isabelle is, too.

"I'm not asking SVAW to come out against gun control," I continue, "because I know the majority of you believe in gun control. But I am asking that we not introduce pro-gun-control slogans in our press releases or on SVAW signs in the march. We agree on ending violence against women. We don't agree on gun control. "

Marla bangs the gavel. "Thank you, Gun Girl."

There's some tittering at that.

Marla smiles. "All in favor of including gun-control demands in our press releases raise their hands," she says.

Which seven of the ten of us do.

When the meeting's over I say goodbye to people one at a time and tell them I'll see them next meeting. No matter what they do, they won't make me be rude, they won't drive me away.

Because people can change. Events can make people change. See things a new way. And I won't write them off until and unless they cross to the other side and support violence against the working class.

Which I know some of them will do. But not all of them.

Jake's waiting for me at the curb.

42 JAKE

LAST NIGHT ROWAN AND I SPENT A LOT OF TIME examining the same five to ten seconds of my video, over and over, trying to see if we could tell who grabbed Rowan and dragged her away. We couldn't. Too many beefy bodies all around Snoddy.

We tried again this morning, and again no luck.

After Rowan takes the El I walk back to my apartment and think about the work I need to do. Some podcasters record their videos in the same room every time, so that viewers develop a feeling of familiarity and comfort with the podcaster. Some wear a shirt with their logo on it. Some unite their various podcasts with a color scheme or a certain video style.

Jake's Takes are filmed everywhere. I've interviewed people in their homes, my apartment, a studio when appropriate, even outdoors. I try to give the podcasts a brand look by color and by my presence, either throughout or intermittently. My logo is in teal and gray, and I always make certain to wear a teal shirt. I've got teal tees, teal Polos, teal button-downs, teal pullover sweaters, even a teal hoodie and a teal jacket. I think I might be getting a bit tired of teal.

I go to work on the first of two videos — a podcast on the need for free health care for everyone. People call it different names, like Medicare for all, or free healthcare, or national health service. For this one I interviewed two MDs, an intern, a nurse, and an EMT. In Chicago the EMTs are part of the

Fire Department, which adds some interesting texture to the information and opinions.

I begin to make edits. Twenty minutes or so into them, I realize I haven't paid attention to what I'm doing. I'm thinking of Rowan.

I go backwards in the video, trying to figure out where I lost my concentration. Once I find it I end up using one of the doctors, the nurse, and the EMT, making sure the viewer sees enough of each, cutting in their answers so they continue or complement each other, and filming myself, here in the apartment, asking them the questions they answer.

After a few more losses of concentration it takes me four hours to get the video looking and sounding smooth and strong. I put it aside to view again tomorrow night, after which I'll post it. Then I make myself a sandwich, grab a beer, and sit on my balcony, chilling out to whatever Siri feels like playing.

An hour or so later I'm fresh enough to edit the video I shot at the Pilsen rally yesterday. Which, as it turns out, requires little work on my part: Titus, Rafael, and Rowan were all succinct. Almost no wasted time, as there usually is in public speaking, and especially so in outdoor rallies.

When Rowan paused in her talk and looked out across the crowd, I followed her glance with the camcorder. Snoddy: standing in an alley, looking directly at her. Then over at me.

I leave him in the video, along with shots of the cops with their riot gear: face masks, truncheons, handguns. I add some of the closeups of drums at the beginning, then again at the end. I add a title frame, Working Class Control, Pilsen Neighborhood, Chicago, IL, and the date.

Then I upload the video to Dropbox and send a link to Titus Longshaw. That done, I drive down to the address Rowan gave me, park, and wait for her to come out of the meeting.

* * *

On Monday morning I cook us an omelet, bacon, and toast, and after breakfast I give Rowan a ride home.

She tells me she wants to bake a bourbon pecan pie for Lyle as payment for her ride.

"I'm giving you a ride," I point out.

"And I'll bake you a pecan pie."

I glance over at her. "Really?"

"Really. You're a better driver than Lyle, so I might, you know, throw a few extra pecans into your pie."

I grin.

"When can we see each other again?" I ask.

It turns out not until Saturday. Rowan works nights, I work days.

Five days. I don't like it.

I drop Rowan off at her house. MaryEllen's sitting on her porch and Deeply's sitting on her front porch railing. I wave to both and then drive to Highland Studios, where there's enough work on my desk to occupy me the rest of the day. I finish at 6:00, then review my health care podcast. No changes necessary, so I upload it to my site and publish it on YouTube, from where it will go out to subscribers.

At home I park the car and walk to Navy Pier for a chicken sandwich.

I don't know what to do with the video I shot at the gun-control rally. Destroy it? Cut out the part that shows the attack on Snoddy? I'm getting uncomfortable carrying this information around. Even having it on my computer.

But it doesn't feel right to destroy it, either.

43 ROWAN

"YOU'RE ON SMALL SORTING TONIGHT," NOLAN TELLS me when I report to work. "Dollar an hour extra. I'm putting you next to Jennica. She's been here twenty years, one of our best. You're doing good, Rowan. Wherever I put you."

"Thanks," I say. Raise ahead in the near future? I'm aiming for that $20 an hour Vic said was possible. Three dollars more an hour than I'm making now. That's $60 a week more if I'm still a part-timer, $120 a week more if I'm full-time. I practically salivate thinking of the extra money. I know the raises won't come the way Vic implied they would. I probably won't be up to $18 an hour until after my probation time, and then to $19 a year later. But maybe there's a full-time position ahead. If there isn't, I'll need to find a second part-time job — whose hours won't conflict with these.

It turns out I met Jennica last week, in the Package Nova cafeteria. She acknowledges me while she sorts small packages — like legal-sized envelopes and those cardboard flaps that books come in — at a fantastic speed. Flips them into different chutes: left, right, above, below.

We're surrounded by conveyer belts, most running parallel to each other, a few running at right angles. Some at waist level, with two more tiers of belts above these. Miles of conveyer belts. Miles and miles. I hear them in my sleep.

Jennica has obviously trained newbies before: she's very systematic about teaching me, showing me how to grab a black nylon bag as it's dumped into a holding area behind me, loosen the cord, dump the small packages onto the conveyor belt, toss the bag into a pile behind me, grab another, do the same. And another. And another. As I dump she sorts the packages as they come toward her, sort of like a sheepdog separating sheep at warp speed.

As I lift the bottom of the bag high, to shake out the contents, I study the way Jennica's wearing compression sleeves on her upper arms, wrist guards on each hand. More stuff I'll have to buy to help myself avoid injury.

After about an hour my shoulders feel like they're gonna fall off. That's when Nolan comes walking by, distributing Hershey bars, granola bars, and bottles of Gatorade. Jennica doesn't even look at Nolan, just takes three bars and shoves them in her pockets. I take four and do the same. Unhealthful food. But the sugar content will sure rev me up. And man, I could use revving up. This work is fast. And non-ending.

I unwrap a chocolate bar and gobble it down, stuffing the wrapping into a pocket.

This work is tedious.

I'm going to stick it out, do a good job this shift. But I'm going to tell Nolan I prefer something else.

"Is small-sorting confined to women?" I ask Jennica as we work. "Men can't have this job?"

"Women have more dexterity. That's what Package Nova tells us. We can do this faster than men can. So we get shoved here." She glances back at me to see how I'm doing, then steps backward in my direction, sorting the whole time. "Let me empty the bags a while and you can try your hand at the flipping and sorting," she instructs, switching places with me.

I notice an intricate tat just above her wrist: an elaborate intertwining of the letters BLM.

"Great tat," I say. "Took me a sec to figure it out."

She glances at me, maybe to see if I really get that it's a Black Lives Matter tat. "I designed it myself."

"Cool," I say. "Intricate."

Now it's my turn to flip the packages so they're address-side up, send them down the line to someone else, try to spot any that should go into the chutes directly behind us, which are zip-code labeled. Anything with a zip starting with 606 I grab and toss backhanded into the correct chute. I do this so well I just know the White Sox are gonna wanna sign me.

As I make the backhanded toss I'm supposed to turn back to the line without missing a beat.

I miss beats. Maybe no more than any beginner, but I don't like the fact that I miss them. And the pace is, like, brutal.

"You're doing a good job, Rowan," Jennica says from behind me.

I am?

Good to know, cause I'm sure trying.

"You interested in full-time?"

"Sure am," I say over my shoulder. "I need it."

"It might take a year," she says, "but you'll get it. You're too good for them to let go."

That cheers me up. I sort with a vengeance.

"We sort a million-and-a-half packages every twenty-four hours," Jennica tells me.

"Just you and me?"

She appreciates that: laughs. "Wrong chute," she tells me, grabbing the piece I'm about to backhand in. She flips it into the chute next to the one I was aiming for.

She not only has great coordination: she has great eyesight, to see the zip code on a package I'm holding.

"Feels that way, doesn't it?" she says. "This facility. This facility sorts one-and-a-half million packages every twenty-four hours. Double that in November and December."

I glance her way to say something, and notice her face is covered in beads of sweat. She doesn't look good.

I step toward her, letting a hundred or more packages go by.

"Are you okay?"

She stands there holding the empty black bag.

I think she's going to fall, so I grab her around the waist. Another couple hundred packages zoom by, down the line to the next sorter.

"Pregnant. First trimester."

"Should I call Nolan? You can take a break, he can take your place?" That's one thing I learned my first day. You need a bathroom break, you call the supervisor and he takes your place. It seems a way of making sure all bathroom breaks are short ones, cause you ain't gonna leave your supervisor at your spot so long that he comments on the length of your break.

A nausea-because-of-pregnancy seems even more important.

"No. I'll be all right." She gives me a look: Don't call Nolan.

"Let's change places," I say. "I'll go back to the bags. Maybe lifting and shaking them isn't good for you."

"You can't empty bags for four hours. You won't be able to use your arms for a week."

I grab a bag and empty it as I kind of nudge Jennica toward her spot. "I have tomorrow off. And Nolan said he might put me on pre-sort the day after. Different kind of lifting."

Jennica sorts packages even as she's walking backwards to her station. "Thanks, Rowan." She frowns. "Buy yourself some arm sleeves. And wristbands. You'll be protecting yourself."

"I will," I say, tossing an empty bag into the bin, lifting and emptying another bag. First on my list is a back belt. Then the wrist guards. Then the compression sleeves. Package Nova should give us an allowance for safety gear. But they don't.

I'm wearing the required leather boots. If I weren't, Nolan would send me home. Too great a risk a package might fall on my foot, breaking my toes. Or, worse yet, ankle. I have only one pair of boots, pull-on leather ones. More sturdy than dressy, so they work well.

And I have my plastic milk jug full of water. Every night when Lyle picks me up I put my jug in the back seat of his car. I wrote *Rowan* in block letters on mine. He wrote *Lyle* in beautiful calligraphy, like old English letters. Lyle has hidden talents.

My shift ends at 1:30 a.m. So does Jennica's, though she started at 5:30, putting in a full eight hours. I walk with her to the time clocks, just to make sure she's okay. She must notice me watching her. "You plannin' on catching me or something?"

"I plan to throw myself on the ground so you can land on top of me. Protect the baby."

She nods. "Not bad." Then she tells me to rub Ben Gay on my arms. Or soak in a hot tub with Epsom Salts.

On the ride home Lyle tells me they put him on small-sorting when he first started. So I guess it's not only women.

"They might try everyone on small-sorting," he says, "just to see how they do. Lotta guys want the job, cause of the dollar an hour extra. But almost no guy can do it. I couldn't." He glances at me. "Guys look over at the small-sorters and say they've got it cushy."

I rub my upper arms and give a snort. "Do you think so, Lyle?"

"No way. That job is, like, *mental*! The tension from all the decisions you gotta make, and make instantly. Cushy? Not! I'd rather lift packages any day. Even as a loader." He shifts lanes, though there's barely any traffic on the road. "Have you been a loader yet?"

"No. Is it hard?" I ask.

"You'll find out."

44   JAKE

I HIT THE GYM THREE TIMES WHILE WAITING FOR Saturday to roll around. On the third night, as I'm showered and about to dress, a text beeps. Unknown caller. I dress, then check to see if this was solicitation or if somebody actually left a message.

He did. **Jake, Titus Longshaw. Great video! Can we meet WCC HQ?** I text back that we can and ask when.

Tonight.

Good. Gives me something to do so I don't spend all my time counting the hours until Saturday.

When I get there he offers me iced tea or coffee, cookies or cake. I accept the iced tea and coconut cake, both far better than I expected.

He sees my assessment of the drink and food and grins. "Brewed-from-scratch tea, made-from-scratch cake. We don't feed the working class the same chemical products the capitalist class tries to convince them they want. Chemical products the capitalist class never eats: their personal chefs would die before serving instant tea or cake made from a box mix." He studies me. "You like Boston cream pie?"

I wipe up the last of the frosting from my paper plate with a finger, lick it off, and wash it down with iced tea. "In Massachusetts it's unpatriotic not to love Boston cream pie. Which, by the way, is the official state dessert. It beat out Fig Newtons, which I can see, but it also beat out Toll House cookies," I inform him. "Hard to fathom."

"Mmm-hmmm. Something to know," he says. "Rowan's mother bakes a fantastic Boston cream pie."

I don't respond, wondering where this is going.

"When she comes back, I'm sure she'll start baking for WCC again. You can taste her Boston cream pie and see."

"Is she coming back?"

Titus rubs a hand across his forehead. "God, I hope so." He looks up at me. "It's hard to see a person you know and love . . . wander off into the wilderness. Alone."

Should I participate in this conversation? Titus is watching me.

"Rowan was alone, too," I say. "Her mother left her alone."

"Was?" he asks.

"Was. Past tense."

"Pretty sure of yourself, are you?"

It's hard for me to read his mood. Or his intent. Is he angry? Happy? And what's this all about anyway?

"I'm always sure of myself," I respond. "Except when I'm not," I give him.

He smiles. "You have confidence, Jake. And courage. I saw what you did to Snoddy and his enforcers. Confidence and courage don't always come in the same package. A lot of people are confident but not necessarily courageous. A lot of people are courageous when the time comes, but not necessarily confident."

He's right. I've seen it at work and in the ring. Titus and I are circling around each other, but our gloves aren't up.

"On top of that, you are a fantastic videographer. I want to thank you for letting us use your video, but I want to thank you even more for the art and understanding with which you put it together."

"I was happy to give it to you," I tell him.

"There's a lot of power in what you put together, Jake, but the greatest of all the powers is that you let us speak for ourselves. Us, the working class.

There was not a single thing you did to condescend to us. For someone from the petty bourgeoisie, that is unusual. It speaks highly of you." He looks at me. "You do know what the petty bourgeoisie is?"

"*Petty's* a corruption of *petite*. There's what Marx called the *haute bourgeoisie*, or the capitalist class. And there's the *petite bourgeoisie*. Aspirers to the bourgeoisie. Which I'm not."

"You've read Marx?"

"Only *The Communist Manifesto*. Not *Das Kapital*. I have a life to live."

He smiles at that, but looks puzzled. "What made you read *The Communist Manifesto*?"

"Suosso's Lane made me read it. My great-grandfather lived there."

Titus looks pole-axed.

"Your great-grandfather lived on Suosso's Lane, Plymouth?"

I nod.

"Your great-grandfather knew Bartolomeo *Vanzetti*?" He's incredulous.

"I'm told he was a neighbor of Vanzetti's and a good friend."

Titus is utterly silent for a minute or more. Finally he speaks. "You are a man of surprises, Jacob Terranova."

I shrug.

"You know they were murdered because they were anarchists."

"And because they were Italian," I add. "Curly-haired, olive-skinned. Hard-working laborers who didn't look Anglo-Saxon and didn't like being exploited."

Titus nods. "Too close to Africa for comfort." He straightens some papers on the table. "I would love to talk to you about Sacco and Vanzetti some day. Some day soon. But we were talking about the petty bourgeoisie.

"In Marxist analysis the petty bourgeoisie stands between the two major antagonists of the capitalist system — the working class on one end, the owning capitalist class on the other. Around the world members of the petty bourgeoisie and members of the middle class who recognized the gross injustices of capitalism threw their lot in with the working class, to help lead it to power. Lenin, Trotsky, Luxembourg. Mao, Castro, Guevera. King was moving toward socialism before he was assassinated." He makes certain I'm following what he's saying. "Most Black leaders have come from the working class. Malcolm. Fred Hampton. Seale, Newton, Cleaver."

His points made, Titus settles back into his chair. "But that's not what I want to talk to you about, Jake."

Sure it isn't.

"I want to ask if you would consider donating some of your time to filming other WCC events. Even to help us create educational videos of various sorts. On systematic police violence against Black people. On the importance of supporting women in their fight for equality. On the way the ruling class uses racism to divide workers into antagonistic camps. Documentaries, maybe, of successful working class struggles, such as the Minneapolis Teamsters strike of 1934. The Amazon warehouse organizing drive. We could make these ourselves, but undoubtedly not as quickly as you could, and definitely not with your skill."

I sit there and think about this. Think about the ramifications of being associated with Working Class Control.

Think about the way the world is going, and how capitalism has brought us here, nearer and nearer to planetary disaster each decade. I'm not sure Earth has much of a future.

"Okay," I say. "I've considered it. I'll gladly help make videos."

Titus rises. I do the same. We shake hands. He has a powerful grip. "You have made my day, Jake," he says as he walks me to the door. Where somebody else is waiting. "Sofia will get in touch with you. She's in charge of WCC publicity."

We say goodbye. Titus turns to the person waiting and talks to him. I leave the building and there's Antwon Harper standing guard.

Just the person I want to see.

45 JAKE

I TELL ANTWON I'D LIKE TO TALK TO HIM ABOUT
Rowan. He studies me for a long moment, goes inside for a couple of minutes, comes out, and we walk to a bar he says is a good place to talk.

I order a Sam Adams, Antwon orders a Guinness. We wait as it's slowly poured. I raise an eyebrow at the Guinness.

"I like my beers dark," he tells me.

"Check."

We find a table and sit down. Antwon waits for me to begin.

"You know Rowan," I say, "so you know she's not afraid to act."

He looks at me without saying anything. Swallows some beer.

"On the day I first met her, the Saturday of the gun-control rally, somebody overturned a trash can on her. Dragged her across the sidewalk. Sat on the trashcan to keep her from getting out."

"How you know that?"

"Rowan told me. A few days ago."

"She know who did it?"

I shake my head. Drink some beer. "She saw him running away from her. Tall. Wearing dark clothes. She couldn't tell if he was Black or White. Or Latino or anything else."

"Damn," says Antwon.

"And then, maybe two weeks ago, she was biking home from dinner at Titus's house. She noticed somebody was following her."

"On a bike?"

I shake my head. "In a car."

"What happened?"

"Couple of things. Rowan went after the car with a tire iron in her hand. At the same time, her parrot came flying out of the house, screeching, kind of going after the guy in the car."

"Damn," says Antwon. "That parrot is something else. Chewed a hole in WCC headquarters. Rowan tell you that?"

I shake my head. "You know Rowan's got great aim," I tell him. "Hits what she aims at." I pause. "She hit me the day of the gun rally."

Antwon's about to swallow more Guinness, but he puts the glass down. "Hit you?"

I nod. "Elbow to the throat. I wanted to talk to her, she wouldn't stop. Mainly cause she was covered with trash. I caught up to her and grabbed her arm. She spun around and hit me in the throat with her elbow."

He smiles at this. Unapologetically.

"When she threw the tire iron, she hit what she aimed at, too."

We sit there in silence a while, communing with our beers. Testing each other.

"I need another beer," Antwon says. "You?"

I hand him a five and two ones. He gets up, goes to the bar, and comes back holding two glasses: my lager and his stout.

"Where we going with this story?" he asks, placing the glasses on the table.

The beer's cold and tastes great on a hot night, especially after my workout at the gym. "Two reasons this is important to me," I tell him. "First, Rowan was — well, I won't say *scared*, though she probably was. But both incidents got her adrenalin pumping. Fight or flight. A lot of stress. Unnecessary stress, as it turns out."

He sits there listening.

"Second," I say, "Rowan doesn't need to waste her time worrying about the wrong things. The trashcan and the car that followed her home — those are the wrong things for her to worry about. I'd like to get them off her plate. Know what I mean?"

"She agree with you?"

I shake my head. "We haven't talked about it."

Antwon stares into the distance. He sighs. "Sometimes a man has to make a quick decision and it turns out to be the wrong decision. Wrong because it had to be made so quick. Protect Rowan from Snoddy and his men. Who were about to grab her."

"I'm not saying it was the wrong decision," I tell him. "Could have been the only one to make at the time. Probably achieved its intended purpose. I'm just saying — decisions have repercussions."

"That they do." Antwon rubs his face. "One was a quick decision, one was careless tailing. Let the subject spot me." He glares at me. "Cost $400 to repair my rear window. Four *hundred* dollars. Talk about repercussions. From now on, Antwon Harper is going to be the most careful tailer you ever saw."

"Good to hear." I swallow some lager.

"Rowan know any of this?" he asks.

"No."

"You going to tell her?"

"Not for me to tell her."

He thinks. "Could be the whole thing just . . . disappears?"

"This is Rowan we're talking about. Sooner or later, she's going to have time to think about these things. She hasn't given them much thought yet, what with her mother gone, Rowan needing a job. Worried about money. But sooner or later . . . she's going to investigate this. She's already studied my video of the rally."

Antwon swallows more beer. He's silent.

I wait.

"You tell Titus?" he asks. "That what you was there for?"

"No. Titus wanted to talk to me about the video I made. I didn't mention it to Titus." I wait to make sure he hears that. "And I don't intend to," I tell him.

"How'd you figure it was me?"

"Rowan said the guy running away from her was wearing long-sleeved dark clothes. On a June day. You were wearing long-sleeved dark clothes at the Pilsen rally."

"That's it?!!" He's indignant. "That's *it*!?? Man, that's not knowing, that's *guessing*." He scowls at me. "Shit!"

I grin. "It's a deduction, Antwon. The dark clothes. The fact that Rowan came to no harm either time. And the fact that Titus is probably looking after her. Seeing to her safety. And Titus trusts you. You're the one he would ask to protect Rowan."

He nods. "Titus and Sam — that's Rowan's father — were tight. Made a promise to each other that if one of them died, the survivor would always look out for the other one's family."

He's silent a while. "You know how hard it is to be a Black man tailing a white woman?" He makes a scoffing sound. "Talk about adrenalin. Talk about stress."

"You must be doing an A-one job, Antwon. Rowan has no suspicions at all, far as I can tell."

"Good to hear," he says. "I see Rowan most Tuesdays. I'll tell her then."

We shake hands and say goodbye.

I walk to my car and drive home.

Where I see a shape on my balcony.

It's Deeply, sitting on the table.

46 JAKE

I OPEN THE BALCONY DOOR. "DEEPLY. WHAT ARE YOU doing here? Is Rowan okay?"

"Rowan at work," he says. "Deeply alone-ly."

I don't correct his grammar. *Alone-ly* is a damn good word.

"Jake alone-ly, too," I confess as I pull the screen door wide. I'm talking like a goddamn parrot.

He flies in and lands on top of a bookshelf. Then he sits there, inspecting the room. "What do when alone-ly?" he asks.

"Well . . . uh . . . drink beer?" Even as I say it, I'm not so sure it would be wise to give Deeply beer.

"Jake have do-nuts?"

I drop down on the couch and study the parrot. This would be the time to ask him questions — about his attack on Snoddy, about where he's from. A few weeks ago, that's what I'd have done. But it would be wrong to proceed without Rowan. We're in this together.

"Jake do right thing," Deeply says.

Is he a mind reader? I'm thinking yes. I'm thinking maybe Rowan and I won't even have to ask him questions: we'll just sit there and think them, and he'll answer.

"Jake try," I tell him, sounding like a parrot again.

Deeply nods. Then prods: "Do-nuts?"

I eye him critically. "I think you've had too many donuts, Deeply. You're getting a little plump."

He hops up and down on the bookcase. "Not!" he squawks. "Not plump! Not!"

I hold up a hand in surrender. "Okay, okay."

He appears mollified by this.

"But," I venture, "donuts are not nutritious."

He paces back and forth on the bookcase. I'm thinking he can't deny what I said . . . but doesn't want to agree, either. I smile at that.

"Movies," I say suddenly. "When alone-ly, we can watch a movie. And eat popcorn. Which is delicious *and* nutritious."

Easy choice for which movie Deeply would like. I get ready to stream *The Day the Earth Stood Still*. Once the movie's set up I go into the kitchen. Deeply follows me.

I could throw some popcorn packs into the microwave, but I decide to pop some high-quality corn in a pan. With truffle olive oil, which I think the parrot will like.

Deeply observes everything, keeping well away from the stove and the hot pan. When the corn starts popping against the lid, he jumps.

"It's popcorn," I explain. "Kernels of corn popping open."

Deeply imitates the sound of the popping corn. I wonder if that's one of the ways he learns: by imitating sounds.

He studies my every move as I dump the popcorn into a huge bowl, drizzle more truffle oil over it, salt it, mix it, and take it into the living room.

I sit on the couch and motion to Deeply that he should perch on the arm, which he does. I put the bowl of popcorn between us, reach in a hand, and put the handful into my mouth. After a moment Deeply uses a claw to do the same.

He crunches the popcorn. Swallows. Smiles. I swear he smiles. Makes a chuckling-trilling sound. "Deeply love popcorn," he announces, reaching into the bowl for more.

I dim the lights and start the movie.

From the first scene Deeply's into it, sitting there with his mouth open, missing his mouth half the time he tries bringing popcorn to it. There's popcorn all over the couch and on the floor. Serious vacuum time tomorrow.

When the movie's over, Deeply's still in awe. Or what looks like awe to me.

"Did you like it?"

"Humans stupid," he answers.

Or that's what I think he says, because he kind of mutters it under his breath. I'm about to protest his assessment when he speaks.

"Again," he says, eyeing the remote. "Again."

I grab the remote off the couch and keep it in my hand. I look at my watch. Only eleven p.m. "Okay, one more time. *Only* one more time."

"Popcorn all gone," he announces, looking around.

I can take a hint.

After I make another batch of popcorn we settle down to watch *The Day the Earth Stood Still* a second time.

With Deeply there beside me, I don't feel so *alone-ly*. I hope he doesn't, either.

47   DEEPLEA

Me: I must report, HOP, that Antwon Harper is not the third person.

HOP: And why is that?

Me: He has wonderful qualities. Honesty. Bravery. Intelligence. And he weaves with beautiful colors and patterns. But . . . he is capable of acting rashly.

HOP: [Pause] Do we know somebody like that, DeePlea?

Me: What is your point, HOP?

HOP: My point is this. I know and love someone who is honest, brave, intelligent, and has been known to act rashly now and then. This quality of sometimes acting rashly has not prevented him from performing his Duty to the Universe.

Me: [Confused] Are you saying I should overlook Antwon's rashness? That he could be one of the three?

HOP: No, Dee, I am not saying you should overlook it and select him as one of your three choices. I am saying that you should not necessarily reject him because of his rashness. Keep observing and assessing him.

Me: You are very wise, HOP.

HOP: As Head of Planet, I am required to be. [Pause] I have given great consideration to your plan, DeePlea — that you visit three other places on Earth and find three other organizations and three other triads who can help people change the Doomsday course. I recognize, Dee, that you are the best judge of what is to be done on Earth. You are there, assessing matters each and every day. I trust you to make the best decision.

Me: Thank you, Fee. HOP, I mean. Your love and trust inspire me.

HOP: I imagine you are very lonely, Dee.

Me: [Swallows hard]

HOP: Regarding your DU. If you cannot determine the third individual within the next five weeks, then perhaps you can modify your plan and travel to three countries during your year there. One every four months instead of one every three months. Based on what you have reported, your duty seems . . . overwhelming.

Me: I sometimes feel that way, FeeOna. But I fight my way out of it.

HOP: That is good. Would you like to talk to the chicks?

Me: Yes. I have been looking forward to seeing and hearing them. And I want them to know me.

48 ROWAN

ON FRIDAY NOLAN ASSIGNS LYLE AND ME TO HELP Mateo load a 28-foot pup trailer.

After Nolan leaves, the three of us look at the huge stack of packages. Tall ones, short ones. Well-wrapped ones, sloppily-wrapped ones. "About 700 packages," Mateo says. "Two hours, tops. And then we do another."

"And then we collapse," Lyle adds.

"We each load about two packages a minute, we'll be half-finished in an hour. But watch your pace," Mateo tells us. "Not too fast. Not too slow, either."

Two packages a minute. Lift a package, turn around, walk into the trailer with it, stack it neatly, turn around, go back, grab another, do the same. The pile we're building starts out at floor level, below our knees, with us bending (properly) to set each package down. The foundation grows quickly as we stack packages on top of one another. Soon it's chest-high. Then eye-level. Then above our heads.

The inside of the trailer is sweltering. We're dripping sweat as we walk back and forth, chugging our water whenever we can.

The packages are of various weights, anywhere from 5 to maybe 40 pounds, with a few 60- or 70-pound outliers. Select the heavy ones first, place them on the trailer floor as a foundation for the next row. Stack increasingly lighter ones, so the lightest are at the top. You can't necessarily tell how much a package weighs by looking at it, so there's some testing and maybe shoving a package aside for later.

The three of us try hard to cooperate with one another, filling the spaces properly, not getting in each other's way.

"Usually a two-man job," Mateo tells us, "but Nolan wants me to train two of you. Watch it there, Lyle, that's not the best use of space right there." Mateo steps in, moves aside a package Lyle has stacked, and moves another one into its place. He's really good at this. Steady pace, good lifting technique. "You want a tight fit," he tells Lyle.

"Yeah, I know," Lyle answers. "Sometimes I, like, can't judge the space until I've put a package into it."

"Comes with experience," Mateo says. "How're the broken arms?"

"Well, they aren't broken any more."

"How's the other guy?" Mateo asks. "He okay?"

Lyle frowns. Maybe he doesn't like the question? But I look at him for an answer.

"Yeah, he's okay," Lyle mutters. "He needed a second operation on the nose. But he's okay. And his friend didn't have to break my arms, ya know?"

Mateo drops the subject.

By the time we finish the first pup I'm drenched in sweat. So are Mateo and Lyle. I guzzle more water. We get a fifteen-minute break between trucks. Which means, really, that we have to work faster on the second one cause we have less time.

"Reward time!" Nolan comes by with a huge pizza and cold cans of Coke. "Good job." He sets everything down on the tailgate of our second pup trailer. We sit there and devour the pizza. Energy. We need energy.

Nolan tosses me something. I grab it.

"Company tee-shirt," he says. "Keep a bunch of them with you so you can change out of your wet ones."

I wonder if I have the energy to walk to the women's room and change my top.

Mateo looks at me as if he knows what I'm thinking. "You can step between the trailers."

I do that. The dry tee feels good. I want more pizza, but I hold back. Loading packages at full speed with a full stomach — not a pleasant combo.

The second trailer's a disaster. So many heavy packages that some of them have to go on the top rows. It takes two of us to lift them, which slows us down.

And then we notice one of the packages is leaking.

"Back away," Mateo orders Lyle and me.

He walks over to a pillar, picks up a red phone, and calls the HazMat team. Which arrives in under three minutes and does an inspection of the leaky package. Nolan comes running to see what the problem is.

"You shouldn't have called HazMat," he shouts at Mateo. "You should have called me."

"Union regulations, Nolan. It's my right to call HazMat any time I encounter a package that might be dangerous. Package Nova regulations say the same thing."

Nolan waves away the regulations with a hand. All of them, I guess. "Next time you call *me*, Mateo. Not HazMat. That's an order.

Nolan's pacing back and forth. He paces until the HazMat team declares the package safe and hauls it away. I wonder what they'll do with it.

"C'mon, move it," Nolan barks to the three of us. "You're twenty minutes behind schedule. C'mon! Move!"

The three of us resume loading. Not one of us moves faster than we have to.

Nolan hovers. Getting in our way.

Mateo and Lyle carry one of the really heavy packages together and lift it into place.

"Faster than that," Nolan orders. "You're lifting like girls."

Mateo's face darkens. Lyle's turns red.

I turn angry. Nolan's insulting me as if I'm not even standing there. I'm invisible. He can say anything he wants because I don't count. Because I'm a woman.

"That's an insult to me, Nolan. You're saying that when you want to diss men, you compare them to women."

Nolan stands there with his mouth open. Stupefied at what I've said. Or that I've said it.

"Hey, Mateo and Lyle are proud to be associated with me," I say lightly, hoping my humor helps them feel better. It's awful to be insulted in front of others.

Lyle gives me an appreciative look.

Nolan studies us a second. "Three hours overtime for each of you on the 55-footer that's backing into Dock Seven. No breaks. No treats."

When he's gone I apologize to Mateo and Lyle for making us work overtime. Until 4:30 a.m.

"Time-and-a-half for me," grunts Mateo as he lifts another package. "Ninety dollars extra."

It's daylight when Lyle and I reach home. "Nolan's going to punish you," he says.

"I thought he just did."

"There'll be more coming."

49 ROWAN

A KNOCKING ON THE DOOR IS WHAT FINALLY WAKES me. I have no idea what time it is. I ache all over. I lay there, my eyes half open, and listen to the knocking. And then I remember. Jake!

I scramble out of bed, run to the door, and pull it open.

Jake's standing there holding two bags, one in each arm.

"Hey," he says, taking in my appearance. "Did I wake you? Wasn't I coming over at ten this morning?"

I move aside to let him in. "You were. You are. I'm sorry. I got off work at 4:30 this morning." I yawn. "What's in the bags?"

He walks into the kitchen and deposits the bags on the counter. Deeply flies from his perch and lands beside them.

"I thought I'd make us breakfast," says Jake. "So: eggs, bread, cheese, bacon, avocado, berries, OJ, a few other things. And I noticed you have a grill in your backyard."

"When you were prowling around, inspecting my garden."

"Exactly. So in the other bag we have two steaks, potatoes, a bottle of wine, and dessert. I figured we could make a salad from your garden."

I look at him. "This is wonderful, Jake. Thank you." I feel a need to reciprocate next weekend. I'll make burgers and fries, and bake that pecan pie for Jake.

We look at each other. He moves toward me. I put up a hand. "Shower," I say. "I'm covered in stale sweat from work. Let me take a shower and I'll make us breakfast."

"You shower," he says, "I'll make breakfast."

Which I do and which he does, and then we have the rest of the day before us. First we make love. Second we make love. Third we walk to Park 571 boathouse, rent a canoe, and paddle upstream. Jake paddles. I couldn't lift an arm if I had to.

We enjoy the beautiful day. Being on the water. Seeing the Chicago skyline.

Then Jake asks: "Should I destroy the video? Not the whole thing, but the part that shows Deeply attacking Snoddy?"

This stuns me: that Jake is willing to destroy what he filmed. That he thinks I have as much a say about it as he does.

I think.

"Rowan?"

"I don't know," I explain. "I don't feel . . . comfortable . . . with destroying pictures that prove something happened. It's like . . . falsifying history. Like under Stalin the Communist Party doctored photos to remove Trotsky, Zinoviev, Kamenev, others. The doctored photos were lies."

Jake lets the paddle idle in the water. "That isn't what I thought you'd say."

"You thought I'd want you to destroy the video?"

He nods. "Yeah. I did."

"I worry about it," I confess. "About your safety. It feels to me like you're safer not having the video."

He goes back to paddling the canoe. He's a great paddler. Strong. Smooth. Good rhythm. He'd be a great package handler.

"I don't worry so much about my safety," he says at last, "as I do yours. And Deeply's."

"Me, too. About Deeply's."

We glide along the Chicago River in silence, each of us lost in our thoughts. Jake paddles all the way to Marina Towers, where the river traffic is thick with tour boats, paddle boats, kayaks, and canoes. He turns our canoe around and heads back toward Bridgeport. With the current rather than against it.

"We don't know what Deeply is," Jake says on the way back. "Alien. Bot. Mutation. But we do know he's highly intelligent."

"So — we ask him?" I say, not sure that's where Jake's going.

He nods. "We ask him." He looks at me to see what I think.

"Agreed," I say. "We ask him."

The *we* makes me feel warm. Strong. I have an uneasy feeling, though. Like I'll need to be strong. Stronger than ever.

We return the canoe to the rental dock and walk back to my house. As we near it, I spot Deeply in the catalpa tree. I wonder if from up there he could see us canoeing the river.

He flies into the house through the open window, and when Jake and I walk in, Deeply is sitting on his perch, trying to groom his orange neck feathers, "Jake de-stroy," he squawks. "De-stroy vid-e-o."

That's when I know for certain that Deeply can read minds.

"Why?" Jake asks. "Why destroy the video?"

"Safety. Jake safety," squawks Deeply, looking at each of us. "Rowan safety."

"Deeply rash in vid-e-o. Rash not always wrong."

Jake takes his camcorder out. "I'll erase it now. Once I do that, there's no going back."

"Not erase all Deeply. Keep Rowan meet Deeply. Keep inter-view."

My eyes flood with tears.

Deeply wants me to remember him.

Deeply is going to leave me.

50 DEEPLEA

JAKE WANTS TO QUESTION ME. EASILY AVOIDED — OUT
the window I fly. On this planet, such a move is called an evasive one. Humans have too many ways of avoiding the truth. I hope I do not pick up any of their bad habits.

Rowan knows that I will leave. Jake did not grasp that as instantly as she did. But she is telling him now.

I perch in the catalpa until dusk, and then I fly another mission. As I have done all nights but one. I did enjoy my night off with Jake.

Popcorn.

I have found many triads, and that makes me happy. Throughout Working Class Control and throughout the organizations of struggle, there are groups of committed people who will fight to save the world.

Many, many triads. But not the third person to match Titus and Rowan. Until I find that person, I cannot move onward to India. Or France. Or maybe Venezuela.

Jake accepted what Antwon did. Perhaps I, too, should write off Antwon's rashness and accept that he is the third pillar.

But perhaps not.

I do not want to be recalled from my Duty to the Universe. Thus far I have admitted nothing to Rowan or Jake — but they are moving closer and closer to accepting the correct conclusion.

Rowan and Jake both seek the truth. Neither would accept a supposition without proof. Not even Jake. They will seek proof. I will not give it to them.

And when I report to HOP, I can evade her questions.

51 ROWAN

"YOU'RE ON THE SMALL-SORTING LINE TONIGHT," Nolan tells me.

Last week when I told him I preferred lifting to small sorting, he said he'd see what he could do. Now he's punishing me for calling him on the sexist remark.

"Dollar an hour more," I say to him.

Tonight I'm with Bri, who's my age and has been there two full years. Bri is a dedicated part-timer: she doesn't want full-time because she's going to college. She teaches me some of the same stuff Jennica did. I'm not as sore as I was last week. Still: I need to buy the compression sleeves, wrist guards, and a back belt. I can get the compression sleeves for maybe twenty bucks, the wrist guards for maybe fifteen. The elastic back brace runs fifty or sixty dollars.

✻ ✻ ✻

Tuesday's my day off. I spend a lot of it in the garden, watching Deeply run around in the sprinkler. Dinner is a salad with more cheese and pecans, and then I bike to Keisha's with Deeply on the rack, a couple of spools of mercerized cotton in the pannier, the three crochet hooks in my back pocket.

"How many feathers did you find in Clari's drawer?" Keisha asks me as we're working.

"Uh, maybe a dozen. Why?"

"Because your feather is getting frayed. Time to change it. I know this, Rowan, because—"

"I'm a year older than you are!" Antwon and I chant in unison.

Keisha sighs as if our humor is too much for her to bear, but we know she's pleased.

"New feather next week, Rowan," she instructs. "Blue looks good on you because of your eyes. What other colors did Clari have?"

"A couple more blue ones. Orange. Turquoise. A white one. A black one. And a mottled one that looks like a pheasant feather or something."

"The black one would look striking," she advises me, sewing away.

We're having fun, expressing ourselves through art. I'm tying off a granny square when Antwon turns to face me. "Rowan," he says, "I have a confession to make."

A confession? Antwon? What is it with men and confessions?

I wait.

And then he tells me that he was the one who dumped the trash can over me *and* he was the one who followed me home that night.

"Don't be angry," he says. "I did it to protect you."

I'm having a hard time accepting this. That it was Antwon.

"From who?" I demand.

"From Snoddy at the rally. You gotta admit he was 'bout to grab you."

"But . . . okay . . . but . . . did you have to hold me prisoner inside an upside-down *trash* can?"

He shakes his head. "I had to protect myself, too. Black man dragging a white woman? In the middle of those racists? Had to get you out of sight yesterday."

I think about this. Part of me is pissed that it was a *friend* who did this to me. The better part of me knows that this isn't easy for Antwon: confessing.

"Okay," I say at last. "We're good about that. As long as it doesn't happen again."

He nods. "And about following you home that night? We're good about that?"

I nod. "We're good."

I'm silent a while. "Titus asked you to do this, didn't he?" I say at last.

"Don't tell Daddy you know this, Rowan," Keisha warns. "He likes the idea of protecting you without your knowing it."

"I won't tell him," I promise. "Is this, like, something he promised my mother?"

Keisha shakes her head. "Not your mother. Your father."

I sit there in silence a while, a lump in my throat. Dad is protecting me still, even beyond the grave. Mom's not protecting me at all.

I can take care of myself. I *am* taking care of myself. But it would be nice to have a mother to talk to. Do things with. Ask advice. Like, I really wanted to ask her advice when Lyle wanted bourbon in his pecan pie. A minor issue, sure . . . but I wanted Mom's take on it

Keisha, Antwon, and I go on to talk about other things. Mainly about the class struggle, but also about our jobs.

"Once your probation is over, you can join the union and start talking about important issues," Keisha says. "Wages, hours, conditions, health care."

"I will," I say, thinking that I'll also talk about the role of foremen and the way they abuse their power. And the patronizing way they hand out pizza and pop and candy bars. I'm looking forward to my probation being over — having a secure job.

The night is hot. Antwon suggests we break early and walk to an air-conditioned bar.

"Wine cooler sounds great to me," Keisha announces as she shuts down her sewing machine.

"Me, too." I gather up my thread and Mom's crochet hooks. My crochet hooks, I guess.

We walk to the bar, order our drinks, and relax.

When I bike home Antwon follows me in the car. As I turn left on Eleanor I give him a wave. He gives me a beep.

* * *

Wednesday night Nolan has me on small sorting again. With overtime. Thursday night it's the same. And Friday. Each at a different station, with a different person.

I keep as neutral a face as possible, so Nolan doesn't know whether I like this or hate it. And I mention the shift differential each time. Fucking with his mind, I hope. I slow down the speed with which I sort, but not so much that it looks like I'm shirking. As Mateo says, you gotta find the right speed.

I want every foreman who sees me on small sorting to report that I'm willing. Friendly. Cooperative. But maybe falling short on the quick mental skills, the dexterity, the concentration, to sort small packages well.

I like the women I work with. They're terrific. I don't know what Package Nova would do without them. They go to their stations and just . . . take charge. Their fingers are flying, their wrists are flipping, their hips are turning, and those packages whiz by like arrows.

But this is a tense job. Much tenser than loading packages. Which is tense enough, but at least it's not constant.

Thanks to the shift differential and the overtime, I'll make $85 extra in next week's paycheck.

* * *

My phone rings early Saturday morning. I'm in some really deep stage of sleep and grope around for it, thinking it can't be Jake, he's coming at ten.

Mom.

I sit bolt upright and shout into the phone. "Mom! Are you okay? Is something wrong?"

"Rowan," she says. "It's so good to hear your voice. I'm all right. I've missed you. I've missed you tremendously."

She has a strange way of showing it. No communication in five months. "Are you . . . coming home?" I ask, holding my breath.

"Of course I am. I told you I was coming back." There's a silence. "Didn't you believe me?"

I shake my head, then realize she can't see me. "No." My mouth is dry. "I . . . I guess I didn't believe you, Mom. You went away. Totally away."

"I know I did." Her voice sounds sad. "I'm sorry for that. But I didn't go away totally. I left a different message every Sunday night, like I promised."

I'm about to launch into how that isn't communication. But I realize that, just like Clari and I had to sort of take care of Mom after Dad died, I have to do the same now. When I get mad at somebody in politics, Titus always says, "Be bigger and better than they are, Rowan."

"Where are you?" I ask.

"Tucson."

"Tucson?" I ask in amazement. "Like, Tucson, *Arizona*?!"

"Yes. I needed to get far away from . . . everything that happened."

"*Mommmmm*! Tucson! You should have taken me with you! I would love to see Tucson!"

As I say this, though, I realize that if I had gone with Mom, I wouldn't have met Jake. The wish to see Tucson evaporates.

She doesn't say anything for a second or two.

"What?" I ask, feeling a sense of trepidation. What's she going to say?

She still doesn't say anything, and when she does, I get the feeling she's changed the subject. "Thank you for all the messages," she says. "They gave me such hope, knowing what you were doing. Your job. That you planted a garden. That a parrot followed you home. And that you were having dinner with Titus and Genevieve. And their messages to me — it all helped me so much."

But I don't think that's what she was going to say.

"I'm glad, Mom. When are you coming home?"

"I've given two week's notice at my job. So I'll leave Tucson two weeks from today. I'll be home three days later, I think. Monday."

I'm, like, stunned.

She really *is* coming back!

"That's great," I shout into the phone. "I'm excited! But if I'm not here, Mom, it means I'm at work. The 9:30 p.m. to 1:30 a.m. shift. If I work overtime, I might not be home until 3:00 or even 4:00 in the morning."

"I'm hoping I can get there before you leave for work. I miss you so much."

My mouth is dry. "I miss you, too, Mom. And Mom — there's a big parrot perch in the living room. Deeply might be sitting on it. He's really big, but he's safe. Just say hello to him and — he'll take over the rest of the conversation."

Mom and I say goodbye.

I shower quickly, get dressed, encourage Deeply to eat some bird pellets, and run across the lawn to MaryEllen's. I tell her and Patrick the news about Mom. Els is almost as happy as I am.

Then I call Genevieve and tell her and Titus.

And then Jake arrives with a large box of donuts and we make breakfast together.

Well, we start out making breakfast together, but when Deeply flies off his perch and out the window, Jake grabs the box of donuts and chases him.

52   JAKE

THE GODDAMN PARROT IS EMPLOYING AN EVASIVE maneuver.

He saw me bring in a box of donuts. I opened the box and carried it to his perch. "Do-nuts, Deeply. Each and every one covered with *sprink-les*!"

Breaking a donut in half, I offered it to him, fully expecting him to stretch out a claw and take the donut. Instead, he flew off his perch and out the window.

"Jake, you can't *bribe* Deeply to talk to you," says Rowan as she flips bacon in a pan. "That won't work."

"We'll see," I say as I exit through the side door.

There's Deeply, perched at the top of the catalpa tree.

"Do-nuts," I call up to him. "Sprink-les. Come-n-get-em."

He ignores me.

I put my fingers between my teeth and send up a shrill whistle: the kind that means, "get your ass down here and be quick about it. Or else."

Deeply sends the exact same whistle back to me.

"C'mon, Deeply," I shout. "We have to talk. You can't avoid me forever."

I realize, though, that the parrot has the advantage. He's up in a tree, I'm down on the ground. He can come to me, but I can't get to him.

I bite into the donut half I'm still holding. "*Mmmmmm!*"

Next thing I know, MaryEllen and a guy I assume is her husband are standing alongside me, looking up at the parrot.

"Hello, Jake," says MaryEllen. "Can we help you with something? And Jake, this is Patrick, my husband."

I put the donut half back in the box and shake hands with Patrick, who's looking amused.

"Deeply will come back inside when he's ready to," Mary Ellen informs me. She looks at the box I'm holding. "You have a lot of donuts there, Jake. I hope you don't intend to feed them all to Deeply."

"Uh, no."

The door to Rowan's house opens. "Breakfast is ready, Jake. Hey, Els and Patrick — want to come in for some coffee and donuts?"

They do.

No sooner do the four of us sit down at the table — bacon, eggs, and toast in front of Rowan and me, donuts in front of everybody — than, *Whoosh*! The bird lands on the hutch.

"Do-nut! Deeply want do-nut!"

Yeah, sure. It knows I'm not going to ask questions in front of MaryEllen and Patrick. Bird's a goddamn conniver.

Rowan's trying to hide the fact that she's laughing at me. She takes a half-donut and holds it aloft. Deeply extends a claw and hauls the donut toward his beak.

He bites and chews. *Cha-haha, cha-haha.*

"That's Deeply's laugh," Rowan informs everyone as she crunches a piece of bacon. Her eyes meet mine, telling me I'm not as smart as I think I am.

"Jake," asks MaryEllen, "did Rowan tell you the good news?"

"No. What good news?"

"Her mother called today. She's coming home."

"I didn't have time to tell you, Jake. You and the donuts came in the door, you and the donuts went out the door. She called me this morning. She says she'll be home two weeks from this coming Monday."

My first thought is a personal one: there goes Saturday morning love making. But I realize how selfish that is. "I'm happy for you, Rowan. I know you thought this would never happen."

She nods. "I did think it would never happen. It's . . . kind of a shock. A happy shock."

We all nod.

"I think — there was something she was going to tell me. But then she backed off and didn't," Rowan tells us.

"Like what?" Patrick asks.

Nobody answers Patrick's question of *Like what*? That's probably because nobody wants to say it. The most obvious like-what is that Rowan's mother remarried.

53 JAKE

ROWAN AND I GO TO A WCC RALLY, THIS ONE IN Woodlawn, then return to Bridgeport. I park in front of Rowan's house, turn off the engine, reach into the back seat, and grab a package.

Rowan eyes it as we walk into the house.

I notice that the parrot is once again at the top of the catalpa tree.

"What's that?" Rowan asks, frowning.

Which means she suspects it's a present. Probably the ribbon and bow give it away.

We walk into the living room. "A present."

She starts to protest, but I place my index finger on her lips. I hand her the box, which I went to The Container Store to buy. Bought the ribbon and bow there, too.

She stands there holding it.

"Just open it," I coax, "and if you don't want to accept it, I'll return it."

She puts the box on top of the piano, unwraps the ribbon, and jiggles the lid off the box. She lifts the tissue paper.

And laughs.

And wraps her arms around me. "Jake, thank you, thank you! I love it!"

I laugh, too. "I thought you would."

"Let me see if the size is right." She pulls out the elastic back belt with removable suspenders. Holds it across her stomach. "Looks good," she says.

Then she pulls out the arm compression sleeves and pulls one on. "Oohh, good fit."

Finally, she removes the wrist bands and tugs one on. I can tell the fit is perfect.

She puts everything back into the box and faces me. "Thank you, Jake. This is, you know, a very working class gift."

I hadn't thought of it that way, but I guess it is.

"I can model these for you," she says with a grin. "If you want."

I definitely want.

* * *

We're lying in bed, arms and legs wrapped around each other, sort of half-asleep, half-awake.

I forgot to close the bedroom door, so I hear the fluttering sound of Deeply landing on his perch.

"Rowan," I whisper, "Deeply's back."

Her eyes open. "Let me be the one to start the questions," she whispers back.

I nod as we untangle and get dressed.

"Hey, Deeply," Rowan says as we walk into the living room. "You're back."

She takes my hand and guides me to the sofa. We sit and face the parrot.

"*Awwwkkk*!" it squawks.

Which is my first clue that we're not going to get answers.

"Deeply." Rowan waits to make certain she has the bird's attention. "Do you remember when I thought you were a bot? I asked you what kind of bird you were. Do you remember what you said?"

"Special," squawks the parrot.

Rowan nods. "That's right. So, Deeps, Jake and I want to know — Special in what way?"

"Smart," squawks the bird. "Brain-y."

I swear it cackles to itself over the *brain-y*. I'm ready to jump in with questions, but when I try Rowan presses her thumb into my thigh.

"That's right. And when I asked if you were smarter than me, you patted my shoulder. That meant you are smarter than me, didn't it?"

"Rowan not bad," Deeply concedes.

"What about Jake? Are you smarter than Jake?"

"Jake not bad. Not as good as Deeply. But not bad."

The bird has an ego the size of the universe.

"What about Rowan and Jake together?" asks Rowan. "Are you smarter than the two of us together?"

The parrot nods. Struts back and forth on its perch.

Rowan studies Deeply for a moment and I think maybe it's my turn to speak, but when I start — the thumb again. I'm going to have black-and-blue thumbprints all over.

"Do you know other parrots as smart as you, Deeply?" she asks.

The bird, still strutting, bobs its head up and down. A bit arrogantly, if you ask me.

"That's wonderful. It means you can consort with your equals."

Consort with your equals — Rowan has some nerve saying I use refined vocabulary.

More head-bobbing and strutting on Deeply's part.

"Do you have a mate?" she asks.

I do a double take. This thought has never crossed my mind: I've always thought of Deeply as singular.

"FeeOna," squawks the parrot. "FeeOna."

"Fiona," Rowan repeats. "That's wonderful. I'm so happy for you, Deeps."

Well, okay. I'm happy for him, too.

"What about chil— what about chicks?" she asks. "Do you and Fiona have chicks?"

Deeply spreads his wings way wide and whistles. "One-hundred-twenty."

Leaving me speechless even if Rowan would let me speak. Who knew the parrot was such a stud?

Even Rowan seems a bit taken aback. But she recovers. "Deeply — will you see Fiona and your chicks again?"

Deeply nods. "Deeply miss them. See them next year."

Rowan's voice thickens. "You're going to leave us, aren't you?" she asks.

Deeply nods. He looks sad.

Rowan swallows and clutches my hand. "When?" she asks.

"Soon," squawks the bird. "One month."

Rowan wipes away her tears. "I will miss you, Deeps. You have been so good to me."

"Deeps miss Rowan."

"Forever?" she asks, not even wiping away the tears. I wrap an arm around her.

The bird nods. "For-ev-er."

It's a while before anybody says anything. I figure I'm free to speak . . . but I can't.

Rowan finally breaks the silence. "Will— will you go home the same way you came?" she asks.

Deeply nods. "Same way."

"The same spaceship in which you came?" she asks.

"Special spaceship. DU-Ovum spaceship," he answers. "Same one. Same day. Same place. One year later."

Holy shit!

Deeply just *admitted* he's from another planet.

This could be the story of the century! It would make my name, that's for sure. Podcast of all podcasts.

But it would result in Deeply's capture and probably his death.

I sigh.

This is a story I'll never tell. At least not while Deeply's here on Earth.

I look at Rowan, thinking she's fucking amazing, the way she got him to tell her.

I'm glad I have no secrets from Rowan. They wouldn't be secrets for long.

Suddenly Deeply screeches. "*Awwwwkkkkkkk*! Deeply tell secret! Rowan trick Deeply! Trick!" He claws the hell out of the perch as he paces in distress.

"There are different kinds of smarts, Deeps. Some of them come from the heart, not the head."

This does't mollify the bird, which still paces. He bites a huge chunk out of his perch and crunches the chunk into splinters. Drops them on the floor. "Deeply tell secret. Deeply fail. Fail! FAIL!" he screeches.

"It wasn't a secret, Deeps," she says. "Jake figured out that you're from another planet. All I did now was confirm it."

"Fail! Fail! Deeply fail," the bird mutters. Softer and softer. And then it goes to the unsplintered end of the perch, hunkers down, and folds both wings over its head.

Rowan stands and walks to the perch. I go with her.

Using just one finger, she gently strokes Deeply's back. "You didn't fail, Deeply. You're too smart to fail at anything. Please don't be upset."

Wings still folded over his head, Deeply turns away from us. "Hop," he mutters. "Hop Hop Hop."

Which makes no sense to me.

After a minute or two, Rowan and I return to the couch. We sit there and keep Deeply silent company, not wanting him to be alone in his misery.

54 DEEPLEA

FAILED. I HAVE FAILED TO KEEP MY ORIGINS A SECRET.
Deeply failed.

Deeply is a failure. Deeply cannot do a DU.

What can I say to HOP?

What will HOP do? She will recall me, that is what. The first parrot ever recalled from a Duty to the Universe.

Ignominious.

Unbearable.

I tighten my wings around my head, shutting out the sounds of Rowan coming home from Jake's.

She strokes my feathers and tells me I have not failed. She smooths down my orange neck feathers. They spring back up immediately. She tells me we will talk later, when I feel better. She tells me she loves me.

I hunker down. Tighten my wings even more. I cannot reply. I do not know what to say.

My wings hurt. They are not meant to be folded up around my head for such a long time.

The pain is good. I deserve the pain.

Hours go by.

A day goes by.

Rowan gets ready for work. She kisses me on my folded wings before she leaves. She tells me I have not failed.

The kiss is soft and warm.

I stay folded up in misery even after she leaves.

Finally, I can stand it no longer: if I do not bring my wings back to their natural position, I will be in such pain that I will topple off my perch.

I fold my wings closed. This hurts.

It is dark outdoors.

Everything is quiet.

I should fly a mission tonight, look into the minds of the people. Check on Titus. See what Antwon is doing and thinking.

Why bother? I have failed to keep my origins a secret. Why bother with anything?

I won't fly my mission tonight.

And I won't contact HOP. Not tonight. Maybe not tomorrow night. Or the next or even the one after that.

I do not want FeeOna to know of my failure.

I rip a huge piece off my already-chewed perch and crack the wood into splinters. This feels good. It strengthens my jaw. It makes me feel powerful.

Could a failure feel powerful? Is that possible?

I don't know.

My stomach rumbles. Loudly.

I must be hungry.

Of course I'm hungry, I haven't eaten for a day and a half.

I fly to the kitchen table, where Rowan has bird pellets in a bowl, with fresh drinking water in another bowl. I drink. I eat.

Not enthusiastically. Failures do not eat with gusto.

Despite the food, my stomach still feels empty. Hollow. Like it wants something soft and sweet nestled inside it.

Do-nut.

Could there possibly be any do-nuts left from what Jake brought two days ago?

I fly to the counter and look around.

No box of do-nuts.

But Jake and Rowan left here Saturday night. I am certain there were still do-nuts in a box. Did Jake take them with him?

Jake would not do that. Jake would leave them for Rowan. And me.

So where are they?

I fly to the top of the hutch. The do-nuts are not there.

Cabi-net.

I fly to the first cabi-net, grab the handle with a claw, and flap my wings backwards to pull the door open.

Awwwwkkkk!

I fall over backwards and land on the floor.

But the door is open. I fly up and look inside.

No do-nuts.

I open the door to the second cabi-net.

Awwwwkkkkk! I fall backwards again, but manage to flap my wings and right myself, so that I land feet-first on the floor.

Cabi-nets are stupid devices.

I fly up and look.

Yes! A box of do-nuts!

I try to open the lid. But it won't go all the way up because a stupid shelf stops it.

Shelfs are stupid devices, too.

This will take a while, but I can do it. I clamp my jaw onto the shelf edge and chomp down. *Crack!* A piece of shelf comes off. *Ptui!* I spit it out onto the counter. I chomp down again, tear a piece off, and spit it out. And another and another.

A dish or two falls off, but I manage to jump out of the way.

Finally! I can open the box of do-nuts.

And I do.

Four!

There are four do-nuts in the box, and each do-nut is covered with sprink-les.

I split one do-nut in half with a claw, grab one of the halves, and fly to the table, where I stand and eat the do-nut. There is no way I can hide the chewed-up shelf from Rowan, so why bother eating on the hutch, where she can't see the crumbs?

Besides, lift-off is difficult when I'm carrying half a do-nut. Jake is buying heavier do-nuts every day.

First I eat the sprinkles, one by one. Then I lick the icing off the do-nut. Then I eat the do-nut.

I feel a bit better.

I fly to the cabi-net and bring the second half of the do-nut to the table.

Eating the second half makes me feel another bit better.

I sit there a while, digesting my do-nut and feeling sorry for myself. Then I fly back to the do-nut box.

55 ROWAN

NOLAN IS ON VACATION, IT TURNS OUT, AND MICHAEL is acting as foreman. "I'm going to put you with Paul tonight," he says, "the two of you unloading a 55-footer."

So that's what Paul and I do: set up the conveyor belt and begin unloading packages onto it. Unloading is hard work. Fast work. But nowhere near as non-stop and tense as sorting the small packages.

No overtime tonight for anyone. Lyle drops me off at my front door around 2:10. I unlock the door and walk into the dark house, noticing Deeply's shape on the perch. His wings aren't over his head anymore, so I think he's feeling better. It's been sad to see him so depressed. I wish I had never gotten him to tell us he's from another planet.

Which is so hard to believe.

I'm hoping that, if Jake and I ask him questions about his planet and why he's here, he'll talk to us. Although, judging from his reaction, I don't think so.

I tiptoe into my bedroom, strip off my clothes, and crawl under the sheet.

My sleep is restless. I wake up groggy. Splash some water on my face and walk into the living room.

Deeply appears to be sleeping, so I let him sleep.

I walk into the kitchen.

What the *fuck*?!

Pieces of wood are all over the counter . . . the floor . . . the table . . . even in the sink. Two cabinet doors are open. I see where the wood comes from — one of the shelves has been chewed to pieces. A broken dish is on the floor. So's a broken cup.

I step carefully around the pieces and up close to the shelf. The donut box has been opened. And there are no donuts left.

Not. One.

I hid those donuts so Deeply wouldn't eat them. He's getting plump. That can't be good for a bird.

I stomp back into the living room, ready to take on Deeply.

But I don't.

Because he's sitting on the perch, eyes closed, wings folded over his stomach. He's kind of slouched sideways, and his feathers are all puffed up. I look closer. There's some sort of crud around his nostrils. Deeply's sick.

I rush to my room, grab my phone, and google "sick parrot." The descriptions match how Deeply looks. I try googling what to do, but don't find anything helpful.

Should I take him to a vet?

I go back to his perch and touch his wing. "Deeply," I say softly. "You're sick. Do you know what's wrong?"

"Do-nuts. Deeply hate do-nuts."

He looks so pathetic, like he's really suffering. "Did you eat all four do-nuts?" I ask, though I'm pretty sure that he did.

"Deeply sorry," he rasps. I have to lean close to hear him.

"Should I take you to a doctor?" I ask. "I'm worried about you." I notice that his wings are crossed in front of his stomach. "Does your stomach hurt?"

"No doctor. Stomach hurt. Deeply stupid."

"Do you want to just rest?"

He nods, his eyes already closed, his feathers all puffed out.

I dash down to the basement and find a cardboard box that's a bit bigger than Deeply. Throwing two clean towels into the dryer, I cut the flaps off the box. When the towels are warm I line the box with one of them, bring everything upstairs, and place the box on the piano. Then I pick Deeply up and put him in the box. I cover the outside of the box with the second warm towel.

"Mmmmm," Deeply sighs. "Warm. Warm good."

After a while I see Deeply open his eyes and rearrange his feathers so they're more natural, less puffy. He sips some water. Then he goes back into his box and back to sleep. Every hour or so I replace the towels with warm ones.

When it's time for me to leave for Keisha's, Deeply is still asleep. I tiptoe out of the room as softly as I can.

* * *

Halfway through an orange-colored granny square I run out of mercerized cotton. I look around to see if there's any linen thread anywhere.

There isn't.

"Whatcha looking for?" Keisha asks.

I swear, she can sew a seam and count the number of threads in my granny square at the same time. "Out of thread. But I think there's some yarn here somewhere."

I stand, stash Mom's crochet hooks in my back pocket, step over Antwon's weaving, and start looking through the neatly stacked plastic bins Keisha keeps her projects in. I see one labeled *Rowan*, carefully remove it from the stack, and look inside.

Yarn. But not much of it. And my G, F, and H-sized crochet hooks. I grab the G hook and the yarn and retrace my steps.

Around 8:30 Antwon announces he has a meeting at headquarters. Keisha says she could go for another wine cooler like last week. I could, too. So Antwon walks with us to the bar, promising to join us soon.

Keisha and I find a table and our wine coolers are delivered.

"So," Keish says after a big sip, "how's it going with you and the boxer?" She breaks into her own rendition of the Simon & Garfunkel tune. Dad loved that song.

"Good," I tell her. "What about you and Antwon? For whom I don't have a song."

"Good," she says. "There is no song to describe Antwon."

"Is that good?" I ask, wondering if we're going to beat *good* to death.

She smiles. "It is not good, girl. It is great!"

We clink glasses and talk about my mom coming back.

"We can't wait," Keisha tells me. "Momma's going to cook up a big Welcome Home dinner." She looks at me. "Lainey sounded good?"

I smile at the *good*. "Actually, she did. She sounded like herself. Like she used to be before Dad died." I sip more cooler. "She started to tell me something, then stopped. I never did find out what it was she wanted to say."

Keisha studies me. "What did you sense?"

"Change. That something is different. Like she wanted to warn me, but then decided not to."

Keisha ponders this. "Change can be good."

I nod.

"You don't think . . . she's remarried?" asks Keisha.

I tell Keisha that I did think this. It was the first thought that crossed my mind. "I just don't know," I conclude.

"How will you take it if she did remarry?"

I slosh the remains of the cooler around in my glass, back and forth, back and forth. "I think I'll be okay with it." It would be . . . weird.

Keisha's phone rings. She looks at it and answers. Listens. Says a few *uh-huhs*. Ends the call.

"Antwon," she says. "He can't join us for at least an hour." She looks at me. "I don't want to stay here another hour. Do you?"

"No way," I say, finishing my cooler.

We leave the bar and walk back to Keisha's the same way we came.

It's dark now. An occasional car goes by. A person walks his dog.

I keep an eye out, like I always do, and I know Keisha does, too. We're on a dark street, few of the street lamps working. Keish is to my right, watching for anybody hiding alongside a porch. Watching the alleys. I'm watching the cars to my left.

We're talking at the same time, cause we've been watching the streets like this since we were ten years old. It's a habit. A precaution.

Up ahead is an old white van, parked at an angle, its front partway into the street. I touch Keisha's hand. Nod at the van.

We slow our steps.

Just as Zeb Snoddy steps out from the front of the van.

A gun in his hand.

56 DEEPLEA

I JOLT AWAKE.

Rowan!

Danger!

I hurry out of the comfort of the box and towels, skitter across the piano top, flap my wings, and lift off. Out the window I fly and over the garage, gaining altitude with each frantic pumping of my wings.

I veer southeast and fly as fast as I possibly can, screeching with rage and fear.

57 ROWAN

"DON'T MAKE A SOUND, EITHER OF YOU." SNODDY motions the barrel of his gun toward the back doors of the van. "Inside. And be quick about it."

Keisha and I slowly move away from each other. Sliding one step apart.

We both know what's waiting for us if we step into that van. Rape. Maybe gang rape. Torture. Death.

If we stay on the street, we might die. But we won't be raped or tortured. The street is an uncertainty. The van a certainty.

Snoddy's wearing a black eyepatch. With his one eye, he stares at us. "Move!" he hisses. "I said *Move*!" He steps closer with the gun.

Keish and I take another slide-step apart.

"We aren't going," I tell him.

"Best you leave us alone," Keisha says.

He looks at both of us in astonishment. And hate. And rage.

Snoddy steps toward Keisha, raises his gun, and smashes it down on her face as she's trying to flinch away from it.

I hurtle myself into him as Keish screams.

My force throws Snoddy off balance. He stumbles. The gun drops and clatters across the sidewalk.

"Keish! The gun! Get the gun!" I shout. "Shoot the fucker! Thigh! Pelvis! Don't hit me!"

Snoddy spins toward me, trying to grab me, but I wrap my arms around his waist, keeping behind him.

As he bends down, going for the gun, I scramble onto his back, wrap my left arm around his neck, pull myself up and try to choke him. Cinching my legs around his torso I grab my left hand with my right, pulling tighter. Harder.

I see Keisha crawling toward the gun. She's hurt bad, blood pouring off her face.

Snoddy lurches forward, toward the gun.

I pull harder and harder against his neck. I want to break every bone in his neck. Crush his larynx.

He stumbles forward, me still clinging to his back. He bends, reaching for the gun.

"No you don't, fucker!" shouts Keisha as she throws herself on top of the handgun. She scrunches up over it, protecting it.

Snoddy straightens and spins away from Keisha.

I scream as he punches something sharp into my right thigh. Blood pours out. Wet. Warm. And then he does it again.

The pain's so great I start slipping from his back. But I'll die if I do that.

I pull myself back up, tightening my left arm around his neck.

He stabs me again and I go light-headed, almost faint.

With my right hand I reach into my back pocket. Grab the steel crochet hooks. Wrap my fist around them. Press forward on Snoddy — and jab the needles into his face with all the force and speed I have in me.

Pull them out as fast as I can, so the hooks grab his skin, his muscles, his cheeks, his teeth, I don't care what the fuck they grab, I've got to stop him. I punch in hard, pull out, punch in, pull out. It feels horrible. Punch, squish, pull. Punch, squish, pull. I'm a frenzied machine. Our lives depend on this. I'm never going to stop. Punch, squish, pull.

Now it's Snoddy screaming.

No more stabbing from him.

Only from me.

And then — *thud*!

Snoddy falls and I fall with him, catapulting over his body onto the sidewalk, which feels wet with blood.

I roll face-up and scoot next to Keisha, who's still huddled over the handgun. I touch her leg. "It's me, Keish. Let me take the gun. You can't see."

She rolls upright, sort of, and lets me do that. I point the gun at Snoddy, who isn't moving. With my other hand I touch Keisha's face, wiping away some of the blood. She puts her hand on mine, and with her other hand wipes blood off her eyes.

"We're okay," I whisper to her, my voice shaky. "We made it."

We both look toward Snoddy, who hasn't moved.

Keisha goes to touch her nose, but I stop her. "Don't touch. Your nose is broken. Tip your head back."

She glances down at Snoddy. Pulls away from him.

"What happened? Is he dead?" Her voice is funny, like she has a stuffed head.

"Don't know. We've got to call someone, Keish, or I'll bleed to death. He might have hit an artery. You call, I'll make a video."

I pull my phone out of my other back pocket and pan it over Keisha's face, my face, my blood-red leg. Then I crawl toward Snoddy and scan the phone over him. That's when I notice two crochet hooks lodged in his eyeball.

I think he's . . . dead.

I lean down to hear if he might be breathing. I can't tell. And I'm not going to touch him to see if I can feel a pulse.

That's when I notice his right arm sticking out. There's some sort of knife on one of his fingers. I film that, too. The blade is covered in blood.

Then I put the gun down, next to Snoddy, far away from Keisha and me, and film that, too. As close as I can get, so it can be identified.

Keisha's talking to someone. Titus, probably.

I send the video to Titus. And then to Jake.

We hear police sirens.

Out of nowhere Deeply comes diving from the sky, screeching loud enough to wake the entire block. Porch lights start flicking on.

Deeply lands on Snoddy's back. He looks as if he's going to rip flesh out of him.

"No, Deeps. Leave him be. Urgent mission." I thrust my phone out to him. "Can you take this to Jake? Right away, before the cops get here?"

Deeply hops toward me, opens his mouth, and I hear a small crunch as his beak grabs the phone exactly in the middle. He flaps his wings to take off, but has to try again.

He flies along the sidewalk at a low altitude, just as five or six cop cars turn onto the street from both sides.

Keisha and I put our backs against the wall and our hands on our heads. We're sitting as close together as possible. Taking and giving comfort.

I don't know about her, but all I'm doing is hoping we don't get shot. And that we get medical attention quick.

Deeply reaches streetlamp height.

As the cops jump out of their cars, guns drawn, I watch Deeply's silhouette over the treetops.

58 JAKE

I'M AT MY COMPUTER, HEADPHONES ON AS I STREAM my podcast-making playlist, tapping my feet to the beat.

Something in the background music doesn't belong. A cacophonous rapping. Tapping. The raven at my window?

With a sigh I lift off the headphones and look around.

Deeply is beating his wings against the balcony door. His beak is tapping the glass. Urgently.

I jump up, pull the door open.

"Rowan!" he screeches.

"Phone!" He alights on the balcony table. On which I see a phone.

I pick it up. It looks like Rowan's. It's blood-smeared. My heart races, my throat goes dry. And then I hear a ping from my own phone, informing me I haven't responded to a text.

The message is from Rowan. A video. Keisha's face fills the frame. Her nose is smashed, her eyes are swelling, blood all over.

Then Rowan's face. Which is not bloody. But which is in pain. Then Rowan's leg. A stream of blood.

A body on the ground. A man. The video goes close up and I recognize Snoddy. Something metal projects from his face.

A closeup of something on his finger. Some sort of knife blade. And then a gun.

And then nothing.

"Where is she? Where's Rowan?"

"Am-bu-lance. We go hos-pit-al."

Deeply hops on my shoulder, I slam the door behind us, run directly to the garage, and roar out of the driveway. Deeply directs me to the hospital. He's a live GPS.

We reach the Emergency Room entrance. I don't bother with a parking space, I just leave the car straddling some yellow lines. "Wait by my car," I tell Deeply.

The first person I see is Titus, a woman I assume is his wife, and Antwon, and somebody I don't know: a Black man dressed in a conservative but well-cut business suit.

Attorney.

"Are they okay?" I ask as I rush toward them.

"Rowan sent you the video?" Titus asks.

I nod, waiting for an answer.

"They're both going into surgery. We were about to leave for the waiting room on the OR level." Titus introduces me to his wife, Genevieve, who looks anguished. And to the attorney, Justin Wells, who Titus says will represent both Keisha and Rowan and will be present at all police interrogations of either of them.

I'm trying to process "police interrogations" as the five of us walk to the main part of the hospital.

"Rowan sent you the video?" Titus asks me a second time.

"Yeah. And her parrot brought me her phone."

Titus stops. "This is good: it means the cops didn't confiscate Rowan's phone." He looks at me to see if I understand.

"They might erase the video?" I ask.

Titus nods. "They're on Snoddy's side, they might do anything. Where's the phone?"

"In my apartment."

Titus puts a hand on my shoulder. "Jake. I'd feel better if you'd turn around, go directly home, get the phone, and put it in some safe place. Some *very* safe place. You have such a place?"

"I do. But I'm not leaving until I know about Rowan. How is Keisha?"

Genevieve turns toward me. "She called Titus from her phone, to tell him what happened, where they were. Antwon and Titus were in the car, and they picked me up, and we got there just in time to follow the ambulance."

"So she was conscious," I say. "That's a good sign."

"We got to see her in the emergency room," Antwon tells me. "And Rowan, too." He looks at me. "Rowan wasn't conscious by then. Loss of blood. But they had her on blood transfusion and IV and everything else that needed to be done. She'll make it, Jake. She's strong," he says, trying to reassure me.

My mouth's so dry I can barely talk.

We take the elevator up to the Operating Room level. The attorney, whose name I have to struggle to recall . . . Justin Wells . . . tells us he'll go down to the cafeteria and bring us coffee and whatever else he can find. Antwon goes to help him.

Titus, Genevieve, and I no sooner sit down than a surgeon wearing scrubs and a mask approaches us. Them, actually. He introduces himself and says he'll be operating on Keisha: setting her nose and reconstructing her cheekbone. He's calm and confident, assuring Titus and Genevieve that their daughter will be well, that they can see her briefly after the operation, and certainly they can see her in the morning.

I understand what I need to do, and I'd better act now. Asking the surgeon if he can wait just one second, I turn to Titus and Genevieve and tell them I want to record everything I can — in case Rowan and Keisha need it.

I pull out my camcorder and explain to the surgeon that I'd like to ask him just one question and record his answer, because it might be vital in helping tell the story of what happened tonight.

"Be quick," he instructs.

The lens trained on him, I ask: "Dr. Podlowski, could you tell by looking at Keisha's face what caused her injury?"

He blinks, then takes control. "Certainly. It was a blunt object like a tire iron or barrel of a pistol, brought down on her face with great force, from somebody who was taller than her and standing close to her." He pauses. "Keisha Longshaw told the ER doctors that she was hit with a handgun."

I thank him, but he's already halfway to the door he came from.

Titus and Genevieve and I look at each other. We return to our seats — just as another scrubs-clad surgeon comes out of the swinging doors. He looks around, seems to reject all other possibilities in the room, and decides we're the people he wants to speak to.

"Rowan Pickett?" he asks us.

"Yes," all three of us reply.

"I'm going to stitch Rowan's wounds, give her antibiotics, and keep her on blood transfusion until she no longer needs it. There's no reason she shouldn't be going home three days from now."

Relief overwhelms me: like I was drowning and somebody pulled me out of the water.

Titus nudges me. "The question," he says.

I give Dr. Goldberg the same explanation I gave to Dr. Podlowski. "What would you say caused Rowan's wounds?"

"A short, wide blade. Maybe a knuckle knife or a finger knife. They can do a lot of damage. Luckily she was stabbed just three times. Her artery was most likely nicked, but not punctured. I'm confident she will recover fully."

I nod. Thank him. Turn off the camcorder.

This time when the three of us return to our seats, there aren't any more interruptions.

"Rowan can't possibly have medical insurance," I say to Titus. "I don't see how she can afford it." It's a question. Who's paying for this?

"She doesn't," Genevieve tells me. "But her mother does. I called Lainey a while ago. Rowan's covered."

That's a relief. "What about Snoddy?" I ask.

"Dead," says Titus.

That's an even greater relief.

I clear my throat. "I don't know what happened," I say, "but from the results, Keisha and Rowan are heroes. I want the world to know that."

"The world *needs* to know that," Genevieve says.

"What you got in mind?" Titus asks.

I lean back in the chair and sweep my hand left to right. "The story I see is two young women who have been friends from childhood, walking home one warm July night, enjoying themselves, and then — Zeb Snoddy, fascist bastard, interferes with their lives. Violently. They fight back. They successfully defend themselves. But at a heavy cost. Serious injury."

I look at Titus and Genevieve. "That's the story I want to get out there. The story of self-defense. Heroic self-defense. Right now. For the 6:00 a.m. news. Later, once we talk to Keisha and Rowan, we can get more details. But I want to call my boss, meet her at the studio, and make use of Rowan's video."

Titus thinks about this, but only for a second. "It's a good beginning," he says. Genevieve nods. "You can add on to the story day by day, if necessary?"

"Absolutely. In fact, if Keisha and Rowan are up to it, I'd like to interview them first thing tomorrow morning."

Genevieve gives a half-hearted smile. "Keisha will be wanting to wear one of her creations. I'll bring one with me tomorrow."

"It would play better if she's in her hospital gown," I suggest.

Genevieve sighs. "I'll try."

"Another thing. Do you have any photos of Keisha and Rowan when they were kids? And also a recent one?"

Genevieve pulls out her phone and gets my number.

"Okay, then." I stand. "I'll call my boss now, go home and put Rowan's phone in a safe place, go to the studio." I hesitate. "I probably won't get back here until maybe five or six a.m."

Titus stands. "Don't worry about that," he says, placing a hand on my shoulder. "We'll be looking in on Rowan all night long. We'll let her know you were here, and that you're coming back."

I go to a corner and call Harita, waking her from sleep. After my brief explanation, she agrees to meet me at the studio in an hour. On my way to the elevator I meet Justin Wells and Antwon, who are carrying two trays of food. I grab a coffee, a spinach pie, and a candy bar and eat them as I drive back home.

Halfway there, I realize that Deeply didn't wait for me by the car. I have no idea where he is.

But Deeply can take care of himself, that's for sure.

59 JAKE

"JAKE. I AM FEELING VERY FAINT."

Harita looks white as a surrender flag. I grab her around the waist, drag a chair over with my leg, and lower her into it, pushing her head down toward her knees. All her bangles jingle, maybe in protest. "Keep your head toward your knees," I say. "Take deep breaths."

Hurrying to the refrigerator, I grab a bottle of water and pour some into a cup. "Take sips of water, but come up slowly, and get your head back down. Slowly."

After two or three minutes Harita carefully raises herself to a sitting position.

"You did not tell me there was blood," she explains. "I feel faint at the sight of blood."

"But — you watch boxing matches." I try to not sound astonished.

"Those are not up close, Jake. The blood looks far away."

"I'm sorry," I say. "About the blood. I guess I'm used to it."

She takes a slow, deep breath. "You have seen this video before, Jake. So I will watch, but please stop it before there's any blood. I will look away, and you describe to me what is on the screen. Yes?"

"Right. Let's start over, and I'll stop it before the bad parts."

Before Harita arrived at the studio I was busy for at least half an hour, putting together something that might run on the news. The first thing we see is a photo of Keisha and Rowan when they're maybe six or seven. They're standing together, smiling: both of them missing their front teeth.

"That is sweet," whispers Harita.

This fades to a picture of the two in their tweens, wearing White Sox shirts and caps. Standing with Titus and Rowan's father, whom I recognize from the photos around her house. I like that Genevieve sent me the middle photo, which I didn't think to ask for. The transition is stronger this way.

Another fade, this time to a photo from Keisha's high school graduation, with Keisha and Rowan mugging for the camera.

"I hear the voiceover something like this," I tell Harita. *"Friends since grade school . . . their lives entwined with love and trust . . . Keisha Longshaw and Rowan Pickett were walking home last night, talking about innocent things. Sewing. Crocheting. When suddenly they were confronted by Zeb Snoddy, head of POW: Patriotic Owners of Weapons. The admitted Nazi worshipper Snoddy stopped both young women at gunpoint."*

"That is an evil picture of Snoddy," says Harita, pointing to a still I created from the gun-control rally. "It would strike fear into my heart, to be confronted by this man."

"The business of him pulling a gun, Harita — I haven't been able to verify that with Rowan or Keisha yet, but Keisha told the medics that Snoddy smashed her face with a handgun." I look at Harita. "Are you okay running with my inference?"

She nods. "I would make the same one. And Highland Studios wants this out ASAP, Jake." She glances at her watch, which is tucked in there somewhere among the bangles. "Six a.m. would be great. Zeb Snoddy is dead, and that is big news."

"We've got to make Rowan and Keisha's heroism bigger news."

She nods. We're silent a moment, thinking.

"Let's continue" she says. "And remember to warn me." She takes a sip of water and wipes her hands on her dress. Her bangles make a soft, jingling sound that I find reassuring.

"I see it going down like this: *Whatever it was Snoddy wanted of Keisha and Rowan, he didn't get it. Because they fought back in this life-and-death struggle.*" I warn Harita to look away, and she does, just as a still of Keisha, her face all bloody, comes up. Followed by Rowan's face and then her leg. Throughout the video we hear the distinct sound of ragged breathing. The breathing adds an undertone of pain.

"*As the struggle went on,*" I continue, "*Keisha and Rowan were badly injured. Zeb Snoddy crushed Keisha Longshaw's nose and cheekbone with the handgun he was pointing at them. He lacerated Rowan Pickett's right leg with the illegal finger knife he was wearing.*" A still of the finger knife on Snoddy's hand.

"Horrible," Harita breathes, sneaking a peek, then quickly lowering her head.

I run down the rest of the rough narrative that's in my head, making it brief because that's what the news networks want. Ending with: "*Although the two young women were unarmed, they fought back. Fought for their lives. When the attack was over, it was Zeb Snoddy who lay dead.*"

I finished with a side-by-side: Snoddy's evil face next to Keisha and Rowan from the high school graduation.

Fade to black.

"Good," says Harita. "The voice track is separate?"

"It's not even recorded. I'm not a narrator. Except maybe in Boston. But I have it written out," I say, handing her the transcript.

She smiles. "It's a bit repetitive about struggle and fighting back. Are you okay with my editing the copy and sending it to the news networks?"

"Absolutely."

"The networks may write their own narrative, but I'm betting they will be guided by what you've done."

She studies me. Long enough that I know something's bothering her.

"Jake, how did you get this video?"

"Rowan messaged it to me."

"So it was she who took it, just seconds after it was over?"

"Must have been," I say.

Harita breathes in. "What presence of mind, Jake . . . to react so quickly . . . at such a horrible time."

"Yeah." I'm thinking I don't know how Rowan did it. Any of it. I'm so grateful she's alive that I haven't spent much time thinking about how it all went down.

Except that Rowan killed Snoddy.

With her crochet hooks.

It's the only explanation.

"She is very much like you," continues Harita. "Great presence of mind."

"*Harita!*" I shout. "I just remembered — I have Rowan's phone, and I need to put it in a safe place. Can we keep it in the office safe?"

"What?" she asks. "Slow down, Jake. What do you mean you have Rowan's phone? The phone with which she took the video? How can that be?"

Think, Jake, think. "Rowan has a trained parrot," I explain, hoping Deeply's nowhere around to hear me. "She gave the phone to the parrot and the parrot flew to me. At home. It knows where I live," I finish lamely as I notice the look on Harita's face.

"I don't believe this, Jake."

I don't say anything.

"Let me see the phone."

I reach into my pocket to bring out the phone in its plastic bag, but then I remember — the phone is covered in blood. I tell as much to Harita.

She shakes her head. "I need to see this, Jake. I cannot take your word on such a preposterous explanation. I cannot release this video if there is something funny going on. Something illegal. Were you there?"

"No, Harita. I wasn't there. And preposterous though it sounds, what I told you is true."

She shakes her head so vigorously that all her bangles set up a tintinnabulation. She doesn't believe me.

I need to get going. I need to leave the video we just created with Harita, need to put the phone in a secure place, need to get home and work on a video for the Facebook page Antwon's probably created by now, and post it on X, YouTube, and everywhere else, need to make a podcast, and then I need to see Rowan and interview her and Keisha and . . .

"I have a video of her parrot," I tell Harita. "Just for fun, I started to interview him one day." I pull out my camcorder, find Deeply Interview-1, and show it to her. Not all of it, but just the first minute or so.

Harita's mouth falls open. When I remove the camcorder to turn it off, she reaches out for it.

I ignore her reach. "I don't have time to show you the whole interview," I say. "But you can see that the parrot is big — big enough to carry a smartphone in its beak. And you can see that the parrot is smart — smart enough to know where I live and smart enough to bring me the phone.

"And," I add, "I wouldn't lie to you about this. What happened with Rowan, Keisha, and Snoddy tonight is too serious for me to fuck it up with a lie."

She looks at me. "I am assuming that she sent you the phone because . . . she didn't want the police to have it?"

"That's what I assume, too."

Harita nods slowly. "In case they might . . . tamper with it. Or lose it. Or deny it exists."

I wait.

Harita stands. "Follow me. We can put the phone in the safe."

I follow, she opens the safe, I put the phone inside, she closes the safe. "What are you going to do now?" she asks.

"Go home, create a video, make a podcast, then interview Rowan and Keisha in the hospital."

"Message me each interview video as you complete it," she says. "I can keep the story alive by feeding it to the news in bits and pieces."

I agree to that and am on my way out the door when she calls me back.

"Jake. The police will question you. They will want to know how you got the video. They may even ask you if you know where Rowan's phone is."

"I'll tell the truth: that Rowan messaged me the video. If they want to know where Rowan's phone is, they'll have to ask Rowan."

She smiles. "Or a large parrot."

"Correct."

She hands me a business card. "That is the attorney for Highland Studios. I will call her at seven this morning, let her know that you might need representation. If you run into trouble, call her immediately. Then call me."

60 DEEPLEA

I CANNOT READ MINDS THAT AREN'T CONSCIOUS.

Rowan's mind is closed to me. As is Keisha's.

I read Jake's mind and know that Rowan and Keisha are alive.

I switch my receptors to Titus and learn that Rowan and Keisha are being operated on, that neither is in danger of dying.

I fly a circle around the hospital, until I know I am close to Titus. I land on a window ledge and see him inside. Antwon is there, too. And Genevieve.

Walking backwards, I wedge myself into a corner of the ledge. A pigeon lands on the ledge, takes one look at me, and flies away.

I will wait here until Rowan is awake. All night and all day if necessary.

61 ROWAN

I SENSE SUNLIGHT ON MY EYELIDS. I SHOULD OPEN MY eyes. But it's easier not to.

Somebody taps my face. Over and over. So annoying.

I force my eyes open for a second. There's a bald-headed person sitting in a chair close to me. Maybe holding my hand, I can't tell. There's a nurse standing next to me. Tapping my face.

"Wake up, Rowan. We let you skip breakfast, but you need to eat lunch. Come on, I'll help you."

I make no effort to get up. Waking up does not interest me.

"Would you rather your mother helped you?" the nurse asks.

Mother?

Mom! The bald-headed person! "Mom?"

She squeezes my hand, leans forward and kisses my forehead. "You're going to be fine, Rowan. But you need to eat. I ordered you scrambled eggs, bacon, and toast." She moves her chair closer to me.

The nurse tilts the bed upward and pushes a tray across the bed. She sort of lifts me by the shoulders and pulls me up.

I see a glass of water with a straw in it. I reach for the glass with both hands, put the straw in my mouth, and drink. And drink. Until the nurse takes it away from me. "Slowly," she says. "Eat a little, then drink more water. Your mother will help you." She leaves the room.

"Mom. You're here." My throat's so dry I can hardly talk. My lips stick together.

"Keisha!" My shout comes out like a croak.

Mom rubs my arm. "She's doing well. And she's just four doors down the hall from you."

I nod. Force away the images. The fear.

Mom squeezes my hand. Tries to get a spoonful of scrambled eggs into my mouth. I push them away. "What day is it? Is it two weeks already?"

"No, of course not," she says, slipping a spoonful of eggs into my mouth as I'm talking. "Genevieve called me and I flew in this morning. It's 1:00 p.m. Wednesday."

She feeds me more scrambled eggs. I eat them. I pick up a piece of bacon and eat it too. It's dry and scratchy and has no taste at all. I sip more water. Nibble on a half-piece of buttered toast. Then I take the spoon from Mom and eat more scrambled eggs. I see the orange juice and drink it. Slowly.

I do everything slowly, but eventually I eat all the eggs, toast, and bacon.

"Mom," I say after a while. "What happened to your hair? Are you sick?"

"I'm not sick, Rowan. I shaved my head, that's all."

"Oh." I see coffee and drink it. Awful coffee. "There's applesauce, too," Mom says. "And what looks like tapioca pudding. Do you want them."

I push myself up more, reach onto the tray, pick up the applesauce, and pull the lid off. Mom reaches over to help me but I tell her I'll do it. The applesauce is sweet and good. There's not enough of it.

Mom has already opened the pudding. She hands it to me.

"You said you might do that," I say, remembering. "You said you might shave your head."

"I'm glad you remember that. I'm so sorry I left you, Rowan. And never called."

"You called last week. Didn't you?" I think she did. Things are fuzzy.

She nods. "Yes. On Saturday. And then again on Sunday and Monday and Tuesday."

I look at her. She looks weird with no hair. But she looks like Mom — Mom with no hair. "Do they mind at your job? That you're bald? It looks kinda weird, Mom."

She laughs. "Yes, I imagine it does. I wear a wig to work."

"Oh." I nod. "That's smart."

Work. Wednesday. I'm scheduled. I'll have to call in, tell them . . . I'm in the hospital.

We sit there a while in silence. My mind goes back to the day Mom left. She said something else. She might shave her head . . . she might . . .

I glance down at her arms. They're covered with cuts, like cutters do at school. Small narrow scars all up and down each arm.

Tears fall down my face.

Mom stands up and hugs me. I hug her back. "Shhh. It's okay, Rowan. They don't hurt anymore. And they helped me heal. I'll be home soon, and that's all I need to be completely better. To be home and to be the mother I should have been, but couldn't be." She strokes my hair. Lingers at Clari's feather. "But I can be now. And I will be."

I kind of blubber a bit. "What about your work?" I ask, trying to sit straighter in the bed. "Do they ask you about the scars?"

Mom sits back down. "I wear long-sleeved shirts."

I remember something else. "You said you might build a shrine."

Mom nods. "And I did." She hesitates. "Do you want to see a picture of it?"

I shake my head. "No. Not now. But later, yeah."

Something to my right attracts my attention. There's Deeply, sitting on the window ledge. "Deeps!" I shout.

Mom looks at me worriedly.

"That's the parrot I was tell—" I stop what I'm saying because two cops walk in the door.

Mom stands and turns toward them. "You cannot question my daughter without her attorney present," she tells them. "At the moment her attorney is in Keisha Longshaw's room. As soon as he finishes there, he'll come here." She moves toward them. "In the meantime, please wait outside this room."

They don't like it, not one bit. But they turn and walk out of the room. Just as Jake steps into it.

"Rowan!" He walks right around Mom, sits on the bed, and puts his arms around me.

And then Jake also notices Deeply on the window ledge. He gets up, opens the window, and Deeply flies onto my shoulder and makes cooing sounds into my ear, nibbling it gently, pecking me gently on the head, pulling my hair in his beak, chirping and cooing nonstop until I laugh and laugh and laugh.

62 JAKE

AFTER ROWAN INTRODUCES ME TO HER MOTHER AND after I tell Deeply he has to either hide under the bed or go back to the window ledge (he chooses the ledge), and after the WCC attorney Justin Wells enters the room, Titus with him, and after two cops enter to question Rowan, I set up my camcorder. The cops don't like that. In fact, they protest. Justin Wells just stares at them.

The cops tell Titus he can't be present.

Rowan says she wants him there.

The cops ask Rowan to describe what happened. She does.

This is the first I'm hearing it from her. I zoom in on her face. And on the blood bag that's dripping into her arm.

It's hard to listen to, what she and Keisha went through. Titus looks grim. He's heard it from Keisha already, now he's hearing Rowan's version. I glance over at Lainey, who's almost as pale as Rowan.

"Where did the video come from?" one cop asks.

"What video?" Rowan asks.

The cop pulls out a phone, makes a few selections, and shows something — the video, I presume — to Rowan. Who flinches away after a couple of seconds.

"I took that with my phone," she says. "The minute Snoddy wasn't moving, I grabbed my phone and took a video of everything around us. Him. His gun. The knife on his finger. Keisha's face. My leg. Everything."

"Why?" asks the cop.

"Filming the crime scene."

Titus nods in approval.

"Then what?" asks the cop.

"Then I messaged the video to Titus. And to Jake. That's Jacob Terranova." She tilts her head toward Titus, then me.

"Why?"

"Because I trust them to preserve evidence of the crime scene."

"There was only one phone present at the scene," the cop informs her. "It belonged to Keisha Longshaw. There was no video on it."

"I took the video with my phone," Rowan says, "and my phone was there with me."

"We found no other phone on the scene."

Rowan shrugs.

"Where's your phone now?" asks the cop.

"I don't know," she answers. Which comes across as the truth, because of course she doesn't know where it is.

They keep this up a while, but not for too long because Justin Wells intervenes, telling them his client has had enough for one day. The cops leave, but not without saying they'll be back.

Wells waits until they're good and gone, then assures us he'll be back tomorrow.

Titus stands, comes over to the bed, and squeezes Rowan's hand. "I am eternally grateful that WCC provides self-defense classes, and that you and Keisha took them."

"Me, too," says Rowan. "How's Keisha?" she asks him. "Is she going to be okay? Can I see her?"

"She looks a lot worse than you do," Titus tells her. "But she'll be okay. Her room is 624. She's been asking about you." He looks at her. "We are very proud of you and Keisha," he says, his voice choking. "Now you get some rest, Rowan. Genevieve and I will visit later."

Titus and Wells say goodbye to me and Lainey and depart as quietly and efficiently as they entered.

Lainey gets up and sits on the bed, stroking Rowan's hair. I get it on the camcorder. "I'll buy you a new phone," she says.

Rowan hesitates. "Can you afford it?"

"I have a few hundred dollars saved up."

I interrupt. "Rowan," I say. "It will be good for you and Keisha if I can interview you now, right after the event. I've already interviewed Keisha and Titus and Genevieve and Antwon. I won't ask you to repeat anything, I've got a lot on video already. But I could ask you an extra question or two. If you feel you need to rest, though, I can come back in a couple of hours. You look like you need to rest."

"Jake," she says back to me. "You look pretty terrible yourself. Are you okay?"

"Just lack of sleep. Barely had time to shower, no time at all to shave."

"After you interview me, will you go home and get some sleep?"

"I promise I'll get some sleep. Might be home, might be here in the waiting room, might be at the studio."

Lainey moves her chair away from the bed, into the far corner of the room. "I'll stay here while you interview my daughter," she says.

My first thought is that this could be a problem. Not here, today, but later, when Rowan and I want to be alone. But then I think that's unfair, that if I were in a hospital bed my mother would want to stay in the room and oversee any interviews, too.

I set up a chair close to Rowan and look at her critically. Her hair's just unkempt enough, her color just pale enough. I lean over and pull up one shoulder of her hospital gown. "Not too much shoulder exposure," I say. "I want people to concentrate on what you're saying."

"What about Keisha?" she asks. "Did you determine her clothing, too?"

"As if." I check what's in the frame, then move the blood drip closer to Rowan so it'll always be in the frame. Then I start the camcorder.

"Zeb Snoddy had a gun aimed at you and Keisha," I say, "with intent to do harm to both of you. Neither you nor Keisha were armed. What do you think enabled the two of you to survive?"

Rowan looks into the camera. "A few years ago Keisha and I took some self-defense classes for women. At the Y, and also at WCC headquarters. That's Working Class Control headquarters. One of the things we learned was, Never go where the man with the gun wants you to go. Don't get in his car. Don't step into a building with him. That is certain death. With rape and torture before your death."

She takes a deep breath. "He might shoot you right there on the street if you don't do what he wants. Maybe he will, maybe he won't. But he will absolutely kill you if you go with him." Another ragged breath.

"So Keisha and I wouldn't get into the van. He ordered us twice, I think. When we refused, he smashed Keisha in the face with his gun." She bites her lips. "That meant he wasn't looking at both of us, which meant I had a second to act. And I did. Because . . .," she says sucking in a ton of air, "I didn't want to die. That was our only chance. To not die."

She turns away from the camera, wipes her eyes.

It's hard for me to stay behind the camcorder. I take several deep breaths. I hear Lainey crying.

Rowan turns back to the camera. Waits.

"Are you sorry you ended up killing a man?" I ask.

She thinks about the question a moment. "I'm sorry we live in a society in which women are victims of violence. In which some men think women are there to be beaten, raped, tortured. That's what I'm most sorry about. I'm not sorry when the intended victims fight back. I'm not sorry when evil is defeated." She pauses. "The only way to a better world is to know who and what is evil. And to defeat it."

She stops. I turn off the camcorder and take Rowan's hand. The one that's not full of IV drip needles. "You gonna be okay?" I ask her softly.

She nods. "Phone?" she mouths to me.

"Safe," I whisper.

I stand. "I need to take a look at this and send it to the studio. Then I've got to meet with Antwon about updating the social media posts." I turn toward Rowan's mother. "But before I leave, I'd like to interview you, Lainey. If that's okay with you?"

Lainey wipes here eyes and seems to think about it. Finally she nods.

I get the videocam rolling and on her own she brings up Snoddy harassing Rowan at the Illinois State Championship when Rowan was sixteen. She mentions the name of the runner-up, who stepped between Snoddy and Rowan. I had intended to look this up, but Lainey is saving me the trouble. I'll find the guy and interview him if he's willing.

When it's over, I realize that Lainey's interview was great. It adds perspective, shows that Snoddy waiting for Rowan was something planned. Something that had been going on for years. He was stalking her.

I thank Lainey and stand up. Sort of stagger up. I've got to catch a few Z's.

I turn to say goodbye to Rowan, but she's asleep.

Lainey gives me a smile. "Good time for me to duck out and buy her a phone."

63   DEEPLEA

HOP: Where have you been, DeePlea? I have been so worried about you.

Me: Rowan was attacked, HOP. Also her friend Keisha, who is the daughter of Titus Longshaw. It was a life-threatening situation . . . I have been very busy. Which is why I didn't report.

HOP: DeePlea, that is terrible.

Me: Rowan and Keisha are alive. The man who attacked them is not.

HOP: If someone must be dead, then I am glad it is the attacker. [Pause] How is it that this was allowed to happen, Dee? Aren't you protecting Rowan?

Me: Do not worry, HOP. I came to her aid. I helped her.

HOP: That is good. [Pause] Were you not tuned in to Rowan's mind? Did you not sense she was in danger?

Me: Yes, HOP, but not in time. As you know, it is difficult to tune in to more than three minds at once. And I must keep at least one of my three channels free, to roam at will on anything that might happen. The other two are reserved for moving between Rowan, Titus, Antwon, and . . . others. However, as I said, I did get to Rowan in time to help.

HOP: Good. [Distracted] I have missed you, Dee, but I'm afraid I must make this conversation brief. The chicks are calling, and you know how loud that can be.

Me: I hear them. Can they see yet?

HOP: Yes, since this morning. [Moving from in front of the mirror.] Say something and they will focus their eyes on you.

Me: Hello, chicks. This is your father, talking to you from Earth. [Excitedly] They are looking at me!

HOP: Of course. And do you see that each of them is covered with very slight fuzz?

Me: Yes! Can you tell yet what colors the feathers will be?

HOP: It is too soon. I must go, Dee. Report to me again tomorrow.

Me: I will. Bye chicks! Bye FeeOna.

[Mirror contact ends]

Me: [Big sigh of relief]

I fly to my perch and pace, avoiding the ragged end where I tore out chunks of wood. As long as FeeOna does not replay this conversation in her head and ask for specifics, I will be fine.

No parrot in the history of our planet has ever had such a difficult DU. I can see why our species left this place millions of years ago.

64 ROWAN

I THINK THAT WHEN YOU'RE IN A HOSPITAL TIME usually passes slowly. For me it zooms by at the speed of a Package Nova conveyer belt. I'd like it to slow down so that I can catch another nap.

Mom gives me a new phone. That excites me. I download all my contact information from the Cloud. Texts all over the place. There's one from Lyle, informing me he told Vic and Nolan why I wouldn't be reporting to work this week. I text him back: **BIG THX!**

A doctor walks in and introduces himself as the person who operated on me: Dr. Goldberg. I thank him and shake his hand.

"When can I go home?"

"Maybe tomorrow, most likely Friday. We need to observe your healing to make certain there's no damage we might have missed."

"When can I go back to work? I'm a package handler at Package Nova."

He frowns. "Can they assign you to desk duty for three or four weeks?"

Desk duty? He's got to be kidding.

"No. But they can probably *not* assign me to heavy sorting for a while. Keep me standing up, sorting small packages as they come down the conveyor belt. Stuff that weighs less than a pound."

He shakes his head. "I don't want you standing on that leg for hours on end. For the next two weeks I want you using a crutch, so it bears most of the weight. I have you scheduled for physical therapy tomorrow. They'll show you everything you need to know.

"So, returning to work," he repeats, "at least three weeks. When you're discharged you'll receive an appointment slip telling you when to see me for a followup evaluation."

I nod.

Mom asks him if there will be any permanent damage from the knife wounds. He says most likely not.

I sit there and worry about not having a job for three weeks.

"Rowan," says Mom, who can probably read my mind, "there's money in the savings account."

"That's for property taxes, Mom. I can't use it."

"You can in an emergency, and this is an emergency."

I shake my head. "The reason I can't use it is that I can't replace it."

She thinks about that. Probably wondering if she should remind me that she told me months ago to find a job.

"I can send you something each week for the next three weeks. Fifty for sure," she says. "And when I come home I'm pretty sure I can get my old job back. Or one like it. So we'll have two incomes."

This makes me feel better. "You'll be home a week from this coming Monday," I say, sort of counting the time in my head.

The look on Mom's face tells me I'm wrong. "What?" I demand. "What aren't you telling me?"

She stands alongside my bed, looking down at me. Advantage of height. I push the bed-raising button until I'm almost as high as she is. "Tell me."

"I have to work longer than the two weeks. Because I want you covered by medical insurance, and we won't have any after I quit my job. You're going to have appointments with Dr. Goldberg, you're going to have physical therapy, and probably follow-ups. I'm going to work in Tucson until you don't need any more physical therapy or doctor's appointments. Then I'll come home, I promise."

She's right. I can't afford to pay for the doctor or for physical therapy.

I sigh. "I was really looking forward to having you home, Mom. But I understand. And I'm sure glad you have health insurance."

She sits down and I lower the bed. We both laugh.

"When do you leave for Tucson?"

"Sunday night," she says. "Assuming you're home and can take care of yourself."

As we're talking MaryEllen walks in the room. She hugs Mom and the two of them talk nonstop. This makes me laugh inside — I'm the patient here. Eventually MaryEllen realizes that and turns her attention to me.

And then — it's like fifteen trucks have pulled into the loading docks at once. Visitors start coming in. So many that the nurses bring two more in every fifteen minutes, asking the previous two to leave. There's a whole stream of comrades from the WCC: Rafael, Sofia, Angela, Max, Devon. I'm so happy to see each of them.

As people come and go I catch glimpses of Deeply outside the window, tucked into the corner of the ledge. Each time I catch his eye, I raise my eyebrow as a kind of greeting. In reply he raises the turquoise feathers just above his eyes. He looks so funny doing this that I laugh. Even through the closed window I can hear him laugh in return. *Cha-haha, cha-haha.*

I'm super surprised when Zari from Package Nova walks in the door. She brings me a huge plastic container full of pierogi she made at home. Just for me. Mom says she'll take them home and I can eat them there.

Zari tells me that all the women at work are talking about what happened to Keisha and me. "You did right thing," she says. "Strong."

I smile at that. "And I'll be stronger after I eat your pierogi. Thank you so much for coming."

"When you come back to work, we have small party. Eat pierogi."

Sounds great to me.

And then Mateo comes. Both Zari and Mateo are such surprises. They've known me not even two months. Mateo brings me an aloe plant.

"For . . uh . . . smaller injuries," he says. He tells me that he's eager for me to return because he likes working with me. That makes me feel so good!

Finally there's a break in visitors, I take a nap, and then Mom wakes me to say that dinner's about to be brought in.

She ordered me a hamburger, fries, salad, and Coke. She knows I like these things. But I'm not salivating over them, mainly because I don't have that much of an appetite.

I eat slowly, making myself chew the food so it's easier to digest. I finish half the burger, half the fries, half the Coke. Then I simply can't eat any more.

And then three women walk in the door at once. Madison, Isabelle, and Ana, from the Stop Violence Against Women steering committee. They give me a dozen red roses and turn the gift card so I can read it. **You struck a blow for all of us.**

I introduce them to Mom, who knows Isabelle from rallies to defend abortion rights. Ana tells me I'm a hero. Isabelle asks when I can attend a steering committee meeting again. Madison says they want me to speak at the planned Stop Violence Against Women rally next month.

"You have to ask Keisha, too. We saved each other."

They assure me they'll visit Keisha immediately and ask her. So I say yes, I'll do it.

And then Lyle walks in the door, carrying what I instantly recognize as a milkshake. I introduce Lyle to everyone. He can't seem to take his eyes off Madison. When he finally does, he hands me the milkshake.

Chocolate. I have no trouble drinking the whole thing.

"Thank you, Lyle. I really appreciate it."

A nurse comes in and tells us we're being too loud and that four people will have to leave. She stands there until they do.

Soon I'm alone with Mom. We look at each other and laugh.

I ring the nurse buzzer, and when she comes in I tell her I want to walk down the hall to see Keisha. The nurse's face says this is not gonna happen.

She tells me I can try walking tomorrow, when I get a crutch in physical therapy. For now I'm required to travel in a wheelchair.

She goes to get one, helps me into it — for which I'm secretly glad, because my leg really hurts. Plus there's the stupid drip tubes to contend with.

The nurse pushes me and a pole with my IV hookups down the hall. Just four doors down, into Keisha's room. Mom follows.

Keisha's room is almost as crowded as mine was. Just not as noisy.

"Keish!" I wheel my chair up to her and grab her hand, the one without tubes in it. I squeeze really hard. So does she. There are bandages all across her nose and halfway across her face. Her left cheekbone is totally covered in bandages and over that there's a plastic shield of some kind. Her nose has a shield on it, too.

"Rowan, you'll never guess what — every single one of my pieces at Kutt Klothes has sold. Today. In one day. Every single piece!" Her voice is kind of muffled.

"Wow, that's great, Keish!"

Titus and Genevieve are in the room and they smile at Keisha's enthusiasm. Antwon's there, too. He looks proud. Mom sits next to Genevieve and they begin to talk.

I notice that Keisha's wearing one of her own designs, a kind of loose blazer with no buttons or closures of any kind. It's in shades of purple, probably some sort of dyed silk. And there's a beautiful collar made out of the "elegant" gray granny squares I crocheted. Wow! If I were into designer clothes, I'd have to say this piece was stunning. And Keisha looks beautiful in it. Even with all the bandages and face shields.

I notice a large paper tablet on Keisha's lap, and a pencil in her hand. I recognize them as what she doodles on when she's designing clothes.

"You're *working*?" I ask in amazement.

"Demand, Rowan. There's a demand for my clothing. And Jake helped create that demand."

Titus guffaws. "I'll say he did."

"Jake?" I ask. "How?"

Keisha rolls the one eye I can see clearly. "Not only did he film me in the piece I'm wearing," she says, pointing to her blazer, "but he filmed every single one of the pieces I had hanging on the wall. Momma brought them for me to choose from." She points to the wall behind her. "My designs were on ABC, NBC, and CBS. And other networks, too. One *day*, Rowan. I had seventeen pieces at Kutt Klothes and every one sold."

She points her pencil at me. "I'll be designing all night long."

"No you won't," says Genevieve. "You will go to sleep when the lights go out, you will get a good night's rest, and you can start designing again right after breakfast. And if you don't, child, I will make certain the nurses give you enough knockout drops to make sure you do!"

"I'm going to need more granny squares," Keisha says to me. "When do you think you—" She stops. "Oh. Maybe you don't . . . ?"

Total silence in the room.

I clear my throat. "I can crochet with the little aluminum hooks. B, C, D . . . ." My voice trails off.

Keisha looks at me. "You sure? You don't have to if you don't want to."

"If I didn't, your sales would plummet. It's all about the granny squares."

She grins. "Okay. I can make something out of your thick, yarn-y granny squares." Then she turns serious. "But I hope you feel strong enough to use the other hooks soon, Rowan. We can't let him win."

I nod. Keisha is right. But just now I'm not ready to pick up a cold steel crochet hook. Aluminum will get me started again, and then . . . I'll see. I'd have to buy new steel hooks anyway. This could be the first time ever I'm grateful for not having enough money.

I squeeze Keisha's hand again. "How are you feeling?"

She shakes her head gently. "No pain right now. But it will come. I'm sure it will come." She looks at me and gives my hand a squeeze so hard I think she's breaking my bones. "How are *you* feeling?"

"Some pain, but not much. I'm sorry you're hurt worse than me, Keish. I'm sorry you'll feel more pain than me."

She's still holding my hand as if she'll never let go. "This is my role in life, Rowan. Because I'm a year older than you are."

Everyone in the room laughs. Nobody harder than Keisha and me.

✳ ✳ ✳

The next day the nurses unhook me from everything. I go to physical therapy and receive a single crutch. More visitors come. When they aren't there, I practice walking on the crutch, back and forth, back and forth. I realize there's no way I can sort packages while on a crutch, so I resign myself to three weeks of no work.

The nurses show Mom and me how to change the bandages on my leg and how to apply new ones.

Late Friday morning I'm discharged from the hospital with a long list of things to watch for on my wounds; appointments here, there, and everywhere; and a list of Do's and Don'ts. Jake picks up Mom in his car and brings her to the hospital and takes the two of us home. He still hasn't shaved. Sexy.

Keisha's also discharged. She tells me she's taking a week off work to heal and sew more clothes, and then she'll go back full-time.

Full-time has such a nice ring to it.

I'll probably have to start my probationary period all over again when I get back to Package Nova.

65 JAKE

I FIGURE ROWAN SHOULDN'T BE STANDING AND COOK-
ing dinner, and I figure Lainey's exhausted, so when I take them home I offer to make an Italian dinner. Lainey hesitates, but Rowan's enthusiastic and that seals it.

Deeply is sitting on his perch, observing everything. He's quiet, though. Maybe doesn't want to talk in front of Lainey? Rowan and I should be talking to him, asking him about his planet and what he's doing here on Earth. But right now that seems weirdly secondary.

And I suspect Deeply wouldn't tell us anyway.

At the Italian grocery store I buy everything I need, plus some. Like biscotti for dessert, fresh strawberries, and a pound of Italian roast coffee. Which I could use a vat of right now.

When I return to Rowan's, MaryEllen is there. Rowan's lounging on the couch, legs extended. Lainey starts to put away the food. I ask MaryEllen about Patrick and she says he's on the road, won't be home until Sunday. I glance at Lainey, wondering if she can read my mind about inviting MaryEllen to dinner.

Lainey smiles and says, "From the look of it Jake's bought enough food so that you could have dinner with us tonight, MaryEllen."

All right — we're cooking on the same burner here.

We move into the living room to be with Rowan. I sit on the couch with her, putting her feet across my thighs. "Elevation," I say. "Good for recovery."

She wiggles her toes in approval.

Deeply turns on his perch so that he's facing us.

"I thought you said your parrot talked," says Lainey. "I haven't heard him say one word."

We all look at Deeply. "Cracker!" he squawks.

Which astonishes Lainey, but after a second she goes to the kitchen and returns with a cracker. She holds it out tentatively. Deeply takes it and bites into it. Lainey seems satisfied with that.

She fluffs Rowan's pillow and asks if she's comfortable. Rowan replies she is. Lainey asks her if she wants anything and Rowan wonders if they could go out to buy mercerized linen thread tomorrow. Whatever *mercerized* is. I look it up on my phone. *Adjective (of cotton fabric or thread) treated under tension with caustic alkali to impart strength and luster.*

Talk about apropos.

"I'll go," Lainey tells Rowan. "You just tell me what you want. You stay home and stay off that leg. Except for your therapy exercises."

There's a knock on the door. A neighbor coming to see Rowan. And then there's another. And another. It seems the whole street comes by to see how she's doing.

By 4:00 everybody's gone except Lainey and MaryEllen, Rowan and me. Lainey walks over to the piano, sits down, and tests a few keys. Then she adjusts herself on the piano bench and next thing I know the room is filled with Joplin's "The Entertainer." Followed by "Maple Leaf Rag," and that's followed by a whole slew of piano boogie-woogie tunes, some of which I recognize, most of which I don't.

MaryEllen smiles. Rowan keeps time with her foot, and I tap my fingers on the arm of the couch. Lainey's a good player.

I happen to glance at Deeply, and he's in parrot heaven, bopping his head in and out, back and forth, swaying left-right, left-right in perfect time to the music. At the end of each number he lets out a whistle of appreciation. Which makes Lainey laugh.

Finally she finishes and spins on the piano stool to face us.

"Mom, that was great!" says Rowan. "I've missed your playing."

"I didn't know if I still had music in me," Lainey answers. "I needed that." She stands. "Jake, I'll be happy to be your sous chef if you want. I've missed cooking real meals, too."

I lift Rowan's feet off my lap and walk toward the kitchen. "Some help will be great."

Lainey takes charge of the garlic bread and I tell her what's going into the salad — escarole, tomatoes, and crumbled Gargonzola, with a dressing of olive oil, red wine vinegar, and mustard. In no time the garlic bread and salad are done. Lainey calls Rowan and MaryEllen to the table, I pour some Pinot Grigio, and we polish off the huge salad.

Deeply flies to the top of the hutch, which startles Lainey.

"It's okay, Mom. Deeply likes to sit and observe."

I started the pasta water before we sat down, so when we're finished with the salad I toss the linguine into the water, and when it's almost done I sauté lots of garlic that Lainey minced, throw in flakes of red pepper and a couple dozen Little Neck clams, cover them for a couple of minutes, splash in some wine, and when the pasta's al dente I drain it and toss it into the pan with the clams for maybe two minutes, so it absorbs the clam juice. Then I toss everything with parsley.

"*Pasta con vongole,*" I announce as I serve it.

Either I'm the world's greatest chef or we're the world's four hungriest people, because every plate is wiped clean with the last of the garlic bread, and two bottles of wine are gone. That's mainly Lainey, MaryEllen, and me: Rowan limits herself to half a glass because of the painkillers she's taking.

Lainey and I clear the table and I make a large pot of coffee while she serves the biscotti and fresh strawberries. I open the bottle of sambuca.

"Sorry, Jake," says Lainey. "We don't have little dessert wine glasses. We'll have to use juice glasses instead."

I feel awkward, her apologizing to me. She probably thinks I drink out of crystal goblets.

"Works for me," I say as I pour the sambuca. A small amount for Rowan.

When all the biscotti and half the sambuca are gone, MaryEllen and Lainey insist on doing the dishes and shoo Rowan and me back into the living room. Deeply hangs around the kitchen and I hear him squawk *Biscot-ti* a couple of times, until MaryEllen finally gives him one.

"How do you feel?" I ask Rowan softly.

"Not bad." She kneads my thigh with her foot. "But a little TLC would make me feel a lot better."

"Sunday," I mouth.

She smiles.

Lainey and MaryEllen finish the dishes and MaryEllen takes her leave. Deeply flies back to his perch.

Rowan gets so sleepy that her mother sends her to bed. She goes without protest. Leaving me alone with Lainey.

I stand and wait until Rowan's door is closed.

"I don't want to leave if Rowan isn't being protected," I tell Lainey.

"She is. Titus has asked for volunteers to guard the house. Just for a few weeks, until I can come home permanently."

"Good. I'm not sure I could stay awake long enough to guard anybody."

"You go home and get some sleep," she says. "And Jake — thank you for everything you've done for Rowan and Keisha. Thanks to you and Antwon, I don't think they'll be prosecuted." She stands there sort of assessing me. "Getting their story out before the cops had released any information at all — that was critical."

I nod. "My boss thinks the same thing: that the cops aren't going to touch them now. There's just too much information out there from their point of view."

"We all appreciate it: Titus, Genevieve, me. Antwon. And so do Rowan and Keisha."

"And," she adds as we walk to the door, "thanks for the fantastic dinner."

I walk to my car, looking around for anybody guarding the house. I don't see them. I drive my car around the block and down the alley, checking out Rowan's garage. I don't see anybody there, either.

But I trust they're there and I trust they know what they're doing.

66 ROWAN

"HOW DID YOU AND JAKE MEET?" MOM ASKS ME AT breakfast.

"He followed me home on the day of the gun-control rally."

She looks puzzled. "And you were okay with that? With a man following you home?"

I slather some jam on my toast, take a huge bite, and sip some coffee. "No, I wasn't. He annoyed me."

Deeply's perched on the hutch. I pass a piece of plain toast up to him.

Mom studies me. Probably wondering how many questions she can get away with. "Well," she says at last, "Jake seems like a good person."

I nod. "He is."

"And he sure knows how to cook," she adds. "I'm not sure you're going to like what I make tonight as well as you liked the pasta and clams."

"Depends. What are you going to make?"

"Chili, slaw with celery seeds, and cornbread."

I love Mom's chili and slaw and cornbread. She sees me being happy about it and smiles.

"And then," she says, "we can have either 5-way chili on Sunday, or chili dogs. I froze the pierogi for you to have after I leave. It was so nice of your friend to bring them."

It sure was. "Chili dogs," I say, getting back to the question of Sunday dinner.

"It would be nice to invite Jake for Sunday. He offered to take me to the airport, and I said yes. But for tonight, it's just you and me."

"That's great, Mom." I look at her. "I really missed you. There were so many times I wanted to ask you a question about what was the right thing to do." I tell her about how I wondered what to do with Lyle and the pecan pie — bourbon or no bourbon?

Mom smiles. "Those kinds of things are hard little decisions in life. What did you do?"

"I went with the bourbon," I say, "cause I didn't feel I should, like, oversee his consumption of alcohol."

"That's what I'd have done."

After breakfast I clear the table, stepping carefully as I carry dishes to the counter. My leg hurts, but it's not super awful. Maybe Dr. Goldberg was right about the three or four weeks.

I miss going to work. Not just for the money, which is absolutely necessary, but for the friendships. Being with other people who are doing the same thing. Working together. Sharing. Laughing. I wonder if when I go back to work Package Nova will make me start over on my 90-days, 200-hours probation.

Probably. That's what they did with Lyle. But they did give him credit for some of his hours.

Mom washes the dishes and then I grab my crutch and we go for a walk to Park 751, which is less than two blocks away. Halfway there I have to stop, a small rest, ten or twenty seconds. Just to give the pain a breather.

Above us, Deeply flies toward the boathouse.

I think about my therapy and make a mental list of what I should do when we get back home. Right now the exercises are relatively easy, but sooner or later the therapists are going to have me doing lunges and squats, just to strengthen my thigh and make sure it can do what it has to do.

I'm so not looking forward to that.

But they said I could use a rowing machine as early as next week, and I'm looking forward to renting one at Park 751 while I recover. If I have the money.

"Mom. Once my therapy and doctor's visits are over, I'll call you. Then you'll give notice where you work and come home two weeks later?"

She stops and holds my face in her hands. "Yes, Rowan. I will come home two weeks after you call. I was always going to come home. I just didn't know when."

I nod. "I believe you, Mom."

"Good," she says, and we continue the walk.

"There's one other thing, Mom."

She looks at me. "Just one?"

"Yeah. If I can't go back to work for four weeks . . . I won't have money to buy food. Or transportation. I know you're going to send me some each week . . . but I'm worried it's not enough." I hate saying this. Mom spent air fare getting here, and she said she'd saved up only a few hundred dollars. Some of which she spent on my phone, the rest of which she probably needs to drive all the way home from Tucson.

"Let's go to that bench alongside the water," she says, pointing.

A rest stop. Good.

We sit on the bench and look out at the Chicago River. Deeply perches on another bench, facing us. Already there are maybe a dozen couples or singles renting canoes.

"You don't have to worry about money, Rowan."

I look at her. "What do you mean? I mean, I know I don't have to *worry* about it. But I do *need* it."

"The reason you don't have to worry about money, Rowan, is because Titus, Antwon, and Jake set up a fund appeal on X and Facebook."

"I didn't know that. The contributions will help Keisha and me out?"

"They've raised thirty thousand dollars so far."

"*What*?!!!" I scream. "Thirty *thousand* dollars????"

"Shhh," she warns. "Yes. And that's in just two days. Antwon says there's more money coming in today than there was the two previous days. A lot more."

"You've talked to Antwon already?"

"While you were sleeping," she says.

"So . . . half will go to Keisha, and half to me?"

"First they'll pay the attorney," Mom explains, "and then they'll give you and Keisha the rest. Antwon will bring you some of the money Monday afternoon."

I don't know what to say.

"Titus was going to ask WCC members for donations," Mom tells me, "but once the public began donating, that wasn't necessary." She looks at me. "I am proud of you, Rowan. What you did was incredibly brave."

"I had no choice. You know that, right?"

Mom hugs me. "Oh, Rowan! Of course I know that!" Still hugging me, she leans away and looks at me. "And I hope you know it, too. I hope you never, *ever* question what you did."

Right then I think about Clari and the other students who were murdered by a hate-filled sociopath, and I wish Clari and all of them had been carrying guns and had the chance to defend themselves. All my life I'm going to wish that.

"Not a chance," I tell Mom. "I'm glad he's dead."

"Me too, Rowan. Me, too."

We sit there a while, looking out at the river.

"So, Mom — if we have all this money, why do you need to go back to Tucson?"

She looks at me sadly. "Because who knows what you and Keisha might need the money for? Who knows if either of you will need further medical attention? I want you to have medical coverage."

She gives me a hug. "Rowan — I *will* come home two weeks after you call to tell me your therapy and doctor's visits are over. Then I'll get a job — with medical coverage. And by that time, you might have your own medical coverage through your job."

We sit there on the bench a while and watch the boaters come and go, and then we walk back home. Deeply gets there before we do. Such a show-off.

Mom asks me what happened to the shelf inside the kitchen cabinet. "Did your parrot chew it up?" she asks. "It looks just like the chew marks on his perch."

"Deeply sorry," squawks Deeps.

This startles Mom, because the only thing she's heard him say is "Cracker" and "Biscotti."

She walks up to Deeply. They look at each other.

"That's okay, then," she tells him. "But please don't do it again." Then she goes to the piano and plays for at least an hour. I'm so glad I didn't sell her piano.

Almost as if reading my mind, she spins around on the bench and asks, "What happened to Clari's bed?"

"I sold it. MaryEllen told me Brigid wanted a twin bed. She paid me $70 for it. I really needed the money. And . . . I sold Clari's bike, too. It was making me sad."

"That's okay," says Mom. She looks at my hair. "I like that you're wearing one of Clari's feathers"

"Yeah. I had another one before this, but it kind of wore out. Keisha told me I'd better change it."

Mom smiles.

"Did Jake help you move my bed into your room?" she asks.

Whoa! Loaded question!

"Nope." I shake my head vigorously. "I moved your bed into my room the day after I started working at Package Nova. I needed to sprawl out and relax my muscles."

Mom clears her throat. "After I fly back to Tucson, I'd like you to buy a new bed for yourself with some of the money Antwon brings; sell the twin bed that's in my room; and move my bed back into my room." She raises an eyebrow in that Mom way, like: *Are you going to do what I'm telling you to do?*

"No problem," I say. "I'll buy myself a humongous luxury king-size bed with a vibrating mattress and a ceiling mirror, and then I'll move your bed back into your room."

"You'll never get a humongous luxury king-size bed with a vibrating mattress and a ceiling mirror through the door." She spins back to the piano and launches into a medley of boogie-woogie tunes. I can see that she's grinning.

I lie on the couch, elevate my legs, and call to Deeply, who comes to perch on my shoulder, tickling me with his beak. I stroke his feathers. For some reason, he doesn't seem to want to talk much while Mom's around.

It makes me sad to know that he's going to leave. But he wants to go back home. Where he has a mate and chicks. I am so lucky to have had Deeply in my life. No matter how sad his leaving will make me, I understand that he wants to go.

Is he here just to investigate us? No . . . I think he's here to help us. Though I'm not sure how he's doing that. Except for helping me.

67   JAKE

THE NEXT THREE WEEKS GO BY FAST. I SPEND MY DAYS at the studio and my nights with Rowan, sometimes at her place, sometimes mine. But I'm always with her at night.

Titus tells me the guards report seeing nobody casing the neighborhood. Not in the daytime, not in the nighttime. So after two weeks the volunteer guards are gone. Not that Rowan or I ever saw them in the first place.

Rowan buys a new bed. We move her mother's bed back into the other bedroom, dismantle the twin bed and sell it, and put together the new bed. Whose bounciness we make the most of.

Every day Rowan gets stronger. I take her to the hospital to have the staples in her leg removed and I take her to and from physical therapy. She spends time on the Park 751 rowing machines practically every day. Her arms are toned, her legs are toned.

"You can paddle the next canoe we rent," I tell her, running a finger down her biceps.

"I intend to," she says.

"How about you paddle upstream and I paddle down?" I suggest.

"Wimp."

The reporters come to her house at all hours, asking for interviews. I step out onto the porch and tell them Rowan's willing to give an interview a day, five days a week, and they can sign up for slots. Which they scramble to do.

During those three weeks the planned Stop Violence Against Women demonstration takes place in Federal Plaza. The place I first saw Rowan. With Keisha and Rowan as the main speakers the crowd is much larger than anticipated. Cops — in full riot gear — line the perimeters of the streets. As for the demonstrators, I see signs from Milwaukee. Madison. Des Moines. Louisville. Indianapolis. They're here for Rowan and Keisha.

Who don't fail them.

"We not only have the right to self-defense," Keisha tells them, "but if we want to end violence against women, an *obligation* to self-defense. We cannot let this violence continue. We need to prepare, and we need to join self-defense groups!"

Standing side by side on the platform, Keisha and Rowan take turns speaking. "Self-defense is a human right," Rowan tells the crowd. "The fight or flight response is built into our DNA. Keisha and I couldn't 'flight.' There was no place to 'flight' to. And Zeb Snoddy was pointing a gun at us. Our choice was simple: agree to die — or fight back.

"I didn't want Keisha to die. And I didn't want to die, either. So I fought back."

I'm roaming through the crowd, taping whatever is interesting. Thinking that moving to Chicago could be the smartest move I ever made. A lot of what I tape, I use for my podcasts. A lot of it I give to Highland Studio. Business-wise, I should be selling my off-duty footage to them, but Harita helped so much to publicize what happened to Rowan and Keisha that I'm willing to give her many parts of the story for free.

On Tuesday nights Rowan, Deeply and I go to Titus and Genevieve's house for dinner, and when dinner's over we help clean up, then go up to Keisha's room and engage in what I call the material arts. There's Keisha on the sewing machine; there's Rowan sitting on the floor crocheting; there's Antwon sitting on the floor weaving on some sort of African loom. And there's me.

Whom they kiddingly start out on a small metal square that I'm supposed to make potholders on.

Potholders.

This is ridiculous. Nothing but over-under. I complete one and then complete another and tell them I've reached peak performance.

Keisha gets up with an exaggerated sigh. "If you've reached peak performance, Mr. Podcaster, we're going to advance you to twills."

"What's a twill?"

She gives an evil grin. "You will soon find out."

Keisha's cheek guard is gone, but she still wears a plastic nose guard.

I'm sitting on the floor between Antwon and Rowan. Keisha tells me to scoot over, then sits beside me. "A twill," she explains, "is a weave that goes under one or more, then over two or more. Repeat that to me, please."

After I repeat it she sets up my baby loom with elastic bands running vertically. She hands me a new loop and tells me to weave my first row. "Under one, over two. That's your pattern. This time around."

This isn't as easy as over one, under one. But it's not rocket science, either. I weave my first row.

Keisha touches a fingernail to one of the crossings. "Is that over two?" she asks.

I look.

Damn!

Missed a spot. Went over one.

Deeply makes a sound something like a laugh.

"You think you could do better?" I ask him.

I take the whole weaver out and start again. Get it right.

"Now," she says, "you're going to weave the second row so that you move the pattern one step to the left each time." She shows me how to do this.

It's not intuitive. I puzzle over it. Instead of going under one, as I did in the previous row, I go over one. Then under one. Then over two, under one, over two, and so on.

Do I grasp this? I'm not sure. I start the third row by going over two, then back to my under-one, over-two pattern.

Keisha approves.

But I mess up again. She points to the diagonal that's supposed to be forming, stepping up toward the left. "You want to advance the over-two each row," she says, "to create this step-up. It's a great look. Once you master it."

Right.

I spend the rest of the night on one goddamn kid-sized potholder, taking out row after row, reweaving until I get it right.

"Peak performance yet, Jake?" Antwon asks.

"In a couple of centuries," I mutter.

Despite my frustrations with the stupid twill on the stupid potholder loom, I have a grand time. I'm in sync. With Rowan, with Keisha, with Antwon. When the evening's over Rowan and I invite Keisha, Antwon, Titus and Genevieve to Rowan's house for dinner on Friday night.

Just about every day Lainey calls Rowan and they talk.

And every day Deeply entertains us with sounds he imitates. Coffee pot. Toaster. My whistling to him. White Sox fireworks. Vacuum cleaner.

We spend time in the garden, weeding and watching Deeply run through the sprinkler.

Rowan and I talk about it. Decide we won't press Deeply about why he's here. I think we would have, before Snoddy tried to murder Rowan and Keisha. But since then . . . it just seems more important to recover, to go forward, and to appreciate what we have. We have each other. And for now we have Deeply. And if he wants us to know more, he'll tell us.

We decide I should interview Deeply every chance I get . . . though neither Rowan nor I think he'll reveal much.

68   DEEPLEA

SOON IT WILL BE TIME FOR ME TO LEAVE. FRANCE. À *bas la guerre, à bas le capitalisme!*

I will miss Rowan. I will miss Jake.

I will not miss do-nuts. They were too good to be true. They tasted delicious. But they addicted me and I lost all sense of the difference between what I wanted and what I needed. I became greedy, just like the ruling class.

There were consequences.

I am not proud of my behavior with the do-nuts. My failure to be with Rowan when she needed protection. Had I been with her I would have read Snoddy's intention and driven my talon into his remaining eye.

Deep. Very deep.

He would have died instantly.

He would not have had time to hurt Keisha or Rowan.

I will try to do better in France.

And for the remaining week of my time here, I will just enjoy life with Rowan and Jake.

Oh. Yes. Before I leave for France, I will come up with a third person.

Not a problem. The WCC has many good people in it and around it. I am thinking perhaps Rafael. Or perhaps Antwon . . . although Antwon wants to be what he is: the best bodyguard possible. He does not want to be a leader.

Titus does not crave to be a leader, but he knows that leaders are necessary, and so he consciously steps up to the job, carrying the burden on his shoulders.

Rowan steps up to the job without even thinking about being a leader or not being a leader. She is a natural-born fighter for justice.

There are many triads. Everywhere. People supporting one another, people creating stronger shapes that help them survive. Help them withstand the onslaughts of this horrific, greedy, violent, self-righteous ruling class.

Whose iron grip on Earth's future must be shattered.

Else Earth will die.

69 ROWAN

YES! THE DOCTOR SAYS I CAN GO BACK TO WORK START-ing Monday!

Today's Friday. Why wait?

Jake already left for work, muttering something about a dog food video. Deeply's sitting on the hutch. I clean out his water dish, refill it, and place it on the table. Deeply flies down to drink.

"You've been a very quiet bird lately," I tell him.

"Deeply thinking."

I stroke his feathers. "You're looking good, Deeps. Nice glossy feathers. Bright eyes."

"Deeply eat better food. No do-nuts. Deeply hate do-nuts!"

I sit down and stare into his eyes. "Deeply."

He tilts his head.

"Before you leave . . . will you tell me. So I can say goodbye?"

"Deeply tell Rowan. Deeply love Rowan."

I fight back the tears and tell him I love him, too.

"And Jake," he says. "Rowan love Jake."

"I do," I say. "I love Jake."

"Jake love Rowan, too," says Deeply. "All good."

He is *such* a character.

I kick off my flip-flops, pull on my boots, grab the back belt and compression sleeves Jake bought me, and walk to the 31st and Archer El stop.

While waiting for the train I go over what's going to happen. Vic's going to tell me my 90 days of probation start all over, just like he told Lyle. So it'll be three months before I can join the union and get protection: unemployment, disability. And representation for any grievances. Probably ninety days before I get a raise. If then.

I sigh. That's the way it goes. At least I have a job. That's more than half the battle.

The El is nowhere in sight, so I call Mom to tell her the good news.

"Then I'll give notice today and start the drive home two weeks from tomorrow."

"Drive safely, Mom."

Finally the El comes. I hop on, and I hop off at the end of the line: Midway. As I walk down Cicero toward Package Nova, I skip along. Testing my leg.

Feels great.

I enter Package Nova by the same door I entered almost three months ago, only this time I know my way around. I enter Vic's office. He looks up when I walk in, then quickly looks away.

Uh-oh. What's wrong?

"Rowan," he says. Uncomfortably.

I pull a piece of paper out of my back pocket and hand it to him. "Clean bill of health," I say. "I'm ready to start whatever shift needs me."

Vic doesn't take the paper. He looks down at his desk, avoiding eye contact.

"You've been let go, Rowan. I'm sorry."

"Let go?" My brain balks: it can't process *let go*.

When the meaning finally kicks in, I react. "Like — *fired*? You're *firing* me?" I ask, leaping from incredulous to angry in a nanosec.

"Why?" I demand. "I have a great work record, and you know it. I go anywhere I'm assigned, do anything, no complaints, I keep up with the pace, I don't fuck up, I'm *reliable*, Vic. Why am I being fired?"

"The company doesn't want . . . some . . . you got into a fight after working hours. The publicity reflected badly on the company."

"I did not *get into a fight after working hours,* Vic! This wasn't some barroom brawl. And what about Lyle, huh? He got into a fight after working hours, and he's still here. I was *attacked*. Keisha and I were *attacked*!"

Vic looks everywhere but at me. "You killed a person, Rowan."

"I defended myself, Vic. Keisha and I *defended* ourselves. Self-defense is a human instinct. It's a human right!"

"You're going to have to leave, Rowan. You don't have a job here anymore."

I take a deep breath. "Package Nova is saying it prefers I were dead. It would be better if Snoddy had raped, tortured, mutilated, and murdered Keisha and me, wouldn't it? Then Package Nova would be happy. This is absolute bullshit, Vic. How can you sit there and do what you're doing?"

He picks up his phone. "I'm going to call security and have you ushered out."

I march up to his desk and point a finger in his face.

He flinches.

"Go ahead. If Package Nova wants a law suit over how you ordered goons to throw me out just hours after doctors released me from care and all I did was come to ask about my working hours — go ahead. Call them." I pull out my phone and turn on the video.

Vic puts his phone down. "Rowan. There's nothing I can do for you. I have to follow orders."

"*No. You. Don't.*" I shout. "You're making a choice, Vic. And it's the wrong one."

I turn my back on him, walk out the door, slamming it so hard I hope it falls off its hinges. I exit the side door to the outside world, turn, and kick a dent into the metal. With the fucking boots I'm required to wear to load Nova's fucking packages so the owners and investors can make their fucking billions.

* * *

I stomp back to Midway and catch the next El into the city. I text Titus. I know he's at work, but he would want to know immediately.

>Me: **Nova fired me. I want to fight back.**

>Titus: **5:00, HQ**

Then I text Jake the same message.

>Jake: **WTF? Why?**

>Me: **Cause I'm woman. Not sposed to fight back. Not sposed to win.**

>Jake: **U fighting this?**

>Me: **WCC 5:00.**

>Jake: **Meet me 4:00 ur place.**

>Me: **HEART**

70   DEEPLEA

NO REST.

There is no rest for a parrot on Duty to the Universe.

As soon as I read Rowan's mind — hear her reaction to what the boss named Vic is saying — I am once again on alert. Battle station.

Out the window, into the sky, and along the El tracks I fly, to Midway Airport, where Rowan is walking to take the El back home. I fly low, so that I'm not mistaken for any kind of aircraft on the Midway radar.

My orange neck feathers, which had been looking good — smooth and glossy — now look as if they've been attacked by electricity. Halfway between Midway and Package Nova I perch high in a tree, where I can watch Rowan. Make certain she is safe.

She is. The sidewalk she is stomping along is not so safe: Rowan is wishing she had a sledge hammer with which to break up the concrete. She is wishing she could hurl the boulders at Package Nova. Rowan has read many books on the French Revolution and the French Commune and knows all about tearing up pavement.

Once Rowan boards the El I fly back home above it, letting its forward energy aid me in my flight. I sense that I will need a lot of energy.

After Rowan exits the El and begins walking home, I fly there myself. Into the window and onto the table — where I know she will be drawing up battle plans. Rowan is not only a fighter for working class justice, she is an organizer. I will study what she does, in case I need to make suggestions elsewhere on Earth.

Earth: a planet in the hands of profiteers.

71   ROWAN

FOUR HOURS BEFORE JAKE COMES HOME, I START TO organize. Since I'm not yet a member of the union, I don't know if they would fight for me, or how hard. Or when they would start. I'm going to fight for my job as hard as I can. Starting now.

Deeply sits on the kitchen table, watching me. I think of asking him to relocate to the hutch, but reconsider: even with all the space I'm going to need, there's still enough room for both of us. And who knows — he might want to see what I'm writing.

So I sit across from Deeply with a pen and paper and start to make lists. There's something about writing on paper that helps me think. And calms me down.

I write fast. Brainstorming.

Women's Organizations

Leftist Political Organizations, Women

Leftist Political Organizations, All

Black Lives Matter

Union organizers, Amazon warehouse

Union organizers, Starbucks

Chicago Teachers Union

Other local unions

Women's Caucuses in Unions

Newspapers

Radio

TV

Facebook

X

Instagram

TikTok

Self-Defense Organizations

Package Nova Workers I Know

Friends

Neighbors

High School Classmates

Wheelers Workmates

OMG. I forgot to text Keisha.

I do it now.

> **Keisha: Fight back!!**
>
> **Me: HQ 5:00**
>
> **Keisha: THUMB UP**

By the time Jake walks in the door I've entered all the lists into my phone. We're ready to roll.

"Antwon texted me," Jake says as he drives us to WCC. "I'm meeting him to put together a plan for all the media."

"I can feel Package Nova trembling already," I joke.

"We'll be merciful."

Jake parks the car and we walk into headquarters: me into the small meeting room where the executive committee meets, Jake into the large meeting room where Antwon's already at work.

Rafael's already there and so are Sarah and Angela. Titus and Jalen arrive within a couple of minutes. That's the whole EC. I'm not on the Executive Committee, but I'm there to give my story and share my battle plan.

Titus gives a brief explanation of what happened, then asks me to report the details. After I do he states the obvious: that I want to fight Package Nova's firing of me. I want to fight to get my job back.

Everybody nods. They've been there. Maybe not getting fired, but having to fight for our rights.

"Every time workers react to injustice they gain strength," Titus explains. "And knowledge. In every fight for equality we gain knowledge, we learn battle tactics, and we gain confidence."

We all nod, then begin the discussion of what to do. After we decide to call for a demonstration in front of Package Nova on Monday morning, we divide up the labor of getting picket signs printed, taking the portable stage to the demonstrations we have planned, getting the news out, and more.

The slogan we decide on is **Defend Women Who Fight Back. Unfire Rowan Pickett**.

I love the *unfire*.

The Executive Committee divides up the labor, everybody calling out what they want. Angela and I agree to split up Women's Organizations, and I offer to take Left Political Women's Organizations. And Friends. And Neighbors. And Fellow Workers at Package Nova. And Wheelers. This is my fight, I'm not going to leave out a single thing on my list.

Titus, Rafael, and Sarah divide the big union-drive places like Amazon, and each takes at least one other category. Jalen takes Black Lives Matter and the Chicago Teachers Union, both of which he's active in.

When the meeting is done and I step out into the big meeting room, Jake and Antwon motion me over.

"We've just uploaded and posted on X and Facebook," Antwon says, "and sent out twenty press releases. TV, newspaper, radio. And Jake's still writing a list of everyone he knows in the media."

I rub my face vigorously. Too much sitting around making lists. "We have a lot of work ahead of us," I say. "How about we grab something to eat first."

"Good idea," says Jake, still typing on his phone.

"Keisha's on her way," Antwon says. "I'll text her where to meet us."

72 JAKE

MY MIND'S BLOWN BY THE SPEED, EFFICIENCY, AND dedication of everyone in WCC. I mean, *I'm* efficient and dedicated and can move fast. But that's me, one person. To get a whole organization which does that — Impressive!

Rowan and I set up combat headquarters in her kitchen, each of us working at one end of the table, she on her computer and phone, me on my phone and camcorder. Deeply divides his time between the back of one empty chair and the back of the other. I guess that way each of his eyes gets its own viewing time.

When Rowan's looking particularly focused on a task at hand, I take videos. I do the same with some of her phone calls, too. I like the part where she asks the person on the other end to join her in the fight for her job, which, she tells them, is a fight for everyone's right to a job, and which, she hammers home, is a fight for women's right to defend themselves. "They fired me because I fought back and won," she says. "They'd rather that women were raped and beaten than that they fight back. We can't let them get away with that." A lot of the time I record, I make certain Deeply's in the frame, too. When he leaves, we'll have video to remember him by.

Organizing work, it turns out, is exhausting. You're on the entire time.

"Lunch break?" I plead at last.

Rowan smiles. "If you insist."

Protein is what we need. I could use a sandwich from Big City Chicken. Hell, I could use three sandwiches from Big City Chicken. But I can't eat a chicken sandwich in front of Deeply.

"How about some submarine sandwiches from that Italian deli you love?" Rowan says over her shoulder as she continues to cross things off her check list.

"Grinders. They're called grinders."

"Not in Chicago," she retorts.

Rowan stands, stretches, and puts her hands on my chest. "Why don't you take a break, drive there, get the subs and donuts? Getting away from the table and out of the house will be refreshing for you. And I'll make us a big pot of coffee. Italian roast."

I put my hands on Rowan's waist. I can think of something else that would be totally refreshing.

But probably not a good idea right now.

"Okay," I say, "but what'll you do for refreshing?"

"Yoga," she says, heading for the bedroom, returning with her yoga mat.

※ ※ ※

I return from my stops just as Rowan's rolling up her yoga mat. The aroma of the coffee is delicious. I grab a couple of plates from the cabinet — which still has Deeply's chewing damage — unwrap three meatball grinders, and serve them. One for her, two for me.

We chow down on the food, both of us damned hungry judging by how fast we eat. Then we sit back a bit and savor our coffee and donuts. Of which I bought only four: Deeply has developed a dislike of donuts in inverse proportion to his former love of donuts.

"Want some popcorn?" I ask him.

"Deeply love popcorn!" He struts back and forth on the hutch.

Rowan reaches into a cabinet and tosses me a microwave popcorn bag. I pop it into the microwave and in four minutes it's ready. I dump half of it into a bowl for Deeply, but I let it cool just a bit before putting it up on the hutch.

Rowan and I consume the rest of the popcorn. Then we clear the table and get back to work.

* * *

Monday morning the alarm goes off at 5:00. We shower and dress, bolt down toast and coffee, and take Archer Avenue to Cicero to Package Nova, where there's already maybe three hundred people gathered on the sidewalks at 6:30 a.m. I'm impressed by the number, to say nothing of their early arrival.

Rowan goes to help set up the stage and distribute picket signs. And to talk to Keisha, who's there wearing both her cheek guard and her nose piece, just as I requested when I texted her yesterday.

We're all standing on the sidewalk in front of Package Nova. Across the street from us is a long line of police in riot gear. Rowan calls it assault gear. Easily two hundred of them, wearing face shields, holding batons, armed as if about to invade a small island. I use the camcorder on them, first sweeping down the long line, then zooming in on the specific weapons. Future podcast on the militarization of the police force.

After I'm done filming the cops I walk among the demonstrators, recording, interviewing. By 7:00 there are at least six or seven hundred people present, and when I look up toward Midway I see more walking our way, carrying their own picket signs.

The Stop Violence Against Women signs are unsettling. They've reprinted the photos from Rowan's video. The one of Keisha's face and Rowan's leg. **Is This What Package Nova Wants? Support Women's Self-Defense! Support Rowan Pickett!** Gruesome signs, but good.

Five different news crews have set up. I know some of them and go over to talk, encouraging them to come back tonight, when the demonstration will be even bigger. Or so I hope.

Rowan and Keisha take the stage. They hold hands and raise their joined hands high.

"Sisters, Brothers, Friends and Fellow Workers," Rowan shouts into the mic. "Thank you for coming. Thank you for your support."

Loud applause.

"Keisha and I are here today because we stood together. Because we fought back against a vile, racist, sexist, *evil* man who wanted to rape us and kill us." She pauses. "And now Keisha and I and all our friends and supporters — like every one of you who sacrificed their time to come here today — are going to stand together and fight back against the corporation that fired me. Fired me because *I'm a woman who fought back!* The only conclusion I can reach — the only one — is that *Package Nova doesn't approve of our fighting back*. Package Nova doesn't approve of women who defend themselves!"

Huge cheers and lots of boos against Package Nova. I'm taping it all.

"In addition to the fact that Package Nova firing me is an attack on women, there's another reason I ask you to help me. That reason is jobs." Rowan pauses. "In their never-ending pursuit for profit, the capitalists have eroded our standard of living. They have moved jobs abroad, they have crushed unions, they have wiped out health care and vacations. This plan meets *their* needs. It does not meet *our* needs! You, me, every member of the working class needs a job with adequate pay, fewer hours, safe conditions, and generous vacations." Loud roars of approval from the crowd. "So we are fighting for me, yes. We are fighting for women, yes. But we are also asserting that *We. Need. Jobs.* All of us."

Rowan steps back a bit. Keisha steps forward.

"Sisters and Brothers and Supporters. Rowan's fight is our fight. It is my fight and it is your fight. Because if they're successful in firing Rowan, they will fire other women who fight back." Keisha turns and points to the street. "They will fire women who fight back on the street, like Rowan and I did." She turns and points to the Package Nova megastructure. "And they will fire women who fight back on the job. Who fight back against sexual harassment, race harassment, and job discrimination. The time to stop them is *now*. Show them they can't get away with this." Keisha looks out at the crowd. "To fight for jobs is to fight for our *lives*."

More loud cheers.

I glance up toward Midway. More people arriving. Mostly women, but maybe as many as 30% men. White, Black, Latino, Asian.

Rowan steps forward again. "This morning, we're going to march up and down the public sidewalk, as is our right, and shout **No Firing of Women Who Fight Back — Unfire Rowan Pickett!** There are close to a thousand of us here, with more coming every minute — we'll have no trouble shouting so loud that those who fired me will hear us."

Applause and cheers from the crowd.

"When we reach the end of the Package Nova complex, we'll turn in place and march north with a different shout, one Keisha came up with."

Rowan hands the mic to Keisha, who gives the same grin she gave when she introduced me to twills. "Listen to our second chant, and give it back to me with all you got." Keisha pauses a second, and then shouts:

> **Package Nova,**
>
> **It's all ovah!**
>
> **Hire Rowan,**
>
> **We be goin'!**

The crowd shouts this back with such fervor I think it wants to start marching north immediately.

Keisha hands the mic back to Rowan.

"And tonight," says Rowan, "from 8:00 to 9:30, we'll be back here with a different shout. One that won't be addressed to the Package Nova bosses. Because, you know, they go home after 5:00. Not us. We work all hours of the day and night, for their convenience." Boos and hisses from the crowd. "If you can come back tonight, that will be great — hugely supportive! Tell others to come. Not each-one-bring-one, but each-one-bring-*two*. And to find out why tonight's chant will be different . . . you have to *be* here!" Rowan raises her fist, as does Keisha. The two of them walk off the stage. And the march begins.

Across the street, Deeply perches on a lamp post and sways to the rhythm of the marching feet, the drum beats, and the chanting.

73 ROWAN

THE MORNING DEMO WENT WELL. WAY MORE PEOPLE than I had hoped for. Antwon and Sarah estimated about twelve hundred people. Jake was able to shoot great signs, record great chants, and interview a lot of supportive people.

No bosses came out to talk to me. Like, give me back my job.

I didn't expect them to. They think this will go away.

It might. But not if I can help it.

Jake drops me off at home, then continues on his way to work. He says Harita will probably use some of his footage as a "continuing story" thing. He also says that Antwon's putting together some video for Facebook, X, YouTube, and the usual places. Mainly, though, Jake's got to work on something about dog food.

As I'm unlocking the side door MaryEllen comes over.

"Sorry I couldn't make it this morning, Rowan. I had to help Mrs. Grundy with her grocery shopping. But I'll be there tonight. JoJo and I are taking the El together."

"So are Jake and I. Too hard to find a parking place," I tell her. "We can all go together if you want. But I have to get there early, around 7:30 or just a little after. You wanna come in for some coffee?" I ask her.

She does. Says hello to Deeply as he flies in the window. "Where does that bird ever go?" she asks. "I've seen him at the top of my tree, but I've also seen him fly off into the distance."

"He flew to the demonstration this morning," I tell her. "I saw him watching from a lamp post."

"I've never been to a demonstration before. Will it be violent?" she asks hesitantly.

"No, Els. We're there to win my job back through peaceful protest." I've told MaryEllen many times that the WCC doesn't engage in provocative violent actions. But the ruling-class media has succeeded in painting a picture of all demonstrations as full of window-smashing anarchists. Violence is almost always initiated by agent provocateurs. Undercover cops or pro-fascists.

"I appreciate your coming, Els," I say over my shoulder as I make the coffee. "But you don't have to if you don't feel right about it."

"No, no," she demurs. "I *want* to support you, Rowan. Their firing you is just awful. I talked to Patrick about it and he thinks I should go."

"Well, who knows," I say. "You might end up being pleasantly surprised."

She looks doubtful about this but doesn't say so. She's a good friend, and I appreciate her coming to tonight's demonstration.

My phone rings. I'll bet it's a reporter.

I excuse myself to Els and take the call. Which lasts ten minutes.

When I'm done, MaryEllen has finished her coffee and is ready to go. We say goodbye just as my phone rings again.

When that call's done I make a dozen of my own, calling more women I know from SVAW. And calling some of Dad's friends from the union he belonged to and Mom's friends from her job. They seem happy to hear from me. Some say maybe they'll come to tonight's demonstration. I thank each of them and go on to the next.

Around 4:00 I go into the garden to pick some greens and veggies, turning the sprinkler on so Deeply can run through the water. I wash all the produce, put together a salad, and season a pork tenderloin. When Antwon brought me the fund-raising money, I took it to the bank and deposited it into the savings account, with the intention of drawing out $500 a week until I start working again. And I told Mom she didn't have to send me any money. Just come home. I'm salivating over the pork tenderloin: it sure feels good to have some high quality meat again.

When Jake comes in I offer him a beer, which he eagerly accepts. I could use a beer. But I'd better not: I want to be as sharp as possible for anything that happens. We have our salad, then I slice the tenderloin into one-inch slices and cook them in a cast iron pan that's been in Dad's family for at least fifty years. I've already made black rice, and I sauté some carrots in butter and honey. Doing all of these routine things calms me down.

As we eat I think about what to say tonight. I assess my morning talk and think I did pretty good talking to my fellow workers about our jobs, our lives, our future — which look bleak and bleaker unless we ourselves take control of industry and the state.

❋ ❋ ❋

I step onto the portable stage, Keisha beside me. "Nice nose guard," I tell her.

"I'm thinking of gluing a granny square onto it," she says. Just to get me loose.

"How many people you think are here already?" I ask, glancing at my watch. 7:40, and we're scheduled to start at 8:00.

"More than this morning. Two thousand. Maybe three? The each-one-bring-two was a good idea. How about each-one-bring-three for tomorrow?" she asks.

"Sounds great," I reply, looking out at the crowd. I spot MaryEllen and JoJo talking to somebody I know but can't place. I think he lives a couple blocks away, down in Lyle's direction. That reminds me: I haven't heard from Lyle since I left the hospital. I notice a huge group of women from SVAW. And lots of people from WCC. And there's Mike Kress, a friend of Dad's from the union. I wave to him and he smiles and waves back. Clenches both hands together and raises them. I see Jake looking for a vantage point from which to tape. I see Deeply on the same lamp post he sat on this morning. He's facing the cops, just as he was then.

More cops than this morning. At least double the number. All dressed in bullet-proof vests, wearing helmets and face shields, carrying canisters of tear gas and pepper spray and who knows what else. Their guns might have rubber bullets, which can be lethal, or real bullets. I don't see any water cannon trucks, at least not yet. All this because one person wants her job back.

All this because the ruling class understands that there ain't no two ways about who controls the means of production and the armed bodies of men — it's either the ruling class, which has controlled them up to now, or the working class, which must control them if we're to have a future.

Somebody calls my name. I look around. Marla, chairperson of the SVAW steering committee. She called me Gun Girl when I proposed the SVAW not carry gun-control signs. I'm surprised she came.

"Hi Marla. Thanks so much for coming. I appreciate it."

She reaches up a hand to me. I shake it.

"This is a violence-against-women issue. We're all here for you, Rowan. You're a hero."

As if they can hear what Marla's saying — they can't, cause it's hard to hear anything above the noise of the crowd — about a hundred women bob their signs up and down, up and down. **Package Nova Fires Rowan — More Violence Against Women.**

I grin and give them a thumbs-up. "*Great* signs, Marla."

She smiles. "I think so, too."

Keisha taps me on the shoulder. "Time," she says.

I step up to the mic, Keisha beside me, just like this morning. This time we don't clasp hands, we stand shoulder to shoulder.

"Sisters and Brothers, Friends and Fellow Workers," I say, "Thank you for coming to support me and yourselves. A fight for one person's right to her job is a fight for *everyone's* right to their job.

"The ruling class and those they employ as our bosses think they have the right to hire us and fire us at will. Their will. To meet their needs of profit. Our needs are different. We need housing, food, health insurance, transportation, and we need leisure time, too, to recover from the work we perform day after day, week after week, year after year.

"We're here today to fight for two things. My right to defend myself against violence, and my right to retain my job after I've defended myself. That's the narrow, specific demand we're making today, and again I thank you very much for your support, because without you I can't win.

"But we're also here to make it clear that we — we, the working class that creates the wealth of the world — need to determine our future. And our present. *We* need to be in control of our jobs and our lives. We don't want to be subject to layoffs or plant closings. We want a say in our work hours and our work pace. *Nobody* knows better than we do what needs to be done on the job and how to best do it. Nobody. But we're given no say in any of this. We're treated like pieces of machinery they can order around.

"This morning we marched and shouted so that the executives in Package Nova could hear us. We shouted **No Firing of Women Who Fight Back — Unfire Rowan Pickett.** We shouted this slogan over and over at the people who think they have power over us. The bosses.

"Not one of them listened. Not one of them came out to say they'd made a mistake. To give me back my job."

As I look out over the crowd, I see it swelling. Growing longer. Wider. Deeper. Maybe four thousand people crowded on the sidewalk and spilling out onto Cicero Avenue. Women and more women and more women! And a lot of men, too.

"Tonight there are four times as many of us as there were this morning. I see signs from everywhere — Madison, Des Moines, Milwaukee, Louisville, even as far away as Pittsburgh! And that's because what affects one of us affects *all* of us. Women know that!"

Loud cheering.

"Tonight we're going to shout louder than we did this morning. But we're going to shout to our fellow workers as they drive into the parking lot. We're going to shout so loud they can hear us through the open bays and loading docks. And here's what we're going to shout: **You Have the Power! You Have the Power!** Turn toward the parking lot entrance. Turn toward the loading docks. Shout it, loud and clear."

I pass the mic to Keisha, who adjusts her cheek guard and speaks. "Friends. Variety is the spice of life. Variety is something they don't give us on the production line, by the way. Variety is something we'll put back into the work process when we have workers' control."

More cheers.

"But for now," Keisha tells them, "we're going to inject variety into our chant, alternating Rowan's chant of **You Have the Power** with something I came up with this morning. Something that tells Package Nova how things stand. And lets them know that when they do the right thing, this particular issue will be resolved."

She raises her fist into the air and begins.

> **Package Nova,**
>
> **It's all ovah!**
>
> **Hire Rowan,**
>
> **We be goin'!**

Half the people are shouting with her from the beginning: they must have been there this morning.

I'm shouting along with everyone when Titus gets my attention, motioning me to the edge of the stage. "Lotta people here," he says. "Good idea to take half of them and march to the south gate. Cover everyone driving in and out that gate."

Great idea!

I get the mic from Keisha and make the announcement, telling them that Titus Longshaw from Working Class Control will help divide the crowd in half, and that Keisha will lead the march to the south parking lot.

In no time at all we're divided and moving. Keisha's about to hop off the stage when I grab her arm. "Keish — each-one-bring-four?"

She nods, Titus hands her a bullhorn, and off they go.

My half of the group stays at the north gate. I walk off the stage and squeeze my way through the crowd until I'm standing where anybody driving into the north parking gate can see me.

Each car that comes through, I try to make contact. A lot of the drivers roll down their windows and want to talk. But that's causing a traffic backup, so they have to leave. Not before I thank them for their support, though. And I know they hear the chant: **You Have the Power! You Have the Power!**

✱ ✱ ✱

Jake and I help gather the picket signs as people leave, and MaryEllen and JoJo help.

"Hey," I say to Rafael, "this looks like a lot more than two hundred picket signs."

He stacks a bunch of signs and puts them carefully into his pickup. "After the way this morning went, Titus and I agreed to order six hundred more."

We pile all the signs as neatly as we can into Rafael's truck for tomorrow morning. Then we help Antwon and Jalen with the dismantled stage, the mics and the bullhorns, all of which go into Jalen's van.

Finally we take the El home.

MaryEllen and JoJo talk about the rally all the way from Midway to the 31st and Archer El stop, to our front door.

By the time Jake and I get to sleep it's midnight. The last thing I hear is Jake telling me the alarm's set for 5:00 a.m.

74   JAKE

HANGING WITH ROWAN PICKETT IS GOING TO DEPRIVE me of half my life's sleep. Hanging with Rowan Pickett makes me feel so alive I think there are vibrations running through me.

No.

That's the alarm.

I roll over, turn it off, and force myself to keep moving. Out of bed, into the shower — hoping Rowan has made her way into the kitchen to put on the coffee.

By 6:45 we're on the El, riding toward Tuesday morning's demonstration. At least I think it's Tuesday . . . yeah, it is. Yesterday was Monday. I pat my pockets to make sure I have my camcorder and a lot of extra cards. When this whole thing is over — and I have no idea which way the chips will fall — I'll have a mountain of video to sort through.

Meanwhile, Rowan's looking at what I posted on social media during my lunch break yesterday.

"Great, Jake. These are great! I love all the different slogans you got in. Shows how everybody came with their own idea of what should be said. I always love that about demonstrations."

She's quiet for a while, clicking and scrolling. "OMG!" she shouts. "The last thing you posted on Facebook has over 85,000 hits!"

"Check YouTube," I say. "What have we got there?"

Rowan checks. "More! Over 100,000!"

I check X and show her the count: 300K. Rowan glances at it, grabs my hand, and squeezes hard. I know what she's hoping for: her job.

We exit the El at Midway and hurry down toward Package Nova. This morning's crowd looks larger than yesterday's. A *lot* larger.

We're walking by the entrance to the north parking lot when Rowan grabs my arm and pulls me to a stop. "Jake. Look. Trailers," she says. "There's three or four waiting in line."

"So?"

"Look at all the bays Nova has. Trailers aren't usually backed up like that. And, Tuesdays are slow days."

I pull out my camcorder and film the three or four trailers waiting in line. I don't think it's such a big deal as Rowan seems to think it is. I know what she's hoping for: a work slowdown. But this is most likely just a coincidence. Traffic's so backed up on Cicero that the trucks could all be arriving late.

I pan across all the cops lined up on the opposite side of the street. As our numbers have gone up, so have theirs. Part of the crowd has lined up to face the cops. Shouting: **Why are you in riot gear? We don't see no riot here!**

Rowan and I shoulder our way toward the stage, which is already up.

A woman reaches out and tugs at Rowan's arm. "Rowan."

Rowan stops, so I do, too. "Jennica," she says.

I notice that the woman, who's maybe in her late thirties, is pregnant.

"I have something to say," Jennica tells Rowan.

"Sure," says Rowan. "I'm listening."

Jennica sighs. "Not to you." She turns around, points to the crowd. Turns back to Rowan. "To them."

"Did you just get off work?" Rowan asks. "Overtime?"

"I came here just for this. I have something to say."

"You want me to introduce you, or you just want to get up and say who you are?"

"I'll do it," Jennica says.

Jennica obviously knows what she wants to do

"Come with me to the platform," Rowan tells her.

I'm taping everything. You never know what will turn out to be significant. I'm also thinking that if I were Rowan, I'd have asked Jennica what she's going to say. Then again, maybe not. Rowan's got to proceed on the basis of trust. That if somebody wants to speak, they're on her side.

At 8:00 on the dot — Working Class Control is more punctual than an atomic clock — Keisha turns on the mic, Rowan nods to Jennica, and Jennica takes the mic.

"I'm Jennica," she tells the demonstrators, "and I've worked at Package Nova for almost fifteen years. All of it on the small packages sorting line."

The crowd is interested. Waiting.

"Almost all women on small sorting. Doin' what we do best — putting things in order."

Laughter and applause.

"Take us away from the job, small packages be backing up all the way to Naperville."

Roars of approval.

"But now," says Jennica, waiting for the crowd's total attention . . . "now we're sick. Sick with worry about Rowan being fired. What does this mean for us? For fighting back against sexual discrimination? For fighting back against race discrimination? For fighting back against sexual attacks? Will fighting back get us fired?" She stops, coughs. "We're sick. Too sick to work as well as we can."

Jennica stops, looking out at the crowd. Wondering if they're intelligent enough to get it.

At first I think they don't get it. But I underestimate them. A few begin to chant and soon thousands chime in: **Sick of violence! Too sick to work!**

Rowan gives Jennica a hug. I can see her say, "Thank you. Thank you!" Jennica gives a proud nod, then walks down the steps and into the crowd.

Rowan consults with Keisha, then steps forward. "Thank you, Jennica. Thank you, women on the small-sorting line! Thank you, fellow workers at Package Nova. You have the power!"

Who has the power? shouts the crowd. **You have the power!**

Rowan waits, then speaks again. "There are a lot more of us here this morning than yesterday, so we'll be a *lot* louder as we march along the sidewalk. Let's shout so that our shouts are the only thing the bosses hear. Let's shout it out, loud and proud — **Sick of violence! Too sick to work!**"

And the crowd moves forward as if it's done this a thousand times.

This all makes me realize the limitations of the visual arts. I can catch the faces, the banners, the shouting, the movement. But I can't catch the feeling: the fighting spirit, the understanding that acting for others is acting for yourself, and acting for yourself is acting for others. Only being here infuses you with that feeling.

After a quarter of an hour I notice that Titus, Rafael, Jalen and a few others are moving the stage away from the parking entrance, down the sidewalk. They center it so that it faces the executive offices of Package Nova.

Rowan steps onto the stage with a bullhorn.

"Come on out!" she shouts. "Come on out and give me back my job."

Come on out! shout the thousands.

Keisha steps up, points to the crowd, and directs them: **Out, Out, Out!**

She turns and points to a line of WCC drummers: **BOOM! BOOM! BOOM!**

Rowan shouts again. **Give me back!**

Keisha directs the crowd. **Back, Back, Back!**

BOOM! BOOM! BOOM!

Rowan again: **My JOB!**

Keisha and the crowd: **Job, Job, JOB!**

BOOM! BOOM! BOOM!

And from there it grows so loud I wish I could cover my ears.

How do Rowan and Keisha do this? — text each other in the middle of the night to come up with these shouts?

* * *

As we board the El back to Bridgeport I tell Rowan that I don't have to work today, Harita gave me the day off.

"That's great. Any particular reason?"

"The dog food video."

We walk into Rowan's house and I deposit my camcorder and all the memory cards on the kitchen table. Make that battle station.

As we're working Deeply flies in the window

At 7:00 p.m. we take the El back down to Package Nova, MaryEllen and four other neighbors coming with us.

If Package Nova doesn't rehire Rowan, they're going to have all of Bridgeport and half of Chicago at their door.

75   DEEPLEA

HOP: What is all that noise, DeePlea? And why are you flapping your wings but not flying?

Me: I am flapping my wings so that I can hover by the street lamp reflector I am using for communication. The noise, HOP — the noise is the sound of people protesting against those who rule the planet.

HOP: [Amazed] A revolution is at hand? So soon?!!

Me: Well, no. This is just one small step, HOP. But such small steps can be coordinated into one medium step, and all those steps can be coordinated into large, significant steps. What you hear is the sound of people angry at injustice — and willing to come out and fight for justice.

HOP: I see. But that is still wonderful, DeePlea. [Pause] Is there hope for the planet?

Me: [Long pause] I don't know, Fee, I mean HOP. It is all a matter of leadership. There are billions of people in other parts of the world. I must visit them and see.

HOP: We know that examples and leadership are key. The great SeeZu taught three whales to enter the water — and they taught the others. BeeBurr taught three crows to sing — and they taught the others. [Pause] Have you found the triad, DeePlea?

Me: I have learned, HOP, that humans are more complex than whales. More complex than crows. [Pause] Therefore, they are capable of more triads. And more complex connections between the triads.

HOP: [Confused] What does this mean?

Me: It means that I have found what may be two key triads: Titus, Rowan, and Jake Terranova. And Titus, Rowan, and Keisha. But there are many other triads within the WCC and outside it, with people such as Antwon, Rafael, and Angela; with Jennica, Mateo, and Lyle; with Madison, Isabelle, and Ana. And many, many more.

HOP: [Pondering] Your analysis . . . your analysis is very different from what we have come to expect from one on Duty to the Universe. But I believe that you have correctly assessed the situation. The more triads the better. The more strong shapes the better. [Pause] When SeeZu and BeeBurr returned from their DUs, they knew they had helped form a triad that would lead to solving the planet's problem. When you return, Dee — will you be able to say the same?

Me: I suspect not, HOP. I suspect that a political revolution to wrest control of the world from the ruling class and place power in the hands of the working class . . . may take several years of struggle. Although . . . .

HOP: Although?

Me: Although revolution can happen very quickly. In a matter of weeks, even. [Sigh] It remains to be seen, FeeOna.

HOP: Yes. I do understand. [Small silence] By the way, you are looking very trim and fit.

Me: [Smile]

HOP: Is it time for you to leave for another country, then?

Me: Yes. I am very sad to leave Rowan. But my Duty to the Universe must take precedence over my heavy heart.

HOP: That is sad, DeePlea. But we are all very proud of you.

Me: Thank you, HOP.

HOP: Where will you go next?

Me: France. The people there believe in the general strike: a powerful weapon in the working class arsenal. From there I will go to India, and then Venezuela. [Pause] I will be very happy to return home, Fee.

HOP: I will be very happy when you do, Dee. Would you like to say something to the chicks? Their feathers are forming.

Me: Yes! I would like to teach them a nestling rhyme.

HOP: Chicks, look at the mirror and repeat after your father.

Me: **Package Nova,**

It's all ovah!

Hire Rowan,

We be goin!

76 ROWAN

THERE ARE SO MANY PEOPLE AROUND THE STAGE THAT I can't get to the stairs. So I shoulder my way forward, grab the top of the stage, and heft myself up.

Keisha's already there. "Nice entrance."

I'm about to say something back when I see Lyle standing at the bottom of the stairs. I jog down the stairs. "Lyle. It's so good to see you. And thanks again for the great milkshake."

"I was here this morning, too," he says, "but you were busy."

"I'm sorry. I always have time for you, Lyle. I wish I'd seen you."

"I heard what Jennica said."

"What she said was great," I tell him. "It took courage to do that."

He nods. "Everybody inside is talking about it. I want to say something, too. Can I?"

I stare at him. "You mean here, on the stage?"

Another nod.

"Sure, Lyle. Do you want me to introduce you, or do you just want to step up and introduce yourself, like Jennica did?"

"Like Jennica did."

"Okay. Hang around. You're on at 8:00 sharp."

From my vantage on the stage I try looking into the Nova parking lot, to see if there are more trailers backed up. This morning might have been a fluke. I don't want to think that, but flukes are possible.

I can't see into the lot. I consider climbing off the stage and shouldering my way through thousands of people. Decide that's not smart.

I hear Titus calling my name. He motions me to come to him. I hop off the stage to stand beside him.

He puts a hand on my shoulder. Pats it. "Doing well, Rowan. Really well. I think you may get your job back."

"Really?" I ask. I mean, I *want* my job back, and I'm determined to fight for it. But I'm worried that Package Nova has the power to hold out forever. And people aren't going to keep coming out here twice a day. The size of the demos will peter out. Though, judging from right now, they're doing nothing but getting bigger.

"This is bad publicity for Package Nova," he tells me. "The crowds are huge. I figure ten thousand or more tonight. Look," he says, pointing toward the street. "We've already filled Cicero Avenue and the cops have put up detour signs. By tomorrow we may be backed up as far as Midway. This is all good."

A big surge of hope floods through me. "Anything special I should do tonight?" I ask him.

He shakes his head. "Just do what you're doing. Talk about violence against women. About a human being's right to self-defense. Talk about the power of the working class. And Rowan — that one of your fellow workers came out to support you this morning? Worth a lot. A whole lot."

Keisha calls me and I heft myself back up on the stage, Jake giving me a boost. Lyle's waiting on the stairs and I motion him to come up. Turn on the mic and hand it to him.

He's really nervous. Pale. Sweaty. I hope he doesn't faint.

"Uh. Hi everyone, I'm Lyle Wallace." He swallows. "I'm a part-time package handler, just like Rowan. And I want to tell you something that happened to me."

He looks around at me. I nod encouragingly.

"A few months ago I went out drinking one night. At a local bar. I probably had too much to drink."

Some laughter from the crowd.

"No, I take that back. I *totally* had too much to drink. And . . . I got in a fight. A bar fight. It was almost one in the morning. All of us were drunk. It was two against one. Two of them. One of me. They were bigger." He pauses. "But I was drunker."

Laughter.

"And that made me, uh, not realize the pain. There was a lot of punching, and when it was over, they each had broken noses. I had two broken arms."

The crowd is silent, wondering where this is going.

"Because of that, I couldn't work at Package Nova. I hadn't yet put in my ninety days, so I was worried they would fire me." He pauses and looks out at the crowd.

"They didn't. They let me come back to work. I had to start my ninety days all over again, but that's not the point. The point is they didn't *care* if I got blasted and broke people's noses and got my own arms broken. They didn't care. They let me come back. Even though I was equally at fault as the other two guys — Package Nova let me come back."

Now the crowd understands. Loud, loud muttering and murmuring.

"Rowan and her friend weren't at fault. They weren't wasted. They were just walking down the street, going home. A guy pulled a gun on them and tried to order them into his van." He breathes raggedly. "Probably a torture chamber."

Lyle coughs, rubs his face. "Rowan should be given a medal — not fired!" he shouts, clenching his fist.

Ten thousand roar in agreement.

My arms have goosebumps. This is a Lyle I never knew existed.

He waits until there's silence. "One other thing. I'm just a white working class guy from Bridgeport. Who likes to go out drinking. At work, I kept to myself and my own kind. Other white working class guys who like to drink. But Rowan and I began riding to work together, and I began hanging with her.

"What Rowan did was meet everyone she works with. Every night, she'd sit with different people. Black, White, Mexican. Asian. Lithuanian. Polish. African. I would never have sat with these people on my own and at first I felt strange. Uncomfortable. But I changed," says Lyle.

"I changed from the person I was. I *liked* the people I was meeting." He pauses. "I'm sitting with them every night. They're just like me, wanting a good job and health insurance and friends. I'm just like them, too. Rowan helped me see that."

Lyle hurries off the stage as the crowd breaks into thunderous applause. I grab him at the stairs and give him a huge hug. Everyone wants to embrace him when he reaches the bottom of the stairs. Jake claps him on the shoulder and shakes his hand.

Probably invites him over for dinner. That's Jake.

I ask Keisha to say a few words, and she does. Then we tell everyone we're going to divide into two teams, like last night, and give encouraging shouts to every worker who drives into the lot or out of the lot. "Remember what Lyle said," I shout. "Everyone in there is just like us, and we're just like them. Here's our shout for tonight: **You in there, us out here. Fight as one for what's fair.**"

Not my greatest chant, but I really want to repeat what Lyle said.

I repeat the chant a couple of times, then half of the march, led by Angela, Marla, and Isabelle — and the entire SVAW contingent with their signs — marches to the south gate, chanting the cry for tonight. Keisha and I jump off the stage and make our way to the front of the people surrounding the north parking entrance gate.

It takes me a while to get a good look into the parking lot, but when I do — I see five trailers backed up. Waiting for a loading dock to clear. On a Tuesday night. Small sorting might not be the only group feeling a bit too sick to work well.

⁂

On the El, MaryEllen can't stop talking about the excitement of the rally. Neither can the neighbors who came with her. Jake long ago asked for permission to tape them — on the ride down, I think — and now they don't even notice him as he moves around the El car. Always looking for the perfect angle.

"We're all coming tomorrow morning," Els says. "And we're bringing even more friends with us."

77   JAKE

WEDNESDAY MORNING AND WE'RE ONCE AGAIN RIDING the El with neighbors and friends. Of whom there are nine in addition to Rowan, MaryEllen, and me. MaryEllen has reached the each-one-bring-nine level all on her own.

When we exit the El and turn south on Cicero, the sidewalk's already full of people marching toward Package Nova.

"Isn't this exciting?" MaryEllen keeps saying to everyone around her.

On the El she convinced one of the Midway-bound passengers that he had enough time before his flight: enough time to join the demonstration. And he's here, walking with us. MaryEllen is a force to be reckoned with.

At the parking lot entrance I glance inside and count six trailers backed up. There's definitely a slow-down going on. Not a major one: Rowan says there'd be dozens of trailers if that were the case. But a noticeable one. I sweep the camcorder across the trailers. One of the drivers is standing on the running board of his truck, waving to the demonstrators. Who are waving back and shouting "Way to go!"

Wait.

Where's the stage?

Just as I'm about to point out the case of the missing stage to Rowan, Keisha finds us and drags us with her. "They asked Daddy to set up the stage near the main entrance," she informs us.

"They?" asks Rowan.

"Package Nova, girl! And look — all the news stations are surrounding the stage."

"They're going to hire you back," I tell Rowan. "And they're going to do it publicly."

We reach the stage and find Titus, who's beaming. He comes to Keisha and Rowan, places a hand on each of their shoulders. "I am *so* proud of both of you."

At moments like this, I step backward and try to blend into the surroundings. With the video running.

"Rowan," he tells her, "they're going to give you back your job. You won an important victory, not just for yourself, but for everybody who works here.

"And Keisha — great work on the stage, in the marches, with the chants. The two of you work like a single unit."

They both hug Titus hard. And then they hug each other. And then they climb the stage and stand there, waiting.

The news crews are filming everybody and anybody. I'm straddling the outside risers of the stairs, as close to the speakers as I can get. The outside risers are pretty damned narrow, and I catch myself swaying backwards a couple of times.

At exactly 6:58 the front doors of Package Nova open and five suited executives come out. They look at the cameras, then climb the stairs to the stage. I catch their grim faces in closeup.

The crowd is as silent as silent can be. I pan the camera over their anxious faces.

One of the execs tries to shake Rowan's hand. She gives him a hard look and points to the mic. Which makes me smile. I know what she's thinking. *The job. Give me back my job.*

Flanked by two fellow suits on each side, the guy in charge — or maybe he's just the guy designated to do the mop-up — speaks. "We at Package Nova are extremely sorry there has been a misunderstanding about our attitude toward women and violence. At Package Nova positive action for women has always been supported and violence against them has been deplored. We are proud to say that many of the women who work here receive a dollar-an-hour extra pay for their valuable work on the small-packages line."

He waits for something. Applause, maybe. Recognizes it's not coming his way and continues. "We at Package Nova regret any misunderstandings that may have arisen because of the violent attack on Misses Pickett and Longshaw. We are happy that they are safe. And we welcome Rowan Pickett back into employment as a part-time package handler."

Cheers roar up and down Cicero Avenue, and across it, too, hitting the cement barrier walls on the other side, bouncing back and doubling in volume. The sound needle on the camcorder has never experienced anything like it.

I film Deeply hopping up and down on his lamppost.

When the noise dies down a bit, the execs look at Rowan. They're smiling. I think they expect . . . gratitude.

Rowan steps up to the mic and looks out at the crowd. "I am so happy to hear this news. Happy to hear that my job, which was unjustly taken from me, is now mine again." She looks over her shoulder at the execs. "I'll report for work at 9:30 tonight, my usual shift."

Turning back to the crowd she raises both fists in the air. "Thank *you*, friends! Thank *you*, sisters and brothers! Thank you, every single one of you who came out here early each morning and late each night, who made your voices heard. *Thank* you — I couldn't have won without you."

She extends the index finger of each hand and points toward the north and south parking gates. "And my heartfelt thanks go out to my fellow workers, who helped make this happen. We workers have the power. We have the power. Raise your voices, everyone, and let's give a five-minute shoutout — **Thank you, package handlers! Thank you, package handlers!**"

The execs are aware this rally might not end for a while. They exit the stage a lot gloomier than they entered it to talk about the "misunderstanding."

The crowd is into this last chant like never before. Package handlers all over the Midwest are going to hear it. Maybe even as far as Boston.

When the five minutes are up Rowan lowers her arms. The chants stop. And then she says, "I think we should all come back one last time, tonight, to thank the night shift workers. What do you think?"

Wild cheers.

"All right, then," she shouts. "You can meet here from 8:30 to 9:30, to thank the workers both coming and going. I won't be with you, because I'll be inside, handling packages."

Even wilder cheers.

"But Keisha will be here." Rowan looks back to confirm this and Keisha grins and nods. "And so will the Stop Violence Against Women Committee." She finds Marla in the crowd and gets an affirmation. "And so will Working Class Control." She looks at Titus, who raises both fists in the air. "Thank you, everyone — I look forward to *hearing* you tonight!"

Wave after wave of happiness emanates from the thousands of people present, as they talk to each other, wave to Rowan and Keisha, or go up to shake their hands.

It's another ninety minutes before we have the stage loaded into Jalen's van and the posters collected and loaded into Rafael's truck. MaryEllen helps, as do the neighbors. Then we walk back to Midway and take the Orange Line home.

We walk.

Rowan practically skips.

78 ROWAN

IT'S HARD TO BELIEVE THAT JUST FOUR MONTHS AGO
I attended the gun control rally to find Titus and ask him for help in getting a job. From that day my life changed in a different direction. Different from the way it changed after Dad's death and Clari's murder, which were deep, sad changes. Losing them changed me. Changed Mom, too. And then Mom left me, too. Changed me in such a way I couldn't climb out of the pit I was in.

Until I saw a colorful parrot in the sky and shouted, "Way to go, bird!"
Until the parrot moved into my life.
Until Jake Terranova followed me home and moved into my life.
Deeply and Jake — they awakened things in me.
I needed a job. I got a job. Worked hard, made friends.
Zeb Snoddy tried to kill Keisha and me.
We fought back. We defeated *him*.
I was fired from my job. I fought back. And won.
Four months. Just four months.
Sometimes change can move like an avalanche.

* * *

Last night Deeply told us he would be gone when we woke up. Jake gripped my shoulders hard, to keep me from crying. It helped. But I felt wet drops on my hair. Nobody was gripping Jake's shoulders.

Deeply reached his beak into his body and pulled out a feather, then gave it to me. No matter how hard Jake gripped me then, it was no use. My tears fell.

"No cry," said Deeply. "No cry."

I finally stopped myself and wiped my face. Took a deep breath. I asked Deeply what he would like to do his last night with us.

"Watch *Day Earth Stood Still*," he squawked. "Eat Jake's popcorn."

Apparently Jake makes better popcorn than the kind in the microwave bags I use. All three of us rode in Jake's car to Jake's place. The way Deeply kept looking at the steering wheel and studying the gearshift, I thought he might try to do the driving himself.

Deeply sat on Jake's shoulder as we took the elevator up.

Then Deeply and I sat on the couch while Jake made a huge batch of popcorn in a frying pan. With truffle oil. Well, no wonder Deeply prefers Jake's popcorn.

The three of us lined up on the couch, ate the popcorn, and watched the movie.

Twice.

* * *

When Jake and I wake up this morning, Deeply's gone.

Jake tries to cheer me up by playing his first interview of Deeply.

And that does cheer me up.

Especially the "Revolt. Revolt! *Revolt*!!!"

ABOUT THE AUTHOR

Barbara Gregorich's interest in writing books began almost at the same time as did her interest in fighting for social justice. When she read contemporary literature or political fiction, she always yearned for it to contain more action and imagination: also some humor. After publishing many books and teaching writing classes for years, Barbara has written *Exit Velocity* — the kind of novel she was looking for.

You can read more about Barbara on her website, her blog, and her Facebook page:

http://www.barbaragregorich.com/

https://barbaragregorich.wordpress.com/

https://www.facebook.com/fwordsya/